Dear Reader,

Last month I asked if you'd like to see more humour, romantic suspense or linked books on our list. Well this month I can offer you all three!

I'm thrilled to bring you the final part of Liz Fielding's critically acclaimed and very popular Beaumont Brides trilogy. But, if we're lucky, maybe Melanie's story won't be the end after all . . .

Two stories which can be classified as suspense, but which are very different in style and plot, are offered by Laura Bradley and Jill Sheldon. These authors have won plaudits from critics and readers alike for their earlier *Scarlet* novels.

And finally, those of you who've asked for more books by Natalie Fox will, we're sure, enjoy reading our exciting new author, Talia Lyon, who brings a delightfully humorous flavour to her story of three gals, three guys and the holiday of a lifetime.

As always, I hope you enjoy the books I've chosen for you this month. Let me have your comments and suggestions, won't you and I'll do all I can to bring you more of the kind of books *you* want to read.

Till next month,

Sally Cooper

SALLY COOPER,
Editor-in-Chief – *Scarlet*

About the Author

Laura Bradley lives in San Antonio, USA, with her husband and three daughters. In 1990 she began her writing career full-time and was delighted to have *Wicked Liaisons*, her first *Scarlet* novel, accepted. When she isn't working on her novels, Laura writes non-fiction articles and is a regular contributor to many American periodicals.

After working her way through university as a television and radio reporter, Laura graduated in 1986. The ABC television affiliate in Honolulu hired her as a weekend news producer and she was quickly promoted to the weekday ten o'clock news. A year and a half later, Laura was KITV's senior producer, a position she held for another two years.

In her spare time, Laura enjoys riding and training horses, hiking, water skiing and reading (of course!)

Other *Scarlet* titles available this month:

GIRLS ON THE RUN – Talia Lyon
WILD FIRE – Liz Fielding
FORGOTTEN – Jill Sheldon

LAURA BRADLEY

DEADLY ALLURE

Enquiries to:
Robinson Publishing Ltd
7 Kensington Church Court
London W8 4SP

First published in the UK by Scarlet, 1997

Copyright © Linda Zimmerhanzel 1997
Cover photography by J. Cat

The right of Linda Zimmerhanzel to be identified as author
of this work has been asserted by her in accordance
with the Copyright, Designs and Patents Act 1988.

All rights reserved. No part of this publication
may be reproduced in any form or by any means
without the prior written permission of the publisher.

This book is sold subject to the condition that it shall
not, by way of trade or otherwise, be lent, re-sold,
hired out or otherwise circulated in any form of binding
or cover other than that in which it is published and
without a similar condition including this condition being
imposed on the subsequent purchaser.

A copy of the British Library Cataloguing in
Publication data is available from the British Library

ISBN 1-85487-723-2

Printed and bound in the EC

10 9 8 7 6 5 4 3 2 1

To Ted and Patt,
who love me like a daughter
and treat me like a friend.

ACKNOWLEDGMENTS

I have many people to thank, but first I want to emphasize that all the characters in this book were born purely of my imagination. This is especially important because Terrell Hills does in fact exist, as a small enclave in San Antonio. Hopefully, I have portrayed the place as accurately as I possibly can with fictional characters in a fictional situation. Terrell Hills Police Chief, Barney Flowers, (who bears no resemblance to Chief Rangel in the book) was extremely generous with facts and figures in helping me get the mechanics and logistics of how his department works correct. Also, I want to thank former fashion model Tammy Putnal for sharing her experiences with the modeling industry. Finally, a big thank you to my brother-in-law, Mike Zimmerhanzel, who answers all my silly civilian questions about the world of the police officer.

PROLOGUE

Her hand shook as she tried to fit the key in the lock. Her heart felt as if it had lost its tether in her chest, suddenly coming loose and beating wildly, bouncing against everything around it – her ribs, her diaphragm, her throat. Her brain felt too big for her head, the anticipation of a migraine more sickening than the pain that was to come.

She brought the back of her left wrist to her forehead, pressing hard, to steady her muscles more than to ward off the headache; she knew better than that. Her dry lips parted and her teeth bit down on the tip of her tongue, hard enough to direct her attention to the source of that sharp pain and from there to the problem at hand – getting the key into the lock.

Finally, after two more failed attempts, the key slipped in and turned. Her hand tried the knob, and when the door opened the relief she felt was physical. Everything was going to be all right.

But the relief was brief. Unjustly so.

She felt the presence the moment she walked in past the laundry room. There, lunch sat ready for her. Lunch that shouldn't have been there. Britt was teaching. She never got home from school earlier than four o'clock.

Panic flared. But it was replaced incredibly quickly

with a sense of inevitability that fell over her like a blanket of peace.

As she hung her keys on the peg next to the alarm control panel and pressed in the code that deactivated the alarm, her mind grasped a single concept. She was going to die.

The emotion that followed was not dread or anger or fear; it was wonder.

Who would be the one responsible for taking her life?

The threats ricocheted in her mind as if they all stood there, whispering in her ear one last time:

'You're not going to get away with this.'

'You're going to pay for what you've done to me, you ungrateful little bitch.'

'I won't let you leave; and I'll do anything – *anything* – to stop you.'

'It don't cost you nothin' to say yes, but it'll cost you more than you know if you say no.'

'You'd better do as I say or somebody's going to have to teach you a lesson you'll never forget and one you'll never have the chance to remember.'

'You aren't going to get rid of me; we'll both die first.'

As she reached for the sandwich that shouldn't have been there, the can of soda she shouldn't have touched, she realized with startling clarity who was to blame after all.

She was.

CHAPTER 1

Her exotic face was flawlessly beautiful, even wearing a mask of death. Britt stared at her little sister, feeling a choking pain rise in her chest. Her breath caught in her throat like a hiccup. She nodded once.

'Yes.' Britt's voice seemed to belong to someone else. 'It's Risa.'

Then – because saying 'it' sounded so cold, so much like a body and not a person – Britt cleared her throat and spoke again. 'She's Risa. My sister.'

The pain in her chest was spreading now, leaving numbness in its wake. She saw the people around her moving, but they seemed to do so in slow motion. A policeman put his hand tentatively on her shoulder. Britt flinched, edging away. The pressure of his hand disappeared.

She looked around the room. Everyone seemed to be watching and waiting for her, without actually looking right at her. Britt stood frozen. Minutes ticked by. But when a paramedic in a blue uniform finally leaned down to touch Risa's too-still body, Britt leaped forward.

'No. Don't touch her.'

Pushing the startled woman out of the way, Britt bent down on one knee and gathered her sister in her arms.

Risa's arms and head flopped like a rag doll's. In a flash of memory, Britt remembered when she would babysit Risa and they would play with Raggedy Ann and Andy for hours. Once Risa had pretended that Raggedy Ann was dead.

'All you have to do is shake her, and she'll come back to life, Bitny,' Risa had explained, with the self-righteousness only a four-year-old can muster.

Risa's face swam before her eyes. Then Britt felt the hot liquid spill over her lower eyelids, coursing down her cheeks. A sob broke from her throat. She began to shake her sister, gently first, then more urgently.

'Wake up, Risa. All I have to do is shake you and you'll come back to life, remember? Remember Raggedy Ann? Wake up now.'

Her tears splashed on Risa's face. A face that would be forever young. It was that thought more than any other that caused Britt to lose control completely. Her fingers gripped her sister's body as her own frame shook with wrenching sobs.

Britt could hear the feet of the police officer and paramedics shuffle nervously around her. Nobody spoke.

Suddenly the front door slammed and heavy feet stomped across the polished oak floor. Britt felt the change in atmosphere. It was charged with immediate electricity. Power. The shuffling around her stopped. But her sobs didn't. Britt sat on the kitchen floor, cradled Risa's head against her chest and began to rock her gently, humming a lullaby.

'Get her up and out of here,' said a hard voice behind her.

'But, Lieutenant . . .' someone began.

'Do it,' was the answer.

Barely aware of the exchange, Britt ignored them.

'What are you guys still doing here?' The hard voice asked.

'We were just waiting to see how she was,' a tentative tenor answered.

'She's dead, isn't she? I don't think you can do her any good.'

Britt kept her eyes pinned on Risa, the conversation around her a dull murmur of voices not quite registering in her mind.

'I meant the sister, sir,' the paramedic answered.

'Oh, how considerate. Well, as long as you're here give her a sedative. The driveway will be crawling with reporters in no time. The last thing we need is to have to worry about getting a hysterical woman through there along with a body.'

Britt stopped humming. She'd belatedly realized that they were talking about her. A hysterical woman? A sedative? A new feeling began to rise from the pit of her stomach. Gently, she laid her sister back on the cold wood floor. With unnatural calm, she stood and turned, meeting the gray eyes that belonged to the heavy feet and hard voice. With black hair liberally laced with gray, a sharply planed face and a tall, lanky frame he looked like a statue made of marble. And he was just as cold.

'I do not need a sedative,' Britt announced in a measured tone.

'You may not think you do, but you do.' The lieutenant snapped his fingers toward the paramedic. He held out his palm. 'Let's have it.'

'I've got to go out to the ambulance,' the paramedic mumbled as he scuttled out the door.

Britt watched him go. 'He's wasting his time.'

'You're going to take the pills,' he ordered her, his gunmetal eyes boring into hers.

'No. I won't.'

'Listen, I know what I'm talking about.' His voice softened slightly.

Britt bristled at his suggestion. 'I suppose you're going to tell me now that you've lost a sister?'

'No, but I know a lot about death.'

'And who are you – you-who-knows-a-lot-about-death?' Britt hated to hear the bitterness in her own voice.

'Detective Lieutenant Grant Collins.' He flipped open a badge that showed the crest of the Terrell Hills Police Department. Shoving it back into the pocket of his chinos, he stuck out his hand. She ignored it.

'Well, Detective Lieutenant, this isn't about death,' Britt stated, with more strength than she felt. 'It's about life. My life and Risa's life. About how hers is over and how I'm going to have a big emptiness in mine. How every time I go to Chester's for a burger I'm going to remember how it was one of her favorite things in the world to do and how she can't do that any more. Ever.'

Britt choked back a sob. 'And when I have children I'll think of Risa and how she wanted that – a family of her own – more than anything in the world. More than being famous, more than being beautiful, more than being rich.

'But the thing that hurts the most is the millions of people who will grieve for Risa thinking they knew her. They didn't know her. The only thing they'll miss is the face that graced a hundred magazine covers. I'll miss her soul. Her laugh. Her touch. Her heart.'

The police detective listened silently to Britt's words as they came out in a rush, the deepening of the lines in his face the only sign that he had heard her at all. When she began to shake with overflowing emotion he took a step toward her and grasped her elbow. She shook him off as if he had a contagious disease and eased into the kitchen chair by herself.

The paramedic reappeared and handed Grant Collins a vial. He strode to the kitchen and got a glass of water. Snatching Britt's hand from her lap, he turned it over and poured a pill into her palm.

He held the water out to her.

'Take it,' he ordered.

Britt raised her eyes from her hand and met his steely gaze with all the strength she could muster. Slowly she turned her palm toward the floor. The pill clattered on the hard wood. The detective's eyes sparked in anger. It was the first sign that he actually felt emotion at all.

'The only thing that – ' Britt looked pointedly at the floor ' – will do for me is put off the grieving. I'd wake up tomorrow and have to remember all over again what has happened: Risa is dead. It won't make it any better. It will just make it fresh.'

Britt stood.

'I know that you don't give a damn how I'll feel tomorrow. I know you want me to take it to make your job easier tonight. Too bad.'

Britt crushed the pill under the soles of her loafers. Then she looked up, and her eyes locked with Grant Collins's hard ones. Heartless, she thought. Finally he broke their gaze and gave a dismissive shrug.

'You'll have to leave, then. We have a lot to do here,' he said as he turned to a uniformed officer standing behind him.

'I'm not leaving Risa,' Britt said quietly.

The lieutenant stopped talking and paused before swiveling to face Britt again. 'You'd better keep out of our way, then.'

A stinging retort jumped to the tip of her tongue, but

Britt held it back. Suddenly she felt guilty. The anger made her feel alive and she didn't want to feel alive. She wanted to feel as dead as Risa was.

Grant Collins nodded once, seeming to take her silence for acquiescence, and turned back to the uniformed officer who'd been first to arrive on the scene.

'Tell me everything – from the top.'

Britt cringed at the flatness in his voice. They were going to discuss her sister's death like a statistic instead of as the loss of a loving, gentle girl. She closed her eyes and tried to concentrate on the men and woman around her, who were gradually retreating from the area with exaggerated quiet. But, instead, her ears kept finding the one conversation she so desperately wanted to avoid.

'Go ahead, Randall,' Collins urged.

'Well, Lieutenant, I was over on Elizabeth, checking out a possible criminal mischief. Y'know – it was just kids playing hooky and they'd – '

'Get on with it.' Impatience gave his voice a sharp edge.

'Yeah. Right. Anyway, Dispatch radioed with a possible . . . uh, y'know . . .'

The young man's voice trailed off and Britt could feel his eyes on her back.

'Get on with it. Now.'

Activity in the room stopped at the detective's bark. Britt looked up to see three pairs of eyes darting between her and the two men behind her. She kept herself unnaturally still. The male paramedic hovered at her elbow, probably ready to shoot her with a tranquilizer if she dissolved into the expected hysterics.

'Well, okay . . . uh, I . . .' The uniformed officer cleared his throat before continuing. 'Dispatch radioed this address as a possible, uh, DOA. 'Scuse me, ma'am.

I'm so terribly sorry about your sister. She was a real pretty thing.'

Britt's stomach clutched at the stark abbreviation – Dead On Arrival – made that much worse by the sensitive young cop's attempt to couch it with a clumsy condolence. A wave of nausea washed over her. She resisted her body's impulse to give in to it. There was no way she was going to break down in front of that stony-faced, rock-hearted detective.

Suddenly Britt shot up and spun around to face the two men, sending the paramedic reeling into the wall.

'I understand your sympathy.' Britt inclined her head briefly at the apologetic young cop, whose gaze shifted immediately to his own feet. 'But don't waste any more of it on me.'

The room had gone silent again. Britt challenged Collins with her look. He held her gaze with an air of bored indulgence.

'In fact – ' Britt still talked to the uniformed officer while she glared at the lieutenant ' – you ought to be feeling sorry for your boss now, because I'm not going to give him a moment's peace until he finds my sister's murderer. And that is a promise.'

Collins's right eyebrow twitched up and his lips thinned at her words. He regarded her for a full minute before he spoke. 'And what makes you think your sister was murdered, Miss Reeve?' He glanced down at her left hand. 'It is *Miss* Reeve, isn't it?'

The understated arrogance in his tone and manner set her teeth on edge. She kept them there as she answered. 'Yes.'

'You haven't answered my first question,' he pointed out bluntly. 'Do you have proof your sister was killed?'

'Isn't that your job, Detective? To find the proof?'

Abruptly the lieutenant broke his gaze with Britt and strode toward Risa's body. 'Yes, you're right, it is my job to figure out what happened to your sister. And your job is – what did you so eloquently say earlier? – to grieve. So, please don't let me stand in your way – and don't you stand in mine.'

Britt stood paralyzed by his callousness. She watched as he leaned over to study the gash on the right side of Risa's head, where the blood had already congealed with her hair into an ugly mass. For a moment she thought she saw him wince, but she knew she must have been mistaken. He *knew* about death. One more body wouldn't make him cringe.

Detective Collins backed up a few steps and motioned for the man who'd introduced himself as the investigator from the County Medical Examiner's office to join him. They conversed in voices so low Britt couldn't hear, but she could see what they were discussing – the doorframe. For the first time since arriving, she saw it was smeared with blood. Why hadn't she noticed that before?

'Did you get plenty of shots of this?' Collins asked Randall.

'Four or five, plus about five minutes of video tape.'

'Take about a dozen more photographs. Every angle you can think of and some you can't.'

Randall nodded and began, then Collins remembered something else. 'And you did get plenty of shots of the body – ' he glanced at Britt ' – the way it looked *before* it was moved?'

'Yes, sir. A whole roll.'

'Good,' Collins commented, then walked slowly through the kitchen and breakfast room before walking back into the living room to wait for Randall to finish the photographs. After a moment he rejoined Collins.

'You know you shouldn't have even let her – ' he cocked his head at Britt – 'into the crime scene. And I'm sure you can see why. She's already messed around with the body before the techs could get to it. This could get sticky if this ever went to trial. Big mistake.'

'I – I know, Lieutenant,' Randall stuttered. 'It's just that the neighbor called her right after she called Dispatch, and she got here as I was checking the backyard for – '

Collins waved him quiet and addressed the Medical Examiner's investigator. 'That gash on her head the only injury?'

'The only *visible* injury, Detective. Of course, you know the doc won't know about internals until the autopsy,' he answered cautiously.

'Of course,' Collins said sarcastically. 'But if you had to guess would you say that whack on the head would be enough to kill her?'

'What "whack" are you referring to?' he asked. 'The doorframe?'

'What else would I be referring to? Nothing else around here has her blood on it, does it?' Collins directed his question at the room.

'Not that we've seen, sir,' was the answer.

'So, what about that doorframe?'

'I wouldn't know for sure, Collins.'

'I'm not asking you for sworn testimony, here,' Collins cut in, 'just your educated guess on what killed the girl. You're a cop – have an opinion.'

As she listened, Britt began to feel all five senses returning. When Rachel from next door had called her at work, her mind had gone blank. Her body had gone into automatic pilot. She had no recollection of telling the principal she was leaving, of getting in her car, of driving home. Her only memory was of the call, and then the way her sister had looked, sprawled on the floor, just the way she sprawled on the bed when she fell asleep. But now Britt noticed the half-eaten sandwich in the kitchen. Peanut butter, banana and mayonnaise – Risa's favorite.

The flesh of the banana was beginning to turn brown.

Britt closed her eyes briefly and struggled to swallow the lump that rose in her throat. Sucking in a breath, she looked back at the counter, trying to reconstruct her sister's last minutes alive. A can of soda was on its side, the brown liquid pooled on the counter and the floor below it. Risa had been eating a late lunch or a snack. What had drawn her the five feet from the kitchen counter to the hall leading to the back door? The blood was smeared on the doorjamb, near the alarm pad. Had she been trying to reach the emergency button?

'I won't venture a guess at this point,' Britt heard the medical investigator answer.

'Okay,' Collins said. 'But, theoretically, she could have slipped and fallen into the doorway, hitting her head?'

Britt started. 'What? You think this was an *accident*? My sister was sixteen years old, not some 93-year-old woman with a walking frame.'

'Look, Miss Reeve, age has very little to do with it. Older people are more likely to fall, but that doesn't mean teenagers don't. She could have slipped on a slick spot, tripped on a shoelace . . .'

They all looked at Risa's white leather shoes. Both were tied.

Britt raised her eyes defiantly to meet Collins's steel orbs. 'Or she could have been pushed.'

A full minute passed. Collins clenched his jaw. Britt could feel everyone in the room listening.

'Or that,' he finally admitted.

The medical investigator leaned his head toward Collins. 'Look, Detective,' he whispered, 'I don't think we ought to be discussing this with the family.'

Enraged, Britt opened her mouth, but Collins beat her to it.

'The girl's family has the right to know what happened to her,' he put in. Britt closed her mouth in surprise. He plowed on, though, crushing her budding sense of gratitude. 'But the family doesn't need to be involved in the investigation. Which is what this is right now. So, if you'll excuse us to do our jobs, Miss Reeve, I'm sure you have calls of your own to make. You guys are done printing in the master bedroom, aren't you?' Grunts of assent answered him, so he turned to another plainclothes cop who'd come in during the debate and had begun inspecting the living room. 'See anything worth looking into in this lady's bedroom, Ortega? The cop shook his shaggy dark head. Collins turned back to Britt. 'So, go ahead and get on with *your* job. You'll be interviewed later.'

Britt had never felt so many strong emotions at once. Grief, anger, hopelessness, outrage. And, of course, the guilt of feeling anything at all. They were all colliding within her, leaving her suddenly paralyzed.

She looked away from Collins and back at Risa. A lock of her rich tawny hair was stuck in the corner of her mouth. Britt itched to pull it away, as she'd done countless times when Risa was a little girl. Britt's eyes filled with tears and she spun on her heel.

'Hey.' His voice stopped her at the threshold.

She didn't turn around.

Undaunted, he continued, 'Don't try to go in your sister's bedroom. That's off-limits. Got it?'

Without answering, Britt escaped into her own room.

* * *

Grant let out a sigh of frustration as he turned back to the waiting investigator and paramedics. Dealing with the grief of the living was a thousand times worse than dealing with the dead. And dealing with the dead was pretty damned bad.

Difficult as it was to be tough with the sister, he knew it was the only way to get her through the next few hours. Experience had taught him that being too sympathetic could cause the floodgates to open and she'd be just another mess to deal with. Grant had had enough of messes while he'd been with the homicide detail of the huge San Antonio Police Department. He told himself he'd transferred to the tiny Terrell Hills police force, where he was one of two detectives, to get away from the body count.

But there was so much more to it.

On one level he'd realized he was running away from the biggest mess of them all – from his colleagues, from himself. For the past six months it had worked. He was slipping into oblivion. But now he was faced with the most sensational death this town of four thousand had probably ever seen. A teenage supermodel. Damn. Though it was looking more and more like an accident, the pressure from the media would be a bitch anyway. Just his luck.

'You're next, Randall.' Grant motioned to the uniformed cop standing stiffly in the corner of the breakfast room. The patrolman's head yanked up. He looked as if he was about to face a firing squad.

Grant decided to let him off the hook over the mistake of letting the sister get to the body. The kid had learned his lesson.

'Tell me the rest,' he said simply.

Randall picked up where he'd left off, still not looking his superior in the eye. 'I got to this location at approximately fifteen hundred hours. The neighbor, who'd called in the report to begin with, was standing outside. She told me she'd heard the sound of a car zooming away from here – she noticed 'cuz the motor seemed really loud as it shifted gears . . .'

Grant looked up from his notebook, still scribbling. 'We'll have to check for skid marks outside.'

'Yes, sir.' Randall bobbed his head. 'Anyhow, the neighbor lady said she walked over to check it out. She says she rang the doorbell, then tried to turn the knob, but it was locked. When she went around to the kitchen door she peeked in and could see the, uh, body. She leaned against the door and the latch clicked.'

'Like it hadn't been quite closed?'

'Right, Lieutenant. The neighbor said she all of a sudden realized she needed to get help so she ran home, called 9–1–1, then ran back over to meet the squad car. She asked to go home right after I got here because her baby was taking a nap.'

'You let her go?'

'Well, uh, yeah. I didn't know what – '

Grant waved him quiet. 'We'll get her statement after you're done telling me what you found.'

'You're seeing everything just like I found it, pretty much. Risa on her right side, sprawled out like that – '

'Risa?' Grant interrupted.

'Well, Lieutenant, I feel like I know her . . . uh . . . knew her. She was in all the magazines all the time and everything.'

'Go on.'

'Course I radioed for an ambulance and back-up, checked her pulse, but I could tell she was already gone. But not long gone. She was still warm as me or you.' Here the patrolman paused, as if he wasn't sure whether the older man really was the same temperature as the rest of the living.

'You know, Randall, bodies take a while to cool off. About a degree an hour.'

'Oh, yes, sir, I studied up on forensics some. But she wasn't stiff then, neither.'

They both glanced through the doorway at the girl's body. Grant could see rigor mortis setting in now, in the small muscles of her face. In her fingers. It always hit faster in the skinny ones. Though this girl wasn't as painfully thin as he'd always imagined models were. She looked as if, on top of being lucky in the genes department, she'd been healthy, had eaten what she wanted, exercised a lot. He felt his chest clutch. He looked away.

'So you're trying to say she hadn't been dead long. Is that what you're figuring?' he continued.

'I'd say so. While I waited for the paramedics I checked the rest of the house and, real quick, the backyard. There wasn't any sign of nobody, sir.'

'You notice any signs of a struggle?' Grant watched the patrolman's face carefully. A lot of detectives treated the reporting officers with disdain, discounting their observations and trying to cut them out of the investigation as soon as possible. Grant liked to get their perspective. Sometimes the first one on the scene saw something or even sensed something that everyone else would miss. In Terrell Hills it was especially important, because the reporting officer detailed the crime scene – a small department like theirs couldn't afford a staff of technicians, so the reporting officer did the fingerprinting and photography, and bagged any evidence before the detectives got there.

'Not exactly a struggle, Lieutenant. Her bedroom's

such a mess, it's hard to tell there. That's probably just teenage-girl mess. But there was . . . I dunno.'

'What?'

'Something not right – like things maybe got searched. Gently, though. And another thing, when you're home and about to have a sandwich, don't you turn things on and leave 'em on? Like you go into the bathroom, leave, and the light's still on? Or you go into the den and turn the TV on and leave it on for company while you're making lunch? Or you flip the ceiling fan on to cool things off? The only thing on was the stereo power light,' Randall offered.

'Some people are particular about turning things off as they leave a room.' Grant liked Randall's observation, but he wanted to test it by playing devil's advocate.

'Not teenagers, sir,' Randall countered. 'I know – I live with two of 'em. My sister and brother.'

Grant nodded. He liked the way this kid backed up what he said. 'Okay, so what do you think happened?'

'Maybe someone turned off the TV and the lights and the fan before he left. So it'd look like no one was home.'

'Or she could have gotten a call and had to leave. She turned off the TV and lights on her way out,' Grant put in.

Randall's shoulders slumped a little; he was obviously disappointed that the detective wasn't completely buying his scenario.

Grant walked around the small living room. He didn't much like his own scenario either. Something about the house didn't feel right, but then again maybe he was making too much of the patrolman's observation.

It was a single story, maybe fifteen-hundred square feet. Grant put it at about fifty years old, but it had been renovated. Its wood floors wore a high shine, the built-in bookcases looked newly painted. The windows looked to be the originals, but they were in good shape and very clean, offering a view of a big backyard shaded by a half-dozen live oaks. It was a home that reflected love from its owner. The only aspect Grant took issue with was the disarray. Some would call it 'lived-in'; Grant called it a mess. He turned back to Randall.

'Whose house is this, anyway? Her parents'?'

'No, sir. It's Miss Reeve's house. Risa's sister.' He inclined his head toward the bedroom, where they could hear her on the telephone. Then he looked back at Grant. 'Her parents split up a long time ago, anyway. Didn't you grow up here, Lieutenant?'

'Yes,' Grant answered cautiously, not sure of what the kid was getting at.

'You don't remember the scandal with Mayor Tabor, 'bout fifteen, sixteen years back?'

Grant would've been deep into the political science department of the University of Texas during the 'scandal' Randall was talking about. But all he said was, 'No.'

'Well, y'know, Marshall Tabor, the guy who owns all those car dealerships? He was mayor, and a pretty good one, I guess. Then in the middle of the night he up and runs off with this gal, leaving his family, his business and the city high and dry. Well, the gal was Risa's momma, Sophia. She left her three little girls and her college professor husband. Risa wasn't more than a baby then. It was a big shocker all around.'

The image of Risa's sister rocking the dead girl in her arms crystallized in Grant's mind. No wonder she was so torn up. She must have raised the girl after her mother ran off. He felt a wave of sympathy, but quickly tamped it down. It wouldn't be right, this feeling sorry for someone who could be a suspect.

'How do you know so much about this, Randall? You couldn't have been more than a baby yourself.'

Randall's face flushed with red. 'Well, it was my momma, see, Lieutenant. She was Tabor's secretary at the car dealership. She talked about it all the time. Still talks about it. I . . . well . . . now that I'm older I kinda suspect she was hoping ol' Marshall would run off with her. My daddy died when I was just thirteen. Left Momma pretty well-off, but lonely.'

This was turning into a soap opera, Grant realized ruefully. He nodded at the young cop to acknowledge his words, but refused to say anything for fear it would elicit another chapter in the saga.

It was a small world, Grant thought, especially in a small town. Although it was almost funny to think of Terrell Hills as a small town. It was one of a dozen cities that existed within the city limits of San Antonio, the ninth largest city in the US. You could move seamlessly from Terrell Hills to San Antonio to Alamo Heights to San Antonio to Castle Hills all in ten minutes' time, never realizing you'd driven through four different cities. Each offered special amenities to its residents, from lower taxes to strict building codes to outstanding schools.

Terrell Hills could brag one of the best school districts in the state, thanks to a rich tax base. Old, well-kept estates and mansions made up nearly seventy-five percent of the residences. And most of the city was residential. Only eight businesses existed within the city's two square miles. The bulk of its residents had grown up in the town and in moving out had only moved down the street. It was a safe place to raise kids. The police patrolled vigilantly, ticketing speeders going two or three miles over the citywide thirty mile-per-hour limit. You knew your neighbors and they knew you.

The flipside of that, Grant reflected was the gossip. He'd hated it as a teenager. Someone who knew someone who knew your mom's hairdresser was always making a midnight run to the grocery store and would just happen to see you driving around in your parents' car – a car your parents didn't know you'd borrowed, until they heard, most likely before the hood was cold.

But, now, as a cop, he'd learned to make the gossip work to his advantage, and he vowed he would with this Reeve case as well.

'I'm done here.' The Medical Examiner's investigator broke into Grant's reverie.

'When can I expect the autopsy results?' Grant asked.

'You want one? You classifying this a homicide?'

'Of course I want one,' Grant shot back. 'The victim was sixteen years old. There are no witnesses. No concrete proof of an accidental death.'

'No concrete proof that it was anything else either,' the investigator put in.

Grant could feel the blood begin to pound in his ears. 'And we won't have any until your boss gets busy cutting up the body – '

They all turned at the sound of a gasp behind them. The victim's sister had emerged from the bedroom. Her hand trembled as she held it over her mouth. Her skin, that had flushed the color of a ripe peach when she'd been angry with him earlier, lost all color. Grant felt a lump form in his throat at the sight of her hazel eyes. They swam with grief. And horror.

'Damn,' he muttered under his breath. 'I'm sorry, ma'am.'

With visible effort, she got a hold on her emotions. Letting her hand drop from her mouth, she squared her shoulders. 'No, I understand. A life has become an investigation.' Grant had the sense she said it more to herself than to anyone else, but suddenly she focused on him. 'I'm just gratified to hear you haven't completely discounted the idea that Risa was murdered.'

At the word, a few of the technicians paused in their work. Murders were as rare as snowstorms in Terrell Hills. Most of the cops there had assumed that this had been just a terrible accident. Grant didn't want to dissipate that assumption. Not yet, anyway. He stepped closer to the woman, intending to placate her while keeping their conversation private.

'Well, ma'am,' he began carefully, 'I try not to discount anything, but I don't want you to get any false impressions.'

'The only one with any false impressions around here is you, Lieutenant,' she retorted, at a normal volume that sounded loud against his whisper. 'And I'm not a ma'am. My grandmother is a ma'am. I'm Britt.'

Grant shifted uncomfortably. He realized he'd probably get more information out of her if he called her by her first name, but he resisted. She'd not said it like an invitation; it had been a demand. If there was one thing Grant hated, it was being ordered around. Why did this woman seem to be constantly testing him? And why was he letting her get to him?

'I'd prefer to keep to Miss Reeve, if you don't mind,' he said, despite his best judgment. Why was he trying to keep her at arm's length?

'Actually, I do mind. My students call me Miss Reeve and I'd like to keep this whole process separated from them – in my mind anyway.'

A teacher. Of course. That explained her bossy way with him. She probably thought she could order him around just like she did her classroom full of teenage hellions. 'What grade do you teach?'

'Kindergarten.'

Grant groaned and shook his head. An added complication. Or rather complications. The tykes would undoubtedly hear about the death of their teacher's sister, which would have the school begging for the police to arrange a psychologist to come out and give them counseling, which would lead to –

'What's wrong, Lieutenant?' Britt cut into his worst-case scenario. 'Don't like kids?'

'No, I love kids,' Grant said defensively, then stopped suddenly. Why was he explaining himself? Why did he care what she thought of him or his opinion of children? 'They're just a problem – '

'A problem?' Britt mocked. 'Oh, yes, I suppose the prospect of interviewing twenty five- and six-year-olds is daunting, because, of course, a hardened cop like you would certainly consider all of them suspects now, wouldn't you?'

'You're being ridiculous.'

'So, I'm ridiculous and – what did you call me earlier? – a hysterical woman, and – '

'I know you're overwrought over your sister's death.'

'An overwrought, ridiculous, hysterical woman.' Britt's voice raised an octave.

Grant ran his palm along his stubble-roughened jaw in frustration. This woman was driving him crazy. He was trying to keep his cool, but she seemed intent on making him lose it. He didn't see the tears welling in her eyes until it was too late and they'd begun coursing down her cheeks. As the tears dripped off her chin, she began shaking uncontrollably.

'Damn,' was all Grant could think of to say as he reached out to grab her before she could hit the floor.

CHAPTER 2

'What the hell are you doing to her?'

In a half-crouch, Grant looked up at the figure which had appeared in the hallway. The afternoon light was streaming in from behind, leaving the new arrival backlit so that all Grant could make out was that he was tall. So tall his head nearly brushed the ceiling.

'Who are you?' Grant retorted.

Britt began to stir in his arms. Or in his lap, really. He'd caught her about halfway in her fall to the floor and, not caring to drop her to the floor, had eased her onto his thighs instead. Just when Grant had begun considering dragging her back into her bedroom, he suddenly had this new obstacle to contend with.

'I'll ask you the same question, young man,' the figure answered. 'And you'll answer me first.'

Geez, it had to be Old Man Reeve. Bossiness must run in the family. Grant could feel his shoulders bunching in irritation. But then he reminded himself that if it was Risa's father he'd just lost a daughter. Grant opened his mouth to answer, but he didn't get the chance.

'Well?' came the insistent demand.

Grant fought to keep his composure. 'I'm Detective Lieutenant Collins.'

A pregnant pause followed in which Grant felt strong, silent disapproval.

'And?'

'And, what?'

'And what have you done to my daughter?'

So it was the patriarch. Whatever his first name was. At this rate Grant was never going to find that out. That or anything else if he was stuck babysitting fainting women and trading verbal barbs with crotchety middle-aged men. And suddenly Grant lost his patience.

'Well, it was either catch her or let her take her chances with the hardwood.'

The man took a few steps forward and peered more closely at Britt's face. As he did, Grant got a closer look at him. His hair was thick and shiny and black. Jet-black, in an out-of-the-bottle way. His face was round and doughy soft, surprising for such a tall, thin man. But his eyes were anything but soft. In fact, they were such a contrast to his pillowy visage that it gave Grant a jolt. They were dark and piercing as they scrutinized his daughter.

'Well, you obviously should have let her hit the floor,' his hard voice clipped out. 'It would have brought her to her senses. She always becomes overly emotional. Always growing faint at the slightest incident.'

Britt moaned and Grant could feel her regaining consciousness. Her father straightened, looking down his nose at the two of them.

'What is it this time? A burglary? Her car get stolen? Officer, you need to tell her that these crimes happen to people all the time. She will just have to deal with it.'

'Wait a minute,' Grant said, 'you don't know what's happened –'

'I don't know anything except Brittany called the department and told the secretary it was an emergency.

She insisted that I be dragged out of my class. I had to leave one of my colleagues in charge and what a disaster that will be. The damage I will have to repair when I return will take up the rest of the week, I suppose. So, let's get on with it. Wake her up. Slap her or shake her. Whatever it takes. She'll thank you later, I feel certain. She knows what's best for her. Her best quality, in fact.'

Rarely could Grant remember being so dumbfounded that he couldn't decide on his next move. Fortunately, he didn't need to.

'Well, good thing *I* knew what was for my own good, because *you* certainly never took the time to know,' Britt croaked.

'Ah, I see you've recovered. Of course with your sharp tongue coming to life before your brain,' her father said.

Britt opened her mouth to retort, but suddenly looked around and realized her position – in Detective Collins's lap. Heart pounding, she scrambled to get her feet underneath her, at the same time digging one elbow into his hard thigh and the other into his chest. She leaned forward, but his hands gripped her. Her eyes sought his, and they held for a moment, his seeming to send a message of support before dropping their cold gray veil again. Yanking herself from his grasp, Britt stumbled into the hall wall. The oil painting behind her slid a bit crooked. Unconsciously Grant righted it as he watched the contest of wills before him.

'Well, rest assured, Dad, that I did not call you out on an idle errand.'

Grant caught the slight tremble in her lower lip as she paused for a breath. For some inexplicable reason he broke in to help her.

'Mr Reeve – '

'Actually, it's *Dr* Neil Reeve, Officer. I'm a professor of marketing at Trinity.'

'Actually, it's Lieutenant, *doctor*. I'm investigating your daughter's death.'

Neil Reeve's razor-sharp eyes darted to Britt, as if checking to be sure she was still breathing. His bushy black brows drew together and the corners of his mouth turned down. Britt returned his stare silently, her eyes filling with more tears with each blink until the salty drops finally spilled over onto her cheeks. Her father shook his head in impatient confusion.

Grant watched him closely.

'I don't understand . . . Who's –?'

'It's Risa, Dad,' Britt almost whispered.

Neil Reeve squeezed his eyelids shut and his whole body tensed. His hands bunched into fists. His arms and legs began to tremble and jump through his tailored cotton button-down shirt and wool-blend suit pants.

'No!' he shouted.

The eruption was so sudden and so loud, ricocheting around the small hallway, that Grant jumped, his right hand flying to the handle of the nine millimeter semi-automatic in his shoulder holster. But as Neil Reeve continued to stand rooted to the floor, shaking, eyes closed, Grant let his hand drop and glanced at Britt. She didn't seem fazed, as if this was the way her father normally dealt with strong feelings. They waited for a full minute before Neil Reeve, his body now still but tense, opened his dark eyes and spoke with a strange dispassion at odds with his physical reaction.

'What was it? A car accident?'

'She was killed,' Britt blurted out.

'Now wait a minute, Miss Reeve – '

'No, you wait a minute, Lieutenant,' Britt interrupted, then addressed her father with a voice full of passion. 'They think she slipped and hit her head. An accident. A healthy teenage girl dying while making a sandwich? No way.'

Grant marveled at her powers of recovery. Was she the same woman helpless in his arms just a few minutes ago? He was just beginning to realize how her unpredictability would make her a dangerous adversary. His eyes narrowed as he studied her.

'Anything is possible in this life, Miss Reeve, and if you don't believe that you're hopelessly naïve. Perfectly healthy babies die in their sleep in their cribs every day while men who've smoked two packs of cigarettes a day live to be a hundred. Where's the sense in that? Nowhere I can see.' Grant turned to Neil Reeve. 'I'm sorry for your loss, Professor. It's my job to find the reason for your daughter's death, not to make sense of it. Now, if you'll excuse me, I need to gather the *facts*.'

Neil moved aside to let Collins pass. 'You will be available for questions, later, won't you, Officer?'

His long, chino-clad legs paused, but he kept his back to them as he answered. 'Sure I will, for the questions *I'll* be asking *you*.'

'A bit of a cold fish, isn't he?' Neil asked as they watched Collins walk through the living room.

Look who's talking, Britt thought. But no, that wasn't entirely fair. She knew her father had feelings – his outburst was proof of that – he just controlled them religiously. She wasn't sure Grant Collins, on the other hand, possessed any emotions to begin with. Big difference there.

'It happened in the kitchen? The police say she slipped and hit her head?' Neil demanded.

Tears threatening again, Britt nodded and opened her mouth to explain, but he jumped in before she could.

'I knew it was a mistake for her to move in here with

you. It was just asking for trouble. You always let her get away with too much – spoiled her. She thought she was smarter than she really was and that's dangerous. You taught her that. You're the one who gave her ideas about quitting modeling and going to college next year. What was the hurry? She was throwing away millions of dollars. And so here she was in your little old house with its uneven floors. She probably tripped on some board sticking out of the floor. If she'd stayed with me this would have never happened. She would be alive right now.' Neil's harangue ended abruptly as he sucked in a breath.

Britt's eyes widened. She felt as if she'd been socked in her solar plexus. 'You think it's my fault Risa's dead?'

Neil carefully considered his answer, which made it that much more painful when it came. 'Yes. Maybe not directly, but indirectly, yes, you caused her death.'

Swallowing, Britt turned away from her father and shuffled down the hall to her bedroom. That detective thought *she* jumped to conclusions, well, what about Dad finding her guilty without ever seeing Risa's body? Of course Britt acknowledged that she had been responsible for Risa her whole life. Maybe she should take some of the blame. Maybe the flooring was in need of repair. Maybe . . .

No, Britt told herself as she stopped in her doorway. This was just a replay of the old dog and pony show – Dad blaming Britt. Britt doubting herself. Others feeding those doubts. Britt taking on martyrdom and pushing everyone away. Everyone but Risa. Risa. Now she was gone. Britt was alone.

Neil cleared his throat. 'You'll make all the arrangements. Call your sister. Tori needs to know before the media starts calling. And your mother. It will look appropriate for her to be at the funeral. Your grandmother must be told. Although we can't let her attend. With her bad hip, she might fall and create a scene. No, that wouldn't do at all. The media would focus on her instead of on Risa.'

Britt felt her anger rising up to replace the pain. She embraced it with relief.

'Grams can make her own decision about whether she'll be there or not,' Britt said, anticipating, with satisfaction, the scene between her father and his mother. No one would keep her 83-year-old grandmother from Risa's funeral; Britt was sure of that.

Neil waved away the suggestion. 'Of course you will convince her she won't.'

Leaning into the bathroom, Neil checked his reflection in the mirror and brushed an imaginary piece of lint from his lapel. Britt watched with incredulous fascination. Was he worried about *his* appearance as he looked at his daughter's corpse?

But as he passed her Britt softened. 'Dad, do you want me to go with you?'

'Go where?' Neil's brow furrowed in irritation.

'To see . . .' Britt swallowed the lump that reformed in her throat, 'Risa.'

Neil shook his head and sighed loudly with exasperation. 'I'm not going to see Risa. I'm leaving.'

'Leaving?'

'I have so much to do.' Almost talking to himself, Neil began checking off his list on his fingers. 'I have to plan the press conference. The media will be clamoring for a family reaction and we must make it perfect. The future depends on just the right touch of grief from the family. I'll handle most of the speaking, but I'll want you there to say a few words – '

'No!' Britt shouted.

'Oh, you're right. You would be terrible for this – much too emotional. Your blubbering would definitely embarrass the audience and off the TVs would go across the country. We'll get Tori to do it. A much better choice. She has been considering launching her acting career and here's her opportunity. An ideal one. If we can keep her sober long enough.'

'You make me sick,' Britt managed to choke out, though the words sounded pitifully inadequate to describe the strength of her revulsion.

But if Neil heard her he didn't show it. 'All the networks will cover it, and if we handle it just right we might be in for a special report. We could get one of the news magazines interested. International media will pick it up – I'm going to have to take at least a week off. Don't you think?'

Neil's focus returned from somewhere inside his internal schedule to Britt's face. The sudden eye contact jolted her. His eyes were glistening – with grief or greed? She couldn't tell, and did she really want to know for sure?

'That's, uh, expected, when a loved one dies. Especially a daughter. You deal with the grief in private.'

'Yes, indeed, there will be plenty of time for that. But first we need to use this opportunity. Remember Grace Kelly, Marilyn Monroe. Risa was even more beautiful and younger, which makes this all the more tragic. There's great potential here.'

Britt was surprised he didn't rub his hands together. Nausea welled up at the back of her throat. She bit the tip of her tongue to keep from throwing up on her father's shoes.

'And we can't forget the movie deals. Hollywood will be calling before nightfall.' Neil marched to the door with purpose.

'Just where do you think you're going?'

Startled, both Britt and Neil looked into the shadows of the dining room. Lieutenant Collins stepped out of a corner. Britt took one look at his assessing eyes and could tell he'd heard all the ugliness. She felt violated.

'Oh, it's you, Officer. I'm going home. I'll have to talk with you later,' Neil said dismissively, as he turned the knob and opened the door inlaid with leaded glass.

'Don't worry, Professor. I'll find you when I'm ready,' the cop responded.

Grant Collins reached forward in one fluid move and grabbed the heavy door before it banged into the wall. Gently, he eased it into its latch. He turned the deadbolt. The click sounded loud to Britt's ears.

An awkward silence followed. Somehow his hard, unyielding presence seemed closer than the fifteen feet from the foyer to the bedroom threshold where she stood.

'You know, it might be better this way,' Collins finally said.

'What's better?'

'That your father not see your sister right now,' Collins explained.

'Is this another of your "he-who-know-a-lot-about-death" observations?' Britt asked. 'Because if it is, I don't need it. I'm learning about death all on my own, thanks.'

Collins's eyes narrowed, but he pressed on. 'We all handle grief in different ways. I've seen people cry for a week non-stop, then pick up and be fine. Others, dry-eyed at the funeral, will lose nearly all their hair six months later. Maybe your father knew the only way he could keep going was by not seeing her body.'

'My father knew the only way to keep going was to make money by turning my sister into an icon. Dying was the best thing she ever did for her career. Now she'll never die. She'll be sixteen forever . . .'

All of a sudden the nausea overcame her. Britt spun around and ran for her bathroom. As she bent over the toilet, she heard the door close softly behind her.

Grant stood in the hallway, wondering what to do next. It was an unusual feeling and one he was not at all comfortable with. Never before in his life had he felt so out of control. He'd been involved in big cases before, when he was with the San Antonio Police Department, so that potential couldn't be what had him so unnerved. Especially since it was looking more and more like an accident – something he could wrap up in a day or two.

Why did that possibility leave him so uneasy?

The house was quiet – Ortega was interviewing the neighbors, the Medical Examiner's investigator had gone along with the body and Randall was outside briefing the officer sent to guard the house – so the sounds of Britt's retching were clear. Instead of making him want to escape to the opposite end of the house, they made him itch to hand her a cool washcloth.

Giving himself a mental nudge, Grant moved down the hallway, past the second bathroom. He paused at the threshold to Risa's room, and took a long look before stepping inside. Randall had been right. The kid's room was a disaster – the double bed not only unmade but looking as if whoever slept in it had wrestled an alligator.

Two of the dresser's six drawers were open, overflowing their contents, and the closet doors were thrown wide, revealing a hodge-podge of clothes hanging not just on the rod but on each other, with hems trailing on the floor. That comfortable look, Grant thought to himself with a tight smile. Actually, he'd always envied the ability to overlook disorder, to have a room like this, but his exacting nature never would allow it. Even now he felt the urge to straighten the concert poster haphazardly stuck up on the wall.

The east-facing window didn't allow much of the late afternoon light in through the well-shaded backyard, but even so Grant could identify the poster's subject purely by the outline. Lyle Lovett. Risa's choice of the singer with the quirky looks and philosophical lyrics impressed him. Maybe there had been more to this girl than smiling for the camera. Then Grant remembered the argument between Neil and Britt. Risa had shown spunk in standing up to her domineering father on the subject of college too.

Grant pulled his thoughts up short. He was starting to like Risa Reeve. That wasn't good. He always studied the smallest details in order to *know* the victim, but not to *feel* the victim. He never allowed his feelings to get involved. That led to error. He would have to be careful.

'What's your take?'

Grant didn't have to turn around to recognize the familiar voice of his partner.

'An accident. Kid hit her head in just the wrong place. Maybe she could've made it to the hospital if someone would've been here to see her do it.'

'And, with a brain bleed, would have ended up a vegetable. It's a helluva lot better this way,' Ortega stated.

Shrugging noncommittally, Grant surveyed the room again. 'Something about this room isn't quite right.'

'More than one something, I'd say,' Ortega joked.

'It's not the mess,' Grant mused. The dresser looked to be a well-restored antique, the unmatching nightstand was crafted of good wood, but old, and the headboardless bed was covered in a handmade quilt. A framed watercolor print of muted spring colors that mirrored the colors in the quilt hung on the wall above the bed. A woven rug of neutral beige lay in the center of the room, over the hardwood floor.

'It's decorated like a guest room, not a teenager's digs,' Grant finally concluded.

'Yeah,' Ortega agreed in a bored tone. 'Look, why are you still here if you think it's an accident?'

Grant turned to look at his partner. 'You know the answer to that. A case with this much heat has got to be handled damned carefully.'

'See any signs the place was tossed?' Ortega asked, glancing around the room.

'Not specifically, but if they were looking it was for something specific, and what would that be?'

Both men's heads snapped to the wall at the sound of a thump on the other side. Ortega cocked his eyebrow. 'The sister holed up in her room?'

Distracted, Grant nodded and crouched down to peer under the bed. Dirty socks and about eight pairs of athletic shoes lurked there.

'So, who's the lucky stiff who gets to do that interview?'

Grant craned his neck to look at Ortega. The guy was so low-key that even after six months of working with him Grant couldn't always tell if he was joking or not. Britt Reeve was physically appealing, and Ortega was a famous ladies' man, so he could be on the level.

Grant stood and slipped by Ortega and back into the hallway.

'I will,' Grant said.

'I'd probably get more outta her. Charm works, y'know.'

'I don't remember them teaching charm in the academy, Chile.'

'They didn't, or you'd've never graduated the top of your class,' Ortega retorted as he followed Grant into the bathroom. 'It's a crying shame. As perfect as you are in everything else, you could use some work in that department, ole Tom.'

Their nicknames for each other – Tom and Chile – had grown out of their first day on the job together. It had been type-A personality meets type-B personality, equaling instant irritation. Grant's intense perfectionism had clashed with Ortega's easy-going demeanor. Grant had tried to push Ortega into working his way and Ortega had responded by ignoring him, intentionally antagonizing Grant. Finally, tired of being bossed, Ortega had called Grant as hard to swallow as a Tom Collins made with cheap gin and sour lemonade. And Grant, who'd been trying to goad Ortega into telling him his first name, had started calling him 'Chile' after the green peppers the Ortega food company was famous for. To Grant's chagrin, Ortega liked the moniker, and even introduced himself using it sometimes – instead of Arturo, his real first name. The 'Tom' still bugged Grant.

Those who eavesdropped on their conversations were often confused.

'I suppose if I have to have a fault, that's the one to have.'

'La-di-da.' Ortega danced his nose in the air.

Ignoring him, Grant pulled a pen out of his pocket and pried open the medicine cabinet. Not much here, over-the-counter painkillers, cough syrup, bandages. Grant collected it all with gloves and bagged it, just in case.

Ortega was going through the drawer to the right of the sink. Using his bare hands, of course.

'Chile, do you think you could be more careful?' Grant asked.

'Why? You said yourself this thing was an accident. Just a bunch of high-dollar buff stuff in here anyway. Oo-hooh, would my Genie love to get her hands on this. One time, her rich sister-in-law gave her some stuff she'd bought and didn't like the "fe-e-e-el" of – if you can believe that. Anyway, you would'a thought it came in a crystal case and was made of crushed-up diamonds, or something. Genie still hoards it. Wears it only when we go out somewheres special. And believe me it's nothing compared to this booty. I bet you lunch the kid has a thousand bucks' worth of junk in here.' Ortega shook his head and let out a sigh like the air let out of a balloon. He leaned against the bathroom wall. 'It's such a waste.'

'I agree. It turns a pretty face into something cheap and an ugly face into a caricature. It doesn't hide anything or fool anyone. Why do women bother? Especially someone with such fresh beauty. It just wrecks it, for God's sake.'

Ortega stared at his normally reticent partner, stunned by the vehemence of his outburst. 'I was talking about the waste of a life, Tom-o – the kid, not her warpaint.'

Grant's eyes snapped up. 'You're too sentimental, Chile. You haven't seen enough and so the little things get to you.'

'And you've seen too much.'

'Ignorance isn't bliss, you know.'

'No, it's not, but it's a damned sight better than seeing so much and knowing so much but never feeling any of it – so that you wake up in a cold sweat every night after your eyes close and your heart wakes up. Y'know Collins, if it goes in it's gotta come out. You're a smart guy, you figure it out. Maybe it'll come to you in a dream.' Ortega flashed his omnipresent grin to indicate a rare lecture from the laidback was over.

Grant moved to the combination tub/shower, sliding

his hand along the edge of the floral shower curtain, pulling it aside to peek around it. His jaw began to ache, and he realized he'd been clenching it since Ortega had started his censure. Ducking his head into the shower, he relaxed his facial muscles. He knew his partner would notice, and he didn't want to give him the satisfaction of knowing what he'd said had got to Grant. He knew Chile had heard the gossip about why Grant had moved from the San Antonio Police Department to the go-nowhere job in Terrell Hills, but he didn't know the truth. Nobody did and nobody wanted to. And Grant didn't want to think about it now.

With an effort he focused back on the case at hand. He didn't notice much of interest in the shower: just some salon-brand shampoo, conditioner, liquid body soap.

'See anything good?' Chile asked.

'N – ' Grant stopped himself and stared hard at the disposable razor in the soap dish. The blades were stained with what looked like blood.

'Hand me an evidence bag,' Grant ordered as he reached into his pants pocket for his tweezers. He carefully placed the razor into the plastic bag Ortega held out to him.

'She probably just cut herself shaving this morning,' Grant mumbled as he zipped the bag closed and slipped it into the pocket of his blazer.

'But ya never know,' Ortega finished. 'She coulda been trying to commit suicide, cut herself up real good in the shower with this cheapo razor, almost bled to death, but got up, got dressed and went to make a sandwich. Right when she was about to eat she felt woozy and passed out, knocking her head on the doorjamb and killing herself anyway.'

Ortega flashed a self-satisfied grin. Grant didn't comment. Ortega was fond of spinning soap-opera-style scenarios that he didn't believe but liked to have fun with. It kept a mostly dull job as a detective in a sheltered community from being eye-glazing. Grant didn't want to tell him that the scenario was more likely than Ortega would have guessed.

But, even if something that far-out had happened, it still didn't make it murder.

Ortega lifted the lid to the toilet tank. 'No drugs,' he deadpanned.

'Of course not. My sister never used drugs in her life. I resent the fact that you'd even consider it.'

Both men turned at the sound of the quiet, yet hostile voice. Britt stood in the bathroom doorway, hands on her hips. Her hair was damp and brushed back from a face that had been scrubbed clean. The tip of her nose and rims of her eyes were red and slightly swollen. But it was the eyes themselves that were on fire.

Grant's eyes locked with hers for several beats. Ortega cleared his throat. Again Grant had to unclench his jaw in order to talk.

'Miss Reeve, I know I asked you to let us do our job. Especially – ' he emphasized the word ' – if you think it was murder. We can't find evidence if you're always popping up telling us what is and what is not important. Usually we like to find what we think is important, then use what you tell us to put it in context later.

'For instance, say Ortega, here, *had* found drugs in the tank. Nobody's saying your sister used drugs. Maybe your boyfriend dumped them in there, your sister found them and called him on it and he came and slammed her head into the doorjamb.'

Britt's face flushed bright pink. She sucked in a breath.

'Hey, take it easy,' Ortega cautioned.

Grant was surprised at himself. He never taunted witnesses or victims' families. He was always scrupulously businesslike and very reticent. What was coming over him? Why did everything this woman say set him off?

Ortega shot Grant a warning glance and stepped up to take Britt's arm. Her chest was rising and falling rapidly and she appeared to be close to hyperventilating. Grant had to wonder if he hadn't hit a nerve with the boyfriend comment. Or was it the drugs?

'I think we're ready to interview you now, Miss Reeve,' Ortega said gently.

'That's right,' Grant concurred, and pushed Ortega away from her side with a hand between his shoulderblades. 'Detective Ortega is going to check through your sister's room for anything we might have missed. You come with me.'

Grant walked between the two and led the way down the hall. Britt glanced at Ortega, who shrugged and ambled off into Risa's bedroom. Britt stood rooted to the floor, looking incredulously at this detective who expected her to jump and run after him. At the end of the hall he stopped and said, without looking over his shoulder, 'Let's get this over with.'

Though she bristled at his tone, Britt had to embrace the thought. The sooner she got him out of her house and investigating, the faster Risa's killer could be caught.

'All right,' she agreed.

He nodded, and turned left instead of right, which put him in her bedroom. Though the technicians had already left their trail of fingerprint dust there, having him in there seemed a worse violation of privacy than their presence had been.

'Can't we go somewhere else?' Britt paused. Where could they go? In the living room and kitchen, even the dining room, she'd have to look at the empty space where Risa had lain. 'Maybe outside?'

His eyes searched her face briefly. 'Why? Do you have something to hide in here?'

He made an exaggerated show of looking around the room, even peering under her four-poster bed.

'No!' Britt answered, too forcefully.

The cop's eyebrows shot up, but he didn't comment again.

Britt took a deep breath. As much as she hated to, she had to plead with him. She couldn't bear the thought of talking about Risa and her death in the only room that hadn't yet been touched by it. And she didn't want him staring at her things, her life.

'Please . . .' Britt cleared her throat. 'I need some air. How about the backyard?'

His gray eyes studied her, and Britt felt as if she was being given a secret test. 'We can't go in your yard; I don't want the neighbors to hear. Plus, the media are starting to descend.'

They were? Britt hadn't noticed. She walked to the front door and looked through the sheer curtain that covered the leaded glass. Sure enough, she could see several news vans with satellite dishes affixed to their roofs. A woman and two men she recognized as reporters on San Antonio television and several other women with notebooks were listening to Mr Zambrino, a nosy old man who lived four houses down the street. He disapproved of women living alone – always said they were asking for trouble. She was sure that he was telling 'Told you so' to anyone who would listen. On the right side of the driveway two men carrying tape recorders and microphones emblazoning the call letters of the local news radio stations milled around near the uniformed police posted along the yellow crime scene tape. She could see one cameraman filming the outside of her house. She knew there must be others out of her sight.

'Let's take a drive,' the cop said. It wasn't an offer, it was an order. Still, Britt jumped at the chance to go anywhere outside the house.

'Okay,' Britt sighed, and reached for the doorknob.

'Wait,' he ordered.

Britt turned to look at him in exasperation. Was he such a control freak that he couldn't even let her open her own door?

He paused in the act of sliding his sunglasses from the top of his head to the bridge of his nose.

'Once you step out that door, the cameras will roll. They'll be taking your picture,' he said, eyes boring into hers.

'I don't care,' Britt spat out. 'My sister's dead. You think I care what I look like? I'm not my father. Don't you forget that.'

His stony eyes softened just a moment before the mirrored lenses covered them. 'You look fine,' he said.

It startled Britt; the comment seemed so uncharacteristic. She looked closely at him, but his eyes were hidden, the unyielding features of his tanned face closed. The emotion was gone. It was as if she'd imagined it.

'And I don't forget anything,' he warned.

Britt turned the doorknob and flung the door open in frustration. Was if he was trying to throw her even more off-balance? Maybe it was a police strategy to get her to spill some secret? If he thought it was just an accident – like he said – then why was he treating her so roughly?

The reporters suddenly noticed their appearance at the door and began shouting. The photographers snapped to attention and pointed their lenses at her face. Even after being forewarned, their intense focus still disarmed Britt. She resisted the urge to bury her face into Grant Collins's convenient, muscular shoulder. *Never* would she do that. Instead she straightened, ignored the reporters' shouts and followed him to the unmarked car in the driveway.

'Don't say a word and look straight ahead,' Collins told her out of the corner of his mouth, before the reporters began shooting off their questions, only a fraction of which Britt actually heard:

'Are you the model's sister?'

'What happened to Risa?

'Is she dead?'

Suddenly a man she recognized from an eyewitness news team broke past the uniformed cop and charged for her, microphone in hand, photographer scrambling to keep up. Several others followed him.

Just as suddenly Grant Collins wrapped his arm around her waist and pulled her in front of him, squeezing her back against his chest, holding her upper arms in a vise grip with his other arm. He propelled her forward, his right leg stepping between her legs, his thigh pressuring her to go faster.

'Move,' he growled in her ear.

What did he think she was doing? She was going as fast as his imprisoning hands would let her. Her anger flared again, racing with the blood already pumping from adrenaline.

'Was anyone with Risa when she died?' a strident tenor-alto that could have been male or female yelled.

'How did Risa die?'

'Are you under arrest, ma'am?'

'Will you make a statement, Detective?'

'No comment,' Collins finally ground out through tight jaws.

They had reached the black car; he opened the door, shielding her body from the reporters and shoving her inside. 'Get in.'

'Tell us, was Risa murdered?'

Britt put her foot against the door Collins was trying to slam shut. She looked at the reporter who'd asked the question – a middle-aged woman with a warm expression in a mocha complexion. 'Yes,' she said.

For a half-second everyone froze. Except Detective Lieutenant Grant Collins, who pushed down the lock, shut the door, elbowed the reporters out of the way and got in on the driver's side. He turned the key in the ignition and, without looking, backed out of the driveway, leaving reporters and photographers scattering in his wake.

Britt looked back and saw a flattened notebook bouncing before finally coming to rest in the street. Its frantic owner raced onto the asphalt to pick it up and throw a middle finger at their tail-lights.

The black sedan struggled to change gears as fast as its driver was putting pedal to the metal. Heart racing, Britt looked up to see the familiar stop sign and wondered if he'd bother to stop for it. Just then she was thrown into the dashboard as he braked. Her forearms braced her until the car had stopped completely. Outraged, she opened her mouth to let him have it – when she saw his face.

It had transformed into a mask of fury – hard on the outside with heat simmering within, almost like the lava she'd seen as a child when her family had visited Hawaii. Its exterior cooled to a black crust while it was still two thousand degrees, molten-red on the inside. But instead of frightening her, somehow this glimpse into his emotion made her feel a brief connection. Maybe he wasn't so unfeeling after all.

As Britt watched, he seemed to struggle inwardly for a moment.

'Why did you do that?' he asked finally.

'She asked a question; I answered it.'

'Don't be flip,' he snapped, then took a quick breath and returned to his usual passionless tone. 'We agreed you wouldn't say anything.'

'No,' Britt corrected. 'You told me not to say anything. I didn't agree.'

Iron eyes met hers across the car. They were unreadable.

'I thought you said you weren't like your father,' he observed with nonchalance. 'What you did back there was just like him. One word that will inflame not only the tabloids but even the usually credible news organizations and will make the case grow into ten times the story it would be if it were mere speculation.'

Britt's eyes widened and she sucked her bottom lip between her teeth, giving it a painful bite. Would her dad have told the reporters what she had? Yes, she had to admit, he would have said it was murder – even if he didn't believe it. It was sensational, good copy, a loaded soundbite. She'd said it because she thought it was true. Her father would have said it because it would make Risa front-page news.

Grant Collins was right. And she hated him for it.

CHAPTER 3

Britt stuck her foot out of the car before he'd slipped the gear shift into 'park'. Slamming the door shut, she stood, turned her face to the sun and closed her eyes. The pungent scent of rosemary filled her nostrils and at once she felt more at peace.

She'd been so angry with herself for acting like her father that she hadn't taken time to speculate on where Grant was taking her for their 'talk'. When he'd turned into the grounds of the McNay Art Museum, she'd been surprised, but pleasantly so.

This bit of culture didn't fit in the stereotypical police detective package that she'd been trying to fit him into. He was arrogant and single-minded and should be taking her to some cold metal fold-out chair in front of a scarred-up table in an interrogation room and offering her cold, burnt coffee. Instead he'd driven her to a haven of art and natural beauty amidst the chaos of the city.

Why?

Did he appreciate the peace and beauty of the gardens or did he simply want to find a quiet place to talk?

Or, more likely, was it just convenient?

Britt opened her eyes and looked at the sparkling water that ran through the grounds of the twenty-three-acre estate that had once been Marion Koogler McNay's home. The main stucco Spanish-style mansion housed many pieces of art, and the hilly grounds, subtly lush, tended more toward perennial green plants and trees rather than splashy colorful annual flowers. The McNay had been one of their favorite places to come, especially when Risa was a child. Risa had loved to dangle her toes in the water and tease the turtles in the Japanese garden. Britt remembered how she'd nagged her to watch out or she'd get her toes nipped. And the turtles *had* gotten hold of Risa's tender little toes, but so what? Why couldn't Britt just have let her be a kid without nagging her? Was it nagging or loving that Risa had remembered of Britt as she died? Britt had nagged out of love, but now she wished she'd just kept her mouth shut.

The scene in front of her began to lose focus . . .

'Are you all right, Miss Reeve?'

Britt pressed her palms into her cheeks where the tears had dropped, as if she could press them back into her skin. She'd need them later; she was sure.

'Please call me Britt,' she sighed, letting down a defense. 'I don't think I want to be talking about . . . all this . . . with someone who calls me Miss.'

His lips thinned and he pushed his car door shut with studied deliberation. She couldn't see his eyes behind the silver mirrored lenses, but she imagined those steely orbs narrowing to slits.

Finally, he said with obvious reluctance: 'If it'll help you talk, then Britt it will be for now. Let's take a walk.'

His long strides had already taken him up the tree-lined trail toward the fountain. Britt followed, unable to keep her eyes off his walk. He consumed the ground. It wasn't so much that his steps were long, they were just so damned confident. He walked as if he owned everything he touched.

Britt envied him that complete self-assurance. Of course with him it often crossed the line into arrogance. Like now.

'Call me Collins,' he sent back over his shoulder as he climbed the hill.

'Oh, what an honor,' Britt mumbled sarcastically.

He stopped. He turned. Sunlight bounced off his shades.

'What?'

For a moment she was intimidated. Then the moment was gone.

'I said, what an honor. I bet you don't let many people call you by your name. Even if it is your last name,' she said as she reached him. She had to look up to meet his eyes, or rather, her own eyes in his glasses. A conversation with herself.

'No, I don't,' he answered with a poker face.

Did this guy possess any sense of humor? Buoyant Risa would have made a project of Grant Collins, Britt thought. Always the optimist, always looking for the best in people, she'd never let anyone take themselves too seriously. Her teasing and cajoling had always worked magic. *Why aren't you here with me now, Risa? You'd have him eating out of your hand.*

A sob caught in her throat. Collins took her elbow without another word and directed her to a bench in the roughhewn wooden gazebo of the Japanese garden. Britt resisted as they ducked through the doorway.

'Would you rather go somewhere else?'

Britt hesitated, then shook her head as she sank down onto the bench. 'No, I feel close to her here. It's okay.'

Collins gave a curt nod and sat down next to her, pulling a notebook out of his blazer's interior pocket. His knee brushed hers. She drew away, pressing her knees together. But he seemed more unnerved by their accidental contact than she was.

'Excuse me,' he said as he inched away from her as far as the short bench would allow. His eyes scanned the page open in his notebook before looking at her.

Suddenly she wished for the open friendly face of Detective Ortega. He seemed caring at least.

'Why didn't you let your partner interview me?' she blurted out.

The muscles in Collins's jaw bunched before he answered, 'Because I'm in charge.'

'And that's supposed to be an answer?'

His eyebrows inched up a notch before falling back into their frozen mask position. The rather violent tapping of his pencil eraser against his knee was the only indication that her answer had irritated him, because his voice was calm and smooth.

'It's not supposed to be an answer; it is an answer. Like it or not, I am in the officer in charge of the investigation into your sister's death and at the moment you are my best witness and best chance to clear up this case. Soon.'

'Well, don't look to me to help you tie it up with a neat little ribbon tonight, because I won't. I want the truth, and the truth isn't always neat and easy and convenient.'

Collins rubbed his palm along the edge of his jawline, calluses audibly scratching across his five o'clock shadow. Then he dropped his hand back to his notebook and opened his mouth, but he must have immediately thought better of it because he shut his mouth again. He scribbled onto the first page without looking at it. Britt peeked, but only saw her name with 'sister of victim' under it.

Couldn't he have written 'Risa'? 'Victim' was so dehumanizing. Britt shut her eyes again to the images that floated to the front of her mind's eye. Risa's inert body. The blood caked in her tawny hair. Her blue lips.

She forced her eyes open and found the silver lenses turned to her.

'Please take off your glasses,' Britt said. She resisted the urge to explain why. The reason should be obvious.

His lips thinned, but he did reach up and move his sunglasses onto the top of his head. Britt couldn't help noticing that the color of the frames matched the streaks of silver in his hair. Everything about him was so metallic.

'Is there anything else I can do for you?'

Britt thought she caught a hint of sarcasm in his voice. But it was so fleeting she wondered if she could have imagined it. She watched a mother and two little girls walk along the pond's opposite bank as she answered.

'Yes. You can catch Risa's killer.'

The knee-tapping started again. Britt was gratified to know that she was getting to him, too.

'All right,' he said. 'Let's get started.'

He cleared his throat, but then had to wait while the little family squealed and skipped its way through the tiny gazebo on the way down the path. The mother apologized, watching her daughters with an indulgent smile. Britt smiled back – the toddlers were so full of the joy of life. They chased a frog that hopped off a lilypad onto the bank. Britt glanced at Collins and saw he never looked at the children. He remained focused on the blank page in front of him until the girls' voices faded into the distance.

Britt's temporarily buffeted spirits sank back down to reality.

'How old was your sister?'

'She's sixteen,' Britt said, then at his look, added, 'I mean was. No, that doesn't sound right. She *is* sixteen. She'll just always be sixteen.'

'Did your sister have any health problems?' Collins asked. 'Ever.'

'No, nothing major.'

'I didn't ask if she had any *major* health problems I said *any* health problems.'

Britt was taken aback, and tempted to give a scathing retort. She knew he was trying to make this into an accident, but did he have to be so blunt about it? Still, she swallowed her pride and reminded herself she was trying to help Risa. Play along, she told herself, and maybe he would be more receptive to her ideas.

'She did have migraines pretty often. Especially when she was under a lot of stress. They'd get so intense she'd have to take something for the pain and lie down for a couple of hours.'

Collins nodded and Britt watched him write 'migraines – stroke?' on the page. Her heartbeat began to speed up. Her sister hadn't had a stroke. She longed to correct him, but she bit her words back.

'Did she have anything prescribed for the migraines or did she just take over-the-counters?' he asked, without looking up.

'No, she never went to the doctor with it. She didn't like taking anything on prescription, but sometimes she had to take an over-the-counter painkiller.'

'And it was always an ibuprofen or aspirin, nothing else – nothing recreational that might have made the pain easier to bear?' His eyes met hers suddenly and Britt realized with startling clarity that he was trying to catch her in a lie, if he could.

'No,' she shouted with outrage. How had he jumped from Risa having a stroke to her committing suicide with a drug overdose? 'I already told you my sister never used drugs. She was a good girl and smart and she wouldn't do that. Not ever.'

'Even parents don't always know what their kids are doing,' Collins said. 'Just because you didn't see it, doesn't mean I can rule it out.'

Britt crossed her arms over her chest and pressed them tightly into her breasts. 'Yes, you can. I guarantee it.'

For a moment their eyes locked, and Britt thought he was going to challenge her bald statement. But instead he stood abruptly and walked to the other side of the gazebo, and looked out over the water with his back to her.

Britt watched as he raised his hand to head level and braced it against the wood supporting the gazebo.

'Unfortunately, there are no guarantees in life,' he said.

He spoke the sentence in the same level voice he seemed to use for everything, but a melancholy essence drifted through his words. Britt opened her mouth to respond, but – for once – held her tongue and waited for him to continue. A minute later, he turned to face her.

'I would like nothing more than to be able to guarantee you that I will find out what happened to your sister. But I can't. And you can't. The only person who knows the truth is Risa. Other people may know parts of the truth – but not the whole. So I'm left to find the pieces of the puzzle and put it together well enough so that I can see the picture it creates. Some pieces will never be found; sometimes they're vital and sometimes they're not.'

His ramrod-straight posture didn't give, but Britt could feel his spirit sagging, as if not being able to finish the puzzle perfectly somehow defeated him. Britt looked into his eyes and for the first time could see a vulnerability beyond their tough outer layer. He was declaring a truce in their war of wills, and she felt herself accepting it.

Instead of accusing him of coming up with an advance excuse for not pursuing Risa's killer, as she'd been inclined to do when he'd begun his monologue, she nodded and said, 'I understand.'

His eyebrows flicked up in recognition of the first exchange they'd had that was not confrontational. He acted as surprised as Britt was by their brief connection.

And brief it was.

'But Risa had a lot of people who loved her – people who really knew her – who'll be willing to help. We'll be able to put it together,' Britt promised.

'We?' Collins slid his sunglasses back down over his eyes and Britt felt a door to his soul closing again.

'Well,' Britt explained, 'you don't expect me to stand by and put justice for my flesh and blood in a stranger's hands.'

'That's exactly what I expect you to do. That's exactly what the law expects you to do. That's what you will do.'

The air seemed charged in the two feet that separated them. Grant struggled with his own emotions that were always so well contained. What had prompted him to share his personal philosophy with this woman? He never did that with an interview subject. But Britt had thrown him so off-balance with her unlikely mix of helplessness and grit wrapped up in a package equally contradictory. Her satin-skinned elfin face with its dimples and dancing hazel eyes set his heart beating one minute while her sexy little hourglass body stopped it the next.

She seemed to thrive on the confrontation. He had to get them back on an even keel, even it meant giving up a little of his control.

'Let's take a walk,' he said.

Britt's eyes searched his face before she nodded. 'Okay.'

As she stood, he stepped back for her to duck out the door of the gazebo. He breathed in the scent she wore. It was either perfume or her soap or her shampoo or just her.

He had noticed it before, as he'd held her unconscious in his lap, but hadn't fully appreciated how well the soft yet spicy scent suited Britt Reeve. It was as contradictory as she was.

And as difficult to forget.

They walked up the path, toward the whitewashed, red-tile-roofed museum in silence. Sneaking a glance at Britt, Grant could see she was distracted, her thoughts turned inward. Suddenly he wanted to hear those thoughts spoken aloud.

'Why don't you tell me about Risa?' he prompted.

'What about her? There's so much to tell I don't know what exactly you're looking for.'

'How she grew up – your family history.'

Britt stopped then, and spun to face him.

'Why are you asking? You heard what went on between me and my father so it's not a great leap to figure out we are a dysfunctional family. Can't we just leave it at that?'

Grant ran his hand back over his five o'clock shadow, across his chin and back over the other side. Talking to her was like dealing with a minefield of nerves, and he kept stepping right on the ones that blew up in his face. He waited for her to dissolve into tears, but she defied his expectations again – staring him down instead, with her back straight, lower lip steady, the wind blowing through her mass of burnished brunette curls.

Where had her dimples gone?

What was he thinking?

'Well?' Britt put her hands on her hips. 'Can we?'

'Look, Miss . . . Britt,' he began. 'If you can go back and give me some history I can do my job that much better. It's likely most of the information will not be useful to me, but there's always the chance that something that seems inconsequential to you will spark my interest or will jibe with some piece of evidence and fill in another piece of that puzzle.'

Britt opened her mouth and Grant braced himself for another challenge. But she surprised him. Again.

'Okay.' With a slight sigh, she turned back to the path and began to stroll. 'Risa was born when I was eleven. Tori was nine. Before that, on the surface, ours had seemed like the perfect family – the successful father, the beautiful young mother who stayed home with the requisite two children, the house in the right city, with the right zip code and the right cars. It was a family model others aspired to. And a perfect façade. Scratch the surface, though, and underneath you'd have seen a father so distant he didn't ask anything deeper than "How was your day?" and didn't listen for the answer, and a mother who was so busy playing tennis and having four-hour lunches that she hardly saw her daughters, and when she did take time out of her busy schedule it was to take the beautiful one shopping to dress up her real live doll.'

'Well, it doesn't seem to have done you any harm,' Grant offered as his eyes scanned her from head to toe, quickly but thoroughly. He couldn't help thinking how she'd look dressed up in silk and lace instead of khakis and cotton.

'Oh, no.' Britt laughed tonelessly at his supposition. 'I wasn't the doll – that's Tori: the perfect combination of my father's height and my mother's beauty. I was the brain. "Brittany does the books and Tori gets the looks" was the family motto.'

Britt seemed lost a moment in reflection that Grant was loath to interrupt. In a moment she continued. 'It rolled along this way for years, until the veneer of the Reeve family began to crack. The university recruited Father out of the business world and into academia, a place perfectly suited to his pomposity, and my mother was a tremendous asset on his arm at university functions. Only Mother didn't see it that way. She'd always hoped the husband she'd hand-picked in college for his overwhelming ambition would take over the multi-billion dollar company he worked for and really begin amassing power and prestige.

'Cunning as she was, she didn't see that his ambition was to control more than achieve. When he couldn't control his colleagues he moved on to college students, who have to revere his every word or suffer at the end of the semester . . .' Britt paused, shifted her gaze to just beyond his shoulder and sucked in a deep breath. The monologue seemed to be taking a lot out of her.

Grant was so fascinated by her story – and the passion and insight with which she told it – that he'd not written down a thing. But somehow he knew he would remember every word.

Britt finally continued. 'At the same time Father took the position at Trinity University Mother had Risa and started spending even more time than usual away from home. It was clear she'd never wanted the baby, but I thought she just didn't want the messy hassle of diapers and feedings. I don't think Dad ever saw what was coming, either. He must still wonder what happened, although he never talks about it.'

'What did happen?' Grant asked, trying not to sound as if he already knew. He wanted to hear this in her words.

Britt gave him a sharp look, as if gauging his sincerity. 'Risa was six months old when Sophia took off with the mayor. She mailed us a postcard telling us she wasn't coming back. And she didn't.'

'You haven't seen her in sixteen years?'

'I've seen her on TV; I've talked to her on the phone

twice. But, that's right, I haven't seen her in the flesh since I was eleven years old.'

'What was she doing on TV?'

'She was standing next to her husband looking as gorgeous as several million dollars can look. I swear money gives her the glow some women gain with motherhood.'

'Her husband?' Grant prompted.

'Senate candidate and land baron supreme Carl Lawrence.'

'Your mother is Sophia Lawrence?' Grant couldn't hide his shock. Sophia Lawrence had been all over the news months before, when she had left her octogenarian millionaire husband to marry Carl Lawrence right in the middle of his decision to campaign for the Senate. Pollsters had predicted a plummet in the polls for the good ole boy candidate from West Texas, but he'd hired a public relations whiz who ruthlessly depicted the jilted old man as a wife-beater. Right or wrong, it had turned the tide of the public's sympathy and had given Carl a cause which he had before so sorely lacked: domestic abuse.

Grant had never quite believed the battered woman story but hadn't had any reason to pursue it at all. Now he might have to.

He noticed Britt looking at him expectantly and realized how long he'd been lost in his own thoughts. Something about her gaze was so penetrating he half wondered if she could guess what he'd been thinking.

'Did Risa have any dealings with your mother?' Grant asked.

'No, not on a personal level,' Britt answered thoughtfully. 'As a baby and little girl she didn't "miss" her. I'd taken care of her more than Sophia ever did so her absence wasn't as traumatic as it might seem. But later, when she began to understand Sophia had left, she began to feel it was her fault in some way. Risa thought she had caused her to run off. After that Risa was almost obsessed about Sophia. She would never have anything to do with her but she would talk about her often and she would follow her in the media. This marriage to Lawrence really upset Risa. She kept saying it wasn't fair that Mother ended up stepping on so many people on her climb to the top of the world.'

Britt stopped suddenly, and her hand flew to her mouth.

'What is it?' Grant asked at the look of sudden realization on her face.

'I just remembered something,' Britt answered distractedly as her hand came away from her mouth but remained hovering in the air nearby, as if standing by if needed. 'How could I have forgotten? I guess it just seemed like more of Risa's obsession about Sophia so I didn't pay much attention at the time.'

'Tell me,' Grant urged.

Britt's eyes met his. 'She said she had to stop Sophia from hurting anyone else. She said, "I'll tell the secret and she and that rhinestone cowboy will never be able to go out in public again."'

'You think she was talking about exposing the way Sophia abandoned you as children?'

'No, the fact that she left my father is public knowledge, but the way she did it is not. I'm sure most people in Terrell Hills remember, but we – the family – made a pact a long time ago – probably the only thing Tori ever backed us on – that we wouldn't talk about it. It sounds too much like whining, and really it's not like she left us on a street corner. We had our father, a roof over our heads, a comfortable life. We were probably better off without her.'

57

Grant couldn't argue with that, but from the wistful expression on her face wasn't sure Britt had convinced herself, despite her words.

'So what could the secret be?' Grant asked, as he began to scribble for the first time in his notebook.

'She didn't say any more,' Britt muttered, shaking her head. She ran her fingers up into her scalp and shook her wild curls with frustration before bringing her hands back over to cover her face. 'And I didn't ask and I should have!'

'Don't get mired in guilt; it won't do any good,' Grant advised.

Britt's eyes flashed and she tossed her head. Something about the defiant gesture made Grant think of the Arabian horses his uncle raised at his ranch north of town. They'd been domesticated animals for countless generations yet there was an element to them that was still so wild and untameable even centuries later. They were so delicate and small, but often harder to control than a thoroughbred twice their size. Their lively spirits were eye-catching, but, in a second, a mincing submissive trot would turn into a crazy buck and headlong gallop.

For years his uncle had been trying to get Grant on an Arabian. He'd never succeeded. Grant liked to ride occasionally but he stuck with his reliable quarter horses.

'Don't worry, I won't,' Britt broke into his reverie. 'I'm going to do something about it.'

With that she left him leaning against the limestone column. Grant had forgotten for a moment what they'd been talking about.

'What is it you're going to do?'

'I'm going to find out what my sister's secret was,' she called back over her shoulder as she disappeared around the corner of the vine-covered mansion.

That got Grant off the column and into action. 'The hell you are.'

'Britt, you could have made a plan before you so dramatically rushed off into the sunset,' she muttered to herself.

Coming around the manicured hedges, she headed toward the parking lot and her car when she realized she didn't have one. She had to come up with a plan – and fast – or she'd come off looking like a hot-headed fool in front of the ultra-cool detective.

And that she couldn't stand.

Remembering Risa's secret had had a galvanizing effect on Britt. She could still feel the grief, but a new sense of purpose blunted its pain and eased its weight somewhat. Finally she had something to do that could help Risa. And her baby sister's spirit seemed strong with her as she hurried into the setting sun.

She paused in the shade of a stand of trees, glancing back to see if Collins was pursuing her. Not finding him, she sighed with relief and relaxed a little. Whipping back around, she launched smack into the middle of his chest. She let out a short scream of surprise and jumped back. He put his hands on her shoulders to steady her and gasped back the breath she'd knocked out of him.

'What . . . are . . . you . . . doing?'

'I could ask you the same thing,' Britt answered, feeling a little smug that she'd recovered so nicely despite her surprise.

Collins dropped his hands from her shoulders immediately and took a half-step back. 'You haven't asked, but I'll answer anyway. I am trying to finish what might rank as the most difficult interview of my career.'

Britt could tell by the set of his jaw that he meant it as a criticism, but she took it as a compliment.

'Now, answer my question.'

He was back to barking orders, but Britt resolved to be patient and she spoke as sweetly as was possible for her. 'I have decided that you were right about the "we" business. After a lot of thought, I agree.'

His straight, strong eyebrows quirked slightly above his mirrored lenses, but otherwise his face remained impassive.

'The "we" business?'

'You said that there shouldn't be "we" in the investigation. You'd do your job and I was to do mine. Well, I've decided you're right and the best way for me to do my job of grieving is through action. I'm going to discover Risa's secret.'

Grant weighed his options as he stared into her hazel eyes that were so changeable – green one moment, golden the next and muddy sepia when her grief overcame her. Right now they were clear and the color of a freshly mown hayfield, and she vibrated with purpose. What could it hurt, he asked himself, if this gave her something beyond the funeral to concentrate on? Plus, maybe it would keep her out of his way and he could finish this up on his own.

'Fine,' Grant finally ruled. 'Just let me know what you find out.'

'Sure – anything I think you'd be interested in, I'll definitely pass on.'

'No,' Grant corrected her, 'you'll pass everything you find out to me. I'll decide what I'm interested in and what I'm not interested in.'

Britt took his measure for a few beats, then her mouth quirked up in a hint of a smile. The dimples were back. But they just as quickly disappeared. 'No problem,' she said, so casually that he knew he wasn't going to hear half of what she gathered.

But really that was all right, because what would she find out anyway? Nothing he could use; that was almost a certainty.

So let her think she was winning this one battle, because he would win the war. She'd thank him later, when her sister's death was settled as an accident and she could go on with her life. And he could get on with his without ever seeing Brittany Reeve again.

She was not good for him at all.

'I'm leaving, and if you want a ride back home you'd better come on or you are going to get left.'

Without pausing, he strode down the path that led to the parking lot, not once looking back to see if she was behind him.

CHAPTER 4

Grant should have looked back.

When he reached his car and unlocked it, he opened the driver's side door but didn't get in. Manners – ingrained or inbred, he wasn't sure – wouldn't allow him to get into a car before a lady. He still opened doors for women, however antiquated that was. Many of the young women he took on dates lately had actually argued with him over his habit, insisting it was not what a feminist should allow. He let them open their own doors after that, but it was a struggle to stay his impulse.

He wondered if Britt Reeve would like having doors opened or whether her headstrong nature would make her balk. He'd opened the car door for her at her house, but, as they were being set upon by the media, she hadn't had the opportunity to argue.

Why did he care if she liked it or not? This should be the first and only time she'd ever ride in a car with him . . .

Suddenly impatient with the direction his thoughts were taking, Grant looked behind him. He saw no sign of the petite brunette. In fact, the entire grounds of the McNay seemed deserted. Even the sun was leaving, the last of its red-gold rays filtering through the trees.

Where had she gone?

'Sir, I am sorry, but the museum gates close in five minutes. You must leave.'

Grant started at the man's voice and turned to see a groundskeeper in a grass-stained khaki uniform. The cop in him was disgusted that he'd let a gardener sneak up on him, even though that had not been the man's intention. What had him so distracted anyway?

'I'm waiting for someone – ' Grant began.

'Ah, yes,' said the groundskeeper. 'The pretty lady you were talking with earlier?'

Grant was taken aback that they'd been noticed, but after all the museum had not been crowded.

'That's right. I thought she was right behind me, but . . .' Grant looked off again in the direction from which he'd come, then turned back to the man. 'Have you seen her?'

'No, sir. I did not see her when I drove all the way around. I am still going to have to lock up at seven o'clock.'

Reaching into his rear pocket, Grant drew out the leather case and flipped open his badge. 'Look, this is police business. I have to find this woman.'

The groundskeeper's dark eyes glittered with interest. 'She did a bad thing? She is under arrest?'

'No, no,' Grant answered impatiently. 'I just need to talk to her and then get her back home.'

'So she is not in trouble?'

'Not yet,' Grant said, with a touch of irony.

'Ah . . .' The groundskeeper's eyes lit up with sudden enlightenment. 'And you need some *privacy* for your talk, yes?'

The man spoke with a heavy accent and the stilted delivery of someone who uses English as a second language, and Grant didn't catch at first why he'd put an emphasis on the word 'privacy'.

'That's right.'

'We-e-e-ell – ' the man stretched out the syllable long enough to get Grant's attention. ' – I think I can find a way all of us can be satisfied. I can lock the gates and you can stay in here until you are finished with your lady and then I open them again. If you like, we can make it a regular arrangement. Yes?'

Grant's eyes had been roaming the grassy knoll where he'd thought he saw some movement, but at the man's last words he looked sharply at him. His hand was open, palm up, fingers wiggling.

Suddenly it all came to Grant. This guy thought Grant was getting a quickie with a suspect or a prostitute. Just the month before a San Antonio cop had been caught by Internal Affairs trading sex for the cuffs, and, of course, the story had spread all over town faster than good news ever did. Grant shook his head at the opportunist before him. One dirty cop out of two thousand made them all look bad.

He considered explaining the situation to the groundskeeper, but knew it was a lost cause.

'Not this time; I have to get back to work.'

'Of course – I see,' was the answer, accompanied by an oily grin.

'No, you damn well don't see!' Britt's indignant voice erupted from behind a rosemary bush at Grant's right shoulder.

She charged around the plant and stopped abruptly in front of Grant. 'Lieutenant Collins, aren't you going to correct this moron?'

Grant slowly pushed his sunglasses back on top of his head. 'No, I'm not. Where have you been?'

'Moron?' shouted the outraged groundskeeper. 'You have no right to call me a moron, with what you are, you – '

'Collins!' Britt interrupted.

Grant put a hand at the small of her back and pushed her to the passenger side of his car. He opened the door. 'Get in.'

'Not until we settle this.' Britt resisted his hand, which forced his hand lower than he wanted it to go.

Emitting an exasperated groan, Grant looked over the hood of the car at the groundskeeper. 'It's not what you think. She's my . . . my wife.'

As Britt's body relaxed in shock, Grant pushed her into the seat and pressed the lock button as he slammed the door.

'Oh, I misunderstood. My apologies, sir,' the groundskeeper mumbled as he shuffled backwards, his eyes downcast.

Grant nodded and got in, turning the key. The sedan had barely rumbled to life before he shifted into reverse. Tires squealed as he shifted again, pressed the accelerator and whipped out the gates. An oncoming car had to swerve to avoid them.

'Why in heaven's name did you tell him we were married?'

Grant cast her a sidelong glance. She ran both her hands through her hair, shaking the tumble of curls angrily.

'Because it was easier than trying to explain.'

'But it's not the truth,' Britt argued righteously.

'The truth. You get too stuck up on the truth. It isn't the way the world operates.'

'So you go around telling lies and half-truths just to get through life easier?'

'It's perceptions that matter. Worry about being truthful to people's perceptions and you'll get a lot further than worrying about the big vague concept that is truth,' Grant declared bitterly. It made him sick to say it but he knew it was the way he should live his life. If he'd worried about people's perceptions more he wouldn't have gone for that bullet . . .

'So you take the expedient route. It must make you a sorry cop.'

Britt could see immediately that she'd struck a chord. His long fingers tensed on the wheel. The muscles beneath the tweed of his blazer bunched. His jaw clenched.

'If that's your perception then I'm not doing a very good job practicing what I preach.' He clipped the words out of tense lips. 'But if it's the truth you care about I do try to be precise and go by the book.' He added *now* in his head.

'You were a cop back there.' Britt cocked her head the way they'd come. 'That was real precise.'

'We were just wasting time there with that groundskeeper. He had misconceptions about cops that no amount of explaining would change. It would be like butting our heads against a wall. You didn't want him thinking you were a call-girl, so we fixed that. You ought to be happy,' Grant swept a look at her cotton T-shirt and belted khaki pants. 'Though where he got that I don't know – you don't look much like any call-girl I've ever seen.'

His dismissive tone insulted her. 'Well, thanks a lot.'

Grant's eyebrows rose. 'You *want* to look like a call girl?'

'No . . . Well . . .' Britt began, then stopped before she could make it worse. 'That's not what I meant.'

What had she meant?

Grant's attention was called away briefly to navigate the road ahead and Britt used the opportunity to try to get a handle on her emotions. She knew she felt things strongly

– maybe more strongly than some people – but usually she wasn't embroiled in such a jumble of different, opposing feelings all at once. It frightened her that she couldn't even identify what she was feeling.

All her life she'd been told her emotional nature was a weakness. Her father constantly berated her when she cried or argued or danced about in joy. She was always too-*too*, he'd lectured. 'Try to show about a tenth of what you are feeling, Brittany, and the rest of the world will be able to live with you,' was his advice.

Her mother, on the other hand, had ignored the emotions and tried to ignore her eldest daughter as much as possible. Her mother's classic reaction to a Britt over-reaction was to turn her back and walk away. Britt's strongest memories were of needing her mother's arms around her, and warm words in her ear, and seeing her thin, graceful back topped with that well-coiffed golden hair walking away.

She'd overheard her mother telling her father once that: 'Britt is just too difficult. She's too much work to try to understand. I don't enjoy being around her. You deal with her, Neil.'

That about summed up her maternal philosophy in the eleven years she'd acted as Britt's mother. Britt considered her to have given up the title when she'd walked out on them sixteen years before. Sophia had given birth to her but she wasn't her mother any more.

'What are you thinking about?' Grant asked.

Brought out of her reverie, Britt blinked and looked around. They sat in the parking lot of a French bakery and café. Pretty far cry from the convenience store she'd envisioned. She didn't want to let their similar taste in food soften her up, though.

'That's none of your business, Detective,' she said.

The corners of his mouth twitched while the rest of his poker face held fast. 'I think that's my line.'

'Well, I got it in first.'

Grant's lips parted to let out what Britt could've sworn was a sigh. He turned the police radio down in his car as the dispatcher announced a numbered code that Britt couldn't understand but guessed was no big emergency by his non-reaction to it.

'I think you need something to eat,' he said as he switched the ignition off.

'Good for you,' Britt shot back. 'But I'm not going to eat. Not right now.'

Collins shoved the ubiquitous glasses on the top of his head again. His gray eyes probed. He lowered his voice slightly. 'You need to keep going. If you're secret-searching, you need to eat.'

Was that sensitivity she heard in his voice? No, it couldn't be. She shook her head.

'Oh, I'll eat eventually, just not right now. I have to call Tori. I've put it off long enough and it's not going to be any easier. In fact, if she's already heard about it, she'll never let me forget it.'

Collins eyed her with sudden suspicion. 'You haven't called her yet? Who were you talking to while you were locked up in your room all that time?'

Anger rose in her throat. Britt twisted in the leather bucket seat to face him, forcing calm into her voice. 'I was calling one of my kindergarten students who I hired as a hitman and telling him what a great job he did!'

Grant didn't react, but when the horror of her words hit her own ears Britt erupted into sobbing tears. She shook so violently Grant couldn't help reaching over and holding her for fear she would fall apart physically, for mentally she was already in pieces.

After a few minutes, when her sobs abated, Grant let his tight hold on her loosen. But even that slight change sent her into a new wave of crying. Grant felt so helpless, yet afraid of what he was doing. It seemed like a natural reaction, and it felt right. But he worried about what she would think once she'd exhausted her grief. She would let him have it, that was what she'd do.

Grant had to smile at that thought and was grateful she couldn't see his face.

Awkwardly, he reached up and began to stroke her hair. It was like spun silk and the color of coffee. Her spicy scent was muted by the essence of the rosemary bush. He took a deep breath.

Her sobs diminished into small hiccups and she pushed out of his arms. They fell empty back to his sides.

'I'm sorry,' Britt whispered, shifting back to her side of the car, her face flushed. 'I apologize. I thought I could get through all this – '

Uncomfortable with her embarrassment, Grant cut in, 'Listen, what you said . . .'

Her eyes shot him a look that said *Don't repeat it*.

'You just have to be careful. I know you didn't mean it, but stranger things have happened and there will be someone out there who would believe it. You have to . . .' Grant paused, for once worried about his choice of words. 'To think before you speak. Especially around reporters. You might say everything right and in the right way and still it comes out wrong. What you don't mean to say will really bite you in the butt once it gets in print. So watch it.'

Britt averted her face to look out the window. She was silent for a long time, then she spoke quietly. 'Thank you.'

Grant sat in stupefaction. He'd expected a spicy rejoinder to his advice. Instead she was grateful and submissive. Would he ever get to a point where he could anticipate her reaction to anything? He almost regretted that this case wouldn't give him enough time to find out the answer to that question.

'I was talking to Grams, my Dad's mother.' Britt continued to look out the window. 'She's a great lady. The best. She told me she'd call everyone who needed calling. Except Tori. She's tough, but talking to Tori makes her crazy. Grams can never come to terms with the fact that none of her genes were passed down to Tori.'

Britt paused with a look of affection on her face. Grant read it as being for the grandmother, not her sister. He was feeling there was no love lost between the remaining Reeve sisters. Gradually, Britt's faint smile faded into a look almost of panic.

'Grams insisted on making all the arrangements. She said a mother shouldn't have to plan . . . that.'

'Mother?' Grant asked.

'Grams always said I raised Risa. And I guess I did – but it was so easy. She was a perfect child. Dad didn't show much interest in her until the modeling industry did.'

'When did she start modeling?'

'When she was thirteen she visited Tori at a shoot and the photographer took a fancy to Risa.' Britt shook her head with wonder. 'It's only been three years but it seems like a lifetime. Risa and I were so close for so long and we still are . . . were . . . in our hearts, but the modeling took so much time. There was so much in her life I don't know anything about.'

'I thought you said you were certain she wasn't into drugs,' Grant challenged.

Britt's faraway look snapped back to the present and her eyes pierced Grant's with intensity. 'I can be certain of that because I know what kind of person she was. When you know someone that well, you can predict what they will or will not do. Now, Tori is another story entirely. I am amazed how I can be related to someone I can't begin to figure out.'

Grant absorbed that with no comment, but made a mental note in case he ever needed to talk to Tori Reeve. It wasn't a likely prospect. The more he listened to Britt Reeve the more he was convinced this nice teenager who'd just happened to be a beautiful model had met with an unfortunate accident. He certainly didn't hear any skeletons rattling around in her closet. And he damn sure hadn't seen any.

'I'm not going to talk you into eating?'

'No.' Britt dropped her head back against the seat's headrest and closed her eyes. Her pixie face was wan and drawn. Her crimson lips seemed almost deflated. Her slender neck convulsed with the lump she seemed to have trouble swallowing. And the dimple was gone. Again.

Something deep in the pit of Grant's stomach gave a twinge.

It was hunger.

Or was it?

Britt watched while her grandmother fixed her a cappuccino. No tea or ordinary coffee for Jewel Reeve. She was a woman who tried every fad but only hung onto what she liked. Currently the winners were animal prints and homemade cappuccino. She wore a shiny rayon sweatsuit that looked as if it had been inspired by the hide of a kinky cheetah-zebra cross. It suited Grams, Britt thought; it mirrored her strong personality that had flair to spare.

'Pickles and peachfuzz,' Jewel grumbled. 'I can't get this rotten thing to work right.'

The state-of-the-art machine was last year's Christmas gift from her son on Britt's advice. Knowing her grandmother wanted a cappuccino maker, and guessing her father had no idea what to get his mother, Britt had suggested the best non-industrial model money could buy. Her father, relieved to be spared the mental anguish of the gift-selecting process, had jumped at the chance. Jewel was thrilled even though she knew Britt was the one she had to thank.

'It's been working okay, hasn't it?' Britt asked. 'Because if it's a lemon we can get a new one; it has about a hundred-year warranty.'

'It ought to have a lifetime warranty for how much it cost,' Jewel put in.

'Grams, you aren't supposed to know how much a gift costs,' Britt scolded affectionately. 'How did you find out?'

'I had to go check it out – see how much your father thinks it's worth to keep me entertained and out of his hair. As if I care about his boring life.'

'Grams!'

'Of course, if I was really in his hair I'd never get out, what with all that goop and hair-dying junk he puts on it. I'd be stuck fast for the duration.'

Chuckling at her own joke, Jewel flipped another switch and the milk she'd planned to froth spewed instead, leaving a fine splattering of milk from the ceiling to the floor. Jewel turned, with dripping hands, to face Britt who'd jumped off the kitchen stool to come help.

'Oh, Grams, look at you.'

'I can't!' Her shiny fuchsia lips broke into a grin.

Milk covered the lenses of her glasses and had left an unusual speckled pattern on her sweatsuit. Jewel took off her glasses and rinsed them.

'Gol'durned, there wasn't that much milk in the cup. Where did all this come from?' She rotated, taking it all in. 'Well, at least we know the blasted machine works.'

Britt laughed at that. 'Grams, you're always so optimistic. I'd be sitting in the middle of the floor crying or storming around swearing. But here you are, looking at the mess like a glass half-full. Just like Risa.'

Jewel didn't let her grin slip but her sharp eyes went immediately to Britt's downcast ones.

Britt felt her gaze, but waited until an arthritic hand gnarled by age and hard work slipped under her chin. Slowly, Britt raised her eyes.

'You want to talk about it?' Jewel asked.

Her grandmother's tone was the one she always used when asking a question, even one as loaded as this one. She put the question on the table with no strings attached. She'd listen if you wanted to talk. She'd accept it if you didn't. No recriminations, no guilt, no expectations.

For the millionth time, Britt thanked God for Grams. She wasn't sure how she would have survived life without her.

'Not right now,' Britt finally answered.

'Well, grab a rag, then, girlie, we've got a job to do.'

As they got busy wiping milk off the whitewash-stained cabinets and corian countertops, Britt thought back to when Detective Collins had dropped her off. They hadn't talked much after Britt asked him to take her to her grandmother's new townhouse. In her driveway, he'd leaped out and opened her car door before she'd even had time to unbuckle her safety belt. Britt had wondered if he was doing it just because she'd broken into hysterics, and he was afraid she was too weak to make it out on her own, or maybe because he just wanted to maintain his precious control. Whatever the reason, she'd been too exhausted to challenge him on it, and somewhere in the back of her mind she'd liked the feeling of having him do it.

Britt shook her head in disgust. That was real consistent with the independence she so fiercely guarded, wasn't it?

As if she'd read her mind, her grandmother broke into her thoughts. 'That policeman seemed very solicitous of you.'

Britt snorted in answer. 'Solicitous' was about the last word she would've chosen to describe Grant Collins.

'Way off base, am I? Well, appearances aren't everything, that's the truth.' Jewel didn't pause in her floor-mopping, unaware that she'd ventured into territory her granddaughter and 'her' policeman had argued over hours earlier. 'Did he happen to mention when we might know more about what happened to Risa?'

'He said the Medical Examiner will turn in his report tomorrow morning and he'll let me know as soon as possible which direction he'll be taking in the investigation.'

Britt stood up from her squat and brushed a curl of hair off her forehead with the back of her hand. She'd tried to keep her voice devoid of judgement because she didn't want to get into the whole debate of accident versus murder all over again. But the look on her grandmother's face told her they were about to get into it anyway.

'Sounds fair to me,' Jewel answered.

It was just like Grams to make such a statement – one easy to consider rhetorical but one Britt's strong emotions wouldn't let pass by without comment.

'To you, it might,' Britt admitted. 'But I already know which way the investigation is going. So when he tells me, it won't be news.'

Jewel rinsed out her rag and wrung it twice while she

waited for her granddaughter to continue. When she didn't, Jewel threw the rag into the sink. 'Well, pickles and peachfuzz, Britt, are you going to tell me or are you going to make me guess what's going on?'

Sighing, Britt leaned against the counter and pulled out a bar stool. 'I'm sorry, Grams, you have a right to know. I'm just so tired of going round and round about this.'

'Who did you go round and round with? Not your father?'

'No, he wasn't too bad,' Britt lied, and Jewel's pencil-drawn eyebrows arched. She knew her grandmother would be outraged by the implications her father had made and would let Neil know in no uncertain terms how she felt. But she had enough to do with planning the funeral service without needing to reprimand her son. 'The one making trouble is Collins, the cop. He thinks it's an accident.'

'And you don't?'

'No.' Britt sat up straighter and reached out to touch Jewel's forearm. 'Grams, I just know something is not right about that theory. I can't explain exactly what beyond the obvious – that she was too young, too healthy. It's more that's stopping me from even considering the accident angle.'

'You've always had good instincts, Britt. Intuition is underrated. You know how I feel about that. How did your policeman treat your suggestion?'

Britt shook her head and lowered her voice to a false, gravelly bass. '"Just the facts, ma'am."'

'I see,' Jewel said gravely. 'A man who has to see it to believe it. Well, you just might make a good team. You need to keep your feet on the ground sometimes and he might do with putting his head in the clouds a little more.'

'Grams, we aren't Holmes and Watson here. He considers me a peripheral figure – the victim's grieving sister whom he hopes will drift into the woodwork.'

'You will do that for a time. We need to put our baby to rest the day after tomorrow.' Jewel's blue eyes grew large and wet behind her lenses for the first time since Britt had walked in. Tears began to trickle in rivulets through the creases in her face. She reached for Britt and held her close, petting her wild hair gently.

'You are my pride, Britt, but Risa was my joy. A pure joy from the moment she was born. Never a speck of trouble, always so easy-going. So happy. She brightened the world around her so much.' Jewel broke into gentle sobs as tears flowed down her cheeks unchecked. She enveloped Britt in a desperate hug.

Britt's heart twisted, for her grandmother's pain so mirrored her own. It was more painful to watch than even to feel herself. Normally sensitive to slights, Britt wasn't hurt by her grandmother's description of her love for Risa. Britt knew Grams loved them equally and unconditionally – albeit in different ways. Risa was a joy. A gift. Had they only known that gift would be such a temporary one.

'Indian giver,' Britt mumbled heavy with rancor as she gazed at the ceiling.

Jewel pulled away and pulled out a tissue from the ever-present supply in her cleavage. Dabbing at the wetness on her face, she took in Britt's expression and knew whom she was referring to immediately.

'No, don't go getting on your high-horse and second-guessing God. He needed her in heaven and called her a little early. Maybe He was running short on angels – and what with the way people are nowadays I can sure as hell see that happening.' Jewel grabbed Britt's hands in her own. Britt felt her heart lighten a little at her grandmother's words – not their meaning, because she wasn't buying that – but the way she tried to make her holy point using such salty language.

'Risa's up there with Him and will be perpetually happy. We couldn't wish for anything better for her. We're left down here to pick up the pieces and go on. We're the ones who got the bad end of this bargain. Good thing we're both tougher than old shoe leather on the outside. We'll need to show that armor a lot in the coming years.'

Jewel put a hand at Britt's collarbone. 'Now, it's this marshmallow inside I'm worried about in you. Mine's dried out and toughened up some over the decades. Yours has got a ways to go yet. And that other sister of yours knows just how to reach in and give it a tweak.'

Britt had called Tori in Los Angeles right after walking in Grams's door. She'd answered after ten rings and had sounded as if she was coming down from a three-day drunk. Tori had whined about Britt talking too loudly, then, when Britt finally got through to her about Risa's death, complained about having to ride on an airplane with a hangover. Britt had wanted to reach through the phone lines and shake her sister senseless right then.

'I'll be okay, Grams.'

'Of course you will.' Jewel paused, looking thoughtful for a moment before continuing. 'You know, losing Risa may bring Tori around. Turn her into a human being.'

Britt shot her a skeptical look. 'Get real, Grams.'

'That bad on the phone?' Jewel asked knowingly.

'Worse.'

'Well, we can hope and pray,' Jewel dismissed the subject optimistically.

'You can,' Britt added with her typical 'half-empty' pessimism.

Jewel snatched another quick hug before giving Britt a last probing look. 'My holy and hallelujah speech doesn't mean we turn the other cheek. You go out and find out what happened if those police aren't going to do it. If it was an accident, so be it. But if it wasn't, then somebody needs to pay before the Devil gets a hold of him.'

'That's my plan exactly, Grams,' Britt declared.

'Good,' Jewel said, as she reached to the sink and began dabbing at the milk stains on her cheetah spots. 'Risa wouldn't want you sitting around and mourning. She always said you needed a project. And now you got one. Go to it, girl.'

Jewel pulled a casserole out of the oven and placed it on the counter. 'But first dinner and bed.'

Britt nodded and grabbed a plate. She didn't argue with her grandmother any more. It had taken her years to learn that arguing with her grandmother was like arguing with herself.

CHAPTER 5

Sophia Lawrence perched on the edge of the pad-free rattan chair and took a first sip of her morning tea, careful not to purse her lips as she brought the delicate china teacup to her mouth. Her plastic surgeon had given her detailed instructions on what not to do in order to preserve the face she had so painstakingly earned on the operating table. It had been three years now since the surgery and she definitely looked better than ever. It was worth every bit of discomfort every time she looked in the mirror, or looked into the eyes of those who gazed at her with undisguised admiration.

It was no small feat to be forty-nine and look twenty-five.

She did not lean back in the chair either, keeping her back ramrod-straight, shoulders pinned back. Sophia was deathly afraid of becoming a 'sloucher', as she called them. A thousand-dollar consultation with an exclusive orthopedic specialist had reassured her somewhat, for he'd given her a list of things to do to prevent such from occurring. He had mentioned his concern about the added weight of her 'surgically enhanced D-cup breasts', but when Sophia had assured him she wouldn't be getting rid of those, ever, he'd shaken his head and advised her to take her calcium, do special back exercises and come in once a year for a bone density test.

She kept the pad off her chair because she'd been warned that the firm pad on such a hard surface could possibly spread what was left of her tiny behind. She'd liposuctioned what had slipped with age and kept just the right few ounces of fat along with the muscle that was shaped to two perfect hand-sized mounds with the help of a two-hundred-dollar-an-hour personal trainer and a minimum of sweat.

Running her tongue along her teeth, Sophia turned her head slowly to the mirror on the far wall and practiced her smile. It was perfect. Dazzling. The corners of her mouth dipped somewhat at the memory of the unpleasantness that had preceded the perfection. Her dentist had wanted to cap her teeth, but she'd balked, not wanting that obvious a change as her picture appeared on television or in some newspaper almost daily. So when she'd found another dentist who could whiten her teeth gradually, she'd blown her other one off and then had to listen to the new one gripe every time they were in bed together. Eventually she broke off the affair, and she could see now her gleaming teeth were worth the sacrifice.

Her hair-stylist had *finally* found the color she'd been looking for: fourteen carat gold. The style was pure Jackie-O. Classy. Her blue eyes weren't brilliant enough without help, not eye-catching, so her optometrist had specially designed a shade of blue that Sophia had desired, the color of bluebonnets. The way her husband would definitely win the Senate seat from Texas, she told him, was if voters saw their state flower every time they looked into her eyes.

With a sigh of contentment, Sophia looked to the

doorway where her husband appeared. Carl Lawrence wasn't a big man, standing only five-foot-eleven, his rounded, taut beer belly made him seem even shorter to the eye, but to the ears he was ten feet tall. His voice boomed, filling Sophia's sun room now, sending the silk flowers on the buffet table quivering.

'Soph, I know you haven't heard the news yet. And I promise you, hon, you're not gonna like it. Not one bit.'

For a moment Sophia didn't answer. The edges of her mouth turned down just slightly – not technically a frown, for that would be bad for the facial muscles – at the rude interruption to her morning routine and the peace of 'her' room. She had spent a hundred thousand dollars redecorating the twenty-by-thirty-foot sun room to her satisfaction, and she didn't like the intrusion of her loudmouthed husband, who by all rights had a games room and an office of his own at the other end of the ten-thousand-square-foot mansion.

'News?' she finally asked with bored sniff, resisting the urge to look back into the mirror.

Carl took two strides into the room and shoved his hands onto his belt loops on either side of his salad-plate-sized silver buckle. 'It's about one of your girls. And it's not good.'

That caught Sophia's full attention. She forgot not to purse her lips as she took a swallow instead of a sip of her tepid tea. Her hand shook as she replaced the cup in its saucer. She didn't trust herself to speak.

'It's Risa,' Carl began, his florid face even redder than usual.

'Oh, God. No.'

'She's dead,' Carl finished.

Relief washed through Sophia like a wave, though she struggled to keep her face impassive. It was quickly replaced with disappointment, which she allowed her face to show. It was close enough to grief to fool onlookers. She willed the tears to come, and with the letdown of her adrenaline, they did.

Carl stood up, nearly upending the glass-top table. He reached out and took Sophia into an awkward embrace. 'It's just not right for a girl that pretty to die so young. It just isn't right. Not right 'tall.'

He leaned back and took her face in his big, square, paw-like hands. 'But, more than that, it's not right for this to be happening to you. You don't deserve to be hurting.'

Gingerly, Sophia lifted her face out and away from his grasp. His roughened hands might scratch her skin, still tender from her morning facial. His hands moved to her upper thighs and stroked her exposed knees through her hose.

'Is there anything I can do to make you feel better, darlin'?'

'Not what you're thinking, certainly,' Sophia snapped, but didn't dislodge his hands. She rolled her shoulders. 'I think maybe a massage might ward off a migraine.'

'That's a good idea, darlin',' Carl agreed, moving his hands up her thighs just a tad. 'It'll relax you before our trip.'

'Trip? What trip? I didn't see anything on the schedule for a flight today.'

'The funeral, darlin',' Carl pointed out with exaggerated patience. 'The funeral for Risa is tomorrow at that Episcopal church there. I thought we'd better head on down there to San Anton this afternoon.'

'But . . .' Sophia paused to consciously smooth the furrow in her brow. The last thing she needed was a permanent line down the middle of her forehead, not with this new hairstyle. 'But I thought we were going to steer clear of the issue of my daughters during the campaign. That was what we decided. We didn't want the voters to think you were grasping for publicity.'

'I know, darlin', but that was before. Risa dying like this is an undeniable opportunity. The public will expect you to go to the funeral – they can't deny you that. I'll accompany you as your husband, not as a politician. This is going to get international exposure and so will we. It'll tug them in the heartstrings like nothing else. It's just too damn bad that it had to come this way.'

Sophia felt an uncharacteristic flash of insecurity. 'I don't know, Carl. I just don't know if I can do it . . .'

'Sure you can, darlin'. You're one of the strongest women I've ever seen. It won't be easy. She was your baby and all; I know that. And you're going to have to face that low-account ex-husband of yours for the first time since he ran you off. But those cameras are going to be rolling, and if we play this right we could set the momentum for the campaign heading into the summer. I know it's awful to be thinking of publicity at a time like this, but it's the game, and just 'cuz you have a tragedy in the family doesn't mean you quit playing.'

As if her words had made it true, Sophia could feel the hint of a migraine beginning to build pressure just behind her right eye. Her hand went to her temple but hovered there instead of touching, because just in time Sophia remembered the advice of her dermatologist. 'Don't touch your facial skin with your hand,' he'd warned, 'because the dirt and oil on your hand will cause blemishes.' Sophia let her hand drop back into her lap.

'What time is our flight?' she asked as she slowly rose from the chair, remembering to tuck her hips in just slightly to put the line of her skirt just right.

'That's the spirit, Soph,' Carl patted her on her tight

behind as if she was one of his prize cutting horses. 'The jet'll be ready around three o'clock. That'll put us there with plenty of time for our arrival to make the evening news.'

Lurching out of his chair, Carl gave Sophia a loud, sloppy smack on the lips and walked away. At the doorway he paused, turned on a heel and dropped his voice. 'Soph, I know you don't want to know the details, but you've gotta know how Risa died. You'll hear eventually, I guess, but you ought to hear now.'

Carl's brown eyes held hers for a beat before she broke the gaze. She tipped her head back – not for divine intervention, for Sophia was much too secular for that. No, she just wanted to find something to think about besides the loss of a beautiful, famous daughter she really only knew from magazine photos. A daughter she had wished just yesterday would be silenced.

Now she had her wish.

She didn't want to think about how that made her feel. Emotions were too messy. And what did they accomplish, anyway?

Instead, Sophia's eyes landed on a cobweb high in the corner of the twenty-foot high ceiling. She'd have to remember to tell the housekeeper about that.

'Soph?' Carl called from the doorway.

Her eyes dropped to the crystal chandelier for an inspection, and she began to second-guess her decision of the Waterford versus the hundred others she'd considered. 'Yes, go ahead,' she told her husband.

'It happened there in your hometown. They say she slipped and hit her head on a wall in the kitchen at her sister's house. That's what they're saying,' Carl paused just a beat. 'The police want to call it an accident, but the media – Goddamned buzzards – they're trying to say it was more than an accident. Why can't they just accept what happened and leave it alone?'

Carl's vehement tone caught Sophia's attention and she slipped him a sharp look. It wasn't like him to rail at the media. Reporters had been very good to him, whether they'd tried to be or not. His down home charm was unusual in that it translated through the camera. He instinctively knew what would look good in print and said it in short, snappy sentences that reporters couldn't help quoting to give their story flavor. And, to top it off, he remembered small details of the personal lives of those he met and mentioned them.

Last week, in a campaign stop in Amarillo, a bland reporter at that town's dinky newspaper had asked an uncomfortable question about Carl's wishy-washy stand on Texas-Mexico border patrolling. Carl had asked about her son who – Carl had overheard on his last visit – had a broken leg. The reporter had been so thrown off balance and flattered by his memory of her son that she forgot to pursue her question. Her story in the following day's paper, while still critical in some areas, had had a positive slant.

That was what was happening all over Texas. Whether they realized it or not, the media was giving Carl good press. They might not like his politics – and many didn't – but he was everybody's Uncle Carl. And they were buying the act and unconsciously getting the voters to do the same.

'What's wrong, Carl?'

Carl looked startled by his wife's question, and then waved it off. 'Oh, nothing, nothing, Soph. I'm just worrying about what this is doing to you. You look pale as a ghost.'

Sophia's eyes flew back to the mirror on the wall, and

she walked up for a closer look. 'I do?'

'Yep. Why don't you go lay down for a while? I'll send Jonesy up to give you a quick massage.' Carl glanced at the untouched dry toast on her china plate. 'And I'll get Martha to bring you up a tray. Scoot.'

'Thank you, I think I will.'

With one more glance at her reflection, which did indeed look too pale, Sophia tapped on her three-inch heels to the secretary next to the window. She looked out on the desert prairie that was their ten-thousand acre ranch in the middle of West Texas. She could barely see the barn in the distance. A dozen ranch hands – all Mexicans with green cards; Carl was careful not to hire wetbacks considering his political aspirations – were stirring up dust in their attempts to brand a herd of about fifty cows. Cattle, Carl liked to call them, Sophia reminded herself. These were the white ones with the grayish humps on their backs. Brouhas, they were called, or something like that. Sophia could never keep the names straight, though it irritated Carl no end.

'Just one thing I don't understand,' Carl said as he turned to walk to the kitchen. Sophia's head spun around. She'd forgotten he was there. Carl continued once he had her attention. 'Why didn't that family of yours call before we saw the news on TV? It was cruel to let you hear this way. Don't they have any decency?'

Shaking his head, Carl left.

'I guess not,' Sophia whispered. 'No decency.'

She looked down at the top page of her stack of messages from the night before and read again: *Urgent. Call Jewel. It's about Risa.*

With a lightning-quick move, Sophia snatched up the pink page and crushed the paper in her petite hand. The tips of her powder-pink lacquered nails bit into her palm.

She studied them and realized she needed a manicure. One more thing she'd have to work in today.

The halls of Alamo Heights High School very nearly vibrated with the emotion of the students arriving for the last day of school before summer. It should only have been the excitement and anticipation of three months' vacation, but instead those feelings were overwhelmed by grief, disbelief, horror and a morbid curiosity over the death of one of their own. Their most famous and, in many ways, most favorite peer was dead. Risa Reeve had taken time for everyone: band nerds, football heros, the nobody-specials. Risa hadn't snubbed anyone, so, when she began to hit it big, no one could fault her. She'd shared her glory as much as she could and, now, overnight, her star had fallen forever.

Jayson Pilchuk walked down the hall to his locker, dragging his feet and wishing he hadn't come to school at all. He probably wouldn't have except that Risa's Grams had told him Risa would have expected him to go face it – no matter how hard it was. Jayson had known she was right, but it didn't make doing it any easier. He felt the stares of strangers and knew what they were thinking. He avoided the eyes of those he knew because he couldn't cope with their pity, for him and for themselves. Ahead of him, Mara and Nicole embraced, their faces wet with tears, their bodies shaking with sobs. As he passed they tried to pull him into their arms, but he shook off their hands and walked on.

'Jayson,' Mara called after him, 'don't shut us out. We want to help. We loved her too, you know.'

Jayson heard Nicole whisper something to Mara before calling out to him herself in a gentler voice. 'We're here, Jayson, when you want to talk.'

That time wouldn't ever come. The only person he wanted to talk to was Risa, and she was talking to God and the rest of the angels right now. Maybe he should be with them up there, because now who did he have left? At his locker, he stopped and, as he'd done all year, looked right, down ten lockers, to where Risa had kept her books. She hadn't always been there waiting when he got to school, but she'd been there more often than not.

She wasn't there today. And wouldn't be ever again.

The whole space in front of her locker was empty, as if the kids were mourning the passing of her daily ritual as well as her soul. Several stood back, against the opposite wall, staring blankly at locker number C48.

Jayson wondered who would be the one to clean out her locker. He knew the combination, so did her two best girlfriends. Suddenly Jayson realized he wanted to be the one to do it. Only he would really appreciate the significance of each scrap of paper, the memories attached to a pencil, what the sticker on page 203 of her trig book stood for. But he couldn't do it now. Maybe not ever, he realized, as he thought of the police investigation. As tears burned against the insides of his eyelids, he forced his gaze back to the lock in his hand. Why wasn't his locker opening? Then it hit him. He'd been trying to open his locker using Risa's combination. Jayson had to consciously wrench his mind from thoughts of Risa in order to recall his own lock combination.

Then, when his locker had opened, Jayson stood there for a full minute before he remembered it was the last day of school and he didn't need any books except for his second period class. Mr Jeter was going over the last two chapters of the biology book, which they hadn't had time for during the school year. As if any of the kids would be paying attention, Jayson thought, especially now. Jayson grabbed the book anyway. It gave him something to do with his hands.

Out of the corner of his eye, Jayson saw someone approaching. He turned, surprised that any one of the guys would have the nerve to actually come up to him and give his condolences. It wasn't that Jayson was disliked; he just wasn't popular. A loner, he didn't have many friends, and those he did have had been Risa's friends first. He wondered now if they'd still be his friends, or whether their friendship would fade along with their memories of Risa.

He'd almost forgotten his visitor when the guy cleared his throat. Jayson looked him over. He was a lot shorter than Jayson's six-foot-two and had a slighter build. Maybe five-eight and one-forty. Risa would've called him wormy. Jayson didn't remember seeing him around, but he didn't notice everyone the way Risa always had.

'Are you Jayson Pilchuk?' the guy asked without preamble.

'Yeah,' Jayson answered warily.

'You Risa Reeve's boyfriend?'

Jayson's hand gripped his biology book tighter. He dreaded having his emotions rise back to the surface with whatever this guy was going to say.

'Uh-huh.'

'Would you mind stepping outside?' He cocked his head toward the front door of the building. 'So we can ask you a few questions about Risa?'

Jayson searched briefly for the 'we' and didn't see anyone around who seemed to be with his mysterious visitor, only a dozen pairs of curious ears which had scooted in for a closer listen. 'Who are you?'

The guy looked startled at the question. 'Uh, I'm Todd James.'

'Which doesn't tell me much.' Risa had always told Jayson he should take more time to be polite, and he thought of that fleetingly now, but just didn't have the emotional wherewithal to put her advice to use.

Todd James leaned closer, cast his eyes about furtively and lowered his voice. 'I'm a producer for an investigative TV show.'

Jayson was already shaking his head and backing away. He should've noticed the guy looked kinda old to be in high school. The blatantly cynical glint in his eyes should've been a dead giveaway. 'Sorry, man. I gotta got to class.'

Undaunted, Todd James put his arm around Jayson's shoulder and propelled him into the boys' bathroom. Once Todd had squatted down to make a check for feet in the stalls, he straightened and pierced Jayson with a knowing look. 'Gonna hold out for cash, are you? Well, can't say that I blame you. You've got a goldmine here while interest is hot – maybe the next week or so. Okay, we're prepared to give you fifty thousand dollars if you grant us an exclusive interview.'

Todd James reached into the pocket of his jeans and drew out a folded sheaf of papers: a contract. Like magic, a pen appeared in his hand as well. 'Sign here.'

'Fifty thousand dollars?' Jayson intoned in shock.

'Playing hardball, are you, kid?' Todd James didn't look surprised. Jayson shook his head, but Todd James forged ahead. 'Okay, a hundred thou is our final offer.'

Putting his hands up to ward off another figure, Jayson backed toward the lavatory door. 'No!'

Todd James advanced on him, shaking his head. Now he looked surprised. 'Wow, kid. Didn't expect you to be this tough a negotiator. You hang loose here while I talk to my boss, see if he'll spring for more bucks.' He paused and gave

Jayson a conspiratorial wink. 'Just between you and me, I think you could name your price. He's hot for this one.'

Speechless, Jayson leaned against the wall and tried to keep his jaw from dropping.

Todd James put one hand on the door handle and held the other out, as if it could keep Jayson put. 'You chill here for a sec. I'll be right back.'

As soon as the door swished shut, Jayson rushed to the sink, let his book slide to the tile floor and splashed cold water on his face. His eyes looked into their reflection in the mirror. *A hundred thousand dollars*? Was the world crazy for asking or was he the crazy one for turning it down?

'Aren't you s'posed to be halfway to hell by now?'

Tori cracked open one eye and groaned. 'I'm in hell already.'

'Hah. This is heaven compared to where you're going, baby-baby.'

Pushing her tangle of long blonde hair off her face, Tori watched through half an eye and a hangover haze as her bed partner threw the covers off and walked naked to the bathroom. The dark hair looked like worms crawling on the white skin on the backs of his skinny legs. She wondered why she found him so irresistible, why lately she kept waking up with him in bed beside her.

Vic Demond was son of a movie producer who, after thirty years of being given everything his heart desired, had grown up to be a spoiled, cruel, directionless braggart. It wasn't his self-absorbed personality that Tori needed, or his wasted body. It was what he brought with him every visit that Tori couldn't live without. The limos, clothes and jewels weren't bad either.

'You haven't ever been to Texas. What would you know

about it?' Tori raised her ragged voice to be heard through the closed door of the bathroom and was sorry as the sound ricocheted around painfully in her own head.

'I know it's sand and dirt and cactus and tumbleweeds and chicks with big hair and big everything,' he shouted through the door. 'So, really, considering that, I guess it's not all bad.'

'You don't know diddly squat,' Tori said, surprised by her own vehemence as she sat up to argue with the closed door and a numb brain. 'Texas is beautiful in a bunch of different ways. There is sand and cactus, but there's pine tree forests and bayous and mountains and rivers and fruit orchards and – '

'I know producers only go shoot their movies there because the state flings itself down on the ground with its legs open for every filmmaker who comes sniffing around. Nobody with brains would say no to something like that,' Vic answered as he emerged from the bathroom, towel wrapped around his scrawny waist as he sauntered past her and down the hall to the kitchen.

'Well, of course you'd only remember something you'd relate to,' Tori mumbled, quickly losing the urge to fight for her home state.

'Takes one to know one, baby-baby,' Vic leered, stretching his lips until his thick mustache parted to reveal his rather pointed set of teeth. 'But I only have to kiss my daddy's butt to get millions and you have to kiss this ugly thing – ' he whipped off the towel to slap his own hairy buttocks ' – to get a lot less – '

Tori put her hand to her ears and screamed, 'Shut up!'

'My, my, touchy-touchy, aren't we, today? A little nervous about going home?' Vic didn't wait for the answer to a dig he'd made only to hurt. Flicking the towel over his shoulder, he sauntered out of the room.

Tori massaged her fingers along her scalp, shaking her hair back over her face. She couldn't see her bedroom and that was fine with her. She didn't want the reminder of what her life had become. This way she didn't have to see the mess she knew was there, because it was always there: the half-finished bottles of wine and gin, the ashtrays full of cigarette butts, the butts that never got into the ashtray and burned holes in the white deep pile carpeting, the clothes that she couldn't remember if they were clean or dirty, just worn or just bought, because she didn't wash anything. It was wear it and pitch it. Vic kept her in clothes. And if it wasn't Vic it was one of the others in her long line of willing and able men with too much money, too much time and an eye for a beautiful model.

Throwing her long legs over the side of the bed, Tori finally stretched her arms and threw her head back, ready to ignore the disaster surrounding her.

'I'm not going home,' she called out. 'This is home. Hollywood.'

She'd moved to California six months ago, when her modeling had begun to slow down. Tori imagined it the perfect time to pursue her dream of becoming an actress. So far she hadn't gotten anything other than a feminine hygiene commercial, but her agent was promising a big break in the movies any day. She'd bought the townhouse in Venice so she could keep up her tan at the nearby beach. Tanning parlors just didn't create the same result as the real thing, Tori thought. The camera didn't lie.

Vic stuck his head around the corner of the doorway and cut into her thoughts. 'What did you say?'

'I said I am home. My home is here.' She pointed at the floor.

'You mean my home,' Vic pointed out. 'My home is here.'

Tori narrowed her eyes. 'What are you saying?'

'I am saying that I own this dump.' Vic paused to rake a frankly appraising look over her bare breasts. His watery, washed-out eyes met hers again. 'Don't play dumb with me, Tori. You're too cunning to be stupid. Remember? I paid the mortgage for the last four months when you lost those two jobs? That makes the joint mine. You gotta admit it's better than the bank throwing you out on your delicious rump. Instead you throw your delicious rump on me.'

'But you said you were loaning the money. That I could pay you back when I got another job – '

'Ha, that's a good one. Who's gonna hire you? You already missed two shoots because you were too drunk and too stoned to stand up straight. That might've been okay in the seventies and eighties, but not now. They're getting gun-shy. But really you could probably get away with it if you were twenty years old, or sixteen, like your babe of a sister. But face it: you're long in the tooth – '

'Shut up!' Tori screamed, swiping up a champagne bottle and flinging it at Vic's head. It landed well off its mark, leaving a dent in the wall at knee level.

Vic, used to Tori's violent outbursts, continued unabated. 'Nope, this joint is mine and you are too, so come here and pay your rent.'

Panic seized Tori like a cold, ungiving hand around her slender neck. Her home wasn't her home any more and it had taken her four months to figure it out. Sleeping with Vic for the dope was one thing, but, for some reason she couldn't explain, whoring herself for a home was another. Bitter bile rose in the back of her throat and trickled onto her tongue. It was all Risa's fault. One look at her exotic almond eyes, tawny hair and olive skin – and youth – and they didn't want the classic, blonde, blue-eyed beauty who'd worked her ass off for ten years.

Oh, sure, they'd all offered to shoot them together – the Reeve sisters in a joint photo session. But that was just lip-service. Tori knew what it really would've been – a way to show how old Tori looked and how young Risa was. Well, Tori had been one step ahead of them; she'd never let Risa get within miles of any of her shoots. And no mention was made of it again until Risa started to get really big, when she hit the cover of *Vogue* two months ago. Then, when that reporter from a celebrity magazine had called about that article in next month's magazine – 'The Risa and the Fall of the Reeves', she'd said it would be titled – Tori didn't have to guess whose fall it was.

She felt the red flame of hatred catching fire in her chest again, just as it had when she'd hung up the phone in the reporter's ear a week before. Racing against time, she searched the room desperately for the only thing that put out the fire – alcohol. Her eyes scanned the bottles on the nightstand and scattered on the floor. Empty.

'What's the hold-up? Get over here,' Vic ordered, pointing crudely at his crotch with one hand, grasping a Bloody Mary in the other.

'Go to hell,' Tori shot back distractedly.

'Oh, thanks for the invite, but you're going there all by your lonesome.'

Then, Tori remembered where she was going this morning and why: Risa was dead. As suddenly as it had risen the red heat of hatred cooled and faded. They'd be begging to take her back – all of them would want her back in front of the camera again. Risa was gone and would be forgotten in the short shelf-life of the latest batch of magazines. Tori could make a comeback, better than ever.

The thought that it would be at the cost of her little

sister's life gave Tori a twinge, which she tried to shake. No one would think it was her fault, certainly. She held her head in her hands as she struggled to remember Britt's phone call of the night before. She and Vic had been drinking and doping for hours. Or had it been days? Britt had said the cops thought it was an accident. Something about the way Britt had insisted she didn't buy into that theory made the twinge in Tori's stomach twist tighter. Tori shrugged it off again, as a symptom of her hangover.

'Hey!' Vic interrupted her thoughts. He stood in front of her, his crotch at eye-level. He grabbed her hair and yanked back as she let out a yelp. 'You'll be lucky if I'm waiting when you get back. You might just find somebody else in my bed unless you can do something to make me remember you real good, baby-baby.'

With the bravado that the idea of her impending comeback gave her, she pushed Vic out of the way with her forearm and stood. 'I've got to get ready.' She glanced at the clock. Its digital dial read 7:03. She grabbed up a pair of tan leather pants and a lime-green satin blouse. Clean or dirty? New or used? She didn't really care. 'I've already missed one flight. Be a doll and make me some coffee for the road.'

'I'll make you something for the road,' Vic spat out as he raised his hand back and brought it down across her cheek before she could do more than close her eyes. Stars burst behind her eyelids as she ran into the bathroom, slammed the door and locked it behind her.

'That's to remember me by. You're mine. Don't ever forget that, baby-baby,' Vic hissed through the door before walking out of the bedroom.

Tentatively she opened her eyes and brought her fingertips up to her cheek. The red welt was already swelling. Tori knew from experience the swelling would be gone by the time she got to San Antonio, but the bruise would have started to show. She reached for her thickest pancake make-up, and, after splashing her face with cold water, tried to smooth it on without wincing.

The sun's first rays began to turn the horizon pink as he looked in his rearview mirror and Skin wondered where the hell he was. New Mexico was a lot of nothing as far as he could tell. Sometime in the middle of the night he'd crossed the border from Texas and since then he hadn't seen anything worth remembering. A couple of cars had zoomed passed his rickety Volkswagen and he'd passed a few poky clunker trucks. An oncoming drunk had swerved into his lane around three o'clock in the morning, and that had been the highlight of the night's drive so far. As more of the dawn filtered out onto the landscape Skin noticed that daylight wouldn't be offering any more excitement. Red dirt, rocks and scrub trees went far as the eye could see.

Where was Arizona anyway?

Travel-weary and in need of a pitstop, Skin pulled off onto the shoulder of the highway, not even bothering to wait until he came upon a tree. He opened the door and didn't take long to stretch his skinny legs before unzipping his fly and watering the red dust next to the highway. The crunch and pop of gravel behind him made him jump in his skin. Whipping his head around, he zeroed in on the lights on the roof and the emblem on the side and knew he was being nailed by a cop.

'What you doing there, son?' the state trooper called out through his window as he angled his car in front of Skin's and stopped.

'It's been a while since the last rest-stop, Officer and, I, uh, couldn't wait.' Zipping his fly, Skin prayed the cop couldn't see his pounding heart through the back of the thin T-shirt he wore. It felt as if it was going to jump out of his body. He took a deep breath and turned around and faced the officer over the hood of the Volkswagen.

The trooper got out and slammed his car door. Skin could hear the police radio squawking through the open window. Was whatever they were saying over the air about him? Had they found out? Was there a warrant out for him already? Skin didn't have much experience with serious law-breaking, and now he shifted from foot to foot in nervous anticipation.

Hiking his polyester pants up by his belt, the trooper came around his car and spat a stream of tobacco juice next to Skin's urine. He raised his eyes, taking in Skin's worn leather sandals, his holey, baggy jeans and his Grateful Dead T-shirt, his ragged dirt-brown goatee and shoulder-length hair. 'You know, son, I got half a mind to take you in for indecent exposure.'

Skin swallowed the lump in his throat. Either the cop didn't know or he was toying with him. He fought to keep his cool. 'Sorry, Officer,' he mumbled. 'I just couldn't hold it any more.'

'Not for that, son. I'd run you in for those clothes. That's downright indecent as far as I'm concerned.' The trooper had himself a chuckle at Skin's expense.

Skin sighed and relaxed slightly. So the cop was playing with him, but just because he was bored and didn't like long-haired guys with California plates. Okay, Skin thought as he took another fortifying breath, I can handle this.

'You a hippie or something, son? Didn't anyone tell you the sixties are over?'

'Actually, Officer, the fashion from the sixties is making a comeback – '

'Fashion, my butt,' he interrupted. 'Maybe it's making a comeback in California, the home of the fruits and nuts, but not here in good ole New Mexico.'

Here comes the drug question. Get ready, Skinny.

The trooper leaned into the window of the car. 'Got anything I'd be interested in in your vehicle, here, son?'

Skin swallowed and slid his hand in his pocket. Everything was there, safe. 'No, sir. But you can go ahead and take a look if you want to.'

Half a minute passed while the trooper measured Skin with a piercing look. He shot a wad of spit out on the ground before finally speaking. 'Nah, I've gotta go.'

Skin remained standing next to his vehicle while the trooper sauntered back over to his cruiser and got in. He leaned over and spoke through the window. 'Just keep your pecker in your pants from now on, son, unless you're in a bona fide restroom. Or at least behind a wide enough tree.'

'Got it, Officer. Will do. No prob. Thanks for the advice.'

The trooper, who'd been shifting into reverse, stayed his hand on the gear shift and narrowed his eyes. 'You nervous about something, son?'

Oops, laid it on a little too thick, there, Skinny. Ease up.

'No, sir, Officer. Just a little embarrassed – getting caught with my pants down and all.'

The trooper guffawed again. 'Yeah. Guess that would do it, huh, son? Unless I'd been one of those new woman troopers – then you might'a liked having one of them write you up. They'd probably have to measure your pecker for their report. Your tough luck you get some old geezer like me stopping by at the wrong time.'

Skin forced a guffaw to share with the trooper and thought he was almost home free when the guy scratched his gray, greasy head of hair and looked sheepish. 'You know, son, I never asked to see your driver's license. Better take care of that right now. Just pass it on through the window, here.'

Heart racing again, Skin reached into his pocket for his wallet and passed the license through to the trooper's outstretched hand. Skin held his breath with the hope that he wouldn't call the number into the dispatch person on the other end of the radio.

But the trooper only ran his eyes across the license and handed it back over. Skin resisted the impulse to snatch it back and casually retrieved it instead.

'So you're from San Antonio?'

'Well, I live in Los Angeles now, but I'm just waiting until my license expires to get a new one.' Skin tried not to fidget.

'San Antonio's where that model just died. Purty little thing. What was her name?' The trooper seemed to be searching his memory bank, intent on making this a morning of gossip. 'It rhymed with Linda, I think. No, Lisa. It rhymed with Lisa. Nisa? Brisa? Risa – that was it. Just a girl, still. It's such a shame.'

Skin felt his thundering heart rise into his throat, dragging his stomach along with it. He swallowed in an attempt to push it back down but it just rose higher, until he was sure it would fall out of his mouth the next time he spoke.

'You didn't know her, did you?' the trooper asked.

Once again Skin felt as if he was a trapped rabbit, being batted at by a large mountain lion. But it was just his imagination running wild. The trooper seemed genuinely clueless as to how close he was coming.

'No.' Skin cleared his throat but didn't dislodge the lump there.

'Well, I guess San Antonio is a big town. City, I guess. A lot bigger than we have around here but not so big as you got there in California. What is it you do there in the city of devils?'

It took Skin a moment to realize where he was talking about: LA – the city of angels. It was as poor a play on words as he'd ever heard, and he was so distracted by that he forgot to watch himself and the truth spilled out. 'I'm a magazine photographer.'

'Photographer, huh?' The trooper looked interested. 'Deer and fish? Stuff like that?'

If he'd been smart, Skin would realize much later, he would've agreed with the trooper and been done with it. But, no, it was a call to his ego. He wanted this guy to know exactly where his blood, sweat, tears and creativity had gone over the last twenty years. 'No. I photograph models. You know . . .' Skin paused, searching for something the trooper would relate to. '*Sports Illustrated Swimsuit Edition*. Like that.'

The trooper's eyebrows shot up. 'Ah. So you *must* know this dead gal – and I think I heard her sister's famous too. Tori something-or-other. My wife had on *Entertainment Tonight* last night and they showed a picture of her doing that swimsuit edition a couple of years back. They said she's having a press conference with the father today sometime, to talk about the little sister dying so sudden.'

Skin's hand gripped the roof of the car to steady his nerves. This guy was sniffing around too close for comfort. Why couldn't he just let it go? 'Where's this press conference?'

'So you do know her, huh? I dunno. I think they said it was there in San Anton. Makes sense – probably have the funeral there too; it is her hometown.'

'Right,' Skin agreed with a bored air. He wished this

guy would get the hint and let him go. Skin made a show of looking at his watch and realized suddenly that it wasn't there. His eyes scanned the ground around the car and peered into the front seat.

'Lose something, boy?'

'Yeah, my watch is gone.'

'Oh, yeah, mine does that too. The expandable band is so old and stretched out, and it gets caught on things. It's time to get a new one.'

'No, mine has leather band. Not stretchy,' Skin commented distractedly.

Had he been thinking so hard about what had happened in San Antonio that he hadn't noticed it slip off in the car? Or had he lost it somewhere else? He remembered putting it on before he went to talk to Risa. But after? He couldn't remember anything but sheer panic and nausea.

'Well, keep your pants zipped in public on your trip home,' the trooper warned as a goodbye. 'You *are* going home to California?'

'Sure, you bet.' Skin nodded as he slipped behind the wheel and turned the key in the ignition. The muffler bucked and the engine died twice before it finally caught. The trooper waved and pulled out. Skin didn't wait long before he did a U-turn and headed back to the east. If he was going to talk to Tori, he was going to have to go back to Texas to do it.

He was so distracted he didn't notice his friendly trooper had stopped to watch and wonder why Skin was heading in the exact opposite direction from the one he'd said he was going.

CHAPTER 6

Staring at the red liquid dripping from her hand, Britt fought off the images that suddenly crowded into her mind for the first time that morning. She squeezed her eyes shut at the vision of the blood on Risa's head, as she'd seen it the day before, then her imagination took over and rewound, recreating what she imagined had happened: a nameless, faceless person pushing Risa into the doorjamb. Risa's head hitting. Her skull crushing. The blood flowing.

'Can't you get the paint off, Miz Reeve?'

Britt's eyes flew open at the sound of the little voice at her right elbow. Julian's deep brown eyes, so guileless, were like a salve to her aching heart. She smiled and he smiled. A grin that lit up his face and lifted her spirits immediately. Britt had told herself she'd come to school because her students needed her. She didn't want to abandon them to a substitute on the last day before summer – the last day she'd be their teacher.

But the truth was – she realized now – she needed them. She needed this smile that Julian was flashing her.

'I haven't even tried yet, Julian,' Britt admitted. If she'd learned one thing after teaching five-year-olds for the past five years, it was not to lie. 'I'm just standing here day-dreaming.'

Julian nodded in acceptance, clambered up on the stool on the floor and stretched his short arms to reach the faucet. Britt could've done it without Julian's help, much more easily and quickly too, but she didn't try. For someone not naturally patient, Britt had cultivated patience with her little charges. She wouldn't dare interrupt his mission of aid and shoot down his self-confidence. She waited, trying not to look back at the blood-red paint collecting in the basin.

Finally Julian, balanced on the edge of the sink with legs dangling, managed to turn the knob and the faucet squirted out water. It came out too fast and splashed watery red spray all over her white blouse, but Britt didn't flinch or comment, not even when she realized he'd turned on the hot water and the rising temperature began to scald her hand. Julian stood by proudly, the look on his face enough to make her suffer almost anything.

'Nice job, Julian. I'm so proud of what a great helper you are,' Britt said quietly. 'I think I'm going to need a towel to dry my hands. Do you think you could find one for me?'

Nodding enthusiastically, Julian hopped off the stool on his new errand while Britt lifted her dripping right hand to turn off the faucet. Julian reappeared, bearing a towel, before she even took her hand off the handle. Thanking him, she dried her hands and turned to watch the rest of the students finish their last project of the school year. Some wielded sponges, cleaning the worktables, and some were closing up the paints. The rest used clothespegs to hang up their paintings on the drying line.

Britt looked proudly at the twenty paintings, each a self-portrait, each a gift to her, their kindergarten teacher. Each year she'd kept this last project as a memento of her precious students. Each one was priceless to her.

Risa had, unknowingly, given her the idea ten years before, when she'd come home from kindergarten with a painted self-portrait and had given it to Britt instead of her father. 'To my best sister and best friend' it had read.

Sighing, Britt flung the towel back into the sink and glanced at the clock. A quarter to twelve. She couldn't put it off any longer. She rang a tiny bell, the signal to the children to take their seats. As soon as they had, she distributed the twenty envelopes she'd brought to school that morning. The twenty children clutched their letters with looks of open curiosity.

'What's the letter say?'

'Can you tell us what it's about, Miz Reeve?'

'Miss Reeve, please read us the letter first.'

Britt held up her hand and the murmurings and demands faded. Forty eyes looked expectantly at her, Britt hated to put them off, but she had to.

'Now, class, you know our rule about honesty,' Britt began.

'Tell the truth and earn respect,' about half the class chanted, while the other half nodded in agreement.

Britt smiled her approval. 'That's right. So I will tell you the letter is some news about me but that's all I'm going to say now. Your mommies and daddies will have to decide whether they want to read my letter to you or whether they want to tell you about it in their own words – '

Jennifer's hand shot up in the air. 'Miss Reeve, are you quitting? My daddy is quitting and we have to move to a different city. Is that going to happen to you?'

A couple of the children looked stricken at this thought. Their eyes bored anxiously into her own. She smiled reassuringly.

'No, Jennifer, I'm not quitting or moving. I'll be right

here next year, for you to come visit when you have time – because you know you're going to be big first-graders next year. You might even have *homework*.' Britt paused to let that sink in. Faces lit up with excitement at that novel prospect. Britt chuckled inwardly, imagining those same faces ten years from now and the groans that would be following the same word.

'Oh, Miz Reeve, I'll always have time to come visit you,' Julian piped up. 'Even if I have days long of homework. I'm not forgetting you, no way.'

'Oh, good,' Britt answered. 'I might even come visit you in your new classes too.'

That was met with cheers and 'yippees'. Britt could feel the energy level beginning to supersede their curiosity about the contents of the letter and she felt relieved. She'd been concerned about doing the right thing when she'd made the decision and written the letter at four that morning. All the kids had known Risa – she'd come in often as a high school helper as part of her early education class. They'd all loved her. But Britt knew each child should probably be told in a different way, depending on his or her previous experiences with death and their own personalities. The parents of each child would best be able to make the decision on how it should be done, if at all.

The chattering was growing louder and Britt could feel the pull of summer growing irresistible. Thank goodness this last day of school was only a half-day. She held up her hand one last time. It took twice as long as usual for her to have their full attention.

'In about five minutes we have to go home, but first I want you to line up in front, here. I have something for each of you and you'd better have a hug for me.'

With that, the children jostled into a semi-straight line as Britt sat down on one of the mini-chairs in the room.

She pulled up a paper shopping bag full of goodies and began sifting through to find the right gift for each individual child.

Along with returning their hug and handing over their special prize, Britt reminded each child of his or her greatest achievement of the year, what she'd miss most about them, and what they ought to work on during the summer.

'Raul, I'm so proud of you working hard to learn how to write every letter in the alphabet. I'm going to miss the way you always hold my hand walking to lunch. Work on your reading this summer!'

'Tina, your subtraction is so impressive. You can keep up the good work by playing card games with your big sisters this summer. I'm sure going to miss those jelly beans you sneak in to me every morning . . .'

Finally, with nineteen children and the class fish, Goldy, sent home for the summer, Britt looked up to see Lucy, not waiting in line, but sitting at a desk, her eyes glued to a paper, her forehead puckered in concentration and her lips moving silently. Britt stood and walked over to see what Lucy was reading. As she recognized her own handwriting, Britt's heart lurched. She gave herself a swift mental kick while at the same time feeling a surge of pride at the ability she'd helped foster. She should have guessed that her one student who was reading at a third-grade level would have tried to read the letter on her own.

Britt put her hand on Lucy's thin shoulder. Lucy looked up. 'This says Risa died,' she said matter-of-factly.

'Yes, she did,' Britt answered, willing herself not to lose control of her emotions now. She sat down at the desk next to Lucy and pulled her chair so they were knee-to-knee.

'Why?'

'We don't really know why,' Britt began, then realized

that Lucy was really asking how Risa died. 'She was home by herself and she might have fallen and hit her head really hard on the doorway.'

Lucy pondered this a moment before speaking. 'My little brother fell and hit his head. He got a big black egg, right here – ' she touched her forehead ' – but he didn't die.'

'No, little kids are pretty tough and their heads are flexible. Remember when Taylor brought in her baby brother for show and tell and we talked about how the bones in babies' heads don't get hard until they're older? That helps protect them when they fall. They bend instead of break.'

'I remember. And Risa was big. A grown-up.'

'Yes, almost all grown up,' Britt admitted.

'You're sad,' Lucy stated. Britt told herself it was the often amazing insight that children possess that let Lucy see this, because she hoped she wasn't wearing her grief so plainly.

'I am sad,' Britt said, reaching out to pat Lucy's knee through her pink-polka-dot pants.

'But Risa's in heaven now,' Lucy said. 'And heaven is nice. Nicer than here on earth, Father Keene says.'

'I hope it is, Lucy. I guess I'm really sad for myself, because I'm going to miss her.'

'I'm sad, 'cuz I'm going to miss her too. But you'll miss her more, 'cuz she was your sister,' Lucy observed.

So true in its simplicity while so unfathomable in reality. Lucy couldn't see the lump growing in her throat, but Britt was afraid the child would soon see the tears that threatened behind her eyes. So she was angling for a way to close the conversation when Lucy's mother appeared at the door and did it for her.

'Of course I knew I'd find my little bookworm in here,

not willing to give up school,' Mrs Hernandez said as she leaned down to kiss her daughter's head.

'I'm afraid Lucy was doing a super job reading a note that I wrote this morning, intending for parents to see first,' Britt explained.

'Her sister died,' Lucy chimed in.

Mrs Hernandez's eyes clouded with sympathy. 'Yes, I was sorry to hear that. If there's anything we can do, please let us know.'

'Just make sure this girl gets out of doors every now and then, or she'll have my job by summer's end with all her reading,' Britt said as she leaned down to give Lucy a hug and her prize; a copy of one of her own childhood favorites, *Charlotte's Web*.

Britt said goodbye to Lucy and her mother and turned to straighten up the room without following them to the door.

In the hallway, Grant Collins nodded to the woman and her daughter as they passed him. He'd taken a step toward the doorway when the little girl stopped in her tracks, forcing her mother, who was holding her hand, to stop as well. Then she turned her serious eyes on Grant. 'Don't bother Miss Reeve. She's sad. And, anyway, she's on vacation now. So you'll have to come back when summer's over.'

Something about the bossy way she talked, or the authoritative tilt of her chin, or maybe her wild dark hair made Grant imagine Britt as a little girl. A smile tickled at the corners of his mouth. But he kept his face impassive. 'I won't talk to her very long,' he said, then impulsively added, 'I promise.'

She gave him a head-to-toe look that would be intimidating in another ten years, then nodded once. 'You better not talk long. And you'd better be nice,' she warned as she marched forward, dragging her mother – who shot Grant an apologetic grin – along behind her.

Grant watched them walk down the hall for a moment, then turned his attention back to the classroom. Her back to him, Britt stood at the window with her arms full of books. She leaned with her thighs pressed against the bookcase under the window, a casual pose that looked as if it was a usual habit, so she could watch as her students headed to the bus and waiting cars, but the wilt of her shoulders told him what she was thinking about. Her unruly cloud of burnished hair kept him from seeing her face, but he imagined the tears running down her silken cheeks silently.

He didn't want to interrupt her grief; he willed his feet to carry him away, back to his car. The information he'd come for he could've gotten when he'd talked to Jewel Reeve that morning, but something else had driven him here to see Britt. The information was an excuse. He wanted to see how she'd survived the night.

When Jewel had told him she'd gone to work, Grant had been shocked. But on further reflection he realized he shouldn't have been. Her spunky determination combined with the way she wore responsibility like a shield would take her to the children she'd taught for nine months. Jewel had had to remind Grant that it was the last day of school. With no children of his own, and knowing no children, he was completely oblivious to school-year rhythms. He'd realized if he was going to talk to Risa's classmates and boyfriends it would be much easier today. So, instead of sitting at his desk waiting for the Medical Examiner to call, he'd left Chile there to sift through evidence and put interviews at the top of his to-do list.

Frustrated with his own inertia, Grant slid his sunglasses back down over his eyes. He'd get out of here, go to the high school and talk to the kids without any background from Britt. He really didn't need it anyway. This was all routine. Once the Medical Examiner ruled it an accident, he could close the file and go back to investigating that stack of burglaries on his desk.

But before he could step away from the doorway Britt turned round. Her eyes, moist around the edges and shining with unshed tears, widened at the sight of him but her voice was flat. 'Detective Collins. You have some news for me?'

'No, actually I came here hoping you'd be able to help me. I'm going to the high school to talk to Risa's friends. I need you to give me a list of her closest friends, maybe any enemies you knew of.' He stopped, taking in the red-paint-splattered white shirt and navy cotton pants. 'Do you always look this good at the end of the day?'

Britt's golden cheeks flushed and she looked down at her still damp shirt and her grandmother's pants she'd borrowed, that were two sizes too big and that she'd cinched in at the waist with her belt from the day before. The rest of yesterday's clothes had gone into the garbage. She'd never be able to wear them again.

Britt had forgotten what she looked like, and didn't care – but, dammit, he didn't have to comment on it. Feeling rising irritation replacing her embarrassment, she studied his impassive face. No telling if he was joking or not. The man was hard to read.

'Do you always wear your sunglasses inside? Or are you trying to slip in to the school incognito, to do some undercover surveillance on the kids?' Britt cringed at the sharpness of her own tone, but he'd forced her into it. Her quick tongue had always been her weapon against giving in to her emotions when she was growing up. And she was falling back on it now.

Moving his forgotten sunglasses to the top of his head, Grant tried to reconcile the soft-voiced, warm woman he'd listened to encouraging a bunch of five-year-olds with the back-talking cynic with the face of a fairy princess who stood before him now. He couldn't; she was simply an enigma.

Her comment about the sunglasses had hit too close to the part of his life he so vigilantly guarded – from himself more than others. He studied Britt for an extra second, to see if she could read him that well or whether he was just a handy target. She was good at target practice, flinging barbs at will. Grant was beginning to understand it as a diversionary tactic. Diverting attention away from what, exactly? he wondered.

He pulled his notebook out of his jacket pocket. 'So can you help me, or am I on my own?'

Britt blew a strand of curly hair out of her face with a sigh. 'Of course I'll help you. As long as you are keeping an open mind about the cause of her death.'

'Britt, I told you before I won't disregard evidence, but until the ME rules, it's hard to know what direction we're headed with this.'

It was too vague for Britt, but she bit back her urge to argue. It would have to do – for now. She gestured to a pair of chairs near the window where she stood. 'Come on in. I'll tell you as much as I can.'

Grant scanned the room and felt suddenly awkward. The tiny chairs, whose backs barely reached his knees, made him feel ten feet tall. The brightly colored drawings and numbers and alphabet on the walls seemed both foreign and vaguely familiar. It tugged at memories of his childhood. Memories of him and his brother, their dreams and the harsh reality thirty years later. Grant shut his eyes briefly.

Britt crouched down, balancing on the balls of her loafer-clad feet to put her armful of books back into the shelf, but she paused as she looked back to see the strained look on Grant's face. The furrows on the sides of his mouth deepened. The muscles of his jaw bunched. His lips tightened to a thin line.

'You really don't like kids, huh?' Britt asked, shoving *The Hungry Caterpillar* into its place next to *The Grouchy Ladybug*. She wondered why she felt a twinge of disappointment as she said it. It was no skin off her nose if this cop didn't take to kids.

'It's not that,' Grant said, a little too loudly.

Britt waited for a moment or two for him to elaborate, but of course he didn't. 'Well, everyone was a kid once, and sometimes it just takes a while to remember what it's like to be young,' Britt pointed out as she held up a blue and white book. 'Surely this brings back a memory or two.'

The Cat in the Hat. Why the hell did she have to choose that one? He suddenly felt out of breath. It had been his brother's favorite book. Evan had read it until it was so dog-eared that his mother had had to buy a new copy. Evan had insisted upon dressing up as the Cat in the Hat three Halloweens in a row. Grant tried to mentally shove away the image that materialized before his eyes – the vision of Evan running, skipping and jumping at age eight. And where was he now, at age thirty-five? In a hospital bed, unable to move anything but his eyes and his mouth. Paralyzed from the neck down.

And it was Grant's fault. For not preventing it. For not seeing the whole thing before it happened. For being the brother up walking around. For not being the one in that bed.

'Well, doesn't it jog the memory bank?' asked Britt.

'It does,' Grant snapped. 'But not anything I care to dredge up. Now or ever. If you're going to help me isn't there a teacher's lounge or someplace outside we could talk?'

Britt swallowed hard. She hadn't meant to touch on sore feelings. He must have had a bad childhood. Abuse, maybe. For the first time she saw a crack of vulnerability in his steely exterior, and she suddenly felt the need to make up for her unintentional error, to ease his obvious pain. She slid *The Cat in the Hat* back onto the shelf and touched Grant's arm, her fingers just grazing his bicep.

'I'm sorry.'

Grant shied away from her touch and walked out into the hall, pulling the sunglasses back down over his eyes. 'You don't have anything to be sorry for.'

'Oh, yeah, I do,' Britt mumbled, feeling as if she'd been slapped in the face. 'Feeling anything more than anger in the great stone heart. I won't make that mistake again.'

Maybe she was wrong about the bad childhood. Maybe he was just a pig. Maybe that was all there was to it. To him.

By the time Britt had turned off all the lights and shut the door to the classroom Grant was already halfway down the hall, which had quickly become deserted after the closing bell. Despite herself, she noticed his confident stride again. It spoke volumes, radiating a power, an unquestioning authority. A lion's walk. Britt wondered for the first time why he would be working in a tiny police department in a tiny suburb of San Antonio, where the most exciting crime that might occur all year would be a robbery at a million-dollar mansion.

Except this year. Britt swallowed hard and willed the tears that sprang instantly into her eyes back down where they came from.

'Britt, what in the world are you still doing here?'

Turning at the sound of the familiar voice, Britt saw the school principal hurrying from the opposite end of the building. He carried a sheaf of papers in his hand, that he beat against his pants leg with each rushed step of his half-walk half-run. Britt glanced back at Grant and saw that he'd stopped, his broad-shouldered, slim-hipped form, with a hand in one pocket of his chinos, a dark silhouette against the noonday light shining from the open doors.

Britt swiveled back to face Principal Joe McGown. 'I expected you to be long gone by now, Britt,' he said, with a bit of censure in his voice.

'I did too,' she admitted. 'But Lucy Hernandez ended up reading part of that letter I sent home for the parents, and we had to have a talk.'

Joe shook his shaggy blond head that always seemed in need of a haircut and reached up contemplatively to stroke his mustache with his free hand. 'I hope we don't have a problem?'

Britt felt herself going tense at his implication. Had she made the wrong decision by giving the children the letter? Joe had let her handle the matter in her own way, but was he reconsidering now? 'No, her mother came to class to get her and seemed fine. Lucy took it philosophically.'

'Maybe you should take a cue from her,' Joe offered.

Britt raised her eyebrows at his rather pompous suggestion, but bit her tongue on a retort. He was more than her boss, he was a friend, and he was just trying to be helpful. She had broken down first thing that morning in the office when all the teachers had come to offer their condolences while she was talking to Joe, but she'd been dry-eyed when she left his office and had kept a lid on her emotions in front of the kids all morning. He couldn't ask for any more.

'I'm doing the best I can,' Britt said in what she hoped was a neutral tone.

'Of course you are. But sometimes doing our best isn't necessarily the right thing to do. Take, for instance . . .' Joe went off on one of his example tangents, and Britt began to tap her foot impatiently. He was always big on long, analogous stories that did have a point, but it never seemed worth the wait. He was well-meaning, Britt reminded herself as she nodded appropriately.

'So, would you?'

Britt had tuned in too late and missed a question somewhere along the way. 'Would I what?'

Joe put a hand on her shoulder, allowing his fingers to massage her tight muscles gently. 'Would you like to come over and talk about Risa, your feelings? Or maybe I can take you someplace quiet, away from all the arrangements – '

'No, she wouldn't.' Grant's voice rumbled low with warning just over her opposite shoulder. How had his ground-consuming stride approached so soundlessly? Britt hadn't heard anything behind her, but – she glanced back, just to make sure he wasn't a ventriloquist – he *was* there. He was so close she could feel the warm energy radiating from his body. It nearly vibrated the air around him.

'She's got a date with the law,' Grant continued, his steely eyes locked on Joe's brown ones.

Joe's hand tightened on her shoulder.

She looked from Joe's solid, stocky body, the easy grin and tousled blond good looks, to the tough sinewy tan figure accented with shades of flint from his salt-and-pepper hair and his malachite eyes. It was Pooh Bear meets Dirty Harry.

Suddenly Britt snapped out of her daze, shook off Joe's

hand and planted her fists on her hips defiantly. 'I don't have a date with anybody or anything.'

'Good,' Grant said, his body moving forward in a way that didn't touch her but urged her in the direction of the door. 'We can get down to work, then.'

Britt furrowed her brow in frustration. She hadn't expected Collins to agree with her. Why did she always end up speechless around him?

Suspicion clouded Joe's friendly features. 'Work? What kind of work?'

'Police work,' Grant snapped. 'Who are you?'

Britt stared dumbfounded at Collins. First he interrupted their conversation, then he was mad because he hadn't been introduced!

'Joe McGown. I'm principal here.' Joe stuck out a hand which Grant shook and dropped just a second too quickly to be polite. Joe's face grew ruddy and he cleared his throat before turning to Britt. 'What's this about police work?'

'I'm just helping the police find out what happened to Risa,' Britt explained.

'But I thought it was an accident,' Joe said.

'We're not certain, yet,' Grant answered.

Britt craned her neck to look at his face. It was the first time he'd sounded anything but sure of the accident theory. Did he have some new piece of evidence he wasn't telling her about? She wished she could see through those damned silver lenses.

'Britt, I think you need to steer clear of this police investigation,' Joe began earnestly. 'No telling what hornets' nests they'll be digging up. It will be a whole lot safer if you just keep to yourself and your family and friends. You need to concentrate on healing. Let the police get the justice. That's not your job. That's his.'

Joe flicked a thumb in Grant's direction while keeping his eyes fixed on Britt.

'She was my sister, Joe, and – hornets or no – I'm going to do all in my power to find out what's behind her death. Thank you for your concern, though,' Britt said, with a finality she hoped would close the conversation.

Grant had listened with rapt fascination to the principal's lecture. He'd given Grant insight into Britt Reeve as a justice-seeker. Of course she'd come out with guns blazing yesterday, but he'd wondered if it might just have been a reaction to the situation. He'd expected her ardor would have cooled a day later. Maybe he'd been wrong. And if he was, she meant trouble.

He should've been thanking the guy instead of wanting to grab him by the collar. That he'd basically made Grant sound like a glorified beekeeper instead of a cop didn't help endear him. But that wasn't it. He could clearly see Joe was angling for more than friendship with Britt. He'd seen that in his body language from down the hall, which was what had driven him to jump into their conversation in the first place. But why? Why did he care that the principal wanted more out of his kindergarten teacher than a spelling bee? Or maybe he'd already gotten more? Grant didn't like the way his stomach contracted at that thought.

Joe shifted from foot to foot, obviously trying to find a way to prolong the conversation. 'Britt, like I told you earlier, no hurry on getting your room put right for summer. In fact – ' he brightened with sudden inspiration ' – I'd be happy to do it for you. You shouldn't have that to worry about on top of everything else.'

Britt shook her head and put her hand on the principal's shoulder. 'Thanks, Joe, but I'd really rather do it myself. I will take a week or so before I can get to it, though.'

Joe backed off, nodding. 'Sure. And call if you need anything – a friendly ear, a shoulder to cry on . . .'

'I think she gets the message,' Grant said over his shoulder.

Britt had been allowing Grant to shepherd her down the corridor, away from the retreating Joe, but now she spun on him. 'Would you *please* mind your own business?'

'Listen,' Grant said, lifting his sunglasses and fixing her with the most intense gaze she'd ever experienced. 'Your life was a big part of your sister's life. Right now it's my responsibility to find out how her life ended, so until this case is closed your life *is* my business.'

For a moment their eyes held, communicating more than either of them understood. Then, abruptly, Grant dropped his sunglasses over his eyes and stalked out, pushing open both of the double doors, which swished closed behind him.

Britt stood immobile in the hall, which suddenly seemed vast and cold once empty of his powerful presence. Joe was long gone, and all she could hear was the drip-drip of a faucet somewhere behind her. The doors in front of her stopped swinging and Britt finally had nothing to think about but what had just happened. And she didn't like it. Not his bossing her around. Not the invasion of her privacy. Not the way his presence sent her into a sense of high physical awareness. And especially not the way his eyes could talk.

Grant pulled his sedan into a side street about a block from the high school. Then quickly maneuvered into a parallel place between a pair of cars that announced, courtesy of white shoe polish, that they were seniors and ready to face the world: 'Was the world ready for them?' The answer was no, as far as Grant was concerned. Teenagers in recent years made him uneasy – with little support in either single-parent or two-parent working families, they were left to grow up on their own, or with the help of television. Even the good kids, from caring but busy families, ended up in trouble. Alamo Heights School District was one of the most exclusive enclaves in San Antonio, yet even it was not immune to the drugs and gangs that plagued other schools. Its PR was just better, so not as many people heard about it.

Grant locked the car and walked around the corner and onto the campus. He wanted to slip in unnoticed so he could pick up what the kids were telling each other about Risa's death. He really wanted to talk to a couple of Risa's friends before he checked in with the school office. No telling what this principal was like. Grant recalled the one other time he'd been on a high school campus as a cop. The principal had gone on the damned public address system to urge students to co-operate with the police officer on campus. Great. That had really cleared the way. Literally. All the kids he'd really wanted to talk to had been long gone by the time he stepped out of the principal's office.

So this time he was coming in unannounced. And, without trying to, he'd timed it just right. It was between classes and Grant blended in with the crowd, hoping he looked like a teacher. Most of the talk was generic complaints about teachers, grades, girlfriends, boyfriends.

Grant's ears sharpened at the sound of Risa's name, but it ended up being two girls who were worried about what they were going to wear to the funeral. He discreetly followed them, hoping for more, but he didn't get much. Finally he leaned into a group of kids and casually asked where he could find Jayson Pilchuk. A cheerleader type, who, by virtue of a push-up bra, expensive make-up and blonde highlights, looked about twenty-five, gave him the once-over and pointed down the hall.

'You'll probably find him in the computer lab. He's one of the techno-nerds.'

Techno-nerd? That was a new one on Grant. He nodded, and had started down the hall when he heard her tell her friends in a stage whisper. 'Another reporter looking for Jayson. I wonder where he's from?'

'That's not a reporter, you idiot,' a male voice chimed in. 'It's a cop. Can't you tell he's carrying a piece?'

Resisting the urge to turn around, Grant marveled over the fact that high schoolers might not know how to compute the square root of 542, but they recognized when a person was carrying a concealed weapon. Well, maybe that would prove a more useful piece of knowledge in the future, he considered ruefully.

'A piece of what?' Cheerleader asked, before Grant got out of earshot.

'Not everything changes,' Grant muttered to himself as he ducked into the door that said 'Computer Lab'.

A kid of about seventeen years old sat at a computer terminal. He was very tall for his age, but skinny and painfully awkward. His hairstyle looked like an outgrown crewcut – dirty blond hair stood out on end at each cowlick – but his eyes were showstoppers: clear and blue and forthright, they met Grant's as the door closed behind him.

'I'm looking for Jayson Pilchuk,' Grant said.

He's not here, no matter what anyone told you.' The blue eyes clouded before dropping back to the screen in front of him.

The kid couldn't tell a lie; that was for sure, Grant thought. Either this was Jayson or he knew where Jayson was. Grant tried to gauge the best approach by combining his own impressions with those he'd collected from Jewel and Britt. He was a good kid. Studious, quiet, sensitive. He and Risa had been dating for two years, since she was fourteen and he was nearly sixteen, and before she'd hit the big time. Not terribly self-confident, Jayson was having trouble coping with Risa's fame. However, Britt had assured Grant that Risa really did love Jayson. She called him her 'anchor'. Despite this, he'd been getting somewhat paranoid and surly about the whole modeling business, especially with the tabloid accounts of the movie stars and producers who'd begun to get interested in Risa in the past few months.

The description fit the kid in front of him. Grant read him to be basically honest but wary about something. He decided to play it straight and hoped the kid didn't go charging to the principal.

'I'm Detective Grant Collins with the Terrell Hills Police Department. I need to ask Jayson some questions about Risa Reeve.'

'Where's your ID?'

Grant sighed and reflected again about the effects of TV on everyday life as he pulled out his badge and held it for examination.

The kid glanced at it, then went back to manipulating the computer's mouse, clicking and double-clicking. Grant tried to see what was on the screen, but the kid turned the monitor away. 'So how can Jayson get a hold of you?' he asked.

Grant was quickly tiring of this game, but he let the kid play it the way he wanted to. With the accident ruling likely, he really wouldn't need to push for information. 'Here's my card. He can give me a call.'

'Okay.' One of his long, slender hands left the mouse

long enough to take the card and slip it into the breast pocket of his plain blue T-shirt.

Grant watched him for a minute more, before turning and letting himself out of the computer lab. Just then his pager vibrated at his left hip. Checking the number, he saw it was Ortega's desk. He walked down the hall, now deserted with the start of a new class. The lockers flanked the hall as far as he could see, along the wall on both sides. He wondered idly which was Risa's locker just as his eye caught on a break in the monotony of row upon row of steel doors and locks: a yellow bow and flowers.

As he got closer, Grant realized this was Risa's locker. Someone had wrapped the door of the locker in happy, yellow gift paper that had little pink babies – babies? Grant made a note – crawling across fields of daisies. Taped to the top half of the locker was a bouquet of fresh daisies. In the middle of the locker a photograph of Risa had been taped up. It was a magazine advertisement for shampoo and showed her looking over her shoulder. Grant suddenly realized that this was the first time he'd seen a picture of Risa. The only time he'd seen her before was when she was lying on the floor, lifeless.

As he looked at her now, Grant was struck by her beauty, but stunned even more by seeing Britt's eyes in a younger, exotic face. Risa had the same almond-shaped hazel eyes that had kept him awake last night – her sister's eyes topped by delicate brows that just barely arched in the middle. But as Grant examined the picture more closely he saw that while they were the same size, shape and color, there the similarity stopped. Risa's eyes were gentle, kind, content, peaceful. They lacked the fire, the raw emotion that Britt's eyes always brimmed with, snapping with life.

As he got beyond the eyes Grant had to admit Risa Reeve

was remarkable. She had just the right combination of girl-next-door appeal and exoticism to make her incredibly alluring. Her tawny hair was straight but full, framing a perfect oval face, and she had just a touch of Britt's olive tone in her peaches-and-cream skin. Her aquiline nose pointed to a pair of lips that might be considered a millimeter too full for classic beauty, but made her face more interesting because of it. He didn't wonder that she'd been on her way to the top in the modeling business. She gave you a warm contentment just to look at her, along with offering hope for the future of the next generation. He wondered if women were jealous of her, but with her completely ingenuous aura he doubted it, and as he read what her peers had written in the space around the picture his impression was confirmed.

Students – girls mostly, judging by the rounded, flowing script – had scribbled their goodbyes:

Risa, what are we all going to do without your friendly smile?

Thank you for being nice to me when no one else would.

To God's newest and brightest angel; we'll miss you down here.

We all love you, Risa.

Our hearts ache.

Grant tested the locker and found it shut tight. No matter, he told himself. He probably wouldn't have any need to get into it. Although he made a mental note to himself to talk to the principal about prohibiting access to the locker until the police could go through it – if that was necessary after the autopsy.

Remembering Ortega's page, Grant roused himself and headed down the hall in search of the principal's office. He could phone from there while making his courtesy call to the head cheese.

For the first time Grant noticed signs hastily posted along the walls that announced that the school counselor would be available to those who needed help in the wake of Risa's death. Adding the counselor's name and number to his notepad, Grant heard the sound of crying. He turned to see a girl, dressed in a T-shirt, denim shorts and sandals, with her knees pulled to her chest, sitting on the floor in the corner, next to a bank of lockers. She looked up, embarrassed.

'Hey, are you all right?' Grant asked.

'I'm okay.' She sniffed and blew her nose. 'You're not a reporter, are you?'

'No,' Grant's jaw tightened. The reporters must have really been all over this place if the kids were so skittish.

'Good. It's just that Risa was just such a good person, and no matter how much you tell them that it seems like they keep digging for something bad. If they find it – and who's perfect, anyway? – there it goes, right there in the headline, and the three hours of nice things you said about her end up in one sentence. I dunno. They're not all bad, just mostly the *National Enquirer* types are really bugging me.' She blew her nose again. 'So, who are you?'

'I'm a cop – a detective.'

'Oh, really?' She sat up, interested. 'I'm Mara, Risa's best friend. Do you know what happened yet?'

'No, not yet,' Grant said as he sank into a squat next to Mara. 'But you know it could just be an accident, or maybe she had a health problem no one knew about.' Grant threw this last piece in order to gauge her reaction.

Mara shook her head sadly. 'I just don't know how. She was on the track team and the swim team, you know, and never talked about feeling bad. I guess accidents happen, but I just hope . . . it isn't something else.'

All his antennae went up at that tentative statement.

Grant reined in his heightened interest. 'What do you mean?'

'I'm not sure – just that Risa was acting different lately. Secretive. There was something on her mind but she wouldn't talk about it. I know there was some guy who was bugging her on one of her shoots in LA and Acapulco, but that was almost a year ago, and I don't think what was going on with her lately had anything to do with that.'

'Were she and her boyfriend having any trouble? Could that be it?'

'Jayson?' Mara looked surprised. 'No. He'd been bumming lately, about all the great-looking stars and stuff who had been calling her and talking to her on shoots. But Risa didn't think twice about those guys; she really loved Jayson. He was a little paranoid, but I think he was finally coming around to believe what Risa was telling him. Anyway, whatever this secret stuff that was going on, Jayson was in on it. But she wasn't telling anybody but him.'

'How do you know?'

Mara shot him a look that was pure woman. It said, *You're a guy, you'll never understand about women's intuition.* 'I just know.'

Grant tried to accept that without grimacing. He flipped his thumb down the hall. 'You decorate her locker?'

'Yeah, it just didn't seem right to come to school and have everything look the same when everything is so different. Yellow was her favorite color, and she loved daisies. Risa wouldn't want me to be sitting around crying about her. She was always looking on the bright side and she would be telling me I ought to be happy that she's getting into heaven early. So I dressed up her locker like we do on birthdays.'

'The babies?' Grant asked.

Mara's lips tightened momentarily, and she swallowed. 'Oh, Risa loved babies,' she said quickly. 'Anybody can tell you that. She was always helping in her sister's kindergarten class and she worked with a program for abused babies.'

Mara looked down the hall one more time, then stood up abruptly. 'I've got to go to class. I'm late.'

As he rose to a standing position to give her room to get out, Grant handed her a business card. 'Call me if you think of anything I might need to know about Risa.'

Mara looked up from rearranging her books. 'Uh, yeah, sure.'

As he watched her walk down the hall in her sandaled feet, he wondered if Mara's sudden nervousness sprang from being late to class or whether it came from talk of Risa's locker or babies.

CHAPTER 7

'What's going on?'

'Geez, Tom, let's dispense with the niceties right away,' Ortega complained.

Grant frowned and fought the urge to chew his partner out. He was sitting in the middle of the chaos of the high school office, with teachers, parents and secretaries within earshot, so he took a deep breath instead. This was the characteristic that bugged him most about the easy-going Mexican-American. He always wanted to make every conversation a tea party. 'Look, Chile, I'm not going to ask after your mother's health and your father's lotto winnings and your sister's babies every time we talk. I just saw you two hours ago.'

'S'kay, Tom, just trying to rattle your cage a little. Thought you might miss me and need a little needling.'

'I'm getting enough needling without you,' Grant admitted grudgingly, thinking of Britt and her saucy tongue.

'Anyhow, the Medical Examiner called.'

'And?' Grant's fingers tightened on the cold plastic of the telephone. Alerted by his tone, a pair of teachers looked over at him. Grant swiveled to show them his back.

'And he wouldn't tell me *nada*, *amigo*. Said I might lose

the information. Hey, I know I lose a lotta stuff, but I do my job. Like this is our only murder in years. Like I would forget the cause of death with the media crawling up our backs? So, anyway, he says he just wants to talk to you and you only, in that prickly tone of his. He used to be a nice guy. I think being around all those stiffs has turned him into one.'

'He didn't tell you anything?'

'Not nothin', man. Just told me to – ' Ortega cleared his throat and assumed a pompous falsetto '"impress upon Lieutenant Collins the urgency of this matter. I must speak with him at the earliest."'

Grant ignored Ortega's not-so subtle plea for sympathy over the official brush-off. That would only get Chile started on the history of injustices dealt to him by the ME's office, which would lead into a related series of departmental gossip and personal stories. Not that it wouldn't be entertaining, for Ortega was a classic storyteller, Grant just didn't have the time or the inclination.

'I'm coming back to the station right now. Sit tight.'

Grant hung up and thanked the principal for her help. Unlike the principal in his last encounter with the public school system, she promised to keep his visit under wraps and keep her ears open for anything around the school she might hear.

Outside the office, the halls were deserted again. As he passed classrooms he could hear the murmurings of teachers and students. At one point Grant thought he heard a footfall behind him, but as he turned a door out of his range of vision opened and shut, and he thought it was probably a kid heading to the washroom. Pushing open one side of the double doors, Grant walked outside and into the sunshine. It already felt ninety-nine degrees, he reflected, as he slid his sunglasses over his eyes. Touching their cold metal frames made him think of his brother. It had been three days since he'd visited Evan, and he had to make time to see him today.

Grant jogged down the front steps of the school and, eschewing the sidewalk, cut through the front lawn and along the side of the building. Still he had the itchy feeling of being followed. A reporter? A criminal with an old grudge? Either wasn't welcome. His hand brushed the lump of his gun against his ribs as he slid his notebook back into his jacket pocket. Then, as he turned the corner, he ducked behind a tall, dense pittisporum bush.

A second later he heard the footfall and saw the movement of a figure stop. The figure that he could only see through the waxy leaves as a mass of white and shades of brown was standing just on the other side of the bush. Its head swiveled, as if looking for where Grant had gone, then it moved off at a run. Grant jumped to the other side of the bush and leaped out, grabbing the figure as it ran past and hauling it behind the bush with him.

'Why are you following me?' he growled.

His arm hooked the figure's middle and his hand closed around a forearm that felt so delicate under his fingers that he momentarily loosened his grip so as to not break the bone. It was enough for his captive to yank her arm loose and begin fighting for freedom with a determined strength that belied her small form, pushing and kicking and stamping on his feet. It took Grant longer than it should have to realize that the wild-haired hellion was Britt.

Her heart thudding in her ears, hurting her chest, Britt didn't know why she was fighting him so, except she was angry at herself for getting caught. And he'd scared her. Once she'd yanked herself loose he'd pinned her arms to her sides and pushed her up against the brick at the side of the building. Slowly the fight began to leave her, until she stood still, her chest heaving with the air she sucked in, her blood rushing with adrenaline.

'Have you calmed down yet?' Grant asked.

When her eyes met his and he caught their golden sparks he saw the answer to his question. She might be worn out physically, but mentally she had a way to go yet.

'Calmed down?' Britt panted, raising her chin defiantly. 'After you abduct and accost me?'

Grant couldn't help the laughter that bubbled up in his throat. She was so self-righteous. 'Aren't you exaggerating just a bit? You were following me, after all.'

Those were fighting words as far as Britt was concerned. As a child she'd always been accused of exaggerating, and she squared her shoulders to fight back with words now as she'd always done then. She might be accused of exaggerating, but she'd never ended up on the short end of any verbal debate.

'I'm overreacting? Do you always drag people who walk behind you into the bushes?'

The laughter in his eyes dimmed and his smiled slipped before Britt had a chance to appreciate them. She'd been so involved in fighting that she hadn't noticed how the humor had softened him, turned him into another person. Someone she wanted to know. But that someone was gone just as quickly as he'd appeared.

'Listen.' His grip tightened on her upper arms and he pressed her slightly into the wall as he lowered his head to look into her eyes. 'You were following me, not just walking behind me. When you want to talk to a cop, you call out and let him know; you don't go sneaking up on him. We've got plenty of people we can think of who might want us gone and you never know when they might be coming to call.'

His flinty voice held another emotion at bay. Fear? Vulnerability? Whatever it was, Grant Collins was trying to hide it. She had a sudden urge to raise her hand and slide her fingertips along the hard muscle beside his jaw, she could almost feel the dark stubble growing there. But he still held her arms. Britt couldn't help baiting him further, to see if the emotion he so closely guarded would rise to the surface where she could identify it.

'Well, I'm not about to let you know I'm around, because all I get then is the runaround. I have to sneak about just to find out what's going on.'

Storm clouds gathered in his eyes and Britt almost shook with anticipation of what he was going to do. But what he did was nothing she'd expected. He dipped his head lower and his lips parted. In some kind of unconscious reaction, Britt's head tilted back and her lips met his. Their kiss began as a tentative taste, his lips resting on hers gingerly for a moment before his tongue ran across their plumpness. Britt gasped at the intimate feel of his mouth, and he took that as an invitation to deepen the kiss.

His hands, which had pinned her arms, was plunged into her hair; his hard, sinewy body molded to hers, pressing her into the cold brick at her back. With an effort, she kept her arms rigidly at her sides, afraid of what would happen if she lifted them around his neck, where they ached to go. Still, not all of her body resisted; her mouth matched the building urgency of his mobile lips and tongue. The shadows around them began to swim and Britt closed her eyes as her body began to feel the most curious combination of weakness and power. Her heart was pounding out of control. Her brain refused to think. Her eyes couldn't focus. Her hand finally reached to wrap around something solid. Grant.

It was her undoing. And his.

With a groan, his lips released hers and moved down to claim her throat, his stubble leaving a burning trail along the soft skin of her cheek and neck. Keeping her eyes closed – what she couldn't see, she couldn't acknowledge, right? – Britt threw her head back. As his mouth moved lower his hands followed, tracing the outline of her bra with a fingertip, barely cupping her other breast with his palm. Britt sucked in a breath and willed herself to tell him to stop. Her voice did not respond. Instead she slid her hands down to rest on his hips, intending to push him away. But the pressure of her hands just drove him closer, a hard ridge pressing into the hollow between her thighs

'No.'

They both stilled. It took Britt a half-second to realize she was the one who'd spoken. Just then her eyes flew open to meet his, just inches from hers. They burned with a desire that made them fascinatingly alive, but, as she watched, reason doused the fire to turn them back to their cold gunmetal color. Cop's eyes. As he shifted away from her the metallic ridge of his gun knocked her in the ribs. With that came the reminder of everything sudden passion had made her forget. Her sister was dead. He was a cop who wanted to close the case. She wanted justice at any expense.

Her hands reached up to smooth the collar of her shirt. How had it gotten unbuttoned? She always left only the top button open. Her fingers felt for the second button down to slip into the hole but it was gone. Her face flamed. She'd been so lost in desire that she hadn't noticed he was popping buttons off her shirt. Pulling her shirt together with her right hand, she turned her fury and shame from herself and onto Grant; she told herself it would be an easier way to get him at a safe distance than apologizing would.

'Do you always take advantage of women behind bushes?'

'I don't think I coerced you.'

'You wouldn't,' Britt pointed out, jutting her chin upward, 'You're the one with the gun.'

Grant's face registered shock for a split second before he covered it up with narrowed eyes. 'You're telling me the only reason you kissed me is because I'm carrying a gun?'

Britt opened her mouth to deny it. Of course it wasn't true. But her eyes drifted to his mouth, now drawn into a hard line, but not so hard that she couldn't see a sheen of moisture left from their kiss. That did it. She had to get more distance between them or she'd be lost again.

'Believe what you want to believe, but this isn't going to happen again.' Britt announced.

Grant's hand rubbed across the stubble of his jaw as he shook his head. 'You've got that right.'

Britt felt a stabbing pain shoot through her chest at his words. What did she want? For him to argue? 'Fine,' she said as she pushed her way through the dense leaves of the tall bush and out into the sunshine. 'I'm glad we finally agree on something.'

'Right,' Grant mumbled as he walked on past her, to his car.

'Wait,' Britt called. 'Where are you going?'

'None of your business,' Grant answered over his shoulder as he broke into a jog.

Britt stared after him helplessly, knowing that her legs could barely keep up with his at a walk, much less a run. Not that she could run, anyway. Standing was pushing it; her legs felt like overcooked spaghetti.

Grant opened the door to the Terrell Hills Police Department so hard that the door flew back and banged the wall with a clang that drew a stare from Paula, the receptionist/dispatcher. Stalking past, Grant stamped up the stairs to the office he shared with Chile. As he opened the door, Chile looked up and waved. Glowering in answer, Grant made his way to his desk. He had to shake off the surrealism of this day, and if violence against inanimate objects was what it took, well, he'd trash his whole office.

Here he was a hard-bitten thirty-five-year-old cop who was running away from a woman half his size. What was wrong with him?

Dropping into his chair, he opened a drawer and extracted his coffee cup. Caffeine would help.

Walking over to the turned-off coffee pot, he splashed the thick black brew into his cup and lifted it to his lips, not caring what it tasted like, just hoping it would restore his sanity. But the immediate shock of the cold, bitter taste did just the opposite. It made him compare it to the last thing in his mouth – the hot, sweet taste of Britt Reeve.

'Damn.' He spat the coffee back in the cup.

'Eh, *loco*, what'd you expect it to taste like? The stuff's been sitting there fermenting for hours. And it's not that tasty to begin with,' Chile said from behind him.

'Leave me alone,' Grant grumbled as he made his way back to his desk.

'Much as I'd like to, in the current mood you're in, we *are* working a case together.'

Grant had half-forgotten the case, but he wasn't going to admit it. He shoved his cold coffee off to the side and reached for the phone. 'Right.'

'Guess those interviews at the school didn't go so well, eh?'

'They went okay. Found out a lot about the girl – a lot of information we probably won't need after I talk to the ME, anyway. Waste of time,' Grant mumbled.

'That's what got you in such a state? Wasting time on the biggest case Terrell Hills has seen for years? Guess it's not that big a deal for a bigshot San Antonio vet like yourself, though,' Chile needled.

'Shut up, Chile.'

Grant had reached for the phone to dial the Medical Examiner's office when the police chief burst into the office. 'You – ' he jabbed a finger in Grant's direction ' – hang up the phone and follow me.'

Grant and Chile shared a look before they got up to follow the chief downstairs.

'What's the rush?' Grant asked peevishly.

'We got trouble,' the chief answered, pointing at the door.

Just then trouble flew in from the main entrance. Britt Reeve. Grant tried to stifle a groan. Why was he not surprised?

The chief's pointed finger became a proffered hand, and the grizzly bear look on his face was replaced with grandfatherly sympathy. 'Miss Reeve, I'm sorry for your loss.'

'Thank you, Chief Rangel.' Britt extended her hand to shake his, then remembered her lost button and put her left hand on her gaping blouse. Grant raised an eyebrow and her eyes met his before her face flushed and she turned back to the chief.

'I'm here to find out what's being done on my sister's case.'

Rangel smiled indulgently, but Grant could see his eyes calculating the best possible route to take. As Chief of Police in a wealthy community, Rangel was in a difficult position. He'd been appointed by a city council sensitive to its four thousand residents. Being a good cop and a good administrator didn't always guarantee job security. From what Grant had seen so far he rode the fence as best he could. Still, there was no love lost between Grant and Rangel – the chief having been forced into hiring outside his department for a detective lieutenant when Chile had failed his probationary period as such and had to slip back to his detective sergeant status. Grant thought it ironic that Rangel resented that more than Chile did.

Now, Rangel's eyes remained on Britt as he inclined his head to Grant. 'You know Detective Lieutenant Collins, who's handling the investigation?'

Britt crossed her arms across her chest. 'I certainly do.'

Grant raised both his eyebrows.

Britt blushed brighter. 'I mean, of course we've met.'

'And Collins hasn't been keeping you abreast?'

Grant cleared his throat and Britt coughed simultaneously. A grinning Chile moved around the side of Paula's empty desk for a better ringside seat in the tiny reception area. After a second or two of uncomfortable silence, Chile pitched in. 'Ah, Chief, I think Collins, here, has been on the move trying to get a handle on this thing.'

'Right.' Rangel nodded, apparently unaware of the undercurrents passing right under his nose. 'Let's go into my office and see if we can bring Miss Reeve up to date – '

Grant shook his head. 'I was just going to get back to the Medical Examiner's Office on the prelim results of – '

'Do that,' Rangel ordered as he ushered Britt toward his office. 'I'll familiarize her with procedure until you can get in there. Soon, I hope.'

With a glare at his boss's back, Grant picked up Paula's phone and began dialing.

'Aye-yi-yi, *mi amigo*,' Chile whispered with a chuckle. 'You in deep *salsa*. And it's definitely the hot, not the mild.'

Shaking his head, Grant listened to the ringing through the phone lines, unable, for once, to tell Chile where to put his colorful verbal expressions.

'Medical Examiner's Office.'

'Lieutenant Collins, over at Terrell Hills, returning Menendez's call.'

'Just a moment, Lieutenant.'

Grant saw Rangel peer through the crack in his door at least three times while he sat on hold. Menendez *was* an idiot. Just because Grant hadn't been there to take his call that morning, he was going to make him suffer now.

'Collins.' Menendez finally came on the line. 'I got some interesting stuff here with this Reeve girl.'

Grant felt his heartbeat pick up, but he kept his voice neutral. 'What is interesting to you might not be so interesting to me. I just want to know how she died. Can we write the whole thing off as an accident?'

'Well, Collins, it is as I suspected from my initial observation of the scene and the body. Risa Reeve did not hit her head on the doorjamb. Her head was hit on the doorjamb.'

'What the hell are you talking about? I'm really not in the mood for subtle language games. Just tell me how she died.'

'I think you ought to talk to Dr Lee. Just a moment.'

It was more like thirty 'moments' before Dr Lee picked up the phone. 'Detective. How are you?'

'Doc, just tell me how the girl died.' Grant stared at the crack in the ceiling.

'I don't know,' Dr Lee said shortly. 'But I suspect.'

Grant held a breath and counted to five for patience. 'What do you mean, you don't know?'

'We need toxicology tests back before I can confirm my final suspicions.'

'Dammit, Lee, stop talking in riddles. She didn't hit her

head; her head hit. You don't know how she died, but you suspect. Get to the point!'

Grant looked up to see the City Hall secretary and one city councilwoman staring at him through the doorway that led to the adjoining City Hall and fire department. Chile put out his hand. 'Down, boy, down,' he mouthed as he picked up the receiver on the other phone and punched in the lit-up line to hear the conversation.

'Are you asking for my opinion?' The doctor's sarcasm weaved through his high tenor speech, making him sound like a dissatisfied schoolmarm.

'Yes, Lee,' Grant spoke deliberately. 'Give me your esteemed opinion as to what happened to the girl, backed up with the facts from the autopsy, of course.'

'Of course,' Dr Lee said smoothly, reveling in his victory. He cleared his throat officiously. 'The girl was in good health. Excellent, I will venture to say –'

'Your *guess*,' Grant emphasized.

'Yes, well, now on to the good stuff. I believe from her pupil retraction to the pinpoint state that she died of narcotic poisoning.'

'Drug overdose?'

'Not in the way you are thinking, Detective. She did not commit suicide or accidentally overdose on drugs.'

Grant wanted to reach through to phone, grab Lee by his scrawny neck and shake the story out of him. He reined in his impatience. 'Why not?'

'Because she was already dead when she hit her head.'

Grant sat up straighter. 'She was already dead?' Grant could almost feel the doctor's smugness through the phone lines. 'How does an already dead person hit her own head against a doorjamb?'

'Stupid question, Collins. I thought you much brighter than that.'

'Okay, Doctor.' Grant paused to will himself some fresh patience. 'So I'm stupid. Humor me and answer my stupid question.'

'If you insist. A dead person can't hit her own head on the doorjamb.'

'Lee, just tell me how you know she was already dead and how you know she didn't hit her head on the doorjamb all by herself. You can even include your theories and let me weed out the fact from the fiction. Okay?'

Grant felt the weight of the pause through the phone lines. Another bridge burning. He could smell it. So much for second chances . . .

Finally Dr Lee spoke, rattling off in a clipped tone, as if he was reading his statement, 'Risa Reeve, female, age sixteen, died at approximately fifteen hundred hours from an as yet unknown cause. Pending the results of toxicology tests, including – '

'Lee, can you just tell me? I can read the damned report by myself. I want your human input. I *need* it. All right?'

He must have said the magic words, because immediately Lee began talking animatedly. 'What I think happened is she died of poison, ingested – for there is no evidence of an injection or inhalation. The exact source of her demise aside, as soon as the killer knew she was deceased he picked her up and swung her body, knocking her head against the doorjamb to make it look like an accident – '

'Hold on, let me play devil's advocate for a minute,' Grant interrupted. 'Could she have died of natural causes or accidentally –?'

'It wasn't natural causes. I can tell you that without a doubt,' Dr Lee interjected.

'Okay, say she took one too many aspirin. Someone comes in and finds her passed out – or he thinks she's passed out but she's really dead – and he picks her up to get her to the hospital and she falls off his shoulder and hits the doorway unintentionally. I know I'm stretching it, but is it plausible?'

'No, I'm afraid not, Detective. The force with which her head hit the wood was such that she'd have had to build up momentum beforehand.'

'And you could testify that the wound wasn't self-inflicted?'

'Not unless she was hanging from the ceiling or jumped headfirst from the ceiling. I'm being facetious, of course. The angle was such that her skull hit the doorway upside down and face-down. The only way that could happen would be for someone to have whipped her against the wall – not unlike the way a baseball bat – '

Chile rolled his eyes and shook his head while Grant resisted the curse that rose in his throat. 'Did the person drop her or place her on the floor in the position we found her?'

'Oh, he placed her immediately after the impact, I would theorize. She certainly didn't lie anywhere else for long after death. The pooling of blood was consistent with the position she was found in. Looking now at one of the photographs, everything about the angle of her limbs indicates a running fall against the doorjamb. Only the forensic evidence doesn't support it in the least. Really a first-rate job, the body placement. Almost as if whoever orchestrated it had studied up, or knew certain aspects of physics, of momentum and of gravity to begin with. I would venture to guess that a less experienced physician would not have caught the discrepancy.'

'Right,' Chile mumbled into the phone.

'What's that, Collins?' Dr Lee asked sharply.

Grant glared at Chile, who widened soulful eyes to look apologetic.

'I said, that's absolutely right. Good work,' Grant responded neutrally. 'Now, which toxicology tests did you order up? Any indication of what we're dealing with?'

'I set up tests for anything consistent with the fatal damage I found on the body, including pulmonary edema and – '

'How soon until they'll be back?' Grant ran his hand across his jaw impatiently.

'Soon.'

Grant bit his tongue on the question of how long 'soon' was because he knew Lee would add a day or two just to be contrary. 'Okay, Lee,' Grant said. 'Anything else?'

'Not at this time.'

'Okay. Give Ortega a call when your report is ready so he can come pick it up.'

Chile's broad face scrunched up in a grimace as he hung up his extension.

He met Grant's eyes as he replaced his receiver in its cradle. Grant ran his right palm over the stubble on his jaw. Someone had murdered Risa. The teenager who'd been rich and beautiful and famous. But, more importantly for what was now a homicide, a girl with no apparent enemies.

And a girl with a headstrong sister who'd been right all along.

'Collins, get in here, pronto,' Rangel shouted from his doorway, before slamming it shut again.

'Hey, that's my line, *jefe*,' Chile called back softly to the closed door.

Shaking his head, Grant stood up slowly to make way for Paula, who'd returned and was shooing him out of her seat. How was he going to tell Britt? And how would she react? Grant surprised himself by caring how the news would affect her. He told himself to be watching for clues in her reaction, but all he could think about was being ready when she fainted again. Or threw something. With Britt he'd put even money on either one. One thing was for sure: whatever she did it wouldn't be passive or accepting.

'There's no getting out of this one easy, Tom-o.' Chile finally broke the silence between them. 'Better go take your lumps so we can get on with it.'

'Yeah.' Grant nodded absently as he strode to his boss's door and Chile headed back upstairs.

'Nice of you to hurry over, Lieutenant,' Rangel said as Grant shut the door behind him and, crossing his arms across his chest, leaned up against the glass wall from where he could see both Britt and his boss without moving his head. He hated conversations that ended up like tennis matches, which was how this one would have been if he'd sat across Rangel's desk, next to Britt.

'The ME finished his examination and it's his opinion that Risa's death was not the result of hitting the doorjamb.' Grant took a breath and decided to plunge on, afraid any break in the action would allow Britt to fall apart. 'Someone apparently – '

'Pushed her?' Britt broke in.

'No. According to the doctor, she was poisoned.'

'Poisoned?' Britt and Rangel asked in unison.

'That's what Dr Lee says,' Grant answered with a faint shrug.

'With what?' Britt asked.

'That we don't know – '

'You're not trying to molly coddle me and really mean she was poisoned by an overdose, are you?' Britt narrowed her eyes.

'I wouldn't think of molly coddling you, Miss Reeve,' Grant answered. 'I think I know better than that.'

Rangel sat up in his chair. 'Watch it, Collins. Don't be flip with her.'

Grant glanced at Rangel without comment. The chief hadn't kept secret the fact that he hadn't wanted to hire him after what had happened at the San Antonio Police Department, and had flatly taken issue with Grant's lack of respect for authority other than his own. But at the same time Rangel hadn't been able to resist the credentials and investigative ability Grant offered.

'It's all right, Chief Rangel.' Britt's husky voice broke into Grant's thoughts. 'I appreciate his insight.'

Rangel looked disappointed that Britt hadn't given him an excuse to chew Grant out, but he accepted her statement with a nod. 'So, now that Miss Reeve, here, has brought up the possibility of drugs, did Lee mention that?'

'Yes,' Grant said. 'He suspects narcotic poisoning, but not from an overdose.'

Grant could feel the air around Britt relax with relief, although she showed little outward sign.

'Well, that's good to hear. She has . . . uh, had . . . a reputation for being such a fine girl. I hope we will be able to preserve that with our investigation. We'll do our best, won't we, Collins?'

Rangel's implication rankled with Grant and he couldn't help elaborating on his nod. 'As long as the facts back that up.'

This time Britt joined Rangel in glaring at him.

'Now, Collins, I want you to keep Miss Reeve up to date on the investigation as it proceeds. We've decided she would work best as the family liaison – all information goes to her first, to be dispensed through the rest of the Reeve family. Just between us – ' he inclined his head to Britt and shot Grant a loaded look ' – Neil Reeve is a loose cannon who could get us in hot water with the press. Already has, as a matter of fact. Let's let Miss Reeve, here, handle him. Outward co-operation while icing him out of as much information as we possibly can.'

Rangel stood to indicate the meeting was over, but Britt ignored him and pinned Grant with a look. 'The hit on Risa's head came when she lost consciousness and fell?'

'No.' Grant paused. He'd thought he could get by without giving her the details, that the poisoning might be shocking enough to keep her occupied.

'Well, don't make us guess, Collins,' Rangel said irritably.

'She was swung against the wall by someone else, after she was already dead.'

Britt looked stunned. 'The murderer was that cold, that calculating – to kill her and then manipulate her body to try and throw us off by making us think it was an accident?' she murmured, half to herself.

Grant hesitated. But Rangel jumped in. 'Miss Reeve, as of this moment your sister's death is classified a homicide. I have the utmost faith in Detective Collins's and Detective Ortega's ability to solve this case and I will reassign additional officers to aid them as needed.'

Rangel opened the door to usher Britt out of his office, but she sat unmoving in her chair.

'We *are* going to get her killer,' she warned, with a steely resolve that was in direct contrast to the lost murmuring of just a moment before.

Both men stopped and stared at her. Rangel spoke up. 'I think you need to leave this to us, Miss Reeve. You handle the arrangements for your sister, provide any information we might need – '

'Of course, that's what I meant,' Britt interrupted

quietly, still staring off at some unseen point. 'I will do whatever I can to *help* you get her killer.'

Grant didn't believe her for a minute.

Right before his eyes Britt had transformed from a grieving sister with unchanneled emotions to a woman with a singular purpose. Her wild grief for her sister had been shelved and in its place stood intense focus. A focus for justice. It was something hinted at before, but then she'd had no facts to stand on. Now she did. And Grant realized whoever had killed her sister would have hell to pay. And so, he suddenly realized, would he.

CHAPTER 8

The glaring afternoon sun hit her full force as Britt pulled open the front door of the police station. Holding her arm up as a shield, she tried to get her bearings. But before she could do so several microphones were shoved in her face and questions from reporters assailed her from all sides. Then, just as she felt the door open again behind her, with a whoosh of air-conditioned air, a white limousine turned into the parking lot and a shout went up from the media horde.

'It's them!'

Like a school of rapacious fish, the group of reporters shifted to surround the limo as it came to a stop along the curb.

'What the hell . . .?' Grant's voice rumbled behind her.

Britt, too, wondered who was inside the limo, but with inside knowledge of the way her family operated she at least could venture a guess. It was either her mother or Tori.

The muscle-bound driver, wearing a white and gold uniform that made him look like an overdeveloped, gilded ice-cream man, hurried around the side of the vehicle. As he opened the door with a dramatic flourish Britt could hear the click of a dozen TV cameras as they began to whir. One petite hose-clad foot wearing a black stiletto heel appeared and found the asphalt. It was Sophia. Of course, Britt admonished herself. This performance had all the earmarks of Carl Lawrence's publicity team. He was playing the hero, coming in to save the day.

The limo driver helped Sophia out of the car and she paused to give the TV cameras and print-writers the chance to absorb the full effect of *her*. A veil over her black hat covered her face. Her black dress – which dipped to hint at her cleavage, nipped in at her tiny waist with a single burnished gold button and ended at mid-thigh with a flared skirt – rode a fine line between mourning and high fashion. It looked like a thousand dollars even from thirty feet away, where Britt stood. She could almost smell the imported Italian leather of her mother's shoes and handbag. Britt tried not to wrinkle her nose in distaste, although even if she had no one would have noticed. All eyes were where they were supposed to be. On Sophia.

All, that was, except two.

A strong hand gripped her elbow.

'Hang on.'

Startled, Britt swung around to her right. Grant had come up to stand beside her. She tried to shake off his hand, despite her initial urge to lean into it and absorb some of his strength.

'What are you doing?'

Removing his hand, he held it up to hold off any more verbal blows. Grant shook his head. 'Sorry. You were swaying a bit and it was just an automatic reaction.'

'Oh,' she answered uneloquently. Why was she so disappointed? She didn't want him to touch her and what he'd said confirmed that he didn't want to touch her either. Of course he would assume she was going to faint; she'd been doing too much of that lately. 'I'm fine. You don't need to worry about me.'

'I'm not.'

Their eyes met and held for a half a beat until, uncomfortable with what she saw there, Britt tore hers away to look back at her mother. The reporters, recovered from their awe at Sophia's entrance, began to shoot off questions. Sophia chose that moment to lift the veil from her face and reveal her bluebonnet eyes brimming with tears.

'Y'all will have to understand that this is a difficult time for me,' she began, in an artificially weak voice and an exaggerated drawl. 'I have lost my daughter, my baby.' Here she paused to bring a lace handkerchief, proffered by the driver, to each damp eye. 'My dear husband has taken valuable time off from his campaign to be here with me, to be my rock of support during this terrible time. I hope all of you will have the decency to let him be here for me and hold off on the campaign questions until we lay my baby to rest.'

'Give me a break,' Britt muttered, glad that none of the reporters could hear her. The sordid details of their family life or lack thereof was not something she wanted to bring up now. Or ever.

'Not the dear, loving mother you remember?' Grant whispered knowingly into her ear.

Britt steeled herself against her body's reaction to his breath against her hair. 'Hardly,' she answered tightly.

Carl Lawrence joined his wife on the curb, wearing a properly somber expression and a black-mourning version of his campaign 'uniform', as Britt had come to call it as she followed his run for the Senate. Most politicians for the nation's most prestigious governing body couldn't – and wouldn't try to – pull off his attire.

It was invariably a western-cut suit – or tuxedo, as occasion demanded – fancy bolo tie with a silver clasp, wide cowboy belt with a blinding silver buckle, lizardskin boots and a Stetson hat. Britt wondered if Carl would dress this way once he made it to Capitol Hill. But he probably hadn't thought that far ahead. This 'uniform' worked with the 'Uncle Carl' image he was projecting for voters, and that was what was important now.

Britt felt a sudden pang of guilt for her harsh appraisal of her stepfather. After all, she'd never met the man. Her judgments were all based on knowledge of her mother and the kind of man she'd dump a billionaire for. And through seeing Carl Lawrence operate throughout his campaign, watching him now – in person for the first time – as he worked the media, the pang of guilt faded. He did seem genuinely friendly, and Britt was certain he would be just as jovial behind closed doors, but at the same time he was slick. It was a unique combination that confused Britt. She didn't feel comfortable with people she couldn't intuitively figure out right off the bat, and she vowed to keep a close eye on Carl Lawrence.

'Do you want to duck back into the station and out the back door?' Grant asked in her ear.

The offer was extremely tempting. But Britt knew she had to face them before the funeral, and doing it in front of cameras and tape recorders, where her mother would have to be on her best behavior, was probably a good idea. No telling which Sophia she would see – the long-lost loving mother, the wronged mother, the distant mother, the vengeful mother . . .

'Might as well get it over with now,' Britt said.

No sooner had the words left her mouth than Sophia spotted her. She put one hand on Carl's forearm and tipped her head in Britt's direction. Britt read the unspoken signal Carl passed to Sophia as his permission to let his wife go to her daughter, and Britt filed that away in her memory bank. Was Sophia really letting Carl control her, or was she just letting him think he was?

Instantly, the brimming tears spilled over onto Sophia's undoubtedly waterproof make-up and ran down her cheek.

'Brittany!' she called, in a voice befitting a Greek tragedy. A sudden, strong fury rose from the pit of Britt's stomach. Sophia was turning Risa's death into another act in the play that was her shallow life. Risa deserved more than that, and Britt would make sure she got it. But she knew she had to be careful. What might be a wholly justified and well deserved reaction to her mother could be interpreted very differently in the out-of-context way it would be played on the evening news or in tomorrow's papers.

Careful, Britt warned herself as her mother moved toward her.

The driver jumped after Sophia, holding a new handkerchief, but Carl held him back as Sophia tip-tapped her way to Britt, with her arms open. The camera operators and reporters cleared a path for her, and before she could properly brace herself Sophia was grasping her eldest daughter in a stiff hug.

That answered one of Britt's questions. She was playing long-lost, loving mother, certainly on the advice of Carl's image guru.

Britt pulled gently but decisively away from the hug. 'Sophia.'

Sophia pushed her collagen-enhanced, magenta-tinted lower lip out peevishly. 'Brittany, is that any way to treat your mother? Especially at a time like this.'

Watch it, Mother dearest, you're on the verge of becoming wronged mother.

One sharp look from Carl, who had taken on a sensitively indulgent look for the cameras' benefit, put Sophia back on track.

'This is a difficult time for all of us. Most difficult for you, dear.' Sophia's eyes met Britt's, and for a brief instant Britt thought her mother might understand. 'You always did have trouble controlling your emotions.'

The white-hot fury of earlier flared, and Britt fought the urge to tell her mother off. She couldn't let herself be manipulated. And acting as her mother expected would do just that.

Instead she checked to make sure Carl's bodyguard was keeping the reporters out of earshot and then turned on the saccharin smile she'd seen on her mother's face all through growing up. 'And you always did have trouble controlling your greed – whether it was for money or publicity or power. Which brought you here now?'

Sophia's stricken look was good, Britt had to admit. Her mother reached up to stroke Britt's dark curls tenderly. Now *that* would really play well for the cameras. 'You don't understand me at all.'

'And there's more to that story. I don't want to understand you. It might erode my basic trust in human nature,' Britt returned, unable to keep her smile from slipping.

Sophia cast about for a diversion and found it three feet away. 'And who is this handsome man? This can't be your boyfriend, Britt.' Sophia cocked her head to the side to run her eyes up and down Grant's lanky frame.

Grant had stood by unmoving during the women's exchange, wanting to come to Britt's defense even though she didn't need it. But now he shifted uncomfortably under Sophia's scrutiny. Glancing at Britt, he saw her face flushing a deep peach. With anger, or something else?

'No, Sophia, this is the police detective in charge of investigating Risa's murder.' Britt stepped back to give her mother a full view of Grant.

'Murder. *Murder?*' Sophia repeated breathlessly, her hand going to her throat. 'But – but I thought it was an accident . . .'

'No.' Britt caught her mother's eye and held it. 'Someone killed Risa in cold blood. Don't look so stricken. A model's murder will certainly garner a lot more publicity than a mere accident. And what's the saying? "Any publicity's good publicity." I'm sure your husband subscribes to that philosophy. And not all is lost. Just one daughter. One you never knew. And never wanted to know, for that matter.'

'That's not true,' Sophia blurted out, some of her cool façade slipping. 'I tried to see her. I called – '

'Sure – only after Risa was on every magazine in America. Fame and fortune got the attention of your black heart.'

Sophia's eyes narrowed, and for the first time Grant thought she might say something that wasn't scripted. The best thing for his case would've been to hear what she'd say, but instead Grant found himself stepping in between the two women, which was the best thing for Britt. This was not a good sign for the rest of this case – that he was letting his personal feelings get in the way of the investigation.

Grant introduced himself and reached out to shake Sophia Lawrence's hand.

Britt slipped behind them and opened the door to the station.

'Where are you going?' Grant asked gingerly.

'I'll leave you two,' Britt threw over her shoulder. Grant couldn't see her face, but he could tell from the stiff set of her slender shoulders that the lightness in her voice was forced. 'I'm sure you have plenty to discuss, and I sure as hell have better things to do.'

'Wait, Brittany,' Sophia ordered. 'We need to talk to you about the arrangements for the funeral service and – '

One hand on the doorknob, Britt turned to look at her mother. 'I'm sure when you turn on the TV to see your performance here today – if you can listen to anything other than news about yourself – you'll hear when the funeral is.'

'You can call me at the hotel – '

'No,' Britt interrupted with a shake of her head. 'You are the guest here. You can call, or come by Grams's house. That's where I'm staying.'

'Oh, we can't do that.'

'Why? Because Grams can always see right through your act?' Britt laughed mirthlessly. 'Can't say that I blame you.'

With that, she disappeared into the building.

Sophia brushed an invisible piece of lint from her lapel. She sniffed, and then looked up to Grant with a smile full of promise and allure. Immediately he was struck by her resemblance to Risa. He hadn't seen it before, with her blonde, blue-eyed fairness and her petite body which were in direct contrast to Risa's tawny, olive-skinned beauty in that tall, athletic package. It was more an aura the two shared, an ability to charge the air around them with a sensual electricity. It was something Risa could do from the page of a magazine. Her mother turned it on now for his benefit.

How could Britt be so different? Grant asked himself. But was she? She charged the air around her too, but not with sensual electricity; hers was an emotional one. You never had to guess what Britt was feeling, because, no matter how hard she might try to cover it up, her emotions were such a powerful force they managed to affect the emotions of those around her. Grant had never seen anything like it before, and he wondered why his sudden understanding came as he stood before her mother. Possibly it was the contrast. Sophia looked as if she didn't have any emotions, other than selfishness and those she manufactured for her own self-interest.

Right now she was manufacturing a combination of come-hither and self-pity. Designed to throw him off-balance?

'Detective Collins, you can't know what a terrible time this is for me. To lose Risa and then, before I'm even able to get used to that knowledge, here I find out – unceremoniously – that she not only died before her time, she was murdered.' Sophia heaved a dramatic sigh.

'You wanted a ceremony? A drum roll, maybe?' Grant knew he shouldn't have said it but he couldn't resist.

Sophia's eyebrows flew up in offense. 'Certainly not. What I meant was Brittany could have been more sensitive to my feelings. Didn't she expect it to be a terrible shock?'

Grant was in no mood to commiserate with this conniving bitch. She wanted sympathy for herself, not for her dead daughter, which was something he was not going to give her, so he moved on to business where he felt much more sure-footed.

'I need to ask you and your husband a few questions, Mrs Lawrence. I'm grateful you came to me instead of letting me look you up. It's certainly saved me valuable time I can use to work on your daughter's case.'

Sophia's face froze for an instant before it fell into a

polite mask. 'Well, I don't know if we can spare the time now. After all, we do have to check into the hotel and prepare for the funeral service. It will take me a while to regain my strength after our flight and this shock. And please call me Sophia. What we are sharing now seems too personal for anything but first names, don't you agree?'

'Mrs Lawrence,' Grant said pointedly, 'if you aren't going to co-operate with me now I'll be forced to inform my boss, who's holding a press conference this afternoon, and he may be asked a question about what you and your husband have done to aid the investigation. He would have to answer that you were unable to co-operate during your trip to the police station this afternoon. Your visit, after all, is no secret.' Grant motioned toward the crowd still held at bay.

Sophia's smile chilled. 'Your boss will do no such thing, Detective. He wouldn't want to alienate a future US Senator.'

Grant clenched his jaw. She was right, of course. Rangel would be out here kissing Carl Lawrence's butt if he knew he was standing just feet from his office. Dammit, he'd forgotten he was dealing with people not only shrewd but politically powerful. That was sure to gum up his case, but good. Suddenly he felt a rush of frustration. This kind of mess – the worst kind, that came from mixing crimefighting and politics – was part of what had pushed him out of San Antonio's police department. And here he was caught in the middle of the same muck. Only this time he wouldn't be personally involved.

Britt's dimpled face formed in his mind's eye. Or would he?

Grant tensed, hoping his vulnerability wasn't showing. 'I'm sure that you can and will throw your political weight around if you want to. I hope you won't find that to be necessary. My job is to find Risa's killer. If you can respect that, I'll be able respect the fact that you're Risa's mother.' Even though you haven't been a mother to her since she was six months old, he added in his head, and wondered why he cared enough to think it.

Because Britt Reeve was under his skin, that was why. And he was going to have to get her out if he wanted to solve this case and get back to the low-profile police work that had brought him to Terrell Hills.

Sophia's hard eyes appraised him, and Grant resisted the urge to pull his sunglasses down over his own eyes. He didn't want her to see what he was thinking and feeling.

'I can see that you have a lot to deal with here, Detective.' Sophia's index fingernail traced the V where her lapels met. 'I think we understand one another, and as long as we continue to do that I don't see any reason to go to your superior. My husband and I must leave now, but I will be contacting you soon to have that little chat you're so eager to have.'

Sophia pulled her black veil back down over her face and gripped his hands wordlessly in a move blatantly designed for the cameras. Her touch was as cold and as stiff as she was, though that wouldn't show thirty feet away. As he heard the clicks of shutters and motors Grant could almost see the caption under the photo, the tease for the next segment of the news: *Tearful mother wishes police detective Godspeed in his hunt for her daughter's killer*.

Fighting the urge to gag, Grant watched Sophia tip-tap back to her husband's open arms. Grant slid his sunglasses down over his eyes and turned away from the rest of the performance. He knew he'd lost this battle, but the war was still on. He had a chance to win if he could just figure out who were the good guys and who were the bad.

★ ★ ★

Skin watched the cop walk around the side of the building to his car. Before he opened the door to the black sedan he scanned the parking lot. He looked as if he was looking for something. Skin slid down in his seat and pulled the visor down. He'd already driven by Neil Reeve's deserted townhouse. The grandmother's house had looked like a better bet at first, but it turned out no one was home. He'd peeked in the window to make sure. Then he'd asked an old bag walking a dog that looked like a long-haired white rat directions to the police station. He had to find Tori, and if she wasn't at her grandmother's or her father's this was the next best place to find the action.

He'd found it all right, but it wasn't any action he needed right now. A cop shop was the last place on earth he needed to be hanging around. Especially with that tall, tan cop who walked around as if he was a god. Skin just bet chicks loved him. The strong, silent type who was such a man he made other men question their own manhood. Skin didn't run across many of them in the modeling business, and it made him squirm in his seat now. Skin had been entertaining the possibility of casually asking the cops for information on Risa's case – kind of like an interested resident, or a student doing some kind of project. Skin knew he was a lot of bad things, but dummy was not one of them. One look at that cop, and it was on to Plan B.

Skin picked up a road map and held it over his face as the cop drove past him.

'Wonder where the hell he's going?' Skin asked the air.

Skin replaced the map in his glove compartment that hung permanently open. He grabbed the soda off the ratty upholstery of the passenger seat. Its tab caught on a torn piece of fabric and ripped it wider, exposing the foam rubber underneath.

'The whole damned world's got it in for me,' Skin spat out, flinging the uncooperative aluminum can against the opposite door. 'Can't even get a sip of soda without some kinda sacrifice.'

Skin looked out the window at the reporters gathered around the Lawrences, at the shining white limo, their backdrop. He felt bitter bile rise in his throat. 'Bet ole Cowboy Carl never had to get his hands dirty on nothing.' Skin paused, trying to remember the stories about Sophia that he'd heard from Risa and Tori over the years. 'And her, she just goes where the money's best. But what's up now, huh? Got a little taste for power, now, do we? Guess even spending money gets tiring, huh? She probably just woke up one morning and decided to get some political power to spice up her life. Can't do it herself, though. Nah, no fun. Gotta grab some man and hang on for the ride.'

Skin felt the acrid taste of injustice settle on his tongue. *He* ought to be the one the reporters were all over. How does it feel to have your book on the bestseller list? How does it feel to have your collection of photographs critically acclaimed by the same photographers who dismissed you for decades? How does it feel to finally be a multi-millionaire after photographing rich bitches all your life for next to nothing? Well, maybe they wouldn't exactly ask the questions that way, but they should.

Then Skin called himself back from his brief fantasy. He was closer to making it reality than he had been twenty-four hours ago. Risa had stolen the negatives from his office two weeks ago, now. The photos that had made her. And Skin had taken them. He'd made her, and all she could do was stick her nose in the air and tell him no.

'No, I didn't steal any negatives. I don't want you to

publish them, Skin, that's true, but I wouldn't steal them,' she'd said. 'We're friends.'

Hah, Skin thought – then and now. A friend would've told the truth, would've returned the negatives and then would've been endorsing his book, letting him make as much money out of her as she was making herself.

Instead, where was she? Dead. Doing him no damn good. He had to find those negatives.

But now, looking at Carl and Sophia, he had another idea. Those pictures Risa had hired him to take of them . . . Wouldn't they be worth something to the esteemed candidate? Maybe Risa had stashed his negatives and those in the same place.

Hot damn. He was about to be richer and more famous than he imagined

His best hope was Tori. She could look on the inside at the grandma's and Neil's houses. Do a more thorough search of Britt's house. She might hear about the negatives. And she'd do it too, for a little dope. Skin frowned. That might be the reason she'd fail, too. A grin split his face again as he remembered his ace in the hole. He reached in his pocket and pulled out the note he'd found the day he'd gone to see Risa. It had fallen under the kitchen table. He read Risa's longhand:

> *My will and testament. All my possessions go to Britt Reeve, my sister. Above all honor this. Britt, you have things important to me and only you will know the right thing to do with them. All my money I know by law has to go to Dad. I'd rather he have it than Sophia. She doesn't deserve a dime. Dad, share with Britt and Tori, please. Britt especially. All my love, Risa.*

Skin tried to remember Britt. He'd only met her once, the dark little spitfire who'd made no bones about how much she hated the modeling profession and photographers especially. If Tori wasn't successful in digging up the negatives then he'd have to go to Britt and do a trade. The will for the negatives.

Then again, maybe he could get some money out of Carl before the negatives turned up. Maybe Carl and Sophia needed a little shock to get them in the right mood.

Skin continued to watch the sideshow, and then an idea hit him. He could pretend to be a reporter. His ponytail and grunge look would fit right in with the photographers and print journalists. He slung his camera over his neck as a prop and walked toward the scene.

'When do you plan to resume your campaign?' a middle-aged reporter who looked as if he was from one of the networks asked.

Carl cleared his throat and answered officiously. 'As soon as we lay my stepdaughter to rest and my wife feels strong enough to go on. And after we see that Risa's affairs are all in order, of course. Thank y'all very much for your interest and support at this time.'

Carl waved at the crowd with a smile that was warm, while sad at the same time. The guy was an image genius; Skin had to give him that. But now, as he watched Carl usher his wife back into the limo, he realized he was about to lose his chance.

'Mr Lawrence,' he shouted from the back of the horde. 'Who is going to be handling Risa's estate?'

Carl froze in place for a moment, and Sophia stared at her husband.

'Who the hell asked such a crass question?'

A tense murmuring went through the media group, and those round him began to inch away, as if they didn't want to be tainted by the bad vibes passing between the candidate and Skin. In unspoken agreement they parted to give Carl an unimpeded view of the stranger in their midst.

'Now, boy,' Carl began, hooking his thumbs into his belt loops, 'everybody has been real decent up to now. You just ruined that.'

Carl let that hang for a moment, obviously hoping the other reporters there would take Skin out then and there, for wrecking the good rapport. The warm smile was gone. He puffed himself up like the lion king protecting his pride – and what a dysfunctional pride it was, Skin thought. He squinted hard at Skin. 'I don't ever remember seeing you around, boy. And I make it a point of knowing the reporters in San Anton.'

'Uh . . .' Skin stammered. He hadn't expected to be called on his masquerade. 'I'm a, uh, freelancer.'

'Well, you just freelance yourself right out of here. And I better not see you anywhere around me or my wife or my wife's family again. You get my meaning?'

I'll show you meaning, you fat-assed old redneck.

'Sorry, sir, just wondering who would have charge of all her things. Such a famous girl would have a lot of things, wouldn't she?'

Skin stared into Carl Lawrence's eyes for just a few seconds before he broke. Skin swallowed and nodded once, dropping his eyes, embarrassed at his own cowardice. He wished he'd waited to see if the realization hinted at in the politician's eyes was real or Skin's overactive fantasy.

Carl yelled some charming platitudes to break the foul mood cast over the crowd and waved as he got into the limo. The reporters and photographers were hurrying back to their vehicles before the limo had even pulled away from the curb, rushing to meet their deadlines. The print reporters, who had a little more leeway, tried to get into the police station but were turned away at the door. They all studiously ignored Skin.

Goddamned vultures thought they were too good for him, huh? Well, he'd show them. A coupla days and he'd have this whole town in the palm of his hand. Then they'd have to eat his droppings.

Britt did think twice about crossing the yellow crime scene tape that stretched across her front door, but it didn't stop her from ducking under it to get into her house. The crime scene might still be sealed, but surely the police, led by the extremely arrogant Detective Collins, would have already gotten all they needed. All that was left were the memories and the mess.

The sooty fingerprint powder seemed to cover every inch – even turning the white-washed walls gray. Britt tried to conjure up the pain she'd felt yesterday but it was buried deep, replaced on the surface by a fury so powerful it kept her muscles taut and humming with need. The need to avenge her sister's death.

Britt walked from room to room, wondering if she was missing some vital clue, anything that would point her straight to the monster who'd done this. But nothing jumped out at her, nothing caught her eye. It just looked like a house, as her house had always looked, clean but not necessarily tidy. A once warm home. Now just a house that would be someone else's soon.

She couldn't ever live here again.

Not in the shadow of her sister's murder.

Britt's loafers thump-swished on the hardwood floor, breaking the complete silence that pushed down on her. She reveled in the company the sound gave her and stepped a little harder. The click of a key in the back door lock froze her in place. She held her breath. She listened. She heard the slight squeak the kitchen door made as it opened past the halfway point. It banged shut.

Looking around desperately, Britt debated between a weapon – the umbrella leaning up against the wall – or a hiding place – the hall bathroom or Risa's room? On tiptoe, she ran into her own bedroom, then to the closet, carefully shutting the door. Britt could clearly feel the footfalls shudder through the pier and beam foundation of the house. The intruder wasn't trying to sneak around, but with the crime scene tape up, he didn't expect anyone to be there.

Britt held herself tense, feeling the rhythm of his steps. Starting, stopping, starting again, pausing, sliding backward. Somehow it seemed familiar, and Britt realized it was what her footsteps must have felt like just moments before. Was this intruder looking for something as well? What? Was the killer back to make sure he hadn't left any clues behind?

Rage welled in the base of her throat at the thought. *How dared he?* The desire for revenge overwhelmed her reason, and Britt eased out of the closet and grabbed the umbrella with the heavy pewter handle which had been a birthday present from her father. She held it by the opposite end, ready to swing as she edged to peek around the corner.

Surprise ran through her like quicksilver, followed by gradual relaxation.

Grant Collins stood there in profile, rubbing his right hand across the dark stubble along his jaw, his other hand stuffed deep into the pocket of his khaki chinos. His starched button-down shirt couldn't hide the tension in his shoulders. His stance radiated frustration as his eyes scanned the room.

Britt's lips parted to call out to him, but she thought better of it. He wouldn't be thrilled to see her there, considering he'd told her not to go home without a police escort.

Retreating back to her bedroom, she weighed her options and decided to stay hidden until he was gone. Just then she sensed more than heard him heading in her direction, and she dived behind the bed.

On her stomach, Britt watched as his loafers – size twelve if she was any judge – roamed the room. She willed him to stay away from her side of the bed. He co-operated and walked toward the doorway. He paused, and then she heard him suck in a deep breath. Britt held hers. He strode with purpose in her direction and Britt grabbed at his ankle before his foot came down on her head.

'Damn,' he shouted as he lost his balance and toppled onto her. Britt tried to roll on her back, out of his way, but she was too slow and his body landed right on top of hers. Luckily she felt his shoulder holster dig into the space just below her armpit, or it could have broken a rib. Heat radiated from his body, sending his scent – not cologne – wafting over her. It was rich and sharp, like newly cut cedar. The hard lines of his lean muscles fit too well against her. That awareness sent her heart pounding even harder than the adrenaline had. Her head began to swim. She needed space – away from Grant Collins – and air that wasn't saturated with his scent.

As she struggled to force a breath into lungs compressed by the two-hundred-plus pounds lying on top of her, Britt met his eyes. They were more alive than she'd ever seen, crackling with blue lights amid the gray. His mouth tightened – to keep from smiling, she thought. It made Britt angry, and she squirmed beneath his weight, using her weakened arms to try to push him away. She could feel her face turning red from the effort. But she sneaked another glance at Grant and he didn't look too cool and composed either. She squirmed harder and was rewarded with a soft groan. Finally she couldn't stand it any longer.

'Get off me; I can't breathe.'

'No.' Grant shook his head. 'I'm going to stay here for a while, as your punishment for trying to break my leg.'

'I wasn't trying to break your leg,' Britt wheezed. 'I was trying to keep you from squashing my head.'

'Believe me, I would have avoided your head had I known it was there,' Grant assured her.

Britt frowned. 'Wait a minute, if you didn't know I was back here, what made you walk this way? There's nothing on this side of the room except carpet and – '

'A man's watch,' Grant added.

Britt met his eyes again and saw they were guarded. He was asking her a wordless question.

'What watch?'

'Don't play dumb, Britt,' Grant said harshly as he rolled off to allow her to sit up. 'Your boyfriend probably left it the last time he spent the night.'

Britt looked up from straightening the shirt that had pulled loose from her pants. Just as it was beginning to cool down, her face flushed hot again. 'I resent that, Detective. My private life is none of your business.'

'That seems to be your favorite phrase,' Grant retorted as he reached into the inside pocket of his houndstooth blazer and pulled out a small plastic bag. 'But, as I told you before, every facet of your life is my business, and you will facilitate my access to those facets if you want your sister's murder solved.'

Britt swallowed hard and looked away, out the window to her beloved backyard – the yard that she and Risa had spent last weekend planting with impatiens and petunias. Sacrificing some of her pride was a small price to pay for the revenge she needed. 'Okay, you're right. I don't have a boyfriend.'

'Oh, sure, Britt. You expect me to believe that?' Grant said bitterly.

'Of course I expect you to believe that; it's the truth.' Britt looked at the hard profile of his face as he stared at the corner of her bed's comforter. 'Why wouldn't you believe it?'

'Because you're too attractive a woman, that's why. You keep men running hot and cold around you all the time. Take friendly Principal Joe, for instance. Don't tell me he's talking about having you to his house to discuss the finer points of public education?'

'We might.' Britt's chin jutted out. 'Joe is my boss and a good friend, that's all.'

'That's not all as far as he's concerned, I can promise you,' Grant said.

'You have a dirty mind, Detective.'

'How do you know? Can you read it?'

'No, and I don't want to either,' Britt retorted, but the words sounded weak even to her own ears. 'And another thing, I may have to open my life to you but I don't have to let you run it, so keep your opinions to yourself.'

'Well, excuse me for calling you attractive. I won't make that mistake again.'

Britt opened her mouth and closed it again. Why did he have to twist around everything she said? He was looking at her with that hint-of-a-smirk look that so infuriated her. His comment demanded an answer.

'See that you don't,' she said righteously.

His eyebrows raised. Then he looked at what had drawn him to that side of the room in the first place, and Britt followed his gaze. A watch sat in the corner of the room, just visible from the other side where he'd stood.

'So if it's not your boyfriend's watch, whose is it?'

Grant got on his hands and knees to get closer to the watch. Britt followed more slowly. She didn't want to be so close to him in this tight corner, but her curiosity over the watch overcame her hesitation. As she crawled up next to him she could see the watch was a man's style, with an extra large face and thick brown leather band. There was nothing unique about it as far as she could see.

'Do you recognize it?'

'No,' Britt admitted with a frown. She felt violated, with a stranger's watch there in her bedroom.

'It wouldn't be your sister's or Jayson Pilchuk's?'

'It's not Risa's; I know that for sure. She refused to wear one on her wrist. She had a watch pendant Jayson gave her. And Jayson? That's sure not his. He's an electronics freak and wears a watch that tells the temperature, wind speed and the time in twelve countries. It's a huge black thing.'

Grant reached over carefully and used the outside of his evidence bag to pick up the watch by the striated dial. He held it up to the light streaming in through the window. No arm hair that he could see; too bad it wasn't a steel expandable band. Those always collected all sorts of helpful forensic evidence. Grant tried to quell his disappointment as he turned the watch around.

'What's that written on the back?' Britt pointed.

Grant twisted the watch for a better view. 'DEF' was carved into the metal.

'Are those initials or a message?'

'Or part of the alphabet,' Grant offered wryly.

Britt wasn't paying attention; she stared harder at the inscription. 'No,' she mused, 'I think it's initials.'

Grant shot her a sharp look. 'Why? Know anyone with those initials?'

'No. I don't. I was just trying to figure it out.'

'It's not your job to figure it out. It's mine.'

Britt sat back on her heels and crossed her arms over her breasts. 'But that could be the killer's watch.'

'That's right. Which is why you stay out of this.' Grant pierced her with a look.

'But your boss told you to co-operate with me, so, like it or not, you can't keep me out of this.' Britt's chin jutted up.

'No, I can't, but I don't have to make it easy for you.'

Golden lights flared in Britt's eyes and Grant couldn't help himself. He cupped her defiant chin in his hand and brought her lips to his. Giving a little moan of protest, she brought her hands to his shoulders, but her push away became an embrace. Their kiss deepened as her fingers wrapped around his neck, inching up into his nape then into his hair. Her touch was like velvet fire, soft while setting him ablaze. Tongues of flame caught and ran along his veins, sending his heart pounding and leaving him hard and aching.

This is wrong, wrong, wrong, he told himself.

But his body wasn't listening. It begged instead to feel her against him again, under him.

Grant moved his hands down her slender neck, over the gentle slope of her shoulders and around her back, where she held all the strength of her petite body in tight, taut bands of muscle. His fingers massaged and he felt her relax. As she did he pulled her to him, until their bodies fit together again. Familiar. It felt familiar. That thought so shocked Grant that he took his lips from hers. But when the empty air touched his mouth and made him miss the feel of her, he dipped his head to her exposed neck. Britt shook her head as she threw it back, as full of contradiction in making love as she was in conversation.

Her tight nipples thrust against the cotton of her blouse, making Grant long to release the buttons and bra and expose her rich, peachy-olive skin. Her hands ran along the waistband of his pants. His slid from the small of her back to her breasts, his thumbs tracing every contour. His lips met hers again, and she answered his kiss with an urgency that matched his.

'Well, I can see why you didn't meet me at the airport.'

Britt and Grant jumped away from each other and peered over the bed at the doorway. Grant's hand had gone to the gun at his side.

The legs were the first things to capture Grant's notice. The longest he'd ever seen. And not much of them was hidden under the smallest micro-miniskirt he'd ever seen. Where legs ended in skirt, so did her hair, straight, long and blonde. She leaned indolently against the doorway.

'Hey, don't shoot me just 'cuz you didn't get some, guy. You can get back at it as soon as my big sis tells me where I can crash.'

Looking between the two women, he saw they were polar opposites. How could two such different-looking women be sisters? Grant rose to his feet and resisted the urge to lean out of the path of Britt's gaze, which was brimming with powerful emotion.

He wished he could decipher exactly what it was.

CHAPTER 9

'Tori,' Britt said through clenched teeth as she rose to her feet. 'You're drunk.'

Hair draped halfway over her face, Tori walked unsteadily on gold four-inch heels studded with multicolored stones to the only chair in the room. She fell into the seat and barked out a single laugh.

'Well, congrats, big sis. All that book learning taught you something. You can rec'nize a drunk sister when you need to. Course, you forgot to read the book on manners. Don'cha know you're supposed to pick up relatives from the airport when they come to visit?'

Britt clamped her teeth down on her tongue to gain control over her temper. Even as out of her mind and as out of practice as she was, Tori was easily picking up where they'd left off ten years before. As a girl, the only time Tori had wasted any time paying attention to Britt had been to antagonize her.

'If you'd called me back last night after you had your plane reservation, like I asked you to, I would've been there to get you.'

Tori waved one hand weakly in Britt's direction. She combed through her sheet of buttercup-colored hair with her three-inch fingernails. Britt noticed that their gold glitter polish was badly chipped, so unlike Tori, who had always taken meticulous care of her number one asset – her appearance.

'Nah, you wouldn't have,' Tori slurred. 'I missed my flight and got put on stand-by all day. They oughta call it bar-by instead, 'cuz all you do is sit in the bar all day until some airline dweeb comes to pour you into the damned plane. At least they paid for my drinks.'

'They did?' Britt asked, amazed.

'Course, big sis. When you're a gorgeous famous model you don't pay for much. Not in dollars anyway.'

The blatant bitterness in Tori's voice made Britt cringe. She felt Grant's gaze on her and ignored it. She didn't want to acknowledge what had happened between them, or his opinion of her stunningly beautiful sister. He was probably asking himself how he could have kissed a little dark, wild-haired midget when he had this Nordic Amazon coming through the door. Britt forced away the image that formed in her mind, of Grant lip-locked with Tori.

Tori threw one leg over the arm of the chair, giving them a clear view of her panties. She bounced her long, slender leg invitingly. Britt battled between the urge to yank Tori up and kick her out of the house and the intuition to give her a hug. She'd always been self-absorbed, but she'd had plenty of self-esteem to go with it. Where had that self-esteem gone in the decade Tori had been away from home? The woman before Britt was a self-absorbed slut, begging for help. Britt wasn't sure she could give it to her. Instead she avoided the issue. For now.

'Tori, I think you're forgetting that you're not here for a social visit. You're here because Risa's dead.'

A shadow passed over Tori's bloodshot eyes ever so

briefly, before she licked her dry lips and threw her head back against the chair to stare at the ceiling. 'It's a bummer. But then again it sure leaves more jobs for the rest of us working girls.'

Britt took the hit as a savage twist to her stomach. She heard Grant's sharp intake of breath. Quickly, she checked him with a sidelong look. He'd gotten over his shock and now studied Tori with narrowed eyes, arms crossed over his chest.

Adding a suspect to his list, no doubt, Britt thought. Inexplicably, Britt rose to Tori's defense.

'You just need to sleep it off,' Britt said.

'Right again, big sis,' Tori agreed sarcastically. She threw her leg back over, Her heel hit the rug with a thump and she frowned slightly in obvious disappointment that her invitation hadn't sent Grant drooling. 'I'll zonk out for a while. Hate to take the bed away from you and your boyfriend, though from the looks of it you two'll do it anywhere, so I don't feel so bad.'

Britt hated to feel the flush racing up her neck and flooding her face. She turned away from Grant, but hadn't realized she was turning right toward her dresser mirror until his eyes met hers in the reflection. She reached down to straighten the comforter for an excuse to look away. 'This isn't my boyfriend. This is Police Detective Lieutenant Grant Collins. He's investigating Risa's murder.'

'Oh, a cop? Was he frisking you for evidence?' Tori put in archly.

'Very funny, Tori,' Britt shot back.

'Miss Reeve, where were you yesterday afternoon?' Grant asked bluntly, to change the subject.

'Wow, don't they teach you stiffs any tact in cop school, or what?' Tori asked as she reached in her tiny gold purse and extracted a cigarette and a lighter. She held the lighter out to Grant. He ignored her unspoken request for a light. Finally, she lit the cigarette herself and took a deep drag.

'I was . . .' Tori paused to blow smoke toward the ceiling '. . . zoned out of my mind. In my apartment with the current man of my dreams, or at least the man of my hallucinations.'

Britt winced.

'He'll vouch for you, then?' Grant asked.

'For me, he'll say anything I want.' Tori slowly licked the base of her cigarette then took it in her mouth, sliding it in and out meaningfully.

Britt couldn't bear watching, but didn't want to give Tori what she wanted – an admonition. So, instead, she looked out the window.

'What's this boyfriend's name?'

'Vic Demond.'

'Oh, Tori!' Britt said, with a combination of disgust and dismay. She had read about Demond. He'd been arrested – but never convicted – a half-dozen times for roughing up his various girlfriends. He had a predilection for models and actresses.

Tori stood up and didn't bother to pull down her gold mini-skirt that had ridden up to where her thighs met. As she stepped into the light filtering in through the window Britt saw the swelling and discoloration under the thick make-up on her sister's cheek. She couldn't help reaching out to brush it with her fingertip.

'What happened?'

Tori's eyes flashed with fear – not at the pain of her injury, but at the discovery of it – then they glazed back over. 'Oh, rough flight. That's all.'

'Where'd you ride? The wing?' Grant said dryly.

Ignoring him, Tori weaved over to the bed and fell into it. 'I'm gonna crash.'

Grant leaned over and grabbed her toothpick-thin arm before Tori's head could hit the pillow. He hauled her off the bed, throwing her arm around the back of his neck and indicating to Britt to support her on the other side.

'You're not going to crash here. This is a sealed crime scene and neither of you should be here. I could arrest both of you.' Grant's eyes met Britt's glare around her sister's lolling head.

'Britt, I'm taking you two to your car. You will drive your sister to a motel or your grandmother's. She can sleep it off there.'

'Not to Grams. She hates me and I hate her,' Tori mumbled. 'Take me to Daddy. Daddy wants to have a press conference. Daddy wants to help me make a comeback. Daddy wants to help me become an actress. Daddy said he'd do anything, . . . anything for me . . .'

Grant caught Britt's eyes again. 'How come Daddy didn't pick her up at the airport?'

'Oh, no,' Tori mumbled again, with her eyes still closed. 'Daddy's too busy making arrangements, giving interviews, talking to . . .'

'Why didn't she go to Daddy's to begin with?' Grant asked a still silent Britt.

'Daddy'll be so mad that I can't do the press conference now. I gotta take a nap first. He's gonna be so mad . . .'

They reached Britt's car, which she'd parked in the next door neighbor's driveway so as to not attract the attention of media vultures and curious citizens. 'Britt, take her to Jewel's house. I know you'd probably rather dump her on your father and let him deal with it, but if you love her don't do it. Don't even tell your father she's here.'

Britt looked up from fitting her key into the lock on the

passenger side. Was this the cop speaking or the man? Was he trying to keep Tori and her father apart for the sake of the case or was he trying to get Tori the love and support she so obviously needed for the sake of her soul?

His gun-metal eyes weren't telling. And, a second later, Grant slid his sunglasses down, thereby ruling out even a guess. Britt wanted to rip them off him and throw them into the middle of the street in frustration. But her sister leaned against her with all her weight, which probably wasn't a hundred and ten pounds soaking wet but felt like two hundred and ten stone-cold drunk.

'Don't let him order you around, sis,' Tori mumbled with a thick tongue as they pushed her into the passenger seat. ''Cuz once they start, it just gets worse and worse and worse . . . They tell you what to wear and where to wear it . . . how to pose and how much money to take for doing it . . .'

Britt shut the door and left Grant without a word, climbing behind the wheel. As she pulled her own door shut she thought she heard Grant answer her sister.

The words didn't register until she'd backed out of the driveway and pulled into the street.

'You don't have anything to worry about, Tori. She doesn't even listen to herself, much less anyone else.'

Grant called Chile from the phone in his car to tell him to meet at the crime scene for another look through. In the first walk-through they'd had accidental death at the front of their minds, and, even though Grant had ordered everyone to treat it as carefully as they would a homicide, he was afraid he and Chile hadn't.

That was standard operating procedure for Chile, but Grant realized in hindsight he'd been just as guilty of letting too much slide. Had he let Britt Reeve get to him, so that, in an effort to be contrary to her insistence on murder, he'd gone too far the other direction? Or had the months away from San Antonio made him lax and sloppy?

Grant slapped his hand against his leg. He'd left the San Antonio Police Department with a cloud over his ethics but no one could ever claim that Grant couldn't do the job. No one doubted he had what it took to get the bad guy more often than any other detective in San Antonio's homicide division.

But that was then. This was Terrell Hills and now. If he was to fail this he might as well quit police work, because without the faith of his colleagues he wasn't going to get anywhere ever again. On the other hand, this case could be a chance to erase the black mark making an impossible choice had forced onto his career.

But did he really want to erase it? Maybe he needed it to help ease the guilt.

Shaking off the introspection, Grant headed to the back door that the neighbor said she had found ajar. If he could retrace the killer's steps maybe he could get a feel for what had happened, how it had happened and be able to extrapolate the 'who'.

Unlocking the door, Grant went through a mental list of clues the killer might have left. He glanced once more at the blood-stained molding. Armed with the knowledge of the Medical Examiner's report, Grant could see the angle of the hit much more clearly, the impact coming from the opposite direction from the way her body was placed. But where had the killer been before that? Where had Risa fallen, victim of a still unknown poison? Grant glanced at the kitchen counter, where the can of diet cola still sat on its side, the brown liquid evaporated to a brown sticky-dry stain on the white worktop. He could see scrapings where the ME's man had collected samples. Had the cola been deadly, and that was why she'd dropped it? Or had she just happened to have been drinking when she'd lost consciousness from another source? The sandwich, too, had been half-eaten, Grant remembered.

He was driving himself crazy with this speculation. Grant told himself to move on to concrete evidence just as Chile came whistling through the door.

'Hey, *amigo*. *Como estas?*' Chile called.

Grant only grunted in answer and went through to the living room and to the telephone. Sitting next to it was a basic answering machine. Its constant red light indicated no messages. Grant lifted the lid. The tape was gone.

'Damn,' Grant muttered. 'Why would the tape have gone?'

'Uh . . .' Chile said from across the room. 'I . . . uh . . .'

'What, Chile?'

'I, uh, took the tape yesterday, thinking I didn't want any of the boneheads wandering around here to accidentally hit the erase button,' Chile's rambling picked up speed, 'Just in case this turned out to be a homicide, which now it is, and – '

'Great. Anything we can use? Who were the messages from?'

'Well . . .' Chile's eyes wandered from the books in the bookcase to a child's clay sculpture of a dog, 'I don't know.'

'You haven't listened to it yet?' Grant asked, surprised. 'Well, I guess we have been tied up with other things. So where is it? We can listen now.'

'That's just it,' Chile paused, still not meeting Grant's eyes.

'What's just it, Chile? Spit it out.'

'Now promise me you're not going to go off the deep end about this, ole Tom.'

'About what, Chile?' Grant's voice threatened menace.

'Well, I don't exactly remember where I put the tape,' Chile explained, in a rush that wouldn't let Grant interrupt. 'I slipped it into my shirt pocket yesterday, but this morning when I remembered about it I looked and it was gone.'

Grant began pacing like a caged lion. 'You sure you didn't stop by somewhere and pick up a *chica* for the night and drop it while you were dropping your pants at her place?'

It wouldn't be out of the realms of possibility, for, though Chile had a steady girlfriend, it didn't keep him from sampling from the buffet line from time to time. 'No, not last night. I was wiped out.' Chile sank into a nearby chair with his head in his hands. 'I'm sorry, *amigo*. It'll come to me.'

Not trusting himself to speak, Grant only jerked his head in a semblance of a nod. He doubted the killer would've left an obvious message on the machine, so it might not be that big a deal. However, there could be a clue there, and they wouldn't know until Chile's *guacamole* memory kicked in.

Breaking out of his pacing route, Grant walked past Britt's bedroom – trying not to think of the soft, firm feel of her in his arms, the sweet, tangy flavor of her mouth – as he stole a look into the empty room. Without pausing a step, he walked into Risa's room. His brain was methodically going through the possible scenarios that had occurred there just the day before. Had Risa known she'd been poisoned? Had she left any clues of her own?

Grant glanced again at the Lyle Lovett poster on the wall. Something jumped from a recess of his mind to the front and he spun on his heel and rushed back to the living room. At the antique oak bookcase that doubled as an entertainment center, Grant pressed the power button of the CD player, then noticed the pause button was depressed. He had seen the CD case bearing the photo of the singer with the quirky hairstyle on the floor near the fireplace. Grant noticed with approval that the CD player was covered with fingerprint dust. What prints might have been there had been documented, but still he couldn't bring himself to replace those with his own. So he used his knuckle to press 'play'. A soulful voice filled the small room.

Not sure whether it was safe to give up his sorrowful act, Chile watched Grant with his chin in his hand. 'Why are you turning this on? Way too intellectual for me. Don't tell me you like this guy?'

Actually, Grant did like the singer, a lot, but he wasn't about to satisfy Chile's curiosity – he was too mad at him for that. 'This stereo was on yesterday. According to Randall, the uniform who got the call, it was the only thing on, as a matter of fact. He thought it was weird, but I really didn't give it all that much thought until now. Risa could have been trying to tell us something.'

'Oh, *bien*. Like, if you listen to it backwards?'

Grant stifled a smile. 'Chile, just listen to the words in forward first. We might not have to go the backward route.'

Grant returned the CD to the beginning of the song, and they were both silent while the song played.

'So what?' Chile asked.

'So maybe nothing. Probably nothing. But let's look at who the song was about. Big Daddy's the Big Boss-man.'

'And there was something about poisoning.' Chile pointed out part of another lyric.

Grant nodded distractedly. 'If this is a message, I think it's the Big Daddy we gotta look at.'

'I think you're *loco*, *amigo*. You think in circles.'

Grant just shrugged, still pondering through the lyrics of the song and the validity of considering it a clue at all.

Chile watched him closely for a minute, then gave him some credence. 'Okay, so you think Neil Reeve's our man?'

'Not necessarily.'

'Aye-yi-yi, so I try to buy into this convoluted tale you're whipping up and you're throwing it out the window?' Chile complained.

'It all might just be a coincidence. We can keep it in the back of our minds, but we can't spend too much time dwelling on the maybes when we've got for-sures to follow up on.'

'Sounds great, but, partner, we ain't got a lot of those for-sures either – unless there's something you're not telling me.'

'Well,' Grant admitted as he pulled the bag with the watch out of his pocket, 'I found this earlier in Britt's bedroom.'

Chile stood up to examine the watch. 'Her boyfriend's, huh? Maybe we ought to find out who she's doing. Maybe we got a guy with a sheet or he's a freaky pharmacist trying an experiment – '

Grant glared. 'Britt isn't *doing* anybody, so forget it.'

Chile's eyebrows shot up. 'Whoa, *amigo*. She tell you that? Since when do you believe what somebody tells you? A girl like that – ' Chile's hands moved to shape an hourglass figure ' – sure as hell has a boyfriend. I'm telling you.'

'She says she doesn't, and that's the end of it.'

Chile studied Grant's rigid face. 'Oh, I see. You wanna

believe that 'cuz you want to be the one she's doing? Okay, good luck, but wait 'til we're done with this case, that's all. We got enough trouble without making more for ourselves.'

Grant crossed his arms over his chest, trying to shake off the feeling of role reversal. Hadn't he always been the responsible one? 'Since when did you become the voice of caution?'

'Since you got stupid over this *chica*. You get enough horizontal boogie without even trying. So go get your black book and call up one of your *sanchas* to satisfy your itch.'

'It's not an itch,' Grant grumbled, looking at a picture of Risa and Britt, smiling, arms thrown around each other.

'*Dios mio*,' Chile whispered, shaking his head slowly. 'I hope this is not what it looks like on your face.'

Grant looked at his partner sharply and ran a hand over his face. 'What? What's on my face?'

'For someone who's so smart, you sure can be so *estupido*, Tom.' Chile, still shaking his head mournfully, stood and walked down the hall to check the bedrooms and bathrooms again.

As Grant stood there, debating whether to go after Chile, his beeper went off. He checked the familiar number and used Britt's living room phone.

'Hey, Mom,' Grant softened his voice in answer to his mother's subdued hello.

'Grant, how are you?' Her voice brightened. 'How is the case going? We've seen you all over the TV. That poor family, to have such tragedy.'

'We know all about tragedy.'

'Yes, but we didn't lose a life.'

Grant wanted to debate that, but didn't. They had lost a

life – the brother he grew up with. In his place was a bitter invalid whom no one knew. And it was Grant's fault.

'I'm glad you called so soon.' His mother rushed to fill the silence. 'It's your brother. You haven't been to see him this week and he's . . . a little restless. If you have a minute to two to spare, you might think about coming to see him. A break might do you good. And I think a visit from you will calm him right down.'

Grant knew that was a lie but he also knew he'd go. Command performance.

'Mom, I'll try to make it after the girl's funeral for a few minutes. But I can't promise anything, so don't mention it to Evan.'

'Oh, thank you, Grant. It'll mean so much to him.'

The funeral service for Risa Reeve was full of surprises, all of them good ones. The arrangements had been made by her grandmother, who had kept all the warring personalities of the Reeve family out of it by asking only the minister to eulogize Risa. He'd baptized her, confirmed her and watched her grow up as an acolyte and then a youth group leader in the St Matthew's Episcopal Church. Even Grant who'd lost sight of God lately, found his eulogy meaningful.

Despite glares and hostile body language, Sophia and Neil did not come to blows. Britt kept a hungover Tori propped up in a semblance of propriety, although she still looked as if she'd drain the holy challis of its wine if given half the chance. The congregation was mainly a combination of well-dressed stoic types, that Grant pegged for university colleagues of Neil's, and semi-hysterical high-schoolers. None of the models Risa had worked with had been able to make it, with the service scheduled so soon after Risa's death. Grant thought Jewel had planned it that way. He got the feeling she didn't like the modeling profession much. Certainly no more than Britt did.

The church itself was overflowing with flowers, spiritually uplifting music, mourners and pictures of Risa. No casket, no urn. Grant approved. It was a way to remember Risa without imagining her body headed for six feet under.

But the best part was that all the reporters were held at bay by the combination of a formidable visiting bishop and the high school football team. Not one camera, notebook, or microphone was in evidence inside the church walls. They could hear the reporters clamoring outside, including a helicopter that hovered over the roof during the whole service, but not one reporter was able to get in.

Grant's eyes scanned the crowd for possible suspects, but he found his gaze repeatedly returning to Britt. She wore a simple non-descript midnight-blue suit which contrasted markedly with Tori's black Lycra top and leopard print mini-skirt. Britt's cloud of mahogany hair was pinned up, leaving her neck bare and somehow vulnerable. Grant saw her shoulders shudder a few times, but, from his profile view of her, he never saw her cry. The tears were gone. In their place was the determination Grant had seen at the station.

The minister announced that Risa would be buried in a private ceremony at an undisclosed time but that mourners were invited to remember Risa in a reception in the parish family center. It sounded terribly depressing to Grant, and he was grateful for an excuse to leave. As the congregation began to file out, he took note of Neil and Sophia vying for control over the proceedings, which Jewel deftly wrested back for herself.

With an inner high-five for Britt's wily, strong grandmother, Grant made for an exit, leaving Chile behind to canvass the crowd for leads. Grant rarely had any luck finding leads in a mass public gathering. In his experience, killers were usually too careful to slip up in such an obvious place.

He headed out a side door and to the street where his car was parked. He noticed a bubble-gum-blue sports car pulling out of the parking lot at the same time he pulled away from the curb, and felt a kinship for someone who couldn't stomach a post-mortem party.

Britt popped the clutch and the car lurched into second gear. Swearing under her breath, she hung onto the steering wheel and wrested the car back under control, keeping an eye on the cars parallel-parked along the road as well as on the one she was following.

'Why did Grams have to get a peppy little sports car, anyway? She's a senior citizen. She has no business driving around like a race-car driver,' she grumbled to herself as she shifted into third.

Having not driven a standard-shift car since high school, Britt was badly out of practice. But they'd come to the service in Grams's car so when Britt whispered to Jewel that she had to escape Jewel had handed her the keys with a kiss and now she was stuck with it. That's what she got for having a go-go granny.

The service had been beautiful and something Risa would've loved. But Britt knew she couldn't face all the mourners. Friends and strangers, either well-meaning or morbidly curious, either issuing platitudes or offering opinions. They'd all be speculating on Risa's death being a murder, which the police chief had confirmed right before the service. Britt couldn't sit and listen to all the talk; she had to have action. She had to feel as if she was doing something to catch Risa's killer instead of standing around talking about it.

When she'd slipped out one of the church's side doors, she'd caught sight of Grant just reaching his car. Where was he going? To interview a suspect? To some break in the case he hadn't told her about?

Britt had run around the back of the church to the parking lot, dropped into the driver seat and roared the engine to life. She pulled onto the side street just as Grant's car turned the corner. So intent was she on following him, she didn't look back at another car that had fallen in behind her.

A few streets later, a sign announced that they were back in the city limits of San Antonio. Grant got on US Highway 281 and headed north, but not for long. He took off, without indicating at the second exit. A right and a left and a right and they were in a lower middle class neighborhood, where the homes were not expensive but were well-cared for. Some showed evidence of modest additions and improvements.

Because Jewel's car was so visible – why couldn't she have gotten something more subtle, like gray? – Britt had to hang back, and almost lost Grant several times. He got two turns ahead of her and Britt thought she'd lost him for good. But, not willing to give up, she went street to street, looking for his unmarked sedan.

Britt saw a pair of headlights half a block behind her, following. For a moment she wondered if it was a San Antonio patrol car; watching to see if she was casing the neighborhood. But just then she spotted Grant's car in a driveway ahead and drove with purpose to the house.

Parking along the curb, Britt looked at the house. It was a one-story traditional brick, and would have been unremarkable except for the extreme care it revealed. The brick looked clean enough to eat off, paint on its trim gleamed like brand-new and its yard was perfectly trimmed, even the grass regimentally all the same length, like a green carpet. Not one weed could be seen, not one piece of garbage, not one gardening spade left out, no toys. Except for the happy irises planted along the borders, Britt would've called it sterile. They looked slightly rebellious, and added just enough of a personal touch to make the home seem lived in.

Britt got out and shut her door. She'd decided to ring the doorbell and improvise. She couldn't afford to wait to find out who Grant was talking to; she might miss some vital evidence. She turned the key in the car's lock and was about to pocket the keys when they were grabbed out of her hand.

'You aren't going anywhere. Not until you talk to me.'

Britt spun around to face a slight, nearly middle-aged man with a stringy goatee and a greasy ponytail. His hollow-eyed, hollow-cheeked, pock-marked face looked vaguely familiar, but Britt couldn't place it. She was too busy trying not to wrinkle her nose because he smelled like five feet four inches of dirty socks. That he was standing too close – in her 'space' – didn't help. Britt took a step back and felt the cool metal of the car against her rump.

'If you're a reporter, I have no comment right now,' Britt said, glancing at the house. 'And no time even if I did have a comment.'

'I'm not a reporter.' He dismissed that notion with a snort. 'I'm Skin, the photographer who discovered Risa.'

Britt narrowed her eyes. She'd been expecting low-lifes to come along, purporting to be Risa's friends and associates for financial gain. She'd expected to see them on TV, making money for manufactured, close-personal-friend tales. What she hadn't expected was for them to approach her or even know who she was. After all, she wasn't the beautiful model sister or the famous candidate's wife mother or the manager father.

'You don't remember me?' he asked petulantly.

Then it hit her. He was that friend of Tori's. He'd been taking the photos of Tori on a shoot that Neil and Risa had visited in Cancun. Skin had told Risa she ought to model. Neil had told Risa many times that she was too curvy, too thick-lipped, too exotic-looking, too hazel-eyed, too mouse-haired to be a model. But Tori had been making Neil a lot of money on her shoot, and he'd felt magnanimous and paid Skin to take some photos of Risa. The rest was history.

The first agent who'd seen the photos signed her up and Risa could've worked full-time since – and would have if her father had had anything to do with it. But Risa hadn't wanted a tutor. She hadn't wanted to give up being a teenager. She'd wanted to live in San Antonio and go to school. That had limited her jobs – ironically upping the demand and her prices in the business she didn't care much about.

Skin saying that he'd discovered her was pushing it. He was no Svengali. That he was trying to take credit for it now, now that Risa wasn't there to set to story straight, made Britt's blood boil.

'I don't think that's quite accurate.' Britt reined in her temper, watching Skin throw her keys up and down in his hand.

'What? My name is Skin. Yeah, it's a nickname, but that's how everybody in the business knows me – '

His whining patter snapped her stretched nerves. 'I don't give a flying fig what your name is. I don't think it's accurate to say you discovered Risa.'

Skin's colorless eyes almost sank back into his skull in shock. His mouth worked wordlessly over his stringy goatee. His hands with their long, dirty fingernails clutched her car keys. 'I – I – I – ' He choked out a sound like a tortured bird. 'I can't believe you'd say that. Who do you say discovered her, then? Huh?'

'No one discovered Risa. She was the same person before you took her pictures and afterward. A sweet, good thirteen-year-old girl.'

'Yeah, but she was a famous and rich thirteen-year-old girl after I got through with her.'

'She was not famous because of you. She was famous because the beauty of her spirit came through on film. Not just your film; everybody's film. That's what made her famous.'

'Yeah, but she never would've hit it if I hadn't found her at just the right time. The time when the industry was moving away from the classic beauties and more to the exotic, athletic – '

'You didn't find her; she dropped in your lap. You did a few hours' work and got paid for it. Move on and go discover another girl. Stay out of my life and my sister's memories.' Britt stared at him defiantly, meaning to go marching straight to the front door behind which Grant was doing goodness only knew what. Then she remembered. 'But first give me my keys.'

Skin's thin lips cracked into a snide grin and he held his hand up, dangling the keys from two fingers. 'Not yet.' He took a step toward her. Britt pressed harder against the car, willing it to move backward. 'Not until you hear me out.'

'I thought I had,' Britt said belligerently.

'Nope. This is the deal.' Pointy incisors pinned an edge of his mustache and chewed for a second to two. He began to fidget. 'I took those pictures and I oughta be able to publish them wherever I want to. And I'm gonna, once you give them back.'

'Give them back?' Britt asked, both mystified and outraged. 'I don't have them.'

'Sure you do.' Skin caught her in his colorless gaze, then broke it off, glancing around with his eyes flitting here and there nervously. 'Risa was at my studio a month ago. She took the negatives then. Stole them, is what she did. So now you got them.'

'Why would she take them?' Britt crossed her arms over her chest.

'Because I told her I'd sold the idea for a book to a publisher, that's why. She tried to talk me out of the whole deal. Like, sure I'm gonna blow off six figures. Anyhow, I got a call that turned out to be bogus and had to run out. When I get back Risa's gone – along with the negatives. I ain't no detective, but I don't have to be to figure this one out.'

Britt tightened her crossed arms, pressing against her chest. 'Those were her favorite pictures ever made and she wanted to keep them private. She mentioned that to me just recently. But she knew the negatives are copyrighted and I can't imagine that she'd take anything that wasn't hers – '

Britt broke off as she was struck with a sudden realization. Risa had come to Britt's class after getting back from her last job, which had been in Los Angeles. Before she'd put on an apron to help the kids with their art project, she'd shoved an envelope at Britt. 'Keep this for me,' she'd said. 'In a safe place away from home.' Britt had wondered what the mystery was all about, but twenty children and their spaghetti spider art had taken precedence. What had she done with the envelope?

Skin fidgeted, rocking from foot to foot and jiggling his leg at the knee, jangling her keys in his fingers. 'I know you know where the negs are, so spill it and I'll leave you alone, and then we'll all go on our happy way.'

Britt was still lost in her recollection. 'Risa did give me something . . .'

Anger and impatience flashed across Skin's face. 'Yeah, sure. Don't act stupid. Everybody knows you're the smart Reeve sister, so act like it, will you?' Suddenly Skin snapped, and his hand shot out like a snake striking and grabbed her around the neck, just below her jaw. 'Tell me or I'll make you sorry.'

Stomach heaving with fear, Britt struggled to keep calm. She threw her arms up, easily knocking his threatening hands away. She put her hands behind her back, so he couldn't see their shaking.

'I'll be sure to tell the cops about your threat.'

Skin swallowed hard, a sheen of sweat breaking out over his face; but he didn't respond.

'And,' Britt continued, 'if I find your precious negatives while I'm going through Risa's things, I will certainly return them to you. Not because I want to but because it's the law; they are your property. I can promise you, though, I'm not going to go to any extra trouble to dig them up for you.'

'Like you don't know where they are,' Skin whined. 'Yeah, they'll end up in some box in the attic for hundreds of years.'

'Maybe,' Britt said optimistically.

Skin measured her with a narrow-eyed look. 'I get it. I deliver and you'll deliver. Okay. I can understand that kind of mentality. A book with photographs of Risa, especially ones never published before, could make a ton of cash. I'll give you a cut of the royalties. Can't share the advance; it's nearly gone. Still, those royalties could make a chunk of change. You can't turn that down, can you?'

Britt resisted the urge to spit in the sweaty face that was trying so hard to look earnest in hopes of getting her okay to earn that 'chunk of change'. She let her eyes fill with the fire she felt burning in the pit of her belly and spoke slowly and deliberately. 'I can turn it down, and I will turn it down. I loved my sister more than anyone else on earth, and I will do anything to see her memory preserved and her wishes honored. And her wish was to keep these photos under wraps. If you're so greedy that you can't honor those wishes, then I hope there's a place reserved for you in hell.'

'Hey, Mother Teresa, haven't you heard only the good die young?' A warning grin that chilled her to the bone spread slowly over Skin's face.

Britt tried not to show her alarm. Gooseflesh rose on her arm beneath her suit coat. Her heartbeat raced as she realized the man before her, who she'd thought of as pitiful, might be dangerous as well. Her eyes darted around as she looked for escape, a way to get around the car and out of his reach. But suddenly Skin looked over her shoulder and virtually hummed with panic.

'I'll show you hell if I don't get those negs,' he mumbled, and ran off full speed for his dingy Volkswagen.

Instead of turning around to see what had spooked him, Britt hurried after him to catch the license plate number as the Volkswagen coughed out of sight.

A hand grabbed and jerked her back. 'No, you don't.'

Swallowing her scream, Britt felt herself falling back and into a hard chest. Instinctively she began struggling. Arms with sinewy, strong-corded muscle banded over her and held her still. Grant's cedary scent enveloped her, and for some strange reason her muscles relaxed. What was wrong with her body? Didn't it have any sense?

'Now I know for sure,' she forced out of lungs still gasping for air.

'You know what for sure?' he said into her hair, which she could feel working loose from its tight bun.

'I know you have a thing for ambushing women.'

'Maybe not all women, just you.' She felt his mouth closer now, brushing the top of her head, his breath hot on her scalp.

'Hah. Just because you think I'm small and defenseless – '

'I would never be fool enough to think that. From what I've seen you're the best fighter I know. Maybe I just like good competition.'

Britt pushed away from his body and was surprised to find a bolt of regret shoot through her as she stood on her own and faced him. His hands still held her loosely, just above her elbows. She lifted her chin, intending to ask him what he was doing at this house, why he'd come back outside so soon, but instead she found herself captured in the intensity of his gunmetal gaze. It was as if she was locked in a force field. His lips dipped to meet hers and the 'resist' messages her brain was sending weren't reaching her body.

Her mouth accepted his. She felt herself responding. But more than responding – initiating. Hot. Hungry. Needy. She despised it and relished it. Grant groaned and pulled her closer. At the contact with his chest, her breasts swelled instantly. Britt pressed them closer. His hands skimmed up her arms and into her hair as his mouth dropped to her neck, scratching a trail with his perpetual five o'clock shadow. Instead of shirking away, Britt threw her head back, inviting more and imagining what that roughness would feel like in other places on her body . . .

'Grant? Where did you go?'

Britt pulled back so quickly at the sound of the woman's voice that she had to scramble to get her feet under her. Grant reached out to steady her. She shook off his hand and tried to look around him toward the house where a woman stood, just barely visible inside the storm door.

'Your girlfriend? I'm sorry I arrived to interrupt,' Britt began, hating to hear the hurt and bitterness in her voice.

Grant's jaw tightened. 'My mother. And she's the one who's interrupting.'

Britt's mouth actually dropped open. 'Your mother?'

'What did you expect – I came over for a quickie?' He straightened his shoulders a little at the thought of her being jealous. 'That's why you followed me here?'

'Don't flatter yourself. I don't care when or where you get your "quickies", and I certainly don't want to lurk around outside while you do. I followed you here because I thought you were on the case.' Suddenly her bravado dissolved into embarrassment. She looked down, feeling the flush in her cheeks intensify. 'But I didn't mean to interfere in your personal time with your family – '

'Grant? Is everything all right out there?' Mrs Collins called.

'Fine, Mom,' he threw over his shoulder impatiently.

'Please bring your friend inside. It's much more comfortable, uh, talking in here.'

'Okay, okay, we'll be right there.' Grant glowered.

'No.' Taking his cue, Britt shook her head, propriety at war with her curiosity about his family.

'I guess you'll have to come in,' Grant offered, though he didn't look pleased with the prospect. 'Mom is pretty stubborn.'

'I don't want to impose.'

'You also don't want to get caught by that reporter,'

Grant pointed out, jerking his head in the direction Skin had driven.

'He wasn't a reporter,' Britt said flatly.

'No?' Grant answered, eyes searching her face while his own reflected a mixture of suspicion, jealousy and curiosity. 'Well, then you have to come in to tell me why the hell you were having a pow-wow outside my parents' house with a twitchy sleaze with California plates.'

Britt shot him a look. 'How did you get all that? You were barely outside the door when he was gone.'

Putting his arm around her shoulder to guide her to the house, Grant let his mouth turn up at the corners in a smile that was both mocking and warning. 'I don't miss much, Miss Reeve. I don't miss much at all.'

CHAPTER 10

Armed with two cups of steaming coffee, Nancy Collins sat down across the square pine kitchen table from Britt. She pushed one of the mugs toward her and Britt picked it up. She almost had it to her lips when she caught sight of the drawing on the side. It was a Playboy Bunny-esque blonde, busting out of her string bikini. She held a jug of milk and some had splashed on her right breast. Underneath were the words: *I like mine with a little cream*.

Britt tried not to grimace, but Nancy Collins must have caught on because she said: 'It's my husband's. I can get you another if you'd prefer.'

'No, this is fine.'

'And I didn't ask you if you wanted anything in your coffee.'

Britt really wanted some milk, but, staring at the woman on the cup, she considered converting to black coffee for good. 'No, thank you.'

The two women sat, sipping their coffee. They'd been left alone. After the requisite introductions, Grant's father had called from down the hall that he needed Grant's help with his brother. Shooting Britt a look that was both regretful and warning, he'd left. Now, sitting under the silent scrutiny of his mother, Britt distracted herself by looking around the kitchen. It, like the yard, was spotless. Although the interior reflected a few more signs of family life. Two dozen magnets were lined up along the side of the refrigerator. Britt imagined they'd once held Grant's and his brother's school work. And there they waited in orderly fashion for grandchildren's art. The table and chairs looked as if they'd been around since Grant was a kid. The table was scarred and showed a few well-scrubbed crayon marks. Down on the leg closest to her Britt could see a heart carved into the wood along with initials. Just as she was angling her head to see whose initials were there, Nancy put her coffee mug down with a clang. Britt looked up.

'So, how did you and Grant meet?' Nancy asked.

'Over my sister's body.'

Nancy went pale. She opened and closed her mouth without a sound, then tears filled her eyes. 'I'm sorry. You're that model's sister. I should have realized . . . I just thought you were another . . .' She reached across the table and took Britt's hands into hers. 'Please accept my sympathy.'

Unnerved by her unexpected reaction, Britt could only nod. In an instant they had gone from uncomfortable to emotionally connected. Britt wondered why a dead sister would make the difference. She wished Nancy had finished her sentence. Now she felt she could ask. 'You thought I was another what?'

'I shouldn't have said that.'

'But you did,' Britt pointed out.

'Yes, I did,' Nancy admitted. 'And you deserve an explanation. Grant has had a lot of women friends. Girlfriends. He doesn't bring many around here, and never the same girl twice. They are all the same, though – gorgeous. And empty-headed. Polite, for the most part, but without character. You're not like that at all.'

Britt should've bristled, her usual defense when someone compared her – no, contrasted her – with her beautiful sisters, but instead she surprised herself by laughing. 'Thanks a lot.'

Nancy smiled. 'You know it was a compliment. And a sense of humor too; I'm pleased.'

Britt sobered. 'I'm glad you're pleased, but I'm also not your son's girlfriend.'

The look in Nancy's eyes told Britt she'd seen their kiss. 'Well, I'm still pleased that he'll be exposed to someone like you. He needs to see that not all women are window dressing.'

'You don't look like window dressing to me.'

It was Nancy's turn to laugh. 'Touché.'

Britt laughed with her. Nancy was a handsome woman, but it was her bearing that made her so more than her appearance, which might otherwise be considered plain. Her salt-and-pepper hair was drawn back in a ponytail that ended between her shoulderblades. Her strong face was relatively unlined. Her gray eyes were much like her son's – appraising one second, warm the next. Her lean height made Britt feel too short and too curvy. Britt sat up straighter in her chair.

'I have to admit I let my husband rule this roost,' Nancy admitted ruefully. 'I am strong-willed, and when we first got married I fought for my way, but I'm ashamed to say that over time I began to pick my battles more carefully. It just wasn't worth the gray hairs he was giving me, fighting over the brand of margarine or how far to pull the car into the garage.'

'That doesn't sound fair.' Britt frowned and shook her head.

Nancy chuckled. 'Marriage isn't about fairness – '

Both women jumped at the sudden sound of breaking glass on the other side of the wall. Britt met Nancy's eyes. Nancy sighed and took a sip of coffee in what looked like a diversionary tactic. She cleared her throat. 'Has Grant told you about his brother?'

'No.' Britt shook her head. 'He hasn't said much about his own life or his own family. It's mine that's taking up his time lately. I followed him here to see what he was doing about the case. My sister's case. He's been pretty close-mouthed, and I feel like I have to do something. I can't just sit around and cry.'

'I can understand that. I'd feel the same way,' Nancy said. 'But Grant is a good cop. Despite what you may have heard.'

Britt drew her brows together. 'I don't know what you're talking about. I haven't heard anything about Grant – '

The sound of raised voices traveled through the wall to interrupt Britt. The women traded a look.

'Well, all this is intertwined – mixed up – overlapping. So to explain one part I have to explain it all. I guess I have to start at the beginning.'

Britt held herself still, afraid if she moved Nancy would change her mind, but at the same time afraid to hear what the woman across from her was going to say about the man she was growing to trust.

'Grant's brother is Evan. Evan is twenty-two months younger. The boys were close growing up.' She paused and looked around the kitchen, the memories tangible. 'We've lived here since Evan was born. My husband is a retired machinist; he worked as a civilian at Kelly Air Force Base for forty years. I stayed home with the boys and he wanted nothing more than to be more, to have more than he had. Ben, my husband, has always felt inferior because he was a blue collar worker. He worked hard and was responsible, never missed a day of work no matter what. He has nothing to be ashamed of but he was, and still is. He lived for his boys to be his pride.'

Nancy shook her head, met Britt's eyes again and continued. 'Both went to college, at the University of Texas. Ben was never subtle in his hopes for the boys, and Grant tried to please him. He majored in political science and worked for some legislators at the capitol. But he kept getting sidelined by the concept of justice.'

'Politics isn't about justice,' Britt interjected.

'No, and it didn't take Grant long to figure that out,' Nancy agreed. 'He spent a semester in law school before he decided that wasn't about justice either. Police work was as close as he could come and he was happy until . . .'

Britt waited a minute, staring into Nancy's faraway eyes then she prompted her. 'Until?'

Nancy's gaze snapped back to the present. 'I'm getting ahead of myself. Excuse me. Let me backtrack. While Grant went with the San Antonio Police Department, Evan took up the gauntlet and went to law school. It suited Evan, especially litigation. He always loved verbal debates, could talk rings around his more direct, analytical brother. In fact, the more obfuscation Evan could throw into an argument the more blunt and direct Grant became. They evolved into opposites.

'Ben didn't help. He was never shy about saying how disappointed he was in Grant, that he had failed and had to fall back on a blue collar job. But at least one boy had made it, he would brag. "Our Evan, he's an attorney." Ben will – still – never refer to Evan as a lawyer. Sounds too cheap, he says.'

'What kind of attorney is Evan?'

'Defense,' Nancy answered, nodding at Britt's grimace.

'It made for combustible family get-togethers. Those got fewer and fewer as Grant testified against several of Evan's clients. They almost couldn't be in the same room with each other without Evan antagonizing Grant into an argument.'

'Pretty violent arguments?' Britt pointed out, with a glance at the now silent wall.

'They didn't used to be violent, just heated. But a year ago everything changed.'

'What happened?'

'Grant as a homicide detective was working with the vice division on a series of drug-related murders on the Southeast side. After a couple of months, he zeroed in on a well-known cocaine supplier who was trying to consolidate his power. It just so happened that he was also a man Evan had successfully defended on a drug charge. When Grant told his boss about it he was taken off the case for conflict of interest. He fought to be there for the collar. His boss reluctantly gave in.

'When they raided the house, the suspect had somehow known they were coming and had an ambush waiting. Two officers were shot. Some cops said that Grant had tipped them off, but the worst was yet to come. Grant felt he had to vindicate himself and went around the back of the house. He and his partner got in. There was Evan, sitting there with the suspect. Grant was shocked. When Evan reached over to pick up a gun from the table next to the suspect – he says now to turn it over to the police – Grant's partner aimed. Grant jumped into the line of fire and onto Evan. The bullet went right through Grant's shoulder and then into Evan, lodging against his spine.'

'Dear God,' Britt whispered, closing her eyes.

'What would you have done?' Nancy asked, with pain and pride shimmering in her eyes. 'His duty as a policeman was to bring his brother to justice. But his instinct as human being was to protect his younger brother, no matter what he might be.'

Britt thought of Tori. She didn't make it easy to love her but still Britt did. She hoped Tori wouldn't put her in that difficult a position. Ever. Just thinking about it made her sick.

'So, with his brother paralyzed, at the hospital with a police guard, Grant underwent the scrutiny of Internal Affairs. The department kept the details from the press, so all they got was that three cops were shot in a drug raid. That was the one blessing in this mess. After weeks he was finally cleared of the charges that he'd tipped off the suspect about the raid. Internal Affairs found that Grant's partner had fired without warning, so Grant was cleared of wrongdoing. Officially. But he'd lost trust by trying to protect a suspect instead of his partner.'

'That's why he left the San Antonio Police Department?'

'No. I think Grant would've toughed it out. Earned their trust back.'

'Then why did he come to Terrell Hills? Did they ask him to leave?'

'He left on his own, as punishment,' Nancy said, her lips pulled into a thin line.

'Punishment? For what?'

'For failing to take that bullet in his own spine,' Nancy said harshly. 'For being able to walk when his brother can't. He couldn't physically paralyze himself, so he paralyzed something he loves more – his career.'

It made a kind of warped sense that Britt could relate to. And it explained a lot about who Grant was – the ambiguity of feeling emotion and not wanting to, the fact that he was angry at finding himself in the middle of the biggest case of his career when he'd been trying to slip into oblivion.

'He comes here to see Evan for punishment too, I've decided, not because he wants to,' Nancy went on. 'Evan abuses him verbally. Subconsciously, Grant thinks he deserves it. It's like a game of emotional sado-masochism. He comes every two or three days without fail. Sometimes, like today, I call and remind him. I keep thinking they'll get beyond the barrier that's grown between them, be like they were when they were boys. But I just don't know. I just don't know.'

Impulsively, Britt grabbed Nancy's hands and held them in her own. Two broken sons. A good mother like Nancy didn't deserve it.

'Dammit, Mom, what do you think you're doing?'

Neither woman had heard Grant walk up in the doorway behind them. As Britt tried to get her heart out of her throat, Nancy turned to face her son. 'I'm telling her something she needs to know.'

'She doesn't need to know that. That's just none of her damned business.' Grant glared at Britt as if she'd coerced the story out of his mother. He shifted his gaze back to his mother, not lightening it by much. 'Evan wants coffee.'

'He knows he's not supposed to have it. Doctor's orders.'

'Well, you go in and tell him that and hear his "poor quality of life" speech. The "poor me and lucky you" diatribe.' Grant's lips tensed to a thin line as he looked out the window, focusing on nothing.

Nancy poured water out of a pitcher into a glass. Grant's pager went off, and he reached down to check the number. 'Rangel.'

Allowing impulse to control her again, Britt reached for the glass of water. 'I'll take it to Evan.'

Nancy looked uncertainly at Grant, who measured Britt with a hard look, then shrugged. Britt marched off, head high, wondering what the hell she was getting into.

'He'll scare her off but good,' Grant said.

'Or draw her in completely,' Nancy said simply.

'How do you figure that? Evan's meaner than a snake,' Grant pointed out.

'Because she cares about you.'

'All she cares about is that I make an arrest in her sister's case. Your little tale may have undermined her confidence in me. So now instead of being on my back all the time she'll be stabbing me in it. Thanks, Mom.' With that, Grant turned and punched out the numbers from his pager on the phone. He tried to ignore his mother's knowing nod that he caught out of the corner of his eye.

Britt knocked lightly on the bedroom door before she turned the knob.

'What took so long? I could've crawled there and back faster with the cup between my teeth. If I could crawl, that is.'

Britt closed the door behind her and faced the man with the voice so like Grant's – except that it resonated with bitterness. Evan lay in a fancy hospital bed, its back tilted up so that he was sitting at a forty-five-degree angle. His pale bare feet stuck out from under the sheet, and that more than his bare chest above his sweatpants made Britt tense with the embarrassment of invading his privacy.

'Oh-ho. What's Grant done now?' Evan asked the question of his father, while keeping his eyes on Britt. But the burly man standing near the window just folded his arms over his chest and didn't respond. 'He's sending a sexy nymph in here to try to regenerate my nerves. Huh. It might work at that. I think I'm beginning to feel . . .' Evan lifted up the sheet and peeked underneath before letting it fall with his face. 'No. But come here sweetheart and maybe it'll work yet.'

Britt was trying to reconcile feeling flattered at being called sexy and feeling repulsed. She arranged her features in what she hoped made a polite face and approached the bed.

'Who're you?' Ben Collins mumbled, stepping over the broken shards of china.

'Who the hell cares, Pop?' Evan cut in before Britt could answer. 'She's a lot better on the eyes and ears than brother dearest. Come here, sweetheart,' he said again, and beckoned her with wiggling fingers.

'Who're you?' Ben repeated.

'Britt Reeve, I'm an . . . an associate of Grant's,' Britt answered unsteadily, not sure how to describe their relationship.

'Associate?' Evan's eyes flashed. 'Not a cop, are you?'

'No, we just met through his work,' Britt answered evasively.

'Oh?' Evan's eyebrows shot up. 'Maybe Grant worked a deal with a call-girl, huh? Hey, they sure do come prettier and better dressed from the highbrow hills than they do slumming it downtown. Course, Terrell Hills has better everything – better houses, better schools, better cops with their noses in the air.'

Britt felt a rush of anger at this description meant to denigrate Grant. After all Grant had done for him his brother did nothing but knock him, even behind his back.

'Evan, don't forget your manners,' Ben admonished mildly.

'Shut up, Pop. Just because I'm lying here like an amoeba doesn't mean you can push me around. I'm thirty-three years old, and I'll say what I want to say even if I can't do what I want to do.'

He looked at Britt, and she was taken aback by how the determination in his face made him resemble Grant. She hadn't thought they looked much alike up until then. Grant was a hard, masculine version of his mother – handsome, hard and lanky. Evan looked like a younger version of his father – pale blue eyes, straight, thin, light brown hair, in a face as mobile as his brother's was stoic. His frame appeared to have once been as thick as a football lineman's, and was still muscular from the waist up. His legs, though, had shrunk from disuse. A beefy frame that was turning weak and wasted.

'And you, beauty, can tell my mother that I don't want water, I want coffee. Caffeinated. The doctor can go to hell.'

Nodding, Britt turned around. Ben Collins followed her, took the water out of her hand and opened the door for her. In the hall, he cleared his throat.

'Excuse my boy. This injury has been hard on him. And when you have to see one of the guys responsible for putting you there all the time it's hard to handle. A constant reminder of what he doesn't have any more. But he does a helluva job, considering. He'll be up dancing in front of a jury in no time. I told him he had to or his old man would have nothing left to talk about. He'll do it. He's never let me down yet. No siree.'

Britt sighed. She could see it was fruitless to argue with him about Grant's responsibility, about accepting his son's injury, about anything. It was none of her business anyway. Not her problem.

'Good luck, Mr Collins.' She stuck out her hand. He looked at it as if she had eight fingers. Obviously not used to shaking a woman's hand. Finally he took it, just for an instant, before he dropped it with a grunt and a nod and walked back into the bedroom.

Before Britt could take a step, Grant appeared out of the shadows at the end of the hall. He walked toward her and stopped just a little too close, so she'd have to look up to look him in the eyes. Guarded eyes. 'Now we're even.' His voice was a low rumble.

'Even?'

'You accused me of spying on your family at its ugliest,' Grant said. 'Now you've had the same honor with my family.'

'I guess you're right,' Britt admitted. 'But my family still wins the ugly award.'

'Not necessarily. It's all a matter of perspective. Your grandmother is okay.'

'Better than okay,' Britt corrected lightly. 'And your mother is great.'

'Most of the time,' Grant admitted with an exaggerated frown. 'When she isn't telling people things about me that are none of their business.'

Britt grinned. He smiled back and suddenly the hall seemed too small. Claustrophobic. Low on oxygen. Britt stepped back to gain distance between her body and his, but the magnetic draw was too strong. He reached to stroke the soft curve of her cheek. She tilted her face to feel the rough ridges of his fingers as they glided across her skin, its sensitivity heightened. His fingertip traced the outline of her ear around to the lobe, where he teased the little gold loop she wore. Then to the line of her jaw and the tendon along her neck, to the exposed tip of her clavicle bone then just inside the lapel of her suitjacket, to the point where the lapels met. His hard fingers stroked so gently . . .

'Grant.' Britt wanted to warn him to stop, but instead

his whispered name sounded as if she was begging. For more.

He dropped his head down. His mouth hung just centimeters from hers. She wasn't sure if it was his lips or his breath that barely brushed her mouth. 'I can't hear you,' he whispered. 'And I'm not sure I want to. You talk too much, Miss Reeve.'

She willed her arms to stay at her sides. Her will wasn't strong enough. Her hands braced against his abdomen, his muscles tightened under her touch, and she felt an intoxicating surge of power. His tongue tasted the swell of her lower lip. She felt it plumping under his slick touch. She closed her eyes to collect her strength and push him away, but instead her lips opened to let him in. His hands cradled her head gently as their kiss deepened. Britt could feel his blood pumping through his veins, and the rhythm of her own pulse rose to meet it. Their kiss built into a crescendo. Britt's hands inched up to Grant's chest . . .

Just before she lost her sense of time and place, Britt brought herself up short and pulled away, backing into the wall with a bump.

'This isn't a good idea.' Britt forced some strength into her breathless voice.

'I agree. I can think of a dozen more comfortable places to be doing this than in my parents' hallway.' Grant leaned down to caress her neck with his lips.

She pushed him away. 'That's not what I meant.'

Crossing his arms over his chest, Grant frowned. 'Oh, I see. You got what you came for so get out of your way?'

Britt was confused. 'What I came for?'

'You came to get the dirty little secrets of my family to hold over me in case I'm not working on your sister's case to your satisfaction. Sorry to disappoint you but our dirt isn't secret. Doesn't give you much leverage, does it?'

Fury replaced confusion. He wanted her but didn't trust her? 'I don't play games, Detective Collins. I came here to see about my sister's case, that's true, but not for emotional blackmail. You're paranoid. I'm sorry your life got screwed up by a tragedy. I'm sorry you keep flailing yourself with guilt – even to the point of manufacturing other people's motivations. But I can assure you I have enough problems with my own family without meddling in yours. And if you aren't investigating the case to my satisfaction, I'm not going to hold anything over you; I'll investigate myself.'

Grant glowered. 'No, you won't. It's too dangerous.'

'Don't give me that. You just don't want anybody stomping on your turf. Too bad. Arrest me if you want, but that's the only way you're going to keep me from doing what I need to do.'

Grant shook his head and rubbed his hand across his jaw as he stared at the woman before him. How had the tone of their passion shifted so dramatically in seconds? It took only a touch to ignite her desire and a word to set off her rage. He'd never encountered a woman so mercurial, so unpredictable, so independent. If he pushed her too far she'd be out of his reach, which would probably be the best for the case, for him. But maybe not for her. Until he could get a handle on what was behind this case he'd do best by keeping her in his sights, or he'd have two beauties on the slab at the morgue to deal with. He tried to ignore the sickening clutch of his stomach at that thought.

'Fine,' Grant ground out through clenched teeth. 'Stomp all over my turf, but you tell me what you find out and who you talk to otherwise I really will arrest you for obstruction.'

'Dandy,' Britt muttered as she turned and walked

down the hall, waving at Nancy as she stomped out the door.

Grant followed behind, stopping at the screen door to watch her head back to the little sports car. But as she reached the street, he caught sight of the telltale glint of broken glass around her rear tire.

'Britt, wait,' he yelled as he pushed open the door and ran down the front walk.

Britt ignored him and walked right into the glass, realizing what he'd been yelling about too late. She looked down at the pieces of shattered glass, then back up at the car to see the gaping hole in the driver's side window.

'Dammit,' Grant swore, taking in the damage as he drew up next to her. Grabbing her arm, he pulled her out of the way and back into the driveway, all the while searching up and down the street on the offchance he'd see who'd vandalized her car. 'Stay here,' he ordered.

Britt was too shocked to respond. She wrapped her arms around her midriff, welcoming the feel of her grandmother's keys digging into her side.

Taking note of every detail, Grant returned slowly to the car. The vandal had broken the window to get the car door open, because it was ajar. Although he knew the odds of finding the vandal were slim to none – the police department probably wouldn't even fingerprint unless he insisted – he still slipped some gloves on before he pulled the door open. He was greeted with a mess: – upholstery ripped to shreds, its stuffing littering the interior of the car like confetti, the glove compartment hanging open, its contents flung around the car, papers ripped, a box of tissues torn open. And on the floorboard sat a navy blue purse Grant recognized as Britt's.

As he knelt on what was left of the front seat and ducked

into the car to collect the purse, he heard a sound behind him and his head shot up, banging against the roof of the car.

'Ow!'

'Sorry for sneaking up on you,' Britt said quietly.

'I thought I told you to stay back there,' Grant pointed out as he rubbed the top of his head.

'You did,' Britt said, looking around him and into the car. 'What happened?'

'Someone was looking for something,' he said as he handed her the purse. 'Is anything missing?'

Britt glanced inside and opened her wallet, making a cursory check. Her eyes met his.

'Nothing.'

'Well, it could have been a vandal who was surprised and didn't have time to take your purse, but I don't think so. I don't think some punk would take the time to trash the car before he had this nice CD player and your purse in his hot hand.' Grant looked at the car once more. The tears in the leather weren't orderly or systematic, they were vicious. He looked at Britt. 'I don't think Jewel is the target. So, what do *you* have that someone wants?'

'Skin . . .' Britt whispered.

'Skin?' Grant asked, perplexed. 'Someone wants your skin?'

'No.' Britt shook her head. 'Skin is the guy you saw me talking to out here earlier. He's a photographer, a friend of Tori's. He was the first photographer to work with Risa. He thinks Risa stole some negatives of that first shoot the last time she was at his studio. He wants them back because he's signed some big contract with a publisher to do a photo book of Risa.'

'So why would he tear up your grandmother's car?'

Britt looked away. She swallowed.

'Because I told him Risa gave me something about a week or two ago. That's all I told him. It was a sealed envelope. I have no idea what's inside.'

'You told him she gave you something?' Grant asked, exasperated. He ran his hand over his jaw. 'Great.'

'Well, I certainly didn't know that he'd be this violent.'

'Where is this envelope?'

'In a safe place,' Britt answered distractedly.

Grant gripped her upper arm. 'Britt, tell me.'

'It's at school. I can't remember offhand where in the class. I didn't think it was anything important . . .'

'Okay, I doubt he'll look there.' Grant relaxed slightly. 'This could be the motive we've been looking for. How much is this Skin guy making on his book?'

'He didn't say.' A look of apprehension crossed Britt's face.

'And what's his real name anyway?' Grant asked impatiently, feeling an adrenaline rush as the first real break in the case clashed with his concern for Britt's safety. 'Surely it's not Skin?'

'I've never heard it,' Britt admitted. 'But someone in the business would know – maybe my father or Tori.'

'Well, we'll call them, but first let me get people over here to print this car.' He reached into his blazer and pulled out his phone. As he spoke, he hustled Britt into the passenger side of his car. He got behind the wheel and called Ortega, getting him to come oversee the processing of Jewel's car.

Britt began to shiver in the seat, although it was eighty-five degrees outside. Grant hung up and reached over to touch her face. She was ice-cold, and her eyes had taken on a faraway look. He turned on the ignition and pulled out of the driveway just as the first unit arrived on the scene. He had to get her out of there before she slipped completely into shock. He looked at his parents' house; his mother would be a help, his father and Evan hindrances. Jewel would still be at the memorial service and would be surrounded by friends and relatives well into the night. Britt needed quiet and calm. That left only one place. He turned the car in that direction and gunned the accelerator.

CHAPTER 11

Britt's sense of smell awoke first. She recognized bacon, browning butter, coffee. She opened her eyes. It was dark. She looked toward the familiar window on the right side of her bedroom. It wasn't there. Symbolic of her life lately, Britt thought with irony. Nothing was where it was supposed to be any more.

An unsettling sense of unease crept up her spine. Was it day or night? Who was cooking breakfast? And whose bed was she lying in?

Pulling the sheet up to her nose, she breathed deeply. Pure cedar-laced cotton was what she smelled. Clean, strong. Grant. The bed smelled like Grant. One question answered.

Britt sat up suddenly. Her hand fumbled to get free of the covers, then she felt for what she was wearing. Cotton, long sleeves, buttons up the front, closing on the wrong side. A man's shirt. Her fingers reached under the sheet to feel her own bare leg, skimmed up her thigh to check for panties. Britt sighed with relief. This would be embarrassing enough without having to search out her underwear.

Throwing the cover back, Britt swung her feet over the side of the bed. Her eyes finally located a dim glow of light coming from the left side of the room. She couldn't see the door until she'd padded across the plush carpet and around a corner. Then she could see a sliver of light along the floor and she could hear voices.

She stopped, heart speeding up. She held her breath and listened. Had one of the many girlfriends his mother had talked about stopped by? How long was she going to have to hide out in the bedroom?

But, listening more closely, Britt realized the conversation Grant was having was one-sided. On the phone, she decided. She recognized a hint of irritation in his tone and marveled at how she could feel she knew him so well after little more than a day. She knew she should look around for her clothes, but the thought of pulling on her hose and tailored suit was not as appealing as the smell of bacon.

Slowly, she pushed the door open and followed her nose through a small living room that was furnished with sparse Scandinavian pieces and was predictably tidy. Even the magazines were stacked in precise order, largest on the bottom and the smallest on the top. Britt smiled to herself as she thought of the disarray of her own home and how crazy that probably made Grant.

Her home. It would be somewhere else soon. The thought made her smile fade to bleakness. The house was just a building; Britt knew a home would be anywhere she made it. But it would be infinitely more difficult to do knowing Risa would never see it.

Standing in the middle of living room, Britt suddenly felt she'd been set adrift. Ever since Risa was born she hadn't made a decision about her own life without considering Risa. The idea of living for herself was overwhelming. Britt shoved the thought away and heeded the call of her growling stomach.

Britt peeked into the kitchen. Grant stood at the stove, spatula in hand, flipping the bacon in its pan. He'd pulled the tail of his white button-down shirt free of his khakis – his concession to relaxation, she supposed. He still wore his shoes. Didn't the man ever really let down his guard completely?

'How do you feel?' he asked, without turning around or pausing in his cooking.

Britt first looked around the kitchen to see to whom he was talking. It was deserted. How had he heard her come in over the spitting fat, the stove fan, the gurgling coffee and the sizzling butter in a pan that looked to be ready to scramble eggs? In the middle of all that Britt wouldn't have heard a brass band tromp through the room.

That he'd sensed her presence gave her gooseflesh.

Grant didn't seem so moved. He continued to flip the bacon with his right hand while he reached up with his left to get a coffee mug out of the cabinet. He poured the extra strong Java into it, put down his spatula and brought her coffee to her.

His eyes finally left the mug's rim and shifted to her feet, up her legs, bare to mid-thigh, then up his shirt, pausing at where it gaped open at the top before meeting her eyes. His face showed nothing but a deepening five o'clock shadow. Britt thought she saw something flare in his eyes as he studied her. But all he said was; 'You look a little better.'

'Wow,' Britt remarked dryly as she reached for the proffered mug. 'I must have looked pretty bad if this is better.'

'You did.' One corner of his mouth twitched up before it was forced straight again.

'Thanks, you charmer,' Britt murmured teasingly.

Grant's face closed up like a trap and he turned away back to the stove. 'Charm's my brother's department, not mine.'

Staring at his back, Britt opened her mouth for a retort, but an image of his physically disabled brother and his emotionally disabled father made her shut it again. She stepped into the kitchen and opened the refrigerator door. Peeking in, she was surprised by the contents: fresh raspberries, kiwi fruit, broccoli, asparagus, a variety of cheeses, a host of gourmet condiments, a couple of bottles of wine and beer. She finally located the milk behind one of these and poured a generous dollop into her mug.

Grant cocked an eye in her direction. 'Thought you drank yours black.'

First taken aback, Britt then remembered that he'd noticed her coffee at his parents' house. 'Sometimes,' she answered archly.

'A schizophrenic coffee drinker – so like the rest of your personality,' he remarked.

Britt put the jug of milk down with a thump. 'What kind of shot is that?'

'It's not a shot,' Grant said. 'Just an observation.'

Britt took a swig of coffee to ward off a hot retort and ended up burning her tongue instead. She tried to put up a brave front as it burned a path down her throat but she could have sworn she saw the corner of his mouth turn up again before he grabbed the skillet of eggs and dished them onto two plates.

'Maybe schizophrenic was a little strong,' he admitted as he added bacon, toast and a fruit salad to their plates. 'I should have said unpredictable.'

'Just because you're rigid as a hardwood tree doesn't mean my flexibility is wrong.'

Grant's eyebrows lifted slightly and he raised his hands in a placating gesture. 'Did I say it was wrong to be unpredictable?'

'No, but I don't think you meant it as a compliment.'

'But of course I did. It's not my problem you don't know how to take a compliment,' he said smoothly, flashing a smile so brief, so brilliant, it was like lightning – and had the same effect on Britt's nerves.

He was wrong, she thought. He *is* a charmer. And a dangerous one at that. He just doesn't know it. Good thing, too, or she'd be in real trouble.

Having taken back his poker face, Grant made a T with his hands. 'Time-out on our ongoing verbal debate . . . for food.' He motioned to the glass-topped wrought-iron kitchen table with its two chairs. Britt was about to sit when she realized her shirt – or rather his shirt – might ride up higher than was proper. But her legs would be under the table, she reasoned, So she pulled hard on the front tails of the shirt and slipped quickly into the seat. Grant had just taken the first bite of his food and he began choking. Britt looked at him with alarm.

'Are you okay?' she asked, and followed his eyes, which had a prime view of her lacy panties through the tabletop. Throwing her napkin into her lap, Britt felt her face catch fire. She avoided his eyes and began eating. Grant recovered with a few coughs and returned to his meal too.

'What's wrong? Never seen a woman's underwear before?' Britt couldn't resist the defensive challenge that jumped out of her mouth.

'I can't say that I have during a meal, and definitely not over bacon and eggs,' He paused, thoughtful. 'Or, rather, *under* bacon and eggs.'

Ready to be crestfallen – if he recounted exactly how many pairs of women's panties he'd seen – or indignant – if he claimed he'd never seen any at all – Britt instead burst into laughter at his answer. She looked up to see the surprise and pleasure that relaxed Grant's face as he, too, chuckled. His laugh was rich and smooth, like an expensive liqueur. The sound washed over her, spreading a strange warmth. As their smiles finally faded, Britt glanced out at the darkness beyond the window. Their shared laughter had made them too close, too comfortable together. She searched for small talk that would put the emotional distance back between them.

'Why are we having breakfast for dinner? Or did I just sleep a really long time and this is really breakfast?'

'It's dinner – a late dinner. This is my comfort food menu.'

'Oh?' Britt asked as she took her last bite of fruit salad. 'You in need of comfort?'

Grant looked up from his plate in surprise, then put his fork down. 'I'm glad to see you're back to normal.' He stood and collected both empty plates. 'Actually I was thinking you'd be the one in need of comfort. Stupid of me. I should've known better.'

The trace of irony in his voice hung between them, leaving Britt asking herself what he meant by that. He'd wanted to comfort her – but with what motive? So he wouldn't have to deal with a hysterical woman? Or because he cared? And why the sarcasm when she'd shrugged off his explanation?

'That was Ortega on the phone earlier. Sorry the ring woke you. They finished processing the car, got some prints, some hairs – probably mostly from you and your grandmother, so the two of you will have to go to the station to be fingerprinted. We'll run the others through the system, looking for a match. It'll take a while, so you'll have to be patient.'

'I'm not good at that,' Britt said with a frown.

'I've noticed.'

Bristling, Britt crossed her arms over her chest. Suddenly the cool air that floated up under her short shirt made her seem vulnerable to his criticism. She lashed out. 'Well, at least I get things done; it's better than going out of my way to let life pass me by.'

'What's that supposed to mean?' Grant looked at her with eyes so ungiving and intimidating she might have cowered had she not been so damned mad. Deliberately he turned off the water halfway through washing the dishes and faced her. She wondered for a second if he meant violence; it lurked there, she could feel it, see it. It materialized in speech. 'Ah, words of wisdom from a woman who's lived her whole life for her baby sister. Now that she's gone who'll you choose to live for now?'

His words hit home with the accuracy of an icepick. Tears welled up in her eyes. Her crossed arms wrapped around her middle. She wanted to run and hide and hated herself for such a weak impulse. Refusing to give him the satisfaction of knowing he'd broken her, she held his gaze through watery eyes and saw it change from challenge to concern. His brows pulled together and his forehead drew into wrinkles she imagined had deepened in a year of visits to his brother. She would not allow herself to be another charity case he felt sorry for and resentful of. She could take criticism and challenge, but not pity or even sympathy. She dropped her eyes to the floor.

A tear ran down her nose and splashed onto the ceramic tile floor.

It dissolved Grant's resolve.

In a step, he was before her. His hands reached out slowly to cup her face and lift it to his.

'I'm a bastard. I'm sorry,' he whispered, in a voice he tried to roughen but failed.

'Don't be,' Britt choked out.

He shook his head. 'Don't you ever just accept what someone says?'

'Only when I don't care enough to argue.'

'Well, this is a good sign, then,' Grant mused playfully as he moved his hands to the back of her head, luxuriating in the feel of her silken hair. 'I should worry when you stop arguing with me. It seems somewhat backward, don't you think?'

'Definitely,' Britt murmured.

'Uh-oh. Agreement. Guess I'd better find something else for you to argue about.' Grant slowly lowered his lips to hers in a teasing kiss. She tasted like nutmeg – sharp, spicy, slightly exotic, strangely familiar. He explored the delicate inside of her mouth with his tongue, searching for the source of the familiarity, striving to solve the mystery of her exoticism. Her response, both reluctant and eager, set his senses on edge.

He slid his hands out of her hair, down her chest, skimming across her breasts, their points beckoning him through the fabric. His fingers broke her hold on herself and her hands settled on his hips as his wrapped around her. She was such an emotional porcupine – putting out her quills whenever anyone go too close – that he was amazed at how soft she felt in his arms. He pulled her body against his – so petite and strong, feminine and antagonistic. Unpredictable and contradictory. And, right now, irresistible.

Grant knew she was bad for him; she wouldn't let him stay emotionally neutral as he wanted to be. He knew she was bad for the case; she distracted him, made him consider her in every decision. But right then as she shifted against him, her mouth pliant and mobile on his, Grant felt his reservations slipping behind his desire. Suddenly what he wanted was more important than anything else.

And he wanted Britt Reeve. All of her.

Making the decision seemed to let loose Grant's restraint. His kiss became more urgent, claiming.

An essence of ambivalence that had settled around Britt when he took her in his arms vanished in the wake of an ardor so intense that Grant suddenly found himself racing to meet it. Her hands moved to the small of his back, then around to his abdomen, pressing, exploring, bold and unashamed, all the way up to his pectorals. He stifled the groan that rose in his throat, quelled the urge to rip his shirt open to have her palms on his bare flesh.

Instead, he closed his eyes and forced his body still. All he could see behind the lids were images of Britt in her bra and panties, as she'd been half-unconscious hours before. Then, he'd only been concerned, hurriedly trying to get her comfortable and warm, in an attempt to ward off shock. But now the strong image of that fantastic body – rounded beneath lacy fabric, firm along the line of her thigh, sweeping down her tender abdomen, sensual in the peachy-olive of her skin – combined in his mind's eye with the hot wildness in his arms, and he could barely keep himself from finding out if the reality would equal his fantasy.

Opening his eyes, Grant met her luminous golden gaze. Words weren't necessary. They were asking each other the same question. And received the same answer. But it promised to be something so incredible, Grant had to be sure it wouldn't be marred by doubts.

'Are you sure?' His voice sounded foreign to his own ears, so ragged was it with his desire.

'Yes,' Britt answered, certain.

And she was certain. More certain than she'd ever been in her life – that this was right. Was it a sense of destiny, or nothing more than her own throbbing need?

Pushing those questions – indeed, all thought – out of

her mind, Britt focused on her feelings. Hadn't Grant said she thought too much? Well, she promised herself, not tonight. Tonight she would do nothing but feel.

Grant's lips feathered kisses along her hairline. Britt threw back her head and his lips traveled to her neck. His hands cupped her buttocks and he hiked her up until her hips were even with his stomach. She wrapped her dangling legs around him for balance, hanging onto his shoulders as he maneuvered out of the kitchen and into the dark bedroom. Somehow he kept his lips working on her neck as he walked over the threshold and laid her gently on the bed, bracing his thigh on the edge as he leaned over her for another deep kiss.

His tongue stirred her passion to a boil. She felt as if she was in the grip of a fever, restless, needy. His weight grew heavier on her, his hips fit against her, and she arched her hips to meet the swollen, demanding evidence of his arousal. Britt bit her lip against the way the feel of him there intensified her ache. He eased her up to the head of the bed, almost reverently cupping each breast in his hands. His thumb traced their contours, sending shooting trails of adrenaline through her body. Britt felt her life teetering on a precipice of something she couldn't define. She reached forward, to touch him the same way, to drive him as wild as she was. He groaned as her fingertips barely brushed the hard heat through his tightening khakis. One hand enveloped hers to still it.

'You could drive me all the way with just a look right now. Let me do all the work for a minute. Just lie there and be your sexy self,' he murmured, placing her hand back on her thigh.

He left it there and stroked upward, along the silky inner swell of her thigh. His fingertips brushed damp lace. Britt's hips squirmed with impatience and need. She could see the pleasing glimmer in Grant's eyes in the light filtering in from the living room; her heart swelled with the feeling of giving him pleasure. His long-fingered hand sneaked up her bare abdomen, under her shirt. It spanned her waist, traced her navel. Moved up to cup her breasts through their lacy encasements, their nubby tips strained against the fabric, and his touch there was exquisite pain. Britt closed her eyes with a deep intake of breath.

Then his hot, wet mouth was on the swell of her abdomen. Her hips tilted upward like an unconscious invitation. Britt swallowed, and buried her hands in his dense hair. His teeth pulled on the elastic of her panties, teasing them across the curve of her hipbone, letting them snap back gently. His hands cupped her hips, bringing her to his mouth, finally tasting her through the lace.

His sensual torture seemed to go on forever and yet not long enough, and then he straightened and began fumbling wildly for the buttons of her shirt. It wasn't going fast enough for him and, though Britt tried to help, he pushed her hands away and with a single move ripped the two sides of the shirt open, buttons flying. The ultra-controlled Grant losing control. Somehow the idea inflamed her passion, the pounding of her heart. She strove to make him even crazier than she was. Despite her own impatience, she shrugged slowly out of the sleeves, and Grant sat back to watch as she reached back deliberately to unhook her bra and let it fall. He sucked in a breath at the sight of her bare breasts that hung heavy and sensitive after his ministrations. He slid his own hands under each side of her panties and swept them off. Then he covered her body with his, pressing urgently.

Britt didn't hide the grin in her voice. 'Aren't you forgetting something?'

'Am I?' Grant's perpetual five o'clock shadow nuzzled her neck roughly and she imagined, with a shot of pleasure, the burn mark she'd have there later.

'Why don't you show me?' he offered.

Smiling wickedly, Britt reached up to unfasten his shirt, button by button. He tried to help, but this time she shoved *his* hands away and proceeded even more slowly. Grant groaned with impatience. Once he was completely unbuttoned, she slid her hands over his shoulders, reveling in the feel of his sleek skin over steely muscle. The shirt dropped off the side of the bed. Reaching for his belt, Britt let her fingers pet the trail of black hair that led from his navel to disappear beneath his pants. She could see him tense his body, the muscles on his abdomen jumping in response. She moved even slower. Her hands unhooked his belt, then, centimeter by centimeter, pulled his belt from the loops.

Heart pounding in her throat, her own nerves humming with need and desire, Britt unfastened the button of his pants. Grant held his breath, sat back on his haunches, straddling Britt, and tipped his head to the ceiling, exposing the strong cords of his neck. Britt sat up and tugged at the zipper made tight by his powerful erection. She could feel it swell even more at her indirect touch as she slid the zipper completely down. Her hand shook as she toyed with the waistband of his jockey shorts. Finally, Grant let out his breath and crushed her mouth in a searing kiss, pushing her back down to the pillow. He shoved off his pants and shorts at the same time, and the length of his body was on hers.

She hadn't imagined that anything could be hotter than the skin along his thighs, his lips on hers, but what he settled between her legs was. She hadn't imagined the ache she felt could get any worse, but it did get much worse as she felt the searing heat and the promising pressure.

As Grant drew his face away from hers she saw the etched planes of his face, so similar yet so different. Tight with control, wild with lust and alive with emotion. That was the difference – the emotion. Suddenly Britt felt a strange sensation of fullness, as if she was giving a gift to Grant. It seemed so odd. How could she feel so content and vibrating with need at the same time?

They seemed suspended in time for a moment. He staring into her eyes and she into his. A sudden and complete connection, before the passion took over. Her hips arched, begging. He responded with a single thrust. The intense rush of sensation Britt felt nearly overwhelmed her, and her instinct took over, meeting his rhythm, matching it, encouraging a new one. Grant drove deeper and deeper until Britt knew they were one – in sublime sensation, in intense emotion – until they both arrived in a mindless, timeless place neither had ever been before.

Britt awoke to the pre-dawn stillness before night gave way to day. She could sense the day there, waiting for the cue to appear, though the sun had yet to lighten the dark sky even to gray. She'd always, even as a child, been sensitive to the earth's rhythms, and now she lay still, feeling the unchanging time and allowing it to give her an anchor. Because this morning not only did she feel set adrift but blown by a storm – tremendous, frightening and exhilarating though it was – so far off course she didn't know where she was.

She and Grant had experienced something so tremendous – in many different ways – it seemed surreal now. It transcended the physical. Time and place lost their meaning. She had no idea when they'd drifted off to sleep, only that they had done that together as well. Had it been in her dreams or before she'd given in to them that she'd resigned herself to the fact that the love they'd made was ephemeral? It could never be replaced or repeated. The pain she wore like a shield had somehow reached the pain he buried deep down inside his soul and they'd connected and healed. Temporarily, she reminded herself. Day would break and so would their connection.

Britt turned her head away from the window and to Grant. He lay on his stomach, his arm flung across her bare midriff. It felt good to push up its weight with her every breath. One leg was cocked possessively over her thigh under the sheets, the other leg was sprawled over the cover. The hardness of his face was gone, as if it had been washed away by sleep. The deep ridges across his forehead and between his eyes had relaxed. The lips he held tight with control when awake were more inviting now, nearly buried in his almost-beard. She skimmed a touch across her abdomen, along the tender skin of her inner thigh, where his stubble had left evidence of their lovemaking.

She looked at the thick black lashes that he used to shadow his eyes intimidatingly when awake. Now they fringed the top edge of his cheekbone, giving Britt the strong image of him as a sleepy little boy. She drew in a deep breath and tried to brush off the nostalgia. She must possess an over-active imagination if she could make that great a leap – from what he was last night to an innocent child.

She had to start putting some distance between her emotions and reality, and thinking about him that way was not doing it. Closing her eyes, Britt ignored the feel of his heavier, rougher skin against hers and did what she always did to escape her emotions. She made a list.

First she had to call Grams, who must be beside herself with worry. Britt reveled in the deep pang of guilt that racked through her. She was never, ever irresponsible, but she had been last night by not calling Grams to tell her where she was. She knew someone would have given Grams and Tori a ride home yesterday. But leaving Grams to wonder what had happened to Britt at a time like this was cruel.

Britt almost bolted up for the phone, but her eyes went to Grant. If she moved, he'd wake up, and she wasn't ready to deal with him yet. *Coward*, she admonished herself.

After talking to Grams she had to arrange for the car to be towed to a garage and repaired. Then she'd go to the school and go through her classroom. Where had she put that envelope that Risa had given her? It could hold the key to everything.

Her heartbeat sped up at the thought that she'd had the piece of deadly evidence. Had Britt looked at it, could she have prevented Risa's death? *Please, God, don't let that be the case*. She couldn't live with herself knowing she could have saved her sister's life. Of course, if she'd come home from school early that day, could she have saved her? Or if she'd had a better security system? A dog?

An anguished moan tore from her mouth. Grant woke and grabbed her in a tight embrace.

'What is it?' he asked urgently in her ear.

Turning her face to his, Britt marveled at how he could go from sleep to consciousness in an instant. His gray eyes were even clear, without a trace of the haziness she always felt until she had a sip of coffee. His big, strong hand stroked along her ribcage. 'Are you all right?'

'Just fine,' Britt answered automatically. 'I just thought of Grams. She'll be worried. I should've called her last night.'

A relaxed smile spread across his face, and Britt's heart stopped. It wasn't the sensual grin of last night, tight with desire and promise. Nor was it the one-sided lip-curl he used when mocking her. This was a leonine beam of contentment and satisfaction. Her heart swelled in response.

'I called her after we got here last night. She got her mechanic to go pick up the car and she told me to keep you here until you seemed steady enough. You know . . .' Grant paused with a twinkle in his eye, as his stroking moved up her midriff. 'Jewel isn't too subtle, and I got the distinct impression she wanted you to stay the night.'

'Oh, great,' Britt muttered.

'What's wrong?' he asked with that mocking lip-curl. 'Does your grandmother often try to fob you off on men?'

'No.' Britt shook head, frustrated. 'It's just she thinks she knows what's good for me . . .'

Grant's hand cupped her breast and he moved halfway on top of her, his mouth inches from hers. 'And it wasn't good for you?'

'Yes, it was,' Britt said, fighting off a flush and her own rising libido in an effort to make herself understood. 'I mean, no. It . . . this . . . isn't good for me. Not now. In the middle of – '

Grant's mouth captured hers in a slow, all-encompassing kiss that left her weak and hot and more confused than ever. She couldn't resist him like this. Pushing him away, she sat up and crossed her arms over her swelled, exposed breasts. Grant leaned on an elbow and looked at her through those thick black lashes, waiting, not making it any easier for her.

'I owe it to Risa to get her justice. What happened between us . . .' She paused, deciding she wouldn't use the word that came to her mind, jumping ahead and leaving it unsaid. 'It's just complicating the investigation. It's complicated enough as it is. And for all I know you're doing it on purpose, to keep me off balance so I won't be in your way.'

As she spoke, she watched as the cold veil slipped down over the eyes that had so exposed what was in his soul just moments earlier. Britt's heart twisted. She wished she could take back her harsh words. She didn't really mean them but her defense mechanism was working too well. She had pushed him away. She just hadn't thought it would hurt this much.

Grant's eyes narrowed. 'Don't you do anything for yourself?'

She met his gaze, willing as much steel into hers. 'I want to do this for myself. I want to get justice.'

'Right,' Grant said, getting up out of bed suddenly. Britt tried not to look, but couldn't resist letting her gaze roam his lanky naked frame as he yanked the tangle of sheets away and strode to the bathroom.

'This whole thing was a mistake,' he called over the running water in the shower. 'We'll forget it happened. Good idea.'

Did he mean it? Britt felt the tears welling in her eyes and was glad he wasn't there to see them. She'd wanted this distance, hadn't she? Then why did she feel so lousy?

The phone shrilled. Britt jumped and stared at it as if it had come alive. Her instinct was to answer, yet she knew she couldn't, shouldn't. It was probably a girlfriend calling. Suddenly feeling that she wanted to hurt him the way his last shot had hurt her, she reached impulsively for the phone on the sixth ring.

'Hello?' She was almost embarrassed at how husky she sounded.

'Uh . . .' a tentative male voice said. 'Is this Detective Collins's residence?'

'Yes,' Britt answered, dread swirling in her stomach.

'Well, can I talk to him?'

The running water stopped and Grant appeared, dripping, towel wrapped around his waist. His eyebrows rose at the sight of her holding the phone. 'Calling a taxi? Shouldn't you dress first?'

The knot in Britt's stomach weighed down a retort. She held out the phone. 'For you.'

His dark brows dropped and drew together. He stepped to her and took the handset, holding it to his wet ear. 'Yeah, Collins, here.'

His face went stiff as his eyes drifted over Britt. 'Don't worry about it, Chief. It's just the cleaning lady. What's up?'

Britt bit down on her lower lip. *This is what I wanted,* she reminded herself.

Grant's hand gripped the receiver tightly. His tan went pale. 'No,' he whispered as the voice on the phone droned on.

'I'll be right there,' he barked, before hanging up.

His eyes, stony now, met hers. 'That was Rangel. The janitor of Turner Elementary just found the school principal dead. In your classroom.'

CHAPTER 12

Even though she'd expected it, the sight of dozens of dark blue uniformed San Antonio and school district police officers on the elementary school campus shocked Britt. Her foot tapped on the brake too hard and too soon. She stared at the open door of the familiar building where she was so used to seeing groups of four-foot-high people skipping joyfully – where now six-foot men and a lone woman stood, grim-faced.

She turned her car into the parking lot and pulled into a space without much conscious thought. One of the uniforms jogged up to her, as if he'd left his post and had been surprised by her sudden appearance. He pointed to the other side of the building, panting slightly.

'All press is supposed to be in the other parking lot. Please move your car over there.' He smiled politely.

'Then that's the last place I want to be,' Britt began, casting a baleful look in the direction he was pointing, half expecting to see the reporters sense her presence and come running around the corner.

'Sorry – '

'No, I'm sorry. I didn't introduce myself. I'm Britt Reeve. Detective Collins of Terrell Hills Police Department asked me to come. I'm a teacher. I guess Joe – uh,

Principal McGown – was found in my classroom.' Her voice thickened and she struggled to retain her composure. She cleared her throat.

He must have interpreted her faltering speech as evidence of a lie, because he gave her the once-over then told her to wait while he checked out her story. Britt sat in her car, trying not to envision the kids climbing the monkey bars. Somehow putting even their memories there seemed to taint them with the ugliness that had visited their haven.

Instead she thought of Grant. After getting the news about Joe, he'd turned cold and businesslike, as if she were in his office instead of naked in his bed. As she'd slipped back into her rumpled suit, she'd watched him put on his requisite white, long-sleeved, button-down shirt with a pair of black twills. It brought out the black strands in his salt-and-pepper hair and the effect was powerful. The only time he'd talked to her was in his car, right before he dropped her off at Grams's house to change clothes. He'd told her to ask for him here. He hadn't even tried to keep her away from the murder scene. Had he learned that it would be a lost cause, or did he need her there? He certainly hadn't acted as if he'd *wanted* her there.

Britt opened her eyes at the sound of a shout. The cop was waving her in at the door to the building. She locked her car, and then wondered why. The lock hadn't stopped yesterday's vandal. She doubted the presence of so many cops would either.

Several of the milling officers looked at her curiously as she walked by but didn't question her.

Once inside the door, she swallowed painfully. She could see the congregation of figures down the hall. She prayed that Joe's body would be gone. He'd been a good friend, a fair boss, and might have wanted to be more. Britt felt the heavy weight of guilt. Not only had she spurned his advances, but now he was dead and it might be her fault. Had the vandal moved from the car to her classroom in search of something? That envelope? What had she done with it?

Britt realized it might be too late to wonder. She should have come here last night to look for it instead of . . . being irresponsible . . . spending the night with Grant.

It might have saved Joe's life.

Or it might have cost her own.

'Miss Reeve. This is tough to take. I feel for you.'

Britt looked to her right suddenly, surprised that her feet had carried her down the hall to her classroom. Detective Ortega stood in the hall. In silent agreement, the plainclothes officers and photographer with him dispersed and left the two of them alone, looking into the room full of evidence technicians. Nodding once to acknowledge his statement, Britt stretched her neck to see around a burly man in the doorway. She gasped as he moved out of the way.

'Yeah, it's some mess,' Ortega agreed. 'I take it you and the rugrats didn't leave it like this?'

'No,' Britt responded numbly, staring at the books littering the floor, some torn apart. Britt could feel her own emotions tearing apart, leaving white-hot anger in their wake. Her kids did not deserve to have their class trashed like this. The blackboard had been taken down and thrown over four desks. Most of the other desks were up-ended. Blue, red and yellow fingerpaint was splashed all over the walls and rug, turning purple, orange and green as it mixed. The chaos and viciousness of it reminded Britt of the attack on the car.

She stepped closer to the doorway, drawn irresistibly to the disaster, but before she even put all her weight on her foot she drew back. She just couldn't bear to see Joe's body. She was barely dealing with his death in the abstract. A visual image would overwhelm her.

Grant looked up abruptly from a conversation with two detectives Britt assumed were from the San Antonio Police Department.

'He's gone,' he said, with an arresting look that drove straight into her soul.

How had he read her mind?

Maybe it was a lucky guess that he knew her hesitancy had to do with Joe. But Grant had looked so deep in conversation she hadn't thought he'd even noticed her presence, much less known what she was thinking. Unsettled further, Britt just nodded. Grant's eyes didn't give anything away and then he dropped them back down to where one of the techs was gesturing, ignoring her as if she'd vaporized.

Britt felt Ortega take her elbow. 'Can you handle looking around? You'll probably notice something out of place before we would. None of us has been around a kindergarten classroom in at least thirty years.'

Feeling like a mute, Britt nodded again, and Ortega guided her into the room. Grant and the techs were huddled in the corner near her desk. Britt stepped over the legs of the overturned desks. Out of the corner of her eye a bulky shape jumped out at them. Britt flinched. Ortega's hand tightened on her elbow.

'Hey, Detective. I said you and Collins could nose around the scene. No reporters. Get her outta here.'

Britt tried not to stare as she realized the burly figure in a shapeless sort of pantsuit was a woman. Her voice was a high soprano, incongruous with her body and made even more ridiculous by her talk-tough language. She held her hands on her hips and glowered at Britt.

'She's not a reporter, Dubinsky,' Ortega explained.

'Yeah?' Dubinsky was unconvinced. 'How come she looks so familiar, then?'

'She's the sister of that model. Y'know, the case we're working? Which is why we're here in the first place. And this is her classroom – ' Ortega began.

'Oh, yeah, that's why I've seen you on TV. Well, I got some questions for you. Care to step back out in the hall with me?' Dubinsky was already stamping toward the door.

'No, I wouldn't,' Britt called to her beefy back.

She spun around. 'What?'

'I just came from the hall, so I don't really want to go back now. Can't you just ask your questions here?'

Dubinsky studied Britt and shook her head. She glanced over at Grant. 'What's the deal with this one?'

Grant shrugged and Britt could detect the hint of a smile at the right corner of his mouth. 'An authority figure phobia?'

Ortega's mouth dropped open a bit. Dubinsky stared, then started shaking with laughter. 'Yep. Collins, you always were a good judge of character.' She walked back to Britt. 'I kind of like you. I like to buck authority every now and then myself. Probably not so much fun when I'm the authority, but we'll see. So where were you last night?'

The sudden change from jovial joking to interrogation caught Britt totally off-guard. She blinked twice. She could feel Grant's tension radiating from the other end of the room. Dubinsky's broad face pushed closer to hers.

'I was, ah, on Meadowlark earlier in the evening. My car, or rather my grandmother's car, which I was driving, was broken into,' Britt began, floundering for a direction that would end up anywhere but Grant's bed.

'Right.' Dubinsky had pulled out a notebook and was

scribbling furiously, filling it with far more words than were coming out of Britt's mouth. 'Collins mentioned that. Cops called out. Possible link with this. Potential suspect. Okay. What were you doing there?'

'I followed Detective Collins there to ask him some questions about my sister's case.'

'And?' Dubinsky's pen made a rare pause.

'And, what?' Britt stalled.

'And what comes next? At this point the night is still young.'

'And we waited there for the police to come – '

'Listen, I know you're not stupid, and I sure as tootin' ain't, so get past where the car's trashed and you finger the photog as the suspect. What next?'

Ortega cut in. 'Hey, you don't consider Britt a suspect, so ease up.'

'I don't know,' Dubinsky said with a pucker-faced glower. 'She might lead the list of suspects if she doesn't answer the question. And I mean right now.'

Britt cleared her throat and tried to force down the flush that was creeping up her neck. Why was she so transparent? She knew telling the truth would get Grant in hot water. It wouldn't look so great for her either. If she could just be vague enough without looking guilty . . .

She cleared her throat. 'I – '

'Britt was with me,' Grant cut in, voice staccato. Everyone turned to look at him. Ortega tried to hide a grin. Dubinsky tried to keep her jaw from falling open too far.

'All night. She was with me all night,' Grant finished in a monotone.

Britt felt a rush of emotion that was exhilaration – he'd come to her defense – and trepidation – he'd put himself on the line. And anger. That he'd had to step in to save her. She didn't need saving. She could take care of herself.

Grant was looking at Dubinsky, probably to avoid Britt's eyes. It was for the best, because Britt couldn't be sure which emotion would take over if he glanced her way. She felt the eyes of the other detectives appraising her in the loose blue jeans and old T-shirt, her hair pulled back in a messy ponytail. She could feel them thinking *What did he see in her?* and resisted the urge to shoot them a withering glare.

'Okay, Collins. You rode in on your white horse. I don't need to know what you were doing with the fair maiden. At least not yet. You know I might need to at some point. Can I assume you didn't leave your crib all night?' Dubinsky asked.

'That's right,' Grant responded tightly.

'Well, let's move on, then, Miss Reeve.' Dubinsky walked to the opposite end of the room, beckoning Britt to follow. Britt could feel Grant's eyes on her back. She didn't turn around.

'We're considering a link between what happened to your sister and the death of Mr McGown, here. You, of course, are the common denominator. You could have been the target for both these murders. You have to keep that in mind. However, it could be something else the murderer is after – something you have. Or these two could be unrelated. That would be a coincidence, and we cops aren't real big believers in coincidence, but first let's try to eliminate that possibility.'

Dubinsky paused to pull another notebook out of one of the jumpsuit's multitude of pockets. Britt's eyes dropped to the floor. She saw a pool of red behind an overturned child-size chair. It was a common enough sight in a kindergarten classroom. She'd thought she'd cleaned up all the paint after the kids had finished their art, but obviously not. One of them must have spilled a pot of paint and she'd missed it. Or the intruder had knocked it over. She leaned over to move the chair, intending to clean it up.

'Stop!'

Britt looked up at Dubinsky's command.

'What do you think you're doing?'

'I was going to mop up this paint before somebody tracks through it,' Britt explained, grabbing at a fingerprint-dusted roll of paper towels.

'Paint?' Dubinsky's eyes bugged out. 'Lady, you're either naïve or stupid, but either way that's blood and you can't touch it right now.'

Britt recoiled and sucked in a breath. The metallic smell she'd attributed to the non-toxic paint filled her nostrils. Feeling herself sway slightly, she grabbed for the cabinet to steady herself. 'It's . . . Joe's?'

'You know somebody's else had their head cracked open like a melon in this room lately?'

Britt leaned heavily into the cabinet. 'What happened?'

'That's what we're doing here, lady. But if you're asking how'd the guy go down – the murderer was hiding in here, we think, and when McGown came in he or she walloped him over the head with a blunt instrument. Then the guy tossed the place – maybe to make it look like it was a struggle or maybe because he was looking for something.'

Britt closed her eyes and tried to block out the image of a faceless person attacking Joe. It faded into a scene of that same faceless enemy slamming her sister's head against the wall. Then she began to sense a support, almost as if someone had put an arm around her, yet she felt no contact. She opened her eyes and looked straight into Grant's. His head was bowed, his hand had paused in the

239

act of writing in his notebook, yet his eyes bored into hers from across the room. He nodded at whatever it was Ortega was telling him but never stopped looking at Britt. She understood the message: *Tough it out*. She nodded and cleared her throat.

'Detective Dubinsky.' Britt wrestled with her manners. 'Forgive me for being obtuse, but I'm a kindergarten teacher and I didn't have any experience with this sort of thing until three days ago.'

'Yeah, okay.' Dubinsky waved off her apology. 'Well, let's get down to business, then. You knew the principal pretty well?'

'I've worked at this school for five years. Joe came about a year ago. We were friends.'

'Did he have any enemies?'

Britt shook her head.

'Any one of the teachers have a grudge against him? A parent upset about a kid?'

'No.' Britt frowned. 'Joe was very diplomatic, and popular with teachers and parents.'

'When was the last time that you saw him?'

'I saw him at my sister's funeral yesterday afternoon. I didn't talk to him, though.'

'Why would he have been in your classroom yesterday evening?'

Britt looked out the window, remembering the conversation they'd had in the hall the last day of school. Joe's thoughtful smile. The concern in his eyes. 'He came here to clean it up – set it up for the summer so I wouldn't have to come back.'

Dubinsky looked up from her notebook sharply. 'Why would he do that?'

'Because he was just that way.' Tears pressed against her lids. 'He was concerned about how I was dealing with the death of my sister. He offered to clean up my room. I told him I'd do it, but I guess he didn't listen.'

'You don't think he was here looking for anything, do you?'

Britt fidgeted. 'There was – maybe still is – something in the room that could be important, but Joe certainly didn't know about it. I didn't ever think about it until last night.'

Dubinsky planted her hands on her ample hips and stared Britt down. 'Am I supposed to guess what this something was – is?'

'It's an envelope – white, standard size. Risa gave it to me here at school about two weeks ago. I didn't look inside, didn't think twice about it, really. In fact, I can't remember exactly where in the room I put it. I was in the middle of a messy project and I must've stuffed it somewhere . . .' Britt surveyed the room worriedly.

'So you're telling me you don't know if the envelope is missing or not, or even if what's in the damn thing is important or not?' Dubinsky demanded, frustration turning her voice into a growl and her face beet-red. 'I have no use for people like you. You can't remember anything, but you make me run around on some half-baked notion forming in your half-baked brain. So I guess you can't even tell me if anything else is missing?'

'It's a kindergarten room. What else could anyone want. Rulers? Crayons? Reading primers?'

'Nothing in your desk, maybe, that someone wanted to get his hands on?'

Britt glanced at the front of the room, where the drawers in her desk were pulled open, papers littering the floor. A surge of anger flowed from a sense of violation. 'I guess you cops would know that better than I would.'

'Hey, lady, we didn't do that. The murderer did.'

Britt swallowed. 'Oh, I guess I'd better go through all that, then. See if I can find the envelope.'

'You do that,' Dubinsky advised as she slipped her notebook in a different pocket. 'In fact, check the whole room. We're done. Guess I'll have to turn you back over to the custody of the Terrell Hills police. House arrest, I guess. Right, Collins?'

Guffawing heartily at her own joke, and completely ignoring Grant's scowl, Dubinsky cocked her head at the other two detectives and they left. Britt walked quickly to her desk and began sifting through the mess.

What had she done with the envelope?

Ortega shook his head. '*Dios mio*, that Dubinsky gives all women a bad name.'

Britt glanced up fleetingly. 'How about all cops?'

Grant looked amused, Ortega shocked. He waggled his eyebrows at Grant. 'You got a libber on your hands?'

'I just don't like the double-standard, Detective Ortega. If a male cop had acted that way you wouldn't say he gives all *men* a bad name, would you?'

''Course not. Men are supposed to act like that,' Ortega answered with his trademark grin.

Britt couldn't help smiling at his sheer audacity. He was like an irresistible little boy – the opposite of his serious-as-a-heart-attack partner. They surely were the odd couple.

Grant watched the wordplay between the two, focusing on the range of emotions on Britt's face. First the embarrassment evoked by Dubinsky's crude comment. Then the fire in her eyes at the opportunity to right the injustice of Chile's comment. Then the dancing amusement at Chile's irrepressibility.

His heart twisted at the sight of her smile.

How did Chile do it? How did he go from insulting her gender to having her eating out of his hand?

If he'd said that, he and Britt would've been at each other's throats.

Or other parts.

Thinking of the night they'd shared evoked a physical reaction in Grant. He straightened his back and tried to will his body back under control. But his eyes returned to the dimple in her cheek, the tilt of her chin that exposed her creamy throat, and he couldn't help the tightening in his groin.

'I hate to disturb your cozy *tête-à-tête* – ' Britt started at the harsh tone of his voice. Her smile faded away. 'But you have to catch up to Dubinsky, Chile. We have to endear ourselves to facilitate the information flow.'

'Say no more, the Charm Patrol is on the way,' Chile said, with a wink in Britt's direction. He looked at Grant. 'I'm sure you two have a lot to talk over anyhow.'

Grant clenched his jaw. Gray eyes darkened. Chile pressed on. 'We're sure looking at a whole new complexion on the case, with all that's happened.'

'Enough, Chile.'

'*Bien*,' Chile responded, and with a wave to Britt he was out the door.

Sighing audibly, Britt dropped her eyes and went back to sifting through the desk. Grant watched her for a moment, then crossed the room to stand before her.

'You don't see it?'

'No,' she answered shortly, then looked up from her papers to meet his thighs at her eye level. She noticed the line of muscle just barely apparent beneath the black twill. She raised her eyes, intending to meet his, but hers were waylaid by admiring the fit of his perfectly starched clothes, which led to the memory of how he looked and how he moved without them. By the time she reached his face she had lost patience with herself and spoke sharply. 'Are you just going to stand there or do you want to help?'

'What do you suggest?'

Britt motioned to the bookcase, in front of which three dozen books lay pell-mell. 'Pick up those books and wipe them off before putting them back. They are the most precious things in the classroom right now.'

Grant groaned inwardly and was about to back out when he saw Britt's face. She was staring at the pool of blood again, her elfin face drained to a sick paste color.

'All right,' he said, more to distract her than because he was willing to do it. Her attention snapped back to him and she nodded.

He squatted down and gingerly reached for the books covered in a fine film of fingerprint dust. *The Hungry Caterpillar*. *Miss Spider's Wedding*. *Rainbow Fish*. *Baby Love*. Grant felt more uncomfortable with each unfamiliar book he put on the shelf. He realized he knew nothing about children. And didn't particularly want to know about them. Yet they were Britt's life. What did they have in common except one night of incredible passion, screwed up siblings and two murders? Great basis for a relationship, Grant thought wryly. Of course, what had he ever had in common with any woman he'd dated? They were each the right gender; that was about it.

This line of thought was getting him nowhere. He redirected his mind to Joe McGown's murder and how it might tie in with Risa's. Britt was the link to the two victims. Was that because she was the intended target in the first place or because she was the one left? That sent a chill through him. There was one other possibility – even more chilling – that Britt was involved with the murderer. He looked over his shoulder. Her grief and confusion were not manufactured – that much he knew – but they could easily be by-products of guilt and fear.

Grant looked at her petite form huddled over a drawer. She sighed, and even across the room he felt her emotional exhaustion. They had enough suspicious characters in this case without adding the least likely candidate. Why was he doing this to himself? To make it easier to push her out of his heart?

'Thank you.'

Grant spun around on his knee at the sound of her diminutive voice. He glanced back at the bookshelf. He had finished and been so lost in thought that he hadn't noticed.

'What were you thinking?' Britt asked quietly.

'Oh . . .' He stalled as he stood and brushed the black powder off his knees. 'Just about the case.'

'What about it?'

'Running through the list of suspects.'

'Which are?'

'Few or many, depending on how thin a thread of evidence I decide to use,' he said evasively. Skin, 'DEF' of the watch, 'Big Daddy' of the song, the uncooperative boyfriend, the car vandal, he thought specifically.

'You're still keeping me at bay,' Britt said, slamming the drawer closed. 'How can you share the ultimate intimacy and not share your thoughts?'

Grant was lost for an instant in her topaz eyes, warm with the memory of the night before. He looked away, out the window. 'It was just sex.'

Silence hung heavy between them. Grant couldn't bear to look at her, though he could feel the power of her anguish.

Or was it his own?

She stood and walked over to him. Controlled, determined steps. He crossed his arms over his chest and kept his gaze pinned on the rusted swing set out the window. Britt wrapped her fingers around his jaw and tilted his head until he was forced to look her in her flashing eyes.

'You can call it whatever you want now. But we both know what it was last night and it was a helluva a lot more than just sex. We didn't try to hide what we were feeling then. I may not want it to ever happen again, and you might want to change your perception of what it was, but you'll never take away my memory of it.'

Her lower lip trembled almost imperceptibly, but she held his eyes a minute longer. He hated to be contradicted. He hated what she'd said. Then why did he want to kiss her?

Suddenly Britt let her hand drop from his jaw, and she expelled a held breath. Grant shook his head, as if he could shake off the spell she seemed to put over him. He followed her eyes down to what she had in her left hand. A black address book.

'What's that?' he demanded, probably too harshly.

'Risa's book, with her schedule and phone numbers.'

'Why do you have it?'

Her face tightened momentarily then she answered, 'Risa left her schedule with me in case I needed to get in contact with her while she was out on jobs. I thought you might like to call her booker.'

'Booker?'

'The woman at her modeling agency who sets up the jobs. Her number is in there. She'd just come back from doing a holiday ad in Dallas.'

Grant snapped to attention. 'Risa had just come back from Dallas?'

'You bastard! I'm gonna kill you!'

Britt and Grant both turned to stare at the tall skinny form hurtling past the uniformed officer at the door to the classroom and headfirst into Grant's midriff.

They crashed into Britt's desk, ricocheting off onto the floor. Grant tried to pull back far enough to see the face of his attacker, but he fought with such crazed energy – kicking and punching like a piston – it was all Grant could do to fend off the blows. He considered reaching for his gun, but never had the chance. He connected his right fist with the guy's jaw just as he recognized him.

'Jayson,' Britt shrieked. 'Stop it. Stop it!'

Jayson paused and looked toward Britt for a split second, just long enough for Grant to grab his forearm and twist it behind his back. He flipped Jayson on his stomach then reached for his handcuffs, and an instant later had them snapped on both wrists. Grant waved off the uniformed officer who hovered impotently nearby.

'Get up,' Grant ordered, yanking at the handcuffs.

Jayson got up on his knees and Britt supported his elbow tenderly as he rose to his feet. Her brow was furrowed with concern as she looked at Jayson's bloodied lip. Grant felt a surge of pique. *He* was the one attacked and she felt sorry for the snot-nosed kid.

'Are these really necessary?' Britt motioned toward the handcuffs and looked at Grant with accusation. 'He's just a kid.'

'A kid who threatened to kill me, if you'll remember.'

'Oh, he didn't mean it.'

Grant raised his eyebrows a fraction. 'He sure acted like he meant it.'

Britt gave up on Grant and turned to the boy. 'Jayson, what were you trying to do?'

Jayson didn't answer. His chin almost rested on his chest, his hair hanging over his face. He was hardly breathing hard at all, which gave Grant another fit of pique as he brushed a bead of sweat off his own forehead and tried to bring his own breathing back to normal.

Finally Jayson cocked one surly eye in Britt's direction. 'He's a bastard.'

'Well, that may be true.' Britt shot a look at Grant. He narrowed his eyes in return. She continued to talk to Jayson. 'But why do you think so?'

''Cuz he and his brothers trashed Risa's locker,' Jayson said venomously.

Britt looked at Grant with a question in her eyes. He shook his head and spoke to Jayson. 'Listen, kid, nobody was authorized to go into Risa's locker. Tell us what you mean by trashed.'

Shaking the hair out of his face, Jayson glared at Grant. 'Like you don't know.'

Grant clenched his hands into fists and tried to keep himself from socking the kid again. He had new respect for high school teachers and parents if this was a 'good kid', as Britt had described him. He took a deep breath and blew it out before speaking. 'Why would I pretend I didn't know if I did it?'

Jayson looked from Grant to Britt and back again. 'So you wouldn't look bad in front of Britt.'

Grant looked at Britt, who shrugged. 'Why would I care how I look in front of her?'

'Hey, man I'm not stupid. I can catch the vibes.'

'The vibes?' Grant asked archly.

'Wrong word – the hormones. You guys are passing hormones faster than a quarterback.'

Britt blushed and avoided Grant's eyes. Grant cleared his throat. 'You come flying in here, beat me up and still have a chance to catch all that?'

'Hey, man, it doesn't take long to pick it up. I got

hormones myself so it doesn't take much, y'know?' Jayson admitted grudgingly.

Grant tried to keep from smiling. He was finally starting to see why Britt liked the kid so much and why Risa might have been attracted to him. He was honest and had a sense of humor. 'Plus,' Jayson continued, 'I've known Britt a long time and I've never seen her look like this. Not ever.'

Grant wanted to ask what 'like this' was, but when he noticed Britt blush more deeply he fell back on some half-hearted sarcasm instead. 'She's probably in shock is what you're seeing – a scrawny kid trying to beat up an old cop in her kindergarten classroom.' Grant got the keys to the handcuffs out of his pocket and unlocked them. Jayson gave him a guarded look of appreciation, then rubbed his wrists.

'So you cops didn't do that to Risa's locker?'

'No. What is "that" anyway? You ever going to tell us?'

Britt looked up with razor-sharp interest as Jayson continued. 'Well, I went over there this morning. I thought if you guys wanted to check the locker you would've done it by now, so I thought it was safe if I got some stuff out I wanted to keep. To remember her by, y'know?'

He was talking to Britt now, and she nodded.

'I thought the building would probably be locked, but I decided to try the door before I went to the janitor to open it up for me. But it opened, then I noticed the lock was scratched up, like it had been picked real hard, y'know? I got mad right there 'cuz I thought the cops were jerks not to just call up the principal and get her to open up. Anyway, so I was half expecting something bad when I walked down the hall and saw the wrapping paper all in shreds around on the floor and the door to Risa's locker hanging on one hinge. So I'm real mad at this point.'

Grant put up his hands in jest. Jayson brushed a lock of hair off his forehead and flashed a sheepish smile. 'Nah. I believe you. Plus, if Britt likes you, you gotta be all right.'

Britt wouldn't meet Grant's eyes as Jayson continued. 'The locker was totally trashed. Books all with their pages ripped. Her folders all torn apart. Like someone was mad 'cuz they couldn't find something. I thought it was you cops, all mad 'cuz you couldn't find anything bad – like drugs or something. Britt told me you guys were trying to make it look like an accident.'

Grant glared at Britt. 'We were trying to find the truth. Still are. Except now we know it was murder.'

'Yeah.' Jayson took a shaky breath. 'So I'm thinking now maybe it was the killer looking for something in her locker – some piece of evidence – '

'Or he's looking for the envelope,' Britt interjected.

Jayson looked confused.

Grant asked, 'Did Risa tell you about an envelope that she was giving to Britt for safekeeping before she went on her last job?'

'No,' Jayson answered, turning to Britt. 'How come she didn't give it to me? What's in it?'

'We don't know,' Britt said simply.

'It was probably some "Dear John" letter to me,' Jayson muttered sullenly, drawing back into his shell of teenage angst.

Grant looked up sharply. 'Why do you say that?'

''Cuz I know she was about to dump me.'

Britt shook her head. 'No. Jayson, she loved you. She said you were the one who kept her in the real world.'

'Yeah, but she was finding out that the fantasy world she worked in was pretty cool, and the guys in it were rich and charming and handsome. The real world doesn't compare too great.'

Grant watched the chip on Jayson's shoulder grow with each word, changing his personality before their eyes. Would it be enough to drive him to murder?

Before Grant could set a verbal trap for the kid, his beeper sounded.

He checked the number, fished the telephone out of his pocket and dialed.

'What's up?'

'I found the answering machine tape, *amigo*. And you're gonna want to hear it, *pronto*.'

CHAPTER 13

'So where did you find it?'

Grant watched Chile try to squirm out of answering. They sat in Britt's kitchen, having decided to play the message tape on the machine on which it had been received.

The front door opened and both men turned at the sound of Britt's voice, which drifted in from the foyer. 'I'm just going into my bedroom.'

Chile waggled his eyebrows. 'Is that an invitation, *amigo*?'

Grant frowned in response. Ortega was enough of a joker without any encouragement. Plus, Grant preferred not to think about what had happened the night before.

When Britt had overheard Grant tell his partner to meet him at her house, Britt had asked to follow him there in her car in order to pack clothes to take to her grandmother's house. Even though he'd known her real reason for coming – to hear the tape – he'd agreed, but only because he wanted to limit their conversations to a minimum. Talking to her seemed to lead to an argument . . . which led to completely illogical responses in both of them . . . which led to . . . well, where they'd ended up last night. And that was the one place Grant would not end up again.

Not with Britt Reeve anyway. It had been a mistake the first time. It would be idiotic to repeat it.

'Reliving your night of passion?' Chile goaded Grant's thoughtful silence.

'Listen, Chile, she was in shock. You should have seen how that car was torn up. I wasn't going to dump her off in the middle of the post-funeral reception in that condition.'

Ortega shook his head slowly with mock adulation. 'You are such a good *hombre*, Tom. I am in awe.'

'Shut up,' Grant warned. 'You're just trying to get out of telling me where you found the tape.'

'Aye-yi, you're too smart. That's why I hate you sometimes, Tom.'

'Well?'

'It was under the jelly jar.'

'The jelly jar? In the kitchen?'

'No, the bedroom – ' Chile began, having the grace to look sheepish.

Grant held up one hand. 'I don't want to know any more about that jar, except that you found the tape under there today.'

'No, actually Genie found it there a coupla days ago.'

Grant shook his head. As if the case wasn't complicated enough, he had to have Cheech as his partner. 'Why didn't she give it to you, then?'

'Well, she thought it might hold some incriminating evidence as to my extracurricular activities, so she kept it to listen to and it took her that long to find a girlfriend with the kind of answering machine that would play it.'

Grant rubbed his palm across his stubble and realized that if he went one more day without shaving he would have a full beard whether he wanted it or not. He wondered idly whether Britt would like it. Then he noticed Ortega watching him expectantly. 'Do you have to have constant prompting to get anything out?' Grant groused.

'Nah, I just like to bug you. Anyhow, she listened and called me, and I called you and – '

'Okay, Chile, I know the rest,' Grant cut in, exasperated. 'How many messages?'

'Three. All call Risa by name. One a woman, who sounds like she works for the modeling agency. One a guy, who doesn't ID himself but is familiar with Risa. The last one is the hot *tamale*. It's from the sister.'

Grant's chest constricted. 'Britt?'

Ortega shook his head. 'Tori.'

Grant nodded, awash in relief. Did he really suspect Britt of something or was the suspicion his mind's way of keeping walls between them? 'Let's hear it.'

Chile got up, brushed off his pants and ambled over to the telephone in the living room. Grant followed, trying not to push him forward. He glanced at the door to Britt's bedroom but it was still closed.

Ortega got settled – finally – in the chair next to the answering machine. He put the tape in and pushed the play button. Grant leaned a shoulder against the wall as the electronic beep filled the room, followed by the date and time announcement.

'Risa, it's Joan. I got a job I'm sure you're going to want. It's in San Antonio, down at the Riverwalk. They want you, being a hometown girl. It's set for next Tuesday. Call me ASAP. Bye.'

Another beep, followed by, 'Seven-forty-five a.m., Wednesday, June third.' And the message:

'I've been thinking about what you said, Risa, and I won't let you do it. I'll do anything – *anything* – to stop you.'

Grant pointed at the machine. 'Play that again.'

Once he heard the voice again he was sure. 'That's Jayson,' he said over the third beep.

A big sniff preceded the final message, received at 9:04 the morning of the murder. Ortega met Grant's eyes as a woman's voice filled the living room. 'Risa, you bitch. It's Tori.' There was a pause as the speaker slurped a sip of some beverage. Alcoholic, if her slurred speech was any indicator. 'I heard about the article in that magazine. "The Reeve sisters: the Risa and the Fall" What a catchy title. You come up with that yourself? I've been thinking about it and it's making me mad all over again so I wanted to call you. You could've warned me, thankless baby sister, before you flushed my career down the toilet. You are such a bitch. You wouldn't even be in modeling if it wasn't for me. And now the whole industry is ready to kiss your ass while kicking mine out the door. And it's not even like you *want* to do this for a living.' Another sniff. Another gulp. 'You're going to pay for what you've done to me, you ungrateful little bitch. You'll pay.'

The threat hung in the air as a tangible presence.

Until Grant heard a gasp behind him.

'Britt,' he muttered under his breath as he spun around.

She stood in her doorway, hand at her mouth, her hazel eyes watery and large in her pale heart-shaped face.

'Had Risa listened to those messages, do you think?' Britt asked as her hand dropped from her mouth.

Grant didn't want to answer her question; an answer would let her relive the horror of Risa's last moments. He shot Ortega a warning look which he characteristically ignored.

'Maybe, maybe not,' Ortega told her. 'The message light wasn't blinking when we were first called to the scene, so if she didn't hear the messages, someone did.'

Nodding absently, Britt gazed out the window. Her knuckles whitened as she gripped the hanger she held in her hands. 'I wouldn't have wanted her to hear that. To die thinking her sister was out to get her. Tori isn't bad, just narcissistic and selfish. She didn't have much of a chance to be anything else – being told beauty was everything from the moment she was born then being pushed as a child into being paid to be beautiful. She just didn't have a chance.'

'She does now,' Grant pointed out. 'Have a chance to be something else.'

Grant was gratified to see her eyes lose their faraway look and snap back to the present. But he should have quit while he was ahead. Instead, he finished his thought aloud.

'It just doesn't look like she *wants* to be anything else.'

Britt's eyes flared with golden lights. 'How sensitive you are. I say that like it surprises me. What else should I expect from Mr Sensitive?'

'What's that supposed to mean?' Grant asked, trying to ignore Chile's silent chuckling.

'It means – ' Britt put her fists on her hips ' – that my sister is crying for help.'

'You don't get along with your sister,' Grant pointed out.

'You're right,' Britt admitted.

'In fact, you don't even really like her, do you?'

'No.'

'Then why would you care if she was crying for help, much less even notice?'

'Because I love her.'

'That doesn't make any sense.' Grant rubbed his jawline with exasperation.

'It doesn't?' Britt stared at him, aghast. She tried to

hold her tongue but couldn't. 'Did you like your brother when you jumped in the path of the bullet meant for him – when he was defending a drug dealer and you thought he might have been worse?' She studied his face, the tight cords in his neck, saw his urge to drop those sunglasses over his eyes to hide what she saw there. She answered for him. 'No, of course you didn't like him. But you took that bullet. Why? Because you loved him. He's your brother. Why do you go visit him now? Because you like him? No. He's not easy to like. But you love him, so you go.'

'I don't have time for this,' Grant ground out through tight lips. Here was his chance to slip the sunglasses down over his eyes, and he did it as he brushed past Britt going toward the door. 'I've got a suspect to chase down.'

'*Hey, amigo. Esperas.*' Chile jumped to his feet, ready to chase down his partner.

Grant stopped, his hand on the doorknob. 'No, you go back to the station and bring Rangel up to date before he starts paging me every ten seconds. But first stay and lock up here after *she* goes.'

'*She's* going right now,' Britt said, on his heels. 'With you.'

'Oh, no, you're not.' Grant spun around, and Britt nearly ran into him. He put his hands on her shoulders to stop her. The electricity that shot through her at his touch was instant and nearly overwhelming. He swore under his breath and let her go as if she was on fire, holding his palms hovering in the air about two feet away, as if he didn't know exactly what to do with them.

'Your boss told you to keep me abreast of the situation.' Britt paused as Chile made a choking sound behind her. His choking turned to chuckling as she went on, unabated, 'And I consider going with you to interview my sister as being kept abreast.'

'I think Collins misunderstood the Chief's order,' Ortega began, laughing outright now.

Grant shot Ortega a look. 'Shut up, Chile.'

'Oh-ho, take down the date,' Chile began sarcastically. 'The *muy* articulate man has resorted to – '

'Shut up,' Britt threw over her shoulder.

'Well, *bien*. You were a perfectly nice girl before you hang out with him for one night and his bad temperament rubs off on you. *Que malo*.'

The buzz of a beeper ended Ortega's brief diatribe. Grant checked the number. 'Great. Rangel already. Just get back to the station, will you, Chile?'

'It might take a while if I have to wait for your *sancha* here,' Chile began sullenly.

'She's not my *sancha*,' Grant argued.

Britt saw her opening. 'I promise not to say a word if you take me with you to talk to Tori.'

Grant raised his eyebrows. 'I don't think that's possible.'

'What's not possible?' she asked with false innocence, trying to buy enough time to keep her temper under control. She wanted to argue, but knew if she did it would ruin her chance to be in on his talk with her sister.

'That you could hold your tongue for any length of time,' Grant answered with a scowl.

'Now,' Chile added, '*you*, on the other hand, holding *her* tongue for any length of time . . .'

'Try me,' Britt challenged, ignoring Chile's snide remark to bore through Grant's mirrored lenses with her most intense look.

Grant's beeper went off again. He looked at Chile and flipped his thumb toward the door.

'I guess I'll have to,' he answered grudgingly.

* * *

'Mother, will you let her come home with me? You don't need this – not with your hip, your poor health – '

'I'm not in poor health. You just wish I were so I'd die and you wouldn't have to put up with me any more.'

'That's not true. I'm horrified, Mother, that you would suggest such an odious thing.'

'Oo-hoo. You must really be upset. You used "thing" in a sentence. The high-falutin' university professor. What would your students think?'

Britt and Grant stood just inside the kitchen door watching Neil Reeve and Jewel square off on opposite sides of the kitchen counter. For Britt it was a common scene, and she almost walked straight past them. But Grant stopped and she hung back with him.

'Do they always go at it like this?' he whispered in her ear.

'This is a polite conversation for these two,' Britt answered, meeting his eyes as he lifted his sunglasses to the top of his head. 'Where do you think I learned my oratorical skills? Certainly not from Sophia and Dad; they hardly spoke to one another.'

Neil slammed his drinking glass down too hard on the counter. His face turned red with the force of his anger. No one belittled his professorship and got away with it. No one but Grams, Britt thought. She gets away with everything.

She glanced at Grant and saw his iron-gray eyes narrow appraisingly. It was his add-one-to-the-list look. She bit her tongue to keep from talking him out of it. Glancing back at her father, she had to admit that despite his starched suit and tie he did look menacing, but the idea that he might hurt Risa was ludicrous. He'd loved her. Hadn't he? Or had it been her ability to make him money that Neil loved? And hadn't Risa told him she was quitting?

Britt stamped her foot, impatient with herself. Ortega was right; Grant was rubbing off on her – she was beginning to be as suspicious as he was, and it had to stop.

Neil finally got a handle on his anger and he cleared his throat. 'Mother, I refuse to play this game any more. I'm going to take Tori with me, argument or no argument.'

For the first time Britt noticed Tori, just visible beyond the kitchen counter. She sat on the couch in the living room. She looked like hell, bundled up in a blanket even though it was ninety-five degrees outside and not much cooler in the house. Her perfect-peaches skin had faded to the color of library paste, her hair hung greasy-sweaty around her face. She was shaking.

Neil continued as if Tori wasn't there. 'It was bad enough that she was so strung out I couldn't put her on at the press conference. Now I've got to get her into shape before her interview. I think the right amount of alcohol, not enough to make her drunk but just enough to get her past the withdrawal symptoms, will work . . .'

'Sorry to cut into your plans like this, Professor,' Grant said as he stepped into the middle of the kitchen floor. 'But Tori has to come with me.'

Everyone looked at Grant in surprise. Britt noticed a twinkle in Grams's eyes as they shifted from the cop to her granddaughter and back. 'Well, Detective, good for you. I hope you have more luck with my bull-headed son than I do.'

'I don't need luck, ma'am,' Grant said. Britt nearly fainted at the polite reverence in his tone. She'd never heard it before. 'I have the law on my side.'

'I guess you need that badge to hide behind, Officer,' Neil cut in. 'You better hang onto it tightly if you plan to keep me from my daughter.'

'I've got news for you, Professor. Tori is of legal age.

She can make her own decisions and fight her own battles and if she wants to see you when I'm done talking to her, that's her business.'

Neil's color began rising again. 'Why do you want to talk to her? Where are you taking her?'

Oblivious to the barrage of questions, Grant strode to the couch and put out his hand. Tori's glazed eyes took a minute to focus. Then slowly she put her slim, shaking hand in his. He put his arm around her waist to help her up. She leaned against him as they walked back toward the kitchen door. Jewel grabbed up a pair of tennis shoes and handed them to Britt, who followed close enough so Grant wouldn't try to leave her behind.

They could still hear Neil sputtering inside, even once they closed the doors to Grant's car. Britt felt a momentary flash of guilt for leaving her grandmother to deal with her father alone. But as she cast a sidelong look at Tori, leaning heavily against the opposite door, she realized that – right now – her sister needed her more.

Grant was amazed they made it back to Britt's house without getting in an accident, the way he kept looking in his rearview mirror – first at one side of the back seat, to make sure Tori hadn't passed out, and then to the other side to see how Britt was dealing with the situation. Britt was wearing her emotions even more obviously than usual, and he could clearly see her vacillate between anger at Tori, then pity, then worry and brief flashes of suspicion.

He'd considered going back to the police station to interview Tori, but then imagined the mess that would be, with Rangel jumping on him the moment he was in the door and reporters camped out on the front steps. There had been so little action at the scene of the crime that they'd abandoned it. Plus, he wanted to see her face when she heard the tape play.

And when she saw where Risa died.

Once inside the house, Grant allowed Britt to settle her sister in an old oversize armchair before he began.

'Tori,' he said loudly to get the attention of her heavy-lidded eyes, 'I'm going to tape this conversation.'

The taping wasn't unusual, for it was policy for all on-duty Terrell Hills police officers to tape every conversation they held with civilians. Grant thought pointing it out would sober her up, but she gave no indication that she'd heard. He watched her closely as he turned on his tape recorder but she seemed so engrossed in her own misery from alcohol withdrawal that he wasn't sure she realized she was even in her sister's house.

'Where were you the morning of June third?' Grant asked, knowing he could get the answer from the long-distance phone records but wanting to compare her answer to that fact.

'Did you arrest me?' Tori looked a little more alert as she tightened her arms around her knees, drawing them closer to her chest.

'No,' Grant answered. 'This is a voluntary interview.'

Tori looked from Grant to Britt. 'I don't remember being asked,' she said, sticking out her lower lip like a child.

'Do you want to leave?' Grant asked.

Any hint of rebellion slipped out of Tori's face. She looked lost. 'Where would I go? To Grams's house to listen to her philosophy on life until I'm sick? To Dad's house to have him tell me how to play the media just the right way in order to "transition" from modeling into acting? Or back to the jerk I live with so he can tell me what a has-been I am and how I should sleep with him every way from Sunday because that's all I'm good at? Maybe he's right.

'Jail doesn't sound so bad after all, copper,' Tori said, holding out wrists so painfully thin that Grant was sure he could get both in one handcuff. 'Go ahead and arrest me.'

'Tori,' Britt admonished from across the room. 'You don't mean that.'

'Damn right I do,' Tori answered sullenly. 'What do you know about me and what I mean anyway?'

Grant glared at Britt. She shut her mouth and held up her hand to show she remembered her part of the bargain.

'Miss Reeve.' Grant stopped pacing and sat in the chair Chile had been in just an hour before. 'Answer my question.'

'Oh, fine. I was in my apartment, or at least I think I was.'

Grant sat up straighter. 'What does that mean?'

'It means, copper, that I was in my apartment when I started drinking and doping and that's where I was when I woke up after drinking and doping.'

'And that's where you were when you called Risa on Wednesday morning?'

Tori's unevenly plucked brows drew together over her aquiline nose. 'What do you mean, "called"?'

'As in on the telephone.'

Tori flashed a look at Britt. 'She said I called her? She's a liar. I hadn't talked to her in six months.'

Grant could see Britt wanted to defend Risa but he was proud when she looked to him for the answer instead. 'You talked to her answering machine,' he said.

He pressed 'play', not realizing Chile had rewound it completely, so they had to listen to all three messages. Grant watched Tori closely. Her eyes brightened at the booker's message, showed no response at Jayson's, but when her message began her gray face went almost white. She began rocking from side to side as she rested her chin on her knees. She ran her tongue along her cracked lips.

'That low-down magazine. How could they do that to me after all the covers I've done for them? And Risa. Some sister she was – '

A sob tore out of Tori's throat. It could've been for the magazine article, but he was beginning to doubt it. Grant bet she wasn't so callous as she let on. Or was it guilt that had driven her to tears?

'So, did you make this call?'

'I don't know. I guess so. I remember thinking a lot about it after my agent told me about the article. I remember calling Dad to tell him about it and him giving me some line of crap like "any publicity is better than no publicity", but I don't exactly remember calling Risa.'

'And you don't remember leaving the apartment from when to when?'

'From . . . Tuesday morning until I left to fly here Thursday.'

'Your boyfriend with you the whole time?'

Tori looked out the window. 'I guess.'

Grant glanced at Britt, who shrugged and glanced at Tori with concern.

'Any other altercations with Risa I should know about?'

'No. We weren't something out of *Little Women*, if that's what you're asking. We didn't sit around doing each other's hair and talking about boys and the meaning of life. But I did my work and she did hers, and we ran into each other now and then and we'd go out to dinner or something. Or at least we used to. We hadn't done that in a long time.'

A wistful expression crossed her face. One minute she seemed so callous, and the next she was tender. Grant wondered how much of it was acting and how much real. Tori was so unlike Britt, who couldn't fake an emotion if her life depended on it. Grant decided to change his tack to see if he could get to the real Tori.

'You're pretty good friends with the photographer known as Skin, aren't you?'

Tori's face tightened. 'I thought we were talking about Risa?'

'This does have to do with Risa.'

Tori looked at Britt for support. Britt crossed her arms over her chest. Tori looked back at Grant. 'I know Skin. He's shot some of my jobs over the years. I haven't seen him lately.'

'When was the last time you saw him?'

Tori swallowed, her Adam's apple convulsing in her thin neck. 'Oh, I don't know. Uh, a month? A few weeks ago?'

'Was that socially or on a job?'

'It was for business,' Tori answered evasively. 'I guess I really didn't see him, though, just talked to him on the phone.'

Grant could see she was hiding something. Talking about Skin had made her nervous. But why? Was she in it with him? Grant had to see if he was headed in the right direction.

'Do you know anything about a book Skin was working on?'

'Book? What book?' The stridency in her tone hit a false note. Grant could see Britt had heard it too.

'One more thing, Miss Reeve, do you know Skin's real name?'

Tori was clearly taken aback by Grant's shift from high-pressure to hands-off. 'Sure, it's D'Wayne Flanders.'

'Middle name?'

'Who knows.' Tori ran trembling fingers through stringy hair that looked as if it hadn't been washed in days. She rubbed her eyes and left dark smudges of old mascara in the deep hollows under them. Her cheeks were sunken below graceful cheekbones. Even with all that she was still a beauty, the kind of classic beauty Grant had always dated. The kind of beauty that he didn't look beyond, because he didn't expect to find anything else. He thought of the way he reacted with Britt – so differently, from deep in his gut. Was it because she was not classically beautiful? Or was it because her emotions and vivaciousness overtook her physical appearance? Grant realized now with a twinge of guilt that he should have tried to see beyond the aesthetics of those other women. He could see there was more to Tori, but it was so damaged, so shrunken from neglect, that she probably didn't even know it was there herself.

'How did he get his nickname?' Britt asked from her seat in the corner, breaking the silence.

Grant snapped back to attention. He hadn't realized he'd been so lost in thought.

Tori laughed mirthlessly. 'Because he got his start shooting girls who were hoping for a big break – the less clothes the better. He used to yell: "Skin. I want more skin." You get the idea.'

'Oh, no,' Britt breathed.

Tori read Britt's stricken expression. 'Still worried about baby sister, even though she's dead?' Tori asked caustically. 'Don't be. His pictures of Risa were always kosher. Dad made sure of that.'

'Is he successful?' Grant asked, more to break up the fight brewing between the sisters than because he really wanted to know.

'Creatively he's talented. But financially he's a disaster. Professionally nobody can stand to work with him because he's so whiny and obnoxious. He's never had two dimes to rub together – he blows it trying to act like a bigshot, trying to impress everybody. Why all these questions about Skin, anyway?'

Ignoring her question, Grant reached into the message machine and plucked out the tape. 'Stick around town, Miss Reeve. I'm sure we'll need to talk again. It sounds like an extended visit with your grandmother might do you some good.'

'Mind your own business.' Tori glared with dull eyes.

'I wouldn't be a very good cop if I did that,' Grant answered.

'Like I care,' she said.

'You ought to,' Grant pointed out as he stopped to stand in front of her chair. 'Because if I'm not, I might just pin your sister's murder on the wrong person. You wouldn't want me to do that, would you?'

CHAPTER 14

Sophia stood at the railing of their hotel balcony overlooking the glittering San Antonio River as it wound through downtown. They were staying on the famed Riverwalk in a hotel that met Carl's specifications; it was a four-star establishment, it was beautifully appointed and it protected its guests' privacy like no other. If you didn't want to be there, you weren't there as far as the staff was concerned.

And so far Carl had decided they weren't there.

Sophia stepped back as a couple walked along the water on the flagstoned path below their fourth-story room. She realized she was more eye-catching and recognizable than usual, after their appearance on the local and national evening news. The all-news station had aired film of the funeral and the encounter outside the police station every half-hour for a day.

So far so good. Carl had come off as sacrificing and solicitous and she'd seemed a tragic figure, mother of a beautiful wasted life. But they had to be careful. Very careful. The whole scene could backfire in an instant.

Which was why they still hadn't called that detective. Carl's advisors were still debating how to deal with the police, and until Carl decided which opinion to go with they were in hiding.

A sharp knock sounded at the door inside, but Sophia didn't even turn to look. It was one of the entourage, surely. Carl's executive assistant could answer the door.

The door opened and Sophia heard the woman arguing with someone. Sophia tuned them out. Her therapist repeatedly warned her away from participating in disagreements. They were bad for her own emotional equilibrium. Taking a few cleansing breaths, she walked back to the railing.

'You're a hard woman to find, Mrs Lawrence. Hiding from something?'

Sophia spun around to face the police detective, as if he'd materialized from her thoughts. He leaned against the frame of the open French door, wearing a light summer blazer and black twills, the collar of his cotton shirt open at the throat to reveal a hint of the black chest hair beneath. He was extremely attractive – powerful in his sensuality – here at close quarters, more so than he'd seemed the other day, standing there with Brittany outside the police station. Sophia liked to compare those she met with the famous, it gave her a way to catalogue them. This detective reminded her of a leaner, tougher version of a TV doctor. Only the cop's eyes weren't sensitive; they were penetrating.

Sophia felt a stir of lust. Maybe there was another way to deal with the police. A way Carl and his cronies had not considered.

'Detective.' Sophia held out a manicured hand as she stepped toward him. 'Can I offer you a drink?'

'No,' Grant responded shortly, ignoring her outstretched hand.

Carl's assistant hovered just behind him. 'I'm sorry,

Mrs Lawrence. He buffaloed in right past me, ma'am. Shall I page Mr Lawrence at his meeting?'

Sophia ran her eyes up and down the man before her, so obviously appraising that he fidgeted. 'Oh, I don't think that will be necessary. Not yet – isn't that right, detective?'

'Right.' His hooded eyes gave nothing away.

'That will be all.' She dismissed the assistant, her eyes never leaving the detective. 'And take a break. Go shopping. Go see the Alamo. Go do something.'

'If you say so, Mrs Lawrence.'

At the click of the hotel door closing Sophia approached him. 'I'll go get that drink now, Detective . . . what was your first name again? I was so distraught when we first met I'm afraid it's slipped my mind.'

'Grant Collins, Mrs Lawrence. And I don't want a drink.'

'Oh, Grant,' Sophia breathed as she ran a finger along the edge of his blazer's lapel. 'You aren't supposed to drink on the job? I won't tell.' Her finger moved back to her own chest to mark an X on her right breast. 'Cross my heart.'

'I certainly appreciate your discretion,' Grant said as he sidestepped around her to an empty spot on the balcony. 'But I don't want anything but the answers to my questions right now.'

'I have answers,' Sophia promised as she eased into the chair next to her, letting her slimline skirt ride high up her bare thigh. 'Answers to a lot of things.'

'Look,' Grant said as he reached into his coat pocket for his notebook, 'the only answers I want are to questions that pertain to Risa. I don't have time to play word games with you. I'm looking for a murderer and you're going to help me do it if I have to get a court order to force you.'

'Oh, force me – such dirty talk,' Sophia cooed, misinterpreting his irritation for sexual excitement. Her invitations were rarely refused.

Grant snapped his notebook shut. Sophia leaned back and curled her foot around her other calf.

'I am sorry,' Grant began in a clipped, controlled tone, 'that you are so hard up but, listen, call for room service when I'm gone. Until then pull your skirt down and try to give some honest answers. That is all I'm interested in here.'

Sophia stared into his gray eyes, flinty with his anger, gauging whether he was into sexual role-playing or whether he was serious. She finally had to admit he meant what he said and tried to find a way to mend her wounded pride and thwarted plans. 'I think you misunderstood my hospitality. I am offended by your implication.'

'Fine,' Grant sighed. 'File a complaint.'

'I just might do that after I speak with my husband about it.'

'You do that,' Grant said, relaxing visibly. 'Now, tell me about you and Risa.'

Sophia struggled to get her bearings. She couldn't seem to get this detective off-balance no matter what she did, and that was leaving her a bit out of synch. Maybe he was gay, she told herself to salve her ego. She'd have to salvage the conversation as best she could. His first question was not a good place to start. What could she say? It was a minefield of possibilities and not many good.

She reached for her cigarettes on the table next to her. She put one in her mouth and waited for Grant to light it for her. When he didn't, she lit her own, trying to hide her pique. She held her burning cigarette in her fingers, hungrily inhaling smoke as it drifted past her nose.

'Well, as you may know, Risa and I were not especially

close. When my life with my second husband took me out of the area, I realized it would be best for her to stay here with her father and sisters. That was my most difficult decision ever. I did it for Risa. Then, when my life with my second husband turned into a nightmare . . .' here Sophia paused, as she always did when telling this story, to let her eyes grow appropriately moist '. . . and Carl came to my rescue, I was kept busy with his preparations to offer himself to represent the people of Texas in Congress. And of course by then she was busy being a famous cover girl. It didn't leave much time for a close relationship with my baby.

'I regret that now, dearly.' Sophia allowed a single sob to escape her lips as she closed her eyes to squeeze out a tear, tipping her head ever so slightly to allow it to travel down her cheek.

Grant watched her performance with fascination. First she was a seductress and now a grief-stricken martyr. And he didn't believe either one was real. She was an opportunist who'd gambled wrong when he'd walked in the door. She'd first thought the way to his mind was through his pants, now she was trying to do it through his sympathies. It seemed unbelievable that Britt, so ruled by her emotions, could be related to a woman who had to manufacture feelings in order to have any at all.

'So you didn't have any contact with Risa?' Grant finally asked.

'Not much. I tried to call and initiate a relationship, but her father and Brittany had poisoned her mind to me. After the lies they told Risa was understandably hesitant to forge a new understanding. I don't think I would have ever given up, though . . .'

'When was the last time you saw or talked to her?'

The hand holding her cigarette shook like a leaf in an

ever so slight breeze. She raised the cigarette halfway to her lips but then let it drop, breathing in the smoky air deeply. She swallowed. She recrossed her legs. 'I don't remember the exact date. It was a while ago. Maybe two years or so.'

'Nothing said then that might help us with what's happened to her now?'

'Certainly not, just idle small talk. Nothing deep or threatening.' Sophia's laugh sounded like breaking glass and was just as shocking, so inappropriate was it.

Grant began to sense he was shaking her out of her act. He could feel truth lurking.

'Where the hell is everybody?'

They both turned their heads at the sound of the booming voice in the hotel room foyer. Carl Lawrence stood, hand shielding his eyes from the daylight coming in from the balcony as he squinted to make out who was there.

'We're out here, Carl,' Sophia called – a little too eager for the interruption, Grant thought.

'Who's we?' Carl said jovially as he filled the doorway. 'Hey, Detective.' He reached out to take Grant's hand and give it a politician's pump. 'I was just about to give you a call. We've been busy as hell or I would've called you sooner. How'd you find us?'

Grant felt the razor-sharp point of his question amid the good ole boy banter. Carl didn't like it that Grant had come looking instead of waiting to be summoned. Grant bet he wouldn't be getting any engraved invitations to Capitol Hill after the election.

Stretching his lips in a polite smile, Grant ignored the question. 'I was asking your wife some questions about Risa.'

Carl's smile slipped a centimeter, and he slid a probing

look at Sophia as he leaned down to smack a kiss on her proffered cheek. He looked around the patio, then over the railing at the light foot traffic below. 'Let's go inside,' he ordered ushering everyone in through the French doors.

'I hope she was able to help you,' Carl said as he took a seat next to his wife. Grant remained standing.

'Not as much as she wanted to,' Grant answered smoothly.

Sophia gasped unintentionally and then tried to hide it in a delicate cough. Carl reached over to rub her shoulder and offer her a glass of the club soda on the glass end-table.

'You okay, darlin'?'

'Fine,' she said, with a sweet smile to Carl and a sidelong glare at Grant.

'I'm finished talking with your wife, now, Mr Lawrence,' Grant said. 'If you can spare a few moments now, I'd like to talk to you.'

'Go ahead, son – and call me Carl.'

'I need to talk to you alone – and don't call me son.'

'Well, now, you're not too tactful are you, s . . . I mean, Detective. But you're honest, and I got to respect that. Don't recommend you run for public office, though. Or at least not till you learn to wrap that honesty in a pretty little package. Not too many people in politics can drink it straight. I could give you a few pointers, though – '

'I won't need them, Mr Lawrence,' Grant interrupted. 'Running for public office is the last thing I want to do.'

Carl smiled good-naturedly and stood. He held Sophia's hand as she stood too. 'Well, darlin', I guess it's time for you to get your daily massage anyhow. Do you want me to call for the hotel masseuse?'

'No, I'll just lay down for a few minutes.' She shot Grant a warning look before she disappeared into the bedroom. But a warning of what, Grant wasn't sure.

Carl watched her leave with admiration shining in his eyes. 'She's one helluva fine woman, Detective, but a thoroughbred – and you know they require more tender loving care. Sometimes I wish I'd hitched up to a quarter horse, but not too damned often. Believe me, she's worth all the trouble.'

Grant didn't respond. Not only because he didn't want to debate the validity of the equine analogy but because he was trying to figure out just who Carl Lawrence was. He was attractive enough to look good on television but not attractive enough to be intimidating. He was friendly and jovial, quick with a smile and a compliment. He was, overall, likable. But Grant could just sense something there under the surface, something malefic he couldn't define. He'd seen a flash of it when Carl had come onto the patio and looked at Sophia. And he'd felt it when Carl had asked him how their secret hideout had been found.

Maybe it was just his politicianism. Maybe Grant's own prejudice against that was coloring his impressions of Carl Lawrence. Maybe he *was* just a good ole boy. But a smart good ole boy. One didn't turn a thousand acres of not much more than West Texas sand and scrub into fifty-thousand acres and a fortune without brains.

Carl had moved to the bar at Grant's right and begun mixing a drink, even though it was only a little after noon. Over drinks was how good ole boys made deals, and Grant figured that was what he was being primed for – a deal.

'You take it straight or on the rocks?' Carl asked, holding up a bottle of very expensive Scotch.

'I guess soda is out of the question?' Grant couldn't resist saying.

Carl looked at him as if he'd uttered blasphemy, then boomed a laugh. 'I like a man with a sense of humor, though I got to say that you never struck me as that kind of man. Glad to see I was wrong.' He poured three fingers of the Scotch into a glass with a Brahma bull etched on the side along with an insignia. It was the same insignia that appeared on Carl's silver belt buckle and Grant took it as his ranch's brand. He wondered what kind of man traveled with his own highball glasses.

Carl handed the glass to Grant. 'Not for me.'

Frowning, Carl seemed at a loss for a moment. Then he grinned, showing his need for some dental work which Grant guessed was carefully avoided in order to make him look like an 'everyman'. 'Suit yourself,' Carl said as he took a swallow of the drink himself and settled in an armchair.

'Now. I want you to tell me why you're here.'

Grant sat on the loveseat, bracing his elbows against his knees. 'I'll ask the questions first; then you can ask yours.'

Carl motioned him ahead by lifting his drink.

'Tell me about your wife's relationship with Risa.'

'There's not a lot I can contribute, since I just married Soph not long ago,' Carl paused to swallow the last of his Scotch. He rose to refill his glass, talking with his back to Grant. 'I actually never met Risa. And unfortunately won't have the chance now. It's such a damned shame. I know Soph is fond of all her girls. She saw Tori every now and then. She tried to contact Risa a time or two but they never could hook up. I really am to blame.'

Carl turned and faced Grant. 'Soph has sacrificed her own life for me. I wanted to run for the Senate and that's a whole helluva lot to ask a wife. She's done it without complaining, but I know she has to regret not being closer to her girls.'

Grant doubted that. He was more interested in why Carl was trying to put a good face on Sophia's actions, other than the obvious image factor. It smelled like a diversionary tactic. But to divert him from what?

'Your campaign keeps you busy,' Grant said, trying to keep Carl off-balance enough to make a mistake. 'Can you run down your schedule for the past week for me, or should I talk to your assistant?'

'Oh, no, no,' Carl said hurriedly, waving his hand. 'No need to bother her. I can tell you. The body's going – ' he paused to pat his bulging stomach ' – but the mind's still there – for the most part.'

Carl waited for some good ole boy appropriate comeback, which Grant didn't give. After a moment Carl's smile slipped a little but held, more frozen than before. 'We were in Amarillo, Lubbock, detoured down to Alpine to see an old friend, then to Midland for a couple of days. Oh, and there was a side trip to Dallas,' he added, too casually.

'A campaign stop?'

'Oh, no.' Carl looked at his watch. 'Just talking to a couple of people who want to join up with the campaign.'

'I see,' Grant said, although he didn't. Something about Dallas had made Carl nervous. He'd developed a tic in the corner of his right eye. He kept looking away from Grant in the hope of hiding it.

'Why all these questions about my schedule?' He furrowed his brow in exaggerated fashion. 'Oh, right – the family is the first suspect.'

'I wouldn't consider you and your wife family, Mr Lawrence,' Grant said as he snapped his notebook shut, stood and headed for the door.

'Oh,' Carl said as he scrambled to his feet. 'Good. That's good.'

Carl's florid face was a mixture of confusion and relief as Grant closed the door.

★ ★ ★

Sophia emerged from the bedroom as soon as she heard the click of the door latch. Her eyes searched her husband's face. She saw . . . It was unfamiliar, so difficult to catalogue . . . Was it uncertainty? It couldn't be. Her husband's single-minded focus was the attribute that had lured her from her billionaire second husband in the first place. Where was that focus now? She sure couldn't see it.

'What happened?' she asked, careful not to show her desperation.

'He wanted to know about you and your girls and then about our schedule for the past week,' Carl said as he went to the bar for another drink.

'Do you think we're real suspects or he's fishing?' Sophia asked. She tightened the sash on her blue silk robe.

'Of course he's fishing. That's what cops do. They fish until someone bites, and if none bite, they grab the fish closest to shore and throw it in the cooler.'

Carl's right eye tic was acting up again. That wasn't good. Sophia hoped that detective hadn't noticed. He was way too observant. Why hadn't they been saddled with a cop who was partial to coffee and donuts, or at least good sex with a beautiful woman?

'Can't we just leave?' Sophia asked as she sidled up to Carl and began rubbing on his chest. She loosened his silver bolo tie and unbuttoned the top two buttons of his western-cut shirt.

Carl made a guttural sound deep in his throat. His hand went straight to Sophia's left breast and he gave it a hard squeeze. She smiled. She had him now.

'We can't leave; we'd look guilty. Everything, all the media coverage, is too good to blow the image now. Let's stick around until Risa's affairs are settled – until we know just which way the police are headed with this investigation. We've been through worse, right, darlin?'

'I suppose, Carl,' Sophia said.

'Who do you want, darlin?'

'I want you,' she purred. 'My Big – ' She couldn't finish as his mouth engulfed hers in a messy kiss and his hands grabbed clumsily at her robe.

'Show me paradise, darlin'. Maybe I'll find some inspiration there.'

Sophia led him, grabbing and groping, into the bedroom. If Carl wanted inspiration she'd give it to him.

It was the least she could do.

'Why didn't you tell me that Risa was being stalked?'

Britt had jumped out at him from behind a wall as he walked through the hotel lobby. How she'd found him there was a question that would have to wait, because right now she had him cornered and wasn't giving any ground.

'What are you talking about?' he asked.

'I don't like you keeping things from me,' Britt continued as if he hadn't spoken. 'I know you're trying to shake me, but keeping secrets is just going to make me stick closer. So forget that strategy.'

Grant didn't want to touch that argument, so he went back to her first statement.

'How could I keep something from you that I didn't even know?' Grant pointed out. 'Where did you hear she was being stalked?'

'Detective Ortega told me.'

Of course. Chile's way of getting back at Grant for having to go back to the station and listen to Rangel rant. Somehow he'd gotten this stalker information and told Britt so she'd make life difficult for him.

Grant blew out a breath, willing his frustration to go with it. It didn't. 'What else did Chile tell you?'

'He said that she'd gone to the police during a job about

a year ago in Acapulco because there was a guy hanging around their shoot. He kept asking her to go out with him, calling her in her hotel room, leaving her messages. "Marry me. I love you." That kind of thing. She told him to leave her alone but he kept on.'

'Well, that doesn't exactly qualify as stalking. Sounds more like an admirer to me.'

'No. According to the Mexican police, he'd bothered her on two other shoots, in LA and New York, but neither one of the police departments there gave it much credence. They told her to ignore him and he'd go away. Acapulco arrested him and kept him in custody until Risa left town.'

Grant felt the anticipation of a break. Interpol might have his prints. But he reminded himself this was second-hand information from Chile, wherever he might have fallen into it. Both Chile and Britt had a tendency to exaggerate. He put a hand on Britt's elbow, spun her around and guided her to where he'd left his car, nodding at the valet whom he'd left on guard.

'How'd you get here, anyway?'

'Grams dropped me off.'

'A senior citizen accomplice,' Grant muttered.

'She's happy to help when she knows I'm right.'

'Which is always,' Grant offered dryly.

'Of course.'

The valet opened the passenger door for Britt. Grant turned the key, the engine roared to life and the car lurched into the bricked street with a squeal of tires.

'Risa never told you about this "stalker"?' he asked skeptically.

Britt read his tone and anger flashed in her eyes before they filled with regret and tears. Grant couldn't imagine what she would say when she finally looked away and opened her mouth.

'I'd probably be the last person she'd tell.'

'But I thought you two were so close.'

'In this case, too close. I tried to tell her what to do too often.'

'Imagine that,' Grant put in.

'Don't give me that,' Britt warned, swiping at her tears with the back of her hand. 'This is hard enough.'

'Okay,' Grant said, not able to resist reaching out and capturing one of her tears on his fingertip. 'I'll restrain myself.'

Britt drew in a deep breath. 'You see, I was vocally opposed to her going into modeling. It's such a superficial business – men manipulating young women, girls, really, to sell products and, worse, their idea of what women should look like . . . what they should wear, how much they should weigh and how long their legs should be. I'm opposed to the whole industry as a social determinator. But on a personal level, which with Risa was more important to me, I saw it as having the potential to destroy her self-esteem. I'd watched it change Tori for the worse.

'Risa had a stronger foundation to begin with but she was at such an impressionable age. It scared me. I tried many times to argue her out of the business. Of course, Dad told her I was jealous that I couldn't model and Tori depicted it as one big party. I don't think what they said had any effect. Risa had decided it was the best way to pay her way through med school. Dad had refused to do it, saying she was too pretty to be a doctor.

'So the first time she encountered a sleazy photographer or a client who thought paying a model meant he was getting more than pictures, she told me and I went ballistic. Then the bad stories stopped and she got more famous, and I thought she'd reached a higher plane. But now I know there's no such thing in modeling, except for the handful of superstars. Since she wasn't quite there yet, she probably was keeping the truth from me.'

Britt's liquid gold eyes met his. 'Why couldn't I have just kept my mouth shut and listened?' she asked desperately.

'Because that's not who you are,' he answered. 'She wouldn't have wanted you to be anything else.'

'But if I had been – more stoic, more understanding – she would've told me about the stalker and I could've taken precautions. Then maybe she'd still be alive.'

'You don't know that, and this might not have anything to do with her being in the modeling industry,' he said, although he wasn't quite sure he believed it. He pulled the car into the parking lot of the police station. 'Let's go inside and talk to Chile.'

Chile was sitting on the desk of the comely temporary city hall secretary, who was filling in while her predecessor was on maternity leave. The temp hadn't learned yet that you didn't smile at Chile if you wanted to get any work done. Chile had his hand over her computer keyboard so she couldn't work if she wanted to. He was telling her a joke in Spanish when he caught sight of Grant.

'Hey, *amigo*, unless you got a signed confession I beat you today.'

Grant cocked his head toward the coffee room, and after a long goodbye to the temp Chile followed. He greeted Britt.

'Haven't you ever heard of sexual harassment, Chile?' Grant asked.

'It's only harassment when they don't want the attention, and who ever didn't want attention from me?' Chile asked with his trademark grin.

Grant shook his head.

'Before we get to the big news, we got a call from a trooper over in New Mexico who said he stopped a guy fitting Skin's description taking a leak by the side of the road the morning after Risa was found. Said Skin seemed nervous and was headed toward California until the trooper mentioned Risa's murder, and then Skin headed back for the Texas border.'

'Strange . . . If he had something to do with her death, why would he head halfway to California before turning back for the crime scene?' Grant mused.

'Maybe he'd just remembered his watch,' Britt put in.

Chile arched his eyebrows. Grant didn't want to encourage her so he didn't tell her she might be right. Instead he changed the subject. 'Tell me about this stalker. How did you dig this up?'

Before Chile even opened his mouth Grant knew he didn't want to hear the story. It was one of those.

'You know Genie's sister's husband, Enrique? Well, his cousin's girlfriend was talking to her mother in Cancun yesterday. The mother told her – Enrique's cousin's girlfriend – that her sister-in-law's granddaughter's second husband was in the *policia* there in Acapulco and he'd been talking big about meeting that model who died. Well, so the mother – '

'Chile, just leave out the people and get to the story.'

'Okay, Tom, just 'cuz you're too *estupido* to follow . . .'

'Chile.'

'Yeah, so this *policia* is the one who took Risa's complaint about this guy bugging her in Acapulco. He thought she was sweet and scared and not getting much help from the people there working with her, so he locked the guy up until Risa was gone. He said the guy was *todo loco*. He hated to let him go because he knew he'd end up finding Risa and bugging her again.'

'He think the guy had potential for violence?'

Ortega shrugged. 'You know those guys who hear voices; they can do anything.'

'Let's get busy finding a name, matching prints . . .' Grant trailed off as Chile held up a sheaf of papers he had in his hand.

'Richard Sorlirk. Twenty-nine years old, unemployed circus worker, small-time record of shoplifting, indecent exposure. An IQ hovering in the eighties.'

Grant shook his head. It didn't fit. Murderers who chose poison weren't stupid. Neither were murderers who tried to throw the police off-track. The evidence just didn't fit with a stalker. Especially not this stalker.

'And . . .' Chile was savoring some juicy piece of information he was about to impart. Grant gave him his attention or he knew he'd never hear it. 'His prints match some on the outside of the hotrod granny's car.'

Britt gasped. And Grant's heart speeded up its beat. He held his adrenaline in check. 'What about the inside of the car?'

Ortega shook his head. 'There's one set we still can't ID. And none in there match this Sorlirk, but he could've put on gloves.'

Rubbing his palm along his bristly jaw, Grant shook his head distractedly.

'It's the best lead we have,' Chile pointed out.

'Right,' Grant agreed reluctantly. 'Let's see if we can find Sorlirk.'

'I'll kill him.'

Britt had only whispered, but her tone was so determined, so strong, so like a prophesy to be fulfilled, that it reverberated around the tiny room.

Grant put his hands on her small shoulders and bored his eyes into hers. 'We didn't hear that.' Her eyes weren't focused on him, so he shook her until she looked at him. 'Don't ever say that again. Don't even think it. Do you hear me?'

'She can't help hearing you. The whole building probably heard you,' Ortega put in.

Grant flicked a look at Chile and nodded once. He'd overreacted, but what Britt had said made him scared. Not for Sorlirk. He'd kill him himself, given the opportunity. He was scared for Britt. She had lost her perspective. He'd done that once before and it should have cost him his life.

CHAPTER 15

'Codeine.'

Britt stared uncomprehending at Grant as he hung up the phone at his desk.

'What about codeine?' Britt asked hesitantly, half knowing the answer to her question even though she'd been downstairs during his conversation with the Medical Examiner's investigator.

'Codeine is what killed your sister,' he answered, watching her carefully. 'The killer used a narcotic analgesic, methylmorphine – what we call codeine.'

Ortega was on the phone at his desk but his eyes were on the two of them.

Grant stood up. 'Let's take a walk.'

Britt nodded and followed him out the back door. She had gone emotionally numb. Dealing with the vague concepts surrounding her sister's murder was easier than the raw facts. Knowing Risa was murdered enraged her, hearing the details of how she'd died was too painful to bear. She felt her body's defense mechanisms kicking in and she tried to fight it, tried to set her mind to accept the facts and process them analytically instead of straight through her heart.

Since Terrell Hills did not have any downtown of its

own – it shared a downtown with the next door bedroom community of Alamo Heights – its police station was set right in the middle of a neighborhood: a mixture of affluent family homes and million-dollar estates. Grant put his hand loosely on the small of her back as they walked along the curb down Garraty Street. The gesture both charmed Britt and irritated her. She was pleased he felt protective of her but irritated because he felt he needed to be.

Irritation won out and she moved away from his hand as they strolled down the road. Grant didn't say anything but she saw the muscles in his jaw bunch. He was obviously waiting for her to indicate she was ready to talk.

'Where . . .?' She swallowed hard, willing the lump in her throat to go away. 'How . . .?'

'It was found in her bloodstream and in the spilled can of diet soda on the counter,' he said in a monotone that Britt appreciated. It helped her distance herself from her emotions.

'But codeine? I didn't realize that it was fatal.'

'It's extremely toxic; just a half dozen drops can be deadly.'

'But wouldn't she have realized she was drinking it?' Britt asked.

'I asked the ME investigator about that; he says it's transparent and doesn't have an odor, but it does have a fairly bitter taste. But so does diet soda, if you think about it, so she might have only thought she'd got a bad can of soda.'

'But how did it get in the soda in the first place?'

'I don't know,' Grant said, looking at Britt with a new element of admiration. 'I hadn't had a chance to even consider that. Did she drink that brand often?'

Britt nodded. 'It was her favorite.'

'Then we may never know. She could have had a visitor who put the drops in,' she could have left the can open in the refrigerator and the codeine was put in by an intruder. There were no signs the can was tampered with, according to the techs.'

'Did he . . .' Britt cleared her throat '. . . describe how she might have died?'

Grant stopped and faced Britt. They had encountered no cars on their walk through the neighborhood. The sun peeked out from the clouds and its light glinted off the silver strands in his hair and the sunglasses on the top of his head. His gray eyes were fringed closely by his black lashes as they squinted in the bright light.

'Codeine suppresses reflexes. Within twenty minutes she would have started feeling drowsy and then would have lost consciousness. Then she would have slipped into a coma and then her heartbeat would have slowed to a stop.'

Britt felt the relief wash over her like a wave. She'd so often imagined a horrible violence in Risa's death, which seemed an unjust end for her peaceful, quiet sister. 'So she wouldn't have felt pain; just the sensation of going to sleep?'

'That's what the investigator said,' Grant said softly. He reached down and took her hands in his. 'Are you all right?'

'Yes,' Britt smiled faintly as she met his eyes. 'For the first time I'm able to imagine Risa beyond the way I saw her on the kitchen floor, beyond my memories of her, to where she is now. I can imagine her as a wonderful, benevolent angel.' Britt gazed at the clouds floating in the sky.

'Good,' Grant said gruffly. 'That's good.'

It took a moment for his words to register. Britt looked

back down at him. 'Yes, it is, but it doesn't mean I don't want the person responsible for her death and Joe's.'

'Oh?' Grant looked caught off-guard by the sudden switch from ethereal to avenging. 'Oh. Right. We'll get the murderer.'

'Not out here taking a stroll, we won't,' Britt pointed out as she turned around and headed back to the police station at a pace Grant's long legs could barely keep up with.

Under the umbrella of a live oak tree, he put one big hand on her shoulder. She stopped and he turned her around. 'Britt, I think you need to go check on your grandmother. She's worried about you.'

Britt waved it off. 'Grams is fine. She's tough as old shoe leather.'

'She's tough when it comes to herself, but not when you're threatened. The incident with her car has her worried. When I talked to her a few minutes ago – '

'You talked to Grams a few minutes ago? Don't go meddling – '

Grant put his hand over Britt's mouth. 'Listen for a second, will you? She called me. You can't get so obsessive about this investigation that you forget those still alive. I think she needs reassurance that you aren't going to do anything stupid. And I certainly couldn't lie to her.'

'Thanks a lot,' Britt muttered behind his hand.

'So, what do you say?' Grant asked, running his thumb along her lower lip as he took his hand from her mouth.

'I say I know you're trying to get rid of me, but I'll do it on one condition.'

Grant narrowed his eyes. 'You're agreeing too easily; that makes me suspicious. What's the condition?'

'That you take me to a late lunch or early dinner – whatever it's called in the middle of the afternoon.'

'That's all?'
'That's it.'
'It's a deal.'

Grant should have known there was more to it than that. Late lunch turned out to be a brain-picking strategy session on the investigation. They sat in a secluded corner of the nearly deserted Alamo Heights café, sipping iced tea and operating on two different planes. Britt was like a pit bull, not letting go of the case. Grant couldn't stop thinking about how bad Britt was for him and how much he wanted her anyway.

Sighing with resignation, Grant watched as her mahogany curls danced in an unruly tangle and her hands flew as she strove to make some point. He had to admit she had good instincts, an investigative intuition, but every time he thought about getting her opinion he worried about putting her in danger by giving her too much information.

Finally he decided, to hell with it. He had a case to solve and then he'd never have to see her again. If he appeased her now maybe he could get Jewel to keep her under wraps until they arrested the stalker and it would be safe to let her out of doors again.

'Liquid codeine is considered a C-two – a substance controlled by the feds. Every use must be registered in triplicate in a database,' he told her, harboring a fantasy that the inclusion of all this authority would scare her off. Hah.

'Who would have access to such a tightly controlled drug?' She leaned forward on her elbows.

'Not your typical pharmacy, but those in hospitals would.'

'What about in Mexico? Would it be easier to obtain there?'

Grant saw what she was getting at. 'Possibly,' he answered, then seeing his attempt at scaring her had failed completely, he steered her into other speculation. 'You see Skin and this Sorlirk character as your prime suspects? Sorlirk because Risa rejected him and Skin because he's after these negatives for the book? Negatives he thinks Risa stole to keep them from being published?'

'Right, and – '

Grant put up his hand. 'Let me put in my two cents. You know Tori is high on the short list.' Britt looked down into her cup as he continued. 'She threatened Risa. She doesn't remember where she was or who she talked to when whacked out of her mind. Her only alibi is a most likely drug-dealing boyfriend who won't return my telephone call.'

'Tori wouldn't do something like that to Risa.'

'Face it, Britt, you don't know Tori.'

Britt looked up to argue. 'And you do?'

'Maybe better than you do,' he suggested. 'And add Jayson to the list.'

'He loved Risa.'

'A lot of killers loved their victims, Britt. Love does strange things to people.'

'What do you know about love?' Britt asked defiantly, a familiar light burning in her eyes. He almost lost himself in their fiery depths, but he extracted his psyche in time.

'Not enough,' he finally answered ruefully.

Britt quirked one eyebrow questioningly before looking back down into her tea cup. Grant thought he saw color rise in her cheeks, but the afternoon sun filtering through the trees kept him from seeing for sure.

'Jayson was paranoid about the male models and actors Risa would see on her shoots. He's shown a penchant for violence and hasn't been terribly cooperative. And there's the threat on the answering machine tape.'

'He's just being a teenager,' Britt said.

'Maybe. But we've got to consider him. He would know Risa's habits – like what cola she drank, when she'd be home. He'd also be someone she'd let in or he'd already have access to your house. Does he have a key?'

Rubbing her temples with her fingertips, Britt nodded once.

'Did you leave a Lyle Lovett CD on "pause" at your house before you left for school the day Risa was killed?'

Britt drew her brows together. 'Risa was the music lover. I hardly ever turn the stereo on. You didn't tell me it was on.'

'I didn't tell you because it could be nothing. Or it could be Risa or the killer sending us a message.'

'Where was the pause set?'

'In the middle of that song about Big Daddy.'

'You don't think . . .?' Britt couldn't finish the sentence for the tightening in her throat.

'You have to admit the possibility, Britt. Neil was angry with Risa for moving out and firing him as her manager. Anger wouldn't be his only motive, either. He apparently thinks Risa will make more money dead than alive.'

'You're talking about his own daughter. It's impossible. Dad may be greedy, but – ' Britt shook her head, caught halfway between outrage and fear.

'I'm not the one who brought this up. This was your condition, not mine. I'd be happy to take you to Jewel's house right now.'

'No. Finish,' she said, burying her face in her palms.

'Last, there's Carl and Sophia.'

Britt took her hands from her face, staring at him in shock. 'What could their motive possibly be? Risa never even met Carl and Sophia hadn't seen her in years. It seems like a famous, gorgeous step-daughter would be an asset for a politician to cultivate, not kill.'

Grant shook his head. 'I can't say for sure. There's just something not right about those two.'

'Sophia doesn't have a heart; that's what's wrong with her. As for Carl, I couldn't say . . .' Britt let her sentence trail off as she remembered a conversation she'd had with Risa the day she returned from her job in Dallas.

'What is it?' Grant asked impatiently.

'I told you Risa had been asking a lot of questions about Sophia in the past year or so, but more recently she'd been making negative comments about Carl. At the time I thought she was just transferring her animosity for Sophia to Carl . . .'

'What kind of comments?' Grant asked, suddenly focused and intent.

'Oh, talking sarcastically to the television or radio when he'd be on, espousing some issue. If he was promoting an overhaul of healthcare, she'd say: "What do you know, Lawrence? You'd euthanize your own mother if it was to your advantage".'

'Sounds like someone I know,' Grant cut in, amusement hinted at in the crow's feet around his eyes.

'What?' Britt asked her train of thought interrupted. It was so unlike Grant to joke that it took her a moment to catch his meaning. 'Oh, thank you, you're full of compliments for me today. But my point is, that comment was unlike Risa. She was always so positive. We always said she could find good in the Devil. So why attack Carl? A man she doesn't even know?'

'I don't know exactly what that means, if anything, but it might make sense sometime down the line.'

Grant stood up, threw some bills on the table and grabbed his blazer off the back of his chair. Throwing his arm casually around her shoulders, he guided her out onto the tree-lined wooden deck that led to the parking lot. Britt liked the feeling but wasn't sure she should. She knew he was being so expansive because he was about to get her out of his way, but she couldn't resist leaning into his hard leanness. The moment the curve of her hip brushed his thigh, they both tensed with the sexual electricity the contact sparked. Grant's hand ran up into her hair. She stopped; he turned her to face him. His other hand caressed her jawline before cupping her face and bringing his mouth down to hers.

Britt's blood sang through her veins, begging for his kiss; her mind resisted, knowing it was emotional suicide. Grant had made it clear that morning he thought their lovemaking had been a mistake. She had to agree. Intellectually. But right now intellect was fading in the sensations of his lips hungry against hers, his fingertips as they drifted slowly down her neck to trace her collarbone, skimming her ribs to rest at the swell below the small of her back, easing her into the pressure of his masculinity against her abdomen. Her own hands, uncertain of where to go with the conflicting signals from her mind and body, rested lightly on the ridge of muscle above his hipbones, unable to resist exploring the contours.

Then, as suddenly as it had begun it was over. Grant pulled away from her with a half-swallowed groan. He shook his head at himself and looked around at the deserted courtyard as if trying to remember where he was.

'This is all wrong.' His eyes were the clouds on a day that couldn't decide whether to rain or shine.

'You're right.'

'Don't agree with me; it makes me nervous,' he said, deadpan.

Britt looked away at a squirrel scampering up the limb

of a tree that grew in a hole in the wooden deck. She could deal with his isolationism better than this dry humor that revealed how well he'd gotten to know her in such a short time. It reminded her of how much she'd miss him when the case was closed, when all she'd look forward to would be seeing which beauty he'd have on his arm by the time Risa's murderer made it to trial.

That was why this was all wrong for Britt.

His mother had said it; Britt wasn't his type. She wasn't a raving beauty, politely empty-headed or at least calmly subservient. She was an overly emotional, acid-mouthed, debate-loving midget with unruly hair and a turbulent temperament. She was a novelty, or maybe he just felt sorry for her. That wouldn't last long.

But that wasn't why Grant thought it was all wrong.

Britt knew he saw her as a career liability. She was the volatile sister of the victim, who meddled in the investigation he was ready to get off his back. He might like a dalliance with her, Britt imagined, to try the chocolate instead of the vanilla for a change, but she just wouldn't sit on the sidelines like a good little girl and wait for him to snap his fingers.

The jangling of keys broke into her thoughts. She watched his fingers wrap around the sticks of metal and swore under her breath at the heat that spread through her body at the sight of his masculine hands.

'I better get you to your grandmother's house. She promised cookies and milk,' Grant said.

'Right,' Britt muttered as she followed him to the car. 'The closest Grams will ever come to that is *biscotti* and cappuccino.'

It turned out to be neither.

When they walked through the kitchen door, Jewel was

at the counter fiddling with a large dome-shaped appliance.

'Grams.' Britt smiled indulgently. 'What do you have now?'

Jewel glanced up at Grant and Britt, grinned mischievously and pushed her glasses up farther on her nose. 'Don't you know a food dehydrator when you see one?'

'Obviously not.' Britt ignored Grant's quiet chuckle and walked up beside Jewel to stare through the clear plastic at the dissected pears, apricots and plums on a wire rack. 'Why did you feel like you had to get one of these? I've never even seen you eat a dried fruit.'

'Never too late to start,' Jewel said reprovingly. 'Plus, hadn't you heard? Dehydrators are all the rage. Saves all sorts of money. You know how expensive dried fruit is.'

'How can it save you money if you never bought dried fruit in the first place?' Britt put her hands on her hips.

'Well, pickles and peach fuzz, Britt. You're entirely too practical for your own good. You need to learn to branch out, take risks, or you're going to go through life with one regret after another. I'd rather regret doing something than not doing something.' Jewel tilted her head in Grant's direction. 'Wouldn't you, Detective Collins?'

Taken aback, Grant was speechless for a moment, and Britt saw a memory she recognized flash across his eyes before they cleared and he smiled at Jewel. The skin around his eyes crinkled in a way that hurt Britt in the center of her chest for some odd reason. 'It seems to have worked for you, Mrs Reeve.'

The dehydrator issued an electronic beep that drew Jewel's attention. 'Pickles and peach fuzz, this dad-blast thing.' She poked and prodded and turned a few knobs.

Grant's eyes drifted to Britt's for a split second, sending her heart leaping, before he looked back at Jewel's fussings.

'I've got to go. Keep her out of trouble, will you, Mrs Reeve?' Grant walked to the door.

'You betcha. Can't you stay for some dried apricots?'

'Grams, I think it takes days for those to dry out, you know,' Britt offered.

Jewel looked at Britt over the glasses that had slipped back down her nose. 'Well, I wouldn't mind keeping him around for a couple of days. He's pretty easy on the eyes.'

Shaking his head, Grant laughed at Jewel as he moved out the door. 'I'll take a raincheck.'

'What a difference a day makes,' Jewel called out as the door closed.

Britt stared at the fruit to avoid looking at her grandmother. 'What are you talking about now, Grams?'

'That young man is smitten if I ever saw smitten. The first time I saw him he could have bitten a nail in two, and now butter could melt in his mouth.'

'You charmed him, all right,' Britt said with forced casualness as she faked a deeper study of the dehydrator.

'It wasn't me, honey. But what I want to know is why he looks so good and you look like you need an air sickness bag.'

Britt had to laugh at that.

Jewel put one arthritic finger under Britt's chin to raise her eyes to meet hers. 'There. That's much better. You know, oftentimes good comes of bad. It's God's plan. Sometimes it takes the good to make us see the sense in the bad.'

'Grams you think you're so tricky, and you're not. I know what you're saying and it's not going to help me get through this.'

'Britt, look at me.'

Britt met her grandmother's eyes, which were all through joking for the moment. 'I know you're sad for

Risa and for Joe, and you will be – and you should be – for a long time. In a way, forever. But you can't let their loss, that sadness, keep you from the happiness you may be meant to gain from this.'

Britt shook her head vehemently. She put her hands over her ears. Gently, Jewel's stiff hands pried them away.

'It is not for us to second guess the work of God. And if you deny yourself, well, whatever this turns out to be with this detective then you could be denying the meaning in your sister's tragedy.'

'But if it wasn't for this we would've never met.'

'My point exactly.'

'No, but I mean, if we had met . . . sometime, somewhere else . . . we wouldn't have even said two words to each other.'

'My point,' Jewel repeated, nodding.

'No.' Britt shook her head with frustration. 'He likes tall, gorgeous women who're seen and not heard and – '

'And you like to live your life for other people – your sister, your students.'

Before Britt could come up with an answer for that, Tori shuffled into the room in an oversize sweatshirt over cut-off jean shorts. If possible, she looked worse than she had earlier that day. The rims of her azure eyes were red-rimmed and swollen. 'I wish you'd live my life for me now, big sis, I feel like – '

'Victoria, if you are going to stay in my home you must observe my rules. No vulgarity.' Jewel waggled a finger up at her six-foot-tall granddaughter. Britt was always amazed at the way Tori brought out the worst in Grams. She became absolutely prim.

'It gets worse and worse,' Tori grumbled. 'First no sex, no drugs, and no rock and roll, and now no swearing. If you're not careful I might cut my visit short, Grams.'

'Oh, I wouldn't be so lucky,' Jewel mumbled as Tori shuffled back out into the living room, where she turned on the television and cranked up the volume.

Jewel turned to Britt. 'I swear I liked that girl a lot better when she was drunk.'

'Grams,' Britt admonished. 'You don't really mean that.'

'I might.' Jewel glared in the direction of the TV noise. 'She's getting on my nerves.'

'Well, you might want to get used to it. She's a suspect.'

'What?'

'She threatened Risa. It's recorded on my answering machine.'

Jewel sighed deeply, took off her glasses and rubbed the bridge of her nose. 'My Lord. Where is this going to end up? Where?'

Tori reappeared, carrying a long package wrapped in brown paper. Britt's name was printed in block letters on the top. Tori shoved it into her hands and turned back to the living room.

'But it's not my birthday,' Britt said dryly.

'It was sitting outside the front door, smart-ass,' Tori snarled.

'Tori,' Jewel warned. Tori waved her off and disappeared.

Britt carried the package to the table. Jewel approached with scissors. 'Do you think your detective is sending you flowers?'

'I doubt it,' she answered, but her rush to get the package opened belied her words.

As she lifted the top off the box she gasped. Bile rose in her throat.

A baseball bat lay in a bed of red tissue paper, its end darkened with dried blood. It was the baseball bat that had been in her classroom. The bat the minor league baseball team had given her children when they'd visited the ball park on a field trip. The bat that must have killed Joe McGown. The bat that she hadn't realized had been missing until now.

CHAPTER 16

Grant walked into the reception nook to see Paula, phone to her ear, glaring at a man perched on the only chair across from her desk. He was as out of place in Terrell Hills as a penguin in a prairie. His longish black hair curled at the neck of his chartreuse silk shirt. His snug black jeans weren't tight enough to keep him from bouncing his leg compulsively up and down. His thin white hand held an unlit, long brown cigarette, and in the few seconds Grant observed him, he adjusted it in his fingers a half-dozen times. He'd been inspecting the fingernails of his opposite hand when Grant walked in.

He was a bundle of nerves, and Grant could see he'd driven Paula to distraction. Her hair crunched against her forehead as if she'd squished it there in an effort to massage away a headache; her glasses sat slightly askew. The door to Rangel's office was closed. Must have done him in, too. Grant wished he could slip by without even speaking to the guy, but the space wouldn't allow that.

'Excuse me,' Grant said as he sidled past.

Paula began to gesture wildly. Grant ignored her, realizing what she was getting at. She finally held the phone receiver to her chest.

'He's waiting to see you.'

The stranger bounded up. 'Lieutenant Collins? Cool. I didn't have to wait long. I'm Vince Demond. You've been calling me and I decided just to fly on over and talk instead of doing it over the phone.'

Now that he was closer, Grant could see the constant movement was drug-induced rather than nerves. Or maybe a combination of both.

'It wasn't necessary for you to make that long flight from LA. We could have easily handled this over the phone.'

Though he was reluctant to take the creep to his office, he didn't see an alternative. Grant walked to the stairs and started up, with Tori's boyfriend close behind.

'No sweat,' he was saying. 'I was on my way to New York to see my dad and took a detour just for you, man.'

The way he said it, Grant knew he was supposed to ask who 'dad' was, but he didn't. 'I have some questions for you that relate to our investigation into the death of Risa Reeve,' Grant began.

'I didn't know her, man.' Vince said defensively.

'You date her sister?'

'Who? Tori? Yeah, she's mine.'

Grant had to repress a laugh at the bravado with which he claimed ownership, like a rancher bragging on the prize in his stable.

'You were with her the morning of June third?'

'Man, sometimes when you're an entrepreneur like me the days kinda run together, but that was last Wednesday, right? Yeah. We were together. As close as you can get, if you know what I mean.'

Grant didn't respond to his ribald comment and Vince's eyes started straying around the room, his gaze flitting from point to point like a fly.

'You heard her call Risa from your condo that morning?'

'Yeah, she called, talked to her dad to find out where Risa was first, and then – '

'She called Neil Reeve?' Grant made a note; Neil hadn't mentioned this to him. Was that significant or had it slipped his mind? 'Did you hear the conversation?'

'Naw, not really, man. They talked about fifteen, twenty minutes. I would've listened closer if I knew this whole thing was gonna be deadly, y'know. You think it could be a made-for-TV movie or a screenplay?'

Holding tight to his temper, Grant continued. 'Do you think Tori was upset enough about this magazine article that she wanted Risa dead?'

Vince pointed his cigarette at Grant. 'You're good, really good. You might even be able to play yourself in the movie – a real Dirty Harry type. Yeah, man.' He paused, sucked on his cigarette and blew smoke toward the ceiling. 'What'd you ask? Oh, yeah. If Tori could kill Risa. Well, she might have wanted her dead for a second or two, before her teeny, tiny brain flitted on to something else. There's no way she could've done it or had somebody else do it; she's just too stupid. And too selfish. She couldn't have put up with a plan that focused attention away from her for more than a minute or two. Forget that angle, man.'

Grant stood to end the interview – he wasn't getting anything useful out of this guy – but Vince stopped before he could be ushered out the door. 'Man, I gotta tell you. You better sign with somebody soon.'

'Sign what?'

'Yeah, to tell your story about Risa's murder – the hunt for the killer. The public's already on heat over the whole deal. Hollywood, New York – they want it. And I can help you there. Just let me know and I'll get my dad to hook you up with a scriptwriter or a ghostwriter. He's a showrunner, y'know. All it'll take is a phone call, maybe lunch. I know it wouldn't look too kosher, you still working the case, but we can do a deal under the table that's ironclad. That's what I do, I'm a deal-maker. And I can promise you some real heavy coin.'

Grant would bet his last dollar this creep's only deals involved drugs and underage girls. He made the whole room feel greasy. Grant jerked his head toward the stairs. 'Get out.'

'Hey, man, just trying to help out. Now you help me out. Where can I find Tori?'

Remembering the yellowy-purple bruise on Tori's cheekbone, Grant's fists bunched. He willed control into his voice. 'If Tori wanted you to know where she is, she would've told you.'

Vince's eyes constricted to dark points. 'Guess we'll have to work a trade – that information for the really juicy stuff I have on Tori.'

'I guess you'll tell me your juicy stuff or I'll have to search you for evidence of what's pumping through your bloodstream right now.'

'Screw you,' Vince spat out, but his eyes darted across Grant's face as if reading the seriousness of his threat and finally believing it. 'Okay, but just because I'm a nice guy. A couple of weeks ago Tori was visiting Skin, this photographer who's working on a book of Risa, and Tori called him, got him out of the studio, waited until Risa left then stole a whole bunch of negatives Skin was going to put in this book.'

Grant felt his pulse pounding in his neck. 'Tori still has these negatives?'

'Yeah,' Vince admitted reluctantly. 'I saw her put them in her suitcase when she was packing to come here.'

Sitting back down at his desk, Grant let his mind race through the ramifications of Vince's revelation. If Tori had the negatives that Skin wanted, then what had Risa given to Britt to hide?

His gaze drifted out the huge picture window on the wall next to his desk. A car he recognized as an unmarked member of the San Antonio Police Department fleet flew into the parking lot, squealing to a stop in a handicapped space. Grant couldn't see who got out of the car but felt the slam of the door below his feet, then Paula's voice raised in anger and another, alto bellow. A half-second later a heavy clomp-cla-clomp-clomp beat up the stairs.

Dubinsky burst into the room.

'Where the hell you come off, not calling me when you recover a murder weapon from my murder in your jurisdiction – when I've been so willing to let you jokers come in and tromp around my murder scene in my jurisdiction and then you don't even call – '

'Whoa, Dubinsky. What are you talking about?'

'Quit jerking me around,' she warned, then studied his face before easing her tone. 'Okay, I got the word from one of the guys on the street that his cousin is one of your volunteer patrolmen, and he's over at Grandma Reeve's house with my murder weapon – some baseball bat that had been in the classroom. What the hell are you doing here, anyway? Letting your volunteer uniform handle my murder weapon?'

'I'm here because I know even less about this than you do,' Grant admitted through a clenched jaw as he punched Paula's extension into the phone.

'Yes, I knew about it, but Detective Ortega told me not

to notify you until you got through with your interview.'

'The next time interrupt my interview and let me make my own decision,' Grant barked as he slammed down the phone and jogged down the stairs.

His stomach heaved, and he was coming dangerously close to hyperventilating. His one thought was of Britt. How had the baseball bat ended up at Jewel's house? Was Britt in danger? Was she hurt? Why had he left her alone when all the signs pointed to her being in the path of this stalker?

'Hold up, Collins,' Dubinsky yelled, and she came panting up as he jumped into his car. 'Don't have a heart attack. Lovergirl is okay. I didn't hear anything about injuries.'

Grant slid his sunglasses over his eyes. 'It's not that.'

Dubinsky issued a cross between a snort and a laugh. 'Right. And I'm Miss Universe.'

Closing the door on her guffawing, Grant started his car and raced the twelve blocks to Jewel's house, Dubinsky barely keeping up behind him.

Fury warred with his concern when he saw Ortega's unmarked car sitting in the driveway along with the repaired sports car. Grant went straight to the kitchen door, leaving it open for Dubinsky. He searched the room for Britt first, but she wasn't there.

'Where's Britt?' he demanded of the room in general.

'Right here,' Britt answered softly, from his right. She stood, a little pale, but in one apparently unmarred piece.

Grant felt all the eyes of the room on them, and he fought his overwhelming desire to take her in his arms. He shoved his sunglasses up on the top of his head instead. 'I need to talk to you,' he said shortly, taking out his notebook. He turned to Ortega. 'And you, later.'

Ortega winked at Jewel. 'Uh-oh. Think I'm in trouble?'

Grant addressed Britt. 'Where's the bat?'

Disappointment clouded her features for an instant before she covered it up. Grant's heart twisted. He gritted his teeth, trying to grind out his reaction to her. 'Let's hear what happened.'

Nodding, Britt walked to the kitchen table where the volunteer patrolman and Jewel stood. 'Grams and I were in here talking, when Tori brought this package in. I opened it and saw it was the baseball bat that the Missions team gave my class. I didn't think about it being missing when we were there this morning.'

Grant poked his pen gently at the red tissue surrounding the bat, but it was stuck to the blood, hair and brain matter that had dried. The killer had packaged the bat very soon after dispensing with Joe. Grant looked to where Tori stood, slouched against the wall. The sweep of her hair hung over half her face. The eye he could see was closed. She was either asleep or meditating.

'Tori,' he shouted. Her eyes opened a crack and closed again.

'What?'

'How did you come by this package?'

'I told them – ' she waved a hand vaguely at Ortega and the patrolman ' – already.'

'Well, you're going to do it again.'

Issuing a heavy sigh, she opened both eyes and looked malevolently at him. 'I was watching TV and heard the doorbell ring. I answered the door and it – the package – was just sitting there on the mat. I picked it up and brought it in.'

'You didn't see anyone? A delivery person?'

'No, and I didn't look, either. I don't want to have to tip for a package that's not even mine,' Tori complained.

Grant glanced at Britt and Jewel. 'You didn't hear the doorbell?'

Jewel shook her head. 'No, but we couldn't have heard an air raid what with how loud the television was playing.'

'How soon after I left?'

'Not more than five minutes or so,' Britt said.

Grant thought about Vince, sitting in the reception area. It was sure a long way to come to answer a few questions, but what an alibi. He could have left the package and arranged for Tori to not 'find' it until a specified time . . .

Or could it be the stalker? Sending a gory prize?

'If you're all through, I'll take this to the lab.' Dubinsky stepped forward. 'And if it's okay I'll send an officer to canvass the neighbors.' Grant nodded.

Dubinsky reached over to close the box, but stopped suddenly. 'What's this?'

Grant and Chile rushed to her side to stare at what was stuck to the underside of the tissue paper. It was a note. 'Cut out newspaper letters,' Dubinsky said, almost sounding disappointed. 'Not very original.'

'"See what can happen if things don't go according to plan?"' Grant read, forcing his voice into a monotone. Britt shuddered and Jewel put a strong arm around her grand daughter's midriff.

'Sound familiar at all?' Dubinsky asked officiously. Britt shook her head. No one else spoke. 'Okay, then, it's off to the lab.' Box in hand, Dubinsky left.

The phone rang. Everybody jumped. At a slight nod from Grant, Jewel answered.

'It's for you, Tori.'

Tori roused herself and took the phone. 'Yes, I called about that job this morning. Of course I still want it.' There was a pause, while everyone relaxed except Grant.

'I'm right at 105.' Pause. 'No. I won't come drunk or stoned.' She punched the 'off' button. 'He can kiss my – '

'What's the job?' Britt interrupted.

'The Riverwalk shoot.'

Britt gasped. 'Risa's job?'

'Well, Risa can't take it, and it would be a shame to let it go to waste when I could very well do it.' Tori shrugged and addressed Grant.

'You through with me now, or am I up for some fingernail pulling now?'

Grant weighed his options on how to deal with Tori. Could he shock her out of her callous armor? 'I just saw your boyfriend.'

Tori's prominent Adam's apple convulsed. 'Really? Here?'

'Yes, he flew in to answer my questions.'

'Did he . . .' she paused, and her armor slipped away to show a scared young woman '. . . ask where I was?'

'Yes,' Grant answered, watching her eyes dart to the front door. 'But I didn't tell him where you were.'

Tori sucked in a breath. 'Okay,' she blew out as she walked to the bedroom.

'She's the only person on God's green earth that can make you want to throttle her one minute and hug her the next,' Jewel observed with a shake of her curly head.

'It runs in the family,' Grant mumbled.

Britt glared at him but spoke to her grandmother. 'Grams, how could you want to hug her when she's as good as dancing on Risa's grave?'

'Britt, she's torn up about Risa, too; she just doesn't show it the way we do. But maybe this job will give her a second chance. She hasn't had a drink since she came home. She's trying.'

Grant dismissed the volunteer patrolman to return to

his home three doors down the street and then got Ortega alone in the living room.

'Why did you tell Paula to keep a lid on what was going on here?'

Ortega wouldn't meet his eyes. 'Well, *amigo*, Rangel asked me to drop all my other cases to help out on this one full-time, with maybe me taking it over eventually.'

'What?' Grant asked, aghast.

'Well, one of his San Antonio cronies told him about you and Britt. He's not going to say anything to you in case you work it all out . . .'

'What does "work it all out" mean?'

'I don't know, ole Tom-o. I guess not letting the entire metropolitan area know you're sleeping with the victim's sister.'

His reputation was still in tatters from the fiasco with his brother, and now here he was having it torn up even worse. Every time he let his emotions rule, his life self-destructed. Why didn't he learn?

'So you didn't call me because Rangel told you to ice me out of the case?'

'No, you know I wouldn't do that. Paula told me about the *gringo malo* you were talking to and I thought it might be this stalker. I didn't want you to hear about your *sancha* getting a special delivery and leave him sitting in your office.'

Grant couldn't argue Chile's reasoning; he would have done exactly that if he'd heard the news while Vince was there. 'It wasn't Sorlirk. It was Tori's boyfriend.'

'Interesting.'

'Especially since he told me where we can find the envelope holding Skin's book negatives.'

'Where is it?'

'In Tori's luggage. According to Vince, she stole them

from Skin's files. Risa never had them.'

'Then what's in the envelope that Risa gave to Britt?'

'We find that out; we find the killer,' Grant predicted.

'Then we better go find it.'

Both men turned at the sound of Britt's whisky voice in the kitchen doorway behind them.

'You have a bad habit of eavesdropping,' Grant said dryly.

'It's the only way I find out anything worth knowing,' Britt retorted.

It didn't take long to convince Tori to return the negatives to Skin.

'They've been nothing but a pain in the ass since I took them,' she complained as she sifted through her suitcase to find the envelope.

Grant planned to work a trade with Skin: the negatives in exchange for Skin telling him why a watch with his initials had been found in Britt's bedroom. Had he come to visit Risa before her demise? Or after? Was he a party to it or guilty only of bad timing?

The house was quiet now. Jewel was making dinner. Rangel had called Ortega out with him on a sighting of Richard Sorlirk. Grant felt the elbow in his side as if he was being nudged out of control of the case.

The doorbell rang. Britt and Tori looked at Grant. 'Should I get it?' Jewel called gingerly from the other room.

'No,' Grant shouted as he hurried to open the door.

Jayson, dressed in his usual crotch-at-the-knee baggy jeans and T-shirt, hung back on the second porch step, looking as if he would've bolted back to his car if Grant had opened the door a second later.

'Detective. I'm glad you're here, I guess. I have something to confess.'

'Do you want to go to my office?'

'Can we do it here?' Jayson asked tentatively.

'All right.' Grant moved back to allow Jayson to enter and bumped into Britt, whom he hadn't noticed standing behind him. 'Britt, I'd ask you to leave, but I know you'd be sitting with your ear to the door anyway.'

'It's okay, Detective,' Jayson said. 'I came here to tell this to Britt first anyway.'

'Great,' Grant muttered as they all sat down.

Jayson's words came out in a rush as he sat looking down at his hands, oversized and awkward for his skinny frame.

'I, uh, one time when I went to your house last week, Britt, I searched through Risa's stuff and found some letters this guy wrote her. You know I was a little paranoid about all the stars and models – those rich, famous guys always asking her out? But they didn't live here, so I talked a lot about it but didn't get too worried. Not until last week. I saw that three letters were postmarked San Antonio. They were love letters. I took them, then I asked Risa about them. She went totally ballistic, told me some guy who'd been bugging her had sent them and she didn't even know him. I asked her why she'd kept them if she didn't care about him. She told me she was tired of me not trusting her and she was going to break up with me. Then I called her that morning . . .' Here he paused for the first time and tried to cough away the tears that sprang suddenly to his eyes. 'The day she died, and left a message for her before I went to school. I told her I wouldn't let her do it.

'I said it so tough and mean, and I didn't mean it that way. I wish now I'd just said I loved her and I was sorry. You don't think she heard that, do you?'

His anguish was palpable, and Grant wrote in his

notebook to avoid being sucked into more emotional quicksand. He had enough of his own to deal with. Britt reached over and put her hand on his gangly one as he started to sob.

'Did this letter-writer sign his name?'

'Yeah.' Jayson sniffed. 'Richard.'

Britt and Grant shared a charged look. 'The stalker,' she whispered with a shudder. Grant could almost feel the chill go through his own body as it traveled through hers.

'Were they threatening?' Grant asked.

'There was one where he said she couldn't get rid of him, that they'd both die first or something. Sounded more like Romeo stuff than a threat, but I dunno. Mostly they were mushy, with "adore" and "love" and "worship" all over them. He went on and on about how gorgeous she was. All his focus was on how she looked. He fell in love with what she looked like. That's sick,' Jayson commented, looking sick himself, with his skin paled to pasty and the whites of his eyes shot with red veins.

'I need those letters,' Grant said with quiet urgency.

'Sure,' Jayson said with a sniff he tried to mask by clearing his throat as he stood. 'They're at my house.'

At the door, Grant turned to face Britt. She looked so tiny and vulnerable, her volatile elfin face pinched with worry. He wanted to envelop her in his arms, but one touch had already gotten them in enough trouble. Plus, she was stronger than she looked. She didn't need him. The thought shot an odd, unsettled feeling through his gut. He shrugged it off and gave her a narrowed look meant to intimidate.

'Stay put. I'll be right back.'

Staring at the back of the closed door, Britt hugged herself in a poor imitation of what she'd hoped Grant would do before he left. He'd been treating her like a stranger, not like a woman he'd woken up with that morning. Had it only been that morning? It seemed so long ago. She knew him so well and so little.

She wished she hadn't known him at all. All he'd done was leave her emotionally raw.

And now he expected her to listen to him? To stay put? Wrong.

Britt spun on the heel of her loafers and kissed her grandmother's cheek on the way to the bedroom. Tori stood at the mirror, holding up a negative of Risa to the light, examining it, then looking at herself in the mirror.

'Stop it,' Britt snapped.

Tori flicked a look at her older sister. 'Well, she *was* on the verge of superstardom. We were related. Maybe I can capture whatever it was that so enchanted the world.' She pushed her lower lip out in an affected pout and observed the effect in the mirror.

'You don't want to do that,' Britt said as she plucked the negatives out of Tori's hand and slid them back in the envelope.

'What do you know about it?'

'I know because I felt like that for a long time. I wanted to be you, my famous model sister. It took me a long time to decide I had to be myself. Only now am I coming to understand that I have to live for myself too.'

Tori's mouth dropped open and she stared at Britt. 'You did? You wanted to be me? But why? You were the smart one, the one who wowed all the grown-ups with your maturity. Why would you want to be stupid me?'

'You're not stupid.'

'That's what I was told. "Just shut up and smile Tori. Do what you're good at. Leave the thinking to someone else."'

Britt felt a surge of love for Tori that she'd never felt before. 'You know, we're sisters, and I love you, but I want to like you too. I hope we get a chance to know each other so we can become friends.'

'Maybe I can hang around here for a while and we'll get the chance,' Tori offered, the mist in her eyes having nothing to do with alcohol withdrawal.

'But right now we've got to locate Skin and get those negatives back to him. Where do you think he is?'

'I know where he is. He gave me his hotel number at the funeral.'

'Great,' Britt said. 'Give it to me. I'll take the negatives back to him and maybe he'll get off my back.'

'I think you should wait for your cop. You don't know if that stalker jerko is out there somewhere.' She sent a furtive glance to the nearest window.

'Well, he's not out there right now, with cops going door to door. And he certainly won't be staking out Skin's hotel room. How would he know that's where I'm headed?' Britt said. 'I have to do something. Sitting around here on my hands all night will make me crazy. Go get the address.'

As Tori disappeared down the hall to find her purse Jewel called from the kitchen. 'Come here, quick.'

The urgency in her voice drew Britt to where Grams stood fixated on the television set. She pointed at the screen, where a sloppy blond man in his twenties was being led to the San Antonio police headquarters downtown. 'They arrested that Sorlirk character. Maybe now this nightmare will be over.'

Britt felt the tightness between her shoulderblades – that she hadn't realized was there – begin to relax. The adrenaline that had been building over the past twenty-four hours eased. Britt was able to let go of the images of the vandalized car, her trashed classroom, the bloodied baseball bat. The man responsible was in custody. She saw Ortega on the television screen and wondered if Grant would miss not being one of the plainclothes police surrounding Sorlirk. A pang accompanied the thought that his protecting her in front of all those cops this morning had caused him problems on the job. Had he been forced out of the case completely?

'He looks rather ordinary.'

Grams's remark drew Britt's attention back to Sorlirk. She was right, he did look harmless, with his shuffling, hunched, almost apologetic stance and his shaggy hair several months over-due for a trim – until his eyes met the camera. They were windows to a deranged mind. Too much white surrounded irises so pale they were colorless.

'Creepy,' Tori offered as she came in holding a scrap of paper.

'San Antonio police say a phone tip led them to Richard Sorlirk, who's wanted for questioning over the poisoning death of teenage model Risa Reeve. The unemployed carnival worker was staying in a downtown motel. He is now being questioned by Terrell Hills police detectives . . .'

'Well, I guess it's safe for you to go see Skin,' Tori said with a shrug as she handed Britt the address.

The doorbell chimed again. Jewel looked at Britt. 'Do you mind, dear? I've got to keep an eye on my couscous.'

Britt paused with her hand on the knob. Even with Sorlirk in custody, a chill of apprehension ran down her spine. When she opened the door she realized why.

CHAPTER 17

'Brittany.'

Staring at the fake and flawless beauty standing on the porch, Britt wished she hadn't opened the door after all.

'Sophia. What are you doing here?'

'That's no way to greet your mother.' Sophia pushed out her lower lip in a pout reminiscent of Tori's practice in the mirror. 'I was hoping we would finally have a chance to have a nice mother-daughter talk.' Sophia's lips curved up in a semblance of a smile that Britt noticed stopped just short of wrinkling the skin around her eyes.

'Finally found a few minutes to spare after sixteen years? Great, come on in.'

Britt stepped back to let Sophia tip-tap in on her red spike heels with gold trim. Her red and gold silk designer suit made Britt feel frumpy in her cotton slacks and T-shirt. In a brief flash she was a little girl again, intimidated by her gorgeous, ultra-dressed mother.

Grams peeked around the corner and gave her the thumbs-up before disappearing. Britt squared her shoulders and tossed her wild mane of hair as her mother arranged herself on the loveseat in the formal living room. She was an adult now, and damned if she'd let her mother make her feel ten again.

'I see you still have that acid tongue of yours. No wonder you're not married yet,' Sophia observed as she smoothed her blonde hairsprayed helmet.

'Not everybody considers being married an occupation – leaving one husband for a better paying one with more perks.'

Sophia gasped, bringing her coral-tipped fingernails up to her perfectly matching coral lips. 'There's no call to be cruel. Just because it took me a little longer to find the right man doesn't make me bad, Britt.'

Britt didn't want to get into a philosophical discussion about love and marriage with her mother. It would be like discussing spiritualism with a used-car salesman.

'Why are you really here, Sophia?'

'Well, if you don't want to have a little chat, fine. I wanted to ask you a favor.'

'What favor could I possibly do you?'

Sophia pulled a handkerchief from her little red purse to dab at her eyes.

'There are no cameras here, so cut the act.' Britt leaned back and crossed her arms over her chest.

Putting the handkerchief back, Sophia closed the purse with a sharp snap. 'Risa was my baby, and I have nothing but magazine cut-outs to remember her by. I think you owe it to me to let me go through her things and choose something that I can keep to remember my baby who's gone – ' big sniff ' – forever.'

Staring at the woman before her, Britt was fascinated. Not only by Sophia's gall, but by her own reaction. Or rather lack of one. Over the past sixteen years Britt had often imagined what her first real private talk with her mother would be like. It was always the emotions she'd feel that she had focused on – fury, regret, sorrow, bitterness, maybe even a little love.

But what she felt inside now was none of those emotions. In fact it was nothing at all.

For the first time she could ever remember, Britt was emotionally empty. The woman before her could have been a stranger and Britt would have felt more. So it was easy to answer Sophia's question.

'No,' Britt said.

First Sophia looked surprised. 'You can't be serious. I won't take anything valuable, or – '

'No,' Britt repeated.

Sophia's too-blue eyes glittered with obvious menace. 'I think you're being completely unreasonable.'

'Actually, Sophia, for the first time in my life I think I *am* being reasonable.'

Sophia shot to her feet, purse clutched in her hand. 'You're making a big mistake, Brittany. You think about that and when you change your mind, you call me. I'll be waiting.'

'You do that,' Britt said lightly as she followed her to the door. 'Wait just the way Tori and Risa did, for years after you left.'

Sophia's back stiffened and she looked over her shoulder. 'You didn't wait?'

'Of course not. Being older and wiser, I knew better,' Britt said. 'And I was right. The only time you've come back is because you want something. What I don't know is exactly what it is you're after.'

'I told you.' She turned to face Britt. 'I just want a little memento – '

'If I didn't believe in you when I was ten, I sure don't believe you now, Sophia.'

'You're going to wish you had.'

With that, Sophia tip-tapped down the front walkway to a rented Cadillac. Britt watched as she got in and eased the car away from the curb. It struck her as an oddly low-key exit for a woman who liked to arrive places in limos with strobe lights flashing. What was she trying to hide?

Skin looked out the exhaust-streaked window of his motel at the waves of heat rising off the street. Ironic, he thought, that this cruddy motel, surrounded by nothing but asphalt and dirty concrete, was only a few blocks from one of the most exclusive, attractive neighborhoods in the San Antonio area. Skin watched the Range Rovers and Mercedes roll by and wondered why they came up this crummy strip to shop when they had a toney town within spitting distance. Maybe, he thought, the seediness made them appreciate the perfection of their own neighborhood.

When he was rich – very soon – he would surround himself with beautiful things, and he would never need to see the bad side of life to appreciate them. Memories of living in dirtbag apartments and driving garbage can cars would be enough to remind him of what he had.

Very soon. He'd kiss all that goodbye very soon.

He'd come to San Antonio to find the negatives Risa had stolen, but in the process he'd run across the potential to make some real coin – more than the book could ever haul in. If it worked out the way he'd planned, it would be like a pension. He'd be set for life.

And the beauty of it was he'd already done most of the work. Now he had one problem to solve and one promise to gain, and then he was paradise-bound.

A short knock rattled the door. Skin leaped up and straightened the bedspread for his guest as he called, 'Be right there.'

Skin hated to smile. He hated to see people stare at his pointy teeth. But right now he was alone and too damn happy not to smile, even if he had a thousand people staring at him. This victory was assured. How could the answer be no?

Skin pulled the door open. The one he'd called that morning stood there, not meeting his grin. Well, why did Skin expect it? This was going to cost a lot of money. But who could put a value on peace of mind?

'Come on in,' Skin invited, stepping back to allow his guest to enter, then closing the door. 'Do you have an offer?'

'A million dollars, all upon receipt of the package.'

'Two mill,' Skin countered.

'One-five.'

'Deal,' Skin said, wondering if he could've gotten even more. He stuck out his hand. His guest stared but didn't reach out for a handshake. Skin let his hand drop.

'When can I expect delivery?'

'Well, as soon as I get my hands on the package, I'll call you,' Skin said.

'Who has the package now?'

'Britt.'

'Does she know what it is?'

Skin shrugged. 'Who knows?'

'It's important that I know.'

'I'm sure you have ways of finding out.'

'I have ways of doing everything that needs to be done.' Skin's guest produced a brown paper bag and pulled out a bottle of Scotch. 'Shall we drink to our deal?'

'Sure.' Skin bobbed his head, his grin returning. They'd seal their pact with a drink. Skin might not like hard liquor, but he'd choke some down in the name of a million and a half.

'You pour.'

'Sure.' Skin bobbed his head again as he looked in the bag and found two plastic cups. He poured the amber liquid in each cup, then picked his up and held it high for a toast. His guest regarded him silently, so Skin finally tapped the other cup, sitting untouched on the nightstand, and took a big swallow.

He tried not to grimace as the liquor burned a path down his throat. He opened his mouth to pull in a breath and nearly gagged at the bitter aftertaste. It was horrible. He peeked in the bag. It was an expensive label. Maybe he should give it another try. The first taste was always the worst. He swigged more. It did seem better, smoother – still bitter, though.

'I'm afraid I have to leave.'

'But you haven't had your drink yet.' Skin waved his cup at the untouched one.

'Unfortunately I won't be able to. Time is running out.'

'Time for what?' Skin asked. His tongue felt thick in his mouth and he wondered how he could be drunk already from three swigs of Scotch.

His guest turned to leave.

'Hey, don't forget your bottle.' Skin held up the bag.

'You keep it. To celebrate.'

'Okay. Thanks. We'll be in touch soon, then.'

'I'll be waiting for news.' The door shut and Skin was alone with the bottle.

'I do deserve to celebrate,' Skin told himself as he looked at the Scotch. 'And, since this is all I got, this will have to do.' He poured a cupful and toasted himself. 'To the next millionaire. D'Wayne Errol Flanders, you are on your way to paradise.'

As he worked his way through the bottle Skin began to tingle, to float, to feel giddy one minute and sleepy the next. He was drunk. His last thought before he drifted off was that he was going to wake up in paradise with a raging hangover.

Britt pulled the car into the parking lot of Mariel's Motel, San Antonio, just as the sun set – a blazing ball dipping beyond the horizon. The majesty of it eclipsed the griminess of her surroundings and for an instant Britt wished she had someone there to share the sunset. Not just any someone. Grant. The glowing twilight reminded her of where she'd been twenty-four hours before, waking up in his bed. Sensing the essence of him all over her. Watching him cook. Sharing breakfast after dark. Transcending time and place in his arms.

These thoughts made her feel at odds – both lazy and comfortable while restless and urgent. And wholly unwilling to go and return some negatives to a sleazy photographer in a seedy motel.

But it had to be done.

Britt didn't care so much that Skin got his precious negatives of Risa. Britt would be just as happy if he didn't. But she wanted something from him – answers. With the stalker the one behind the murders, vandalism and terrorism, she didn't fear Skin. He just made her angry and disgusted, rapaciously trying to benefit from Risa's fame. But if that was indeed his watch that had been found in her bedroom, then he had to have been in the house sometime after Britt left that morning. Had he come to talk Risa? Britt wanted to ask him how she'd looked, how she'd seemed.

Britt still missed not getting to say goodbye.

She got out of the car and activated the alarm. The answering beep sounded loud in the desolate parking lot, sparsely scattered with mostly dilapidated cars. Britt walked past Skin's old Volkswagen at the front door of number eighteen.

She knocked.

No answer.

She looked down the walkway to the left, and thought about going to the office to ask if he was in. With trepidation, she glanced at the dank stairway just beyond her right shoulder. It was darkening quickly in the fading light.

She had nothing to fear, she reminded herself.

It was just a dirty, pitiful motel.

That was all.

She cursed her too fertile imagination.

She knocked again and softly called his name. Then she tried the knob. It turned. She took a step into the room. A hand clamped down over her mouth from behind. Her heart felt as if it was bursting out of her chest. Her head tried to crank around to see who had her.

'I thought I told you to stay put.'

Britt relaxed for an instant against Grant's hard frame, then her adrenaline transformed into fury and she spun around. 'Do you make a habit of scaring me?'

'Do you make it a habit of doing stupid, dangerous things?'

'They're only stupid and dangerous when a certain someone interrupts my plans and blows my cover.'

'I don't think cover is going to matter. I don't think he's here.'

Britt glared at Grant, then peeked in the darkened room. 'Skin, you here? I have those negatives you wanted.'

She pushed the door farther open and in the half-light she could barely make out his form on the bed. 'Skin. Wake up.'

Her eyes flew to Grant, who'd drawn his gun and advanced into the room, shoving Britt against the wall as he did so. 'Don't move,' he ordered, in a voice she'd never heard him use. He quickly checked the bathroom and the rest of the tiny bedroom before walking over to Skin and checking his pulse.

Steely eyes rose to meet hers. 'He's dead.'

Britt started to walk toward him from her position just behind the door, but Grant stopped her. 'Don't. Not yet.'

Using a handkerchief to wrap the handset, he dialed the emergency number. The motel was just outside the Terrell Hills city limits and so was San Antonio's jurisdiction. As he talked, Britt pored over the room, looking for any clues to what had happened. She didn't see any marks on Skin's body. It looked as if he'd died in his sleep.

In his sleep.

Her gaze landed on the overturned brown paper sack on the nightstand; it was wet, a brownish liquid spread across the tabletop.

It was too familiar. A trickle of dread coursed through her body. She held her arms tightly around her, pressing her fingernails into her ribs just to feel the sensation of being alive.

Why Skin?

Grant hung up the phone. He peered in the bag. 'Scotch,' he said. 'Expensive.'

A thoughtful scowl tightened his face.

'What is it?' Britt asked.

Grant shook his head.

'There's only one glass,' Britt pointed out. 'Suicide? Accidental alcohol poisoning?'

Britt knew her voice sounded pathetically hopeful. She couldn't help it. She didn't want another body. The murderer was supposed to be in custody. If Sorlirk hadn't done this, what did it mean?

'Could Sorlirk have –?'

'No, Britt,' Grant said, the planes in his face standing out harshly in the glare of the light from the parking lot. 'The body is still warm. And we've had Sorlirk under surveillance since just after noon.'

Grant walked over to ease the door shut with his foot. As he did, a scrap of paper skidded across the threadbare carpet. Britt leaned down to pick it up.

'No.' Grant's voice cut through the air like a shot.

Hand outstretched, Britt froze.

'Prints,' Grant warned.

Britt nodded and studied the paper. It was written in the same scrawl as the motel address. Skin's writing, she assumed.

'What does it say?' Grant asked as he crouched down alongside her.

'Photos for Risa two years ago. Evidence worth paying for! Where? Older sister, Britt? Checked: house, car, locker, sister's classroom (interrupted, search there again?). Blackmail subject? How much? A million? Contact: yes. Meeting: Tues. 6 p.m. Deal . . .'

Her skin pricked as she realized she was reading the thoughts of a dead man. A man who had violated her privacy. She thought of his watch in her bedroom, the vandalism of her grandmother's car, the deadly destruction of her classroom. Footsteps of a ghost now. What had he been in search of? The negatives she had in her pocket now? It didn't seem to make sense.

Britt could feel Grant's breath on her neck. His arms pressed against hers as he leaned in to see the writing. She could feel his excitement over the new clue transferring though their contact. She looked in his eyes and she also saw fear.

'I need to get you out of here. To your grandmother's home, with a uniform with you at all times.'

'What are you talking about? I'm not following.' Britt said, unwilling to be let out of what was unfolding.

'I'd say Skin was poisoned, same as with Risa with the exception that he didn't try to hide his crime. When he didn't succeed in fooling us the first time with the hit on the head, he probably skipped that step this time. That's common in killers; they learn from their mistakes, revise, retaining certain aspects of their operating procedure while perfecting others. Maybe he felt the alcohol would mislead us in the same way Risa's head injury did.'

'But Joe's murder – it was different.'

'Right – totally different. Skin killed Joe. It was an impulse, using a weapon of convenience. Skin writes here he searched the classroom but was interrupted. Joe walked in on him and he knocked him out, maybe not intending to kill him.

'What this means, Britt, is the killer is still out there. The killer is the person being blackmailed. Risa had something the killer wanted, Skin seems to have realized what it is and now he's dead. The killer thinks you know it too. You have it. It's not those pictures of Risa. It's in the envelope Risa gave you. That will tell us who is about to come after you.'

Grant grabbed her shoulders. His eyes burned with intensity. The lines in his face were tight with tension. 'You have to remember: what happened to that envelope?'

'I can see that day clearly in my mind,' Britt reflected. 'Risa coming, the kids greeting her, so happy to see her as always. We were involved in our spider spaghetti project and my hands were sticky from the newly cooked spaghetti. I don't remember taking that envelope. Grant, I really don't think I ever touched it; I would have had to wash my hands first, and I didn't.' She pressed her palms to her forehead, until finally lifting them. She looked at

Grant with hope. 'I know who would know, though. Lucy Hernandez.'

'Lucy?'

'She was the little girl you met in the hall the day you came to school. She adored Risa, never left her side anytime she was in the class. She would've seen what Risa did with that envelope. I just hope she can remember.'

'We'll go see her.'

Sirens approached. He stood and helped her to her feet. He pulled out his notebook and quickly copied the contents of the note. He walked back over to Skin's body and reached for a piece of paper just peeking out of Skin's pocket.

'Britt,' he called, the intensity in his voice more compelling than its volume.

She looked at what he'd pulled out of Skin's pocket. '"My will and testament,"' she read, her voice thickening as her eyes scanned the familiar writing. 'It's Risa's. Can I have it?'

Grant shook his head. 'It evidence for the cops now, Britt. You'll get it back later.'

'But how did Skin . . .?'

Grant paused before finally answering. 'He probably found it when he came to your house. Maybe he didn't arrive until after Risa lost consciousness, or even after she was already dead.'

Britt bored Skin's body with a look of loathing. 'He deserves what he got, then.'

Grant took her elbow and guided her to the door.

'Don't you need to stay here?' Britt hung back.

Grant hustled her outside. 'I should, but it would take the rest of the night and we have things to do. Let me pacify the uniforms and get out of here before the detectives get here.'

The first two uniformed officers got out of their cars, hands on their weapons, looking fresh out of the Academy, pumped up and ready for action.

Grant gave one a brief account of what had happened. 'I've got to chase down a lead on a case of my own, now. I'll catch up with your detectives later for a statement.'

'What about her? She ought to stay.' The reporting officer cocked his head at Britt.

'Just tell them I took her with me against your recommendation.'

'Got it, Lieutenant.'

Britt was already halfway to her car when Grant called her back. 'We'll take my car.'

Britt followed him around the back of the building.

They zoomed out of the parking lot just as the first detectives arrived. Britt watched as Grant called back to Dispatch to tell them where they were going. He jammed the receiver back into his holder. His jaw clenched and unclenched. His hand gripped the steering wheel so tightly she wouldn't have been surprised if it had broken off in his powerful hands.

Suddenly it occurred to Britt that Grant should be interviewing Sorlirk with Ortega. She'd assumed that was where he'd go after picking up Sorlirk's letters from Jayson's house. He'd so surprised her that she hadn't had time to consider why he'd come after her.

'Why aren't you interviewing Sorlirk?'

'Chile can handle it.' His hooded eyes told the rest of the story. He was being edged out of a case that could re-establish the respect he deserved.

'I'm sorry.'

'Why? It's not your fault. My own stupid mistakes have gotten me into this mess.'

Britt bit the inside of her lip to distract her from the pain in her chest. He might as well have reached in and a yanked out her heart, Britt thought. Except he didn't want it, so why would he do that? She was nothing more than the object of his mistakes.

Fighting back tears, Britt looked out the window at the streetlights as they flew past. He was entirely focused on unearthing the mystery, solving his case . . . He was putting up with her just because she was the only way to lead him to next piece of the puzzle. She was just a facilitator.

So why did she think of him as a lover?

It did seem ironic that their lovemaking, which had felt so right, so unique, so incredible could have been so wrong. When it had been happening Britt had known in her heart it was a once in a lifetime experience.

Why did she always have to be right?

Britt almost laughed out loud at the bitter irony. Here they were on the verge of discovering the identity of Risa's killer and all she could think about was romantic rejection. The one time in life she could have fallen in love and the obstacles were insurmountable.

Her grandmother's words came back to her: *Oftentimes good comes of bad. It's God's plan. Sometimes it takes the good to make us see the sense in the bad.*

'What are you thinking about?'

Grant's question brought her suddenly out of her reverie. His gray eyes looked at her knowingly. Could he have read her mind? Did he know how vulnerable she was to him? Britt couldn't let that happen. She had to find a way to get through the rest of the investigation with her pride intact.

'Oh, scouring my mind for where that envelope could be.'

'You said Lucy would know. Why don't you go in and find out. This is her address.'

Britt looked around as if she'd just landed on another planet. Had she been that out of it that she hadn't noticed they'd parked in front of the Hernandez house?

'Would you like to talk to her alone?'

Britt considered for a moment. 'No. She seemed to like you.'

'She did?'

A strange expression that looked like pleasure crossed Grant's face. Couldn't be, Britt thought. He said he didn't like children.

They got out of the car and walked to the door. Lucy's mother was willing to let her daughter help, as long as she didn't know why she was helping. She hadn't told her about the principal's death. She brought her daughter to the door.

Britt crouched down to give her a hug and ask about her summer vacation. Then she asked, 'Do you remember the day Risa came to help us make our spaghetti spiders?'

Lucy nodded solemnly.

'Did you notice if she had an envelope with her?'

'Yes, she tried to give it to you, but you couldn't take it with your hands all icky, so she put in a book.'

'A book?' Britt asked. 'Do you remember which one?'

Lucy wrinkled up her forehead and pressed her plump lips together. Grant fidgeted. Britt ignored him and waited silently for Lucy to answer. Finally she frowned. 'I'm sorry, Miss Reeve. I just know it was on the second shelf on the bookcase.'

'You have such a great memory, Lucy.' Britt smiled and squeezed her hand. 'Do you remember what was on the shelf above it?'

'Oh, yeah,' Lucy's face lit up. 'Goldy. The book was under our fishy.'

'That's terrific, Lucy. You've helped us a lot.'

Lucy flashed a wide smile at Britt, then made her face serious before she looked way up at Grant. 'You're being nice to her. I'm glad you listened to me.'

Grant's eyebrows flew up. For some reason Britt felt the need to jump in to save him. 'What makes you think he's being nice to me?'

Lucy looked from Grant to Britt and back again. 'Oh, I can just tell.'

Going back to the car, Grant kept his distance from Britt. Geez, if a six-year-old could tell he was falling in love with Britt, what about the rest of the world? Was he that obvious? Had Britt suspected?

He'd have to be careful for the rest of this case – resist the casual touches that were becoming almost second nature. He couldn't ask her to become involved in a relationship with a man who did nothing but make one mistake after another. A cop who couldn't be a good cop but didn't know how to be anything else.

She was so emotionally rich; he couldn't recognize emotions of his own even if they slapped him in the face.

He couldn't give her love because he wasn't sure what it was.

She deserved better. Someone as sensitive and as giving as she was.

Grant knew he wasn't that man.

The one thing he could do for her was to solve her sister's murder. To provide her with closure so she could get on with her life.

With someone else.

Out of habit, Grant opened her car door. Britt regarded him guardedly and got in without speaking.

He slipped in behind the wheel. 'Any ideas which book?'

'No, but who's to say Skin didn't find the envelope and the killer has it now?'

'Skin told us that in his note. He said he was interrupted, hadn't found it, but was going to blackmail the killer on spec. "You give me the million, I'll find the stuff" was probably his angle. The killer figured why pay when he or she could get the stuff on his own. Exit Skin. We could wait for the killer to come to you, because that will happen in his search for the envelope. But I won't do that. It puts you in too much danger. Let's find the envelope, which hopefully contains an obvious motive, then collar the killer.'

'Okay. Let's go to the school.'

Grant turned the key in the ignition. He hated how much he wanted her to go with him. But it was irresponsible. He would be putting her in danger.

'No,' he forced out, careful to keep his eyes on the road and not on her face. He could picture in detail first the shock and then the beseeching look that would overtake the shock just about now. A beat or two more and it would be outrage. All he had to do was wait. He could handle the anger. It was when her face said *please* that he wouldn't be able to resist.

'What do you mean, no?' Britt's voice sliced through the silence in the car. 'After all this "us" and "we" you've been talking about? Who's the other half of the "we"? I thought you were talking about me.'

'I wasn't thinking. I apologize. Not we; I should've said *me*. Me. Me. Me. I'm going alone to the school and I'm taking you back to Jewel's. She promised me she won't let you out of her sight again. Between her and the volunteer patrolman down the street, you should have plenty of bodyguards.'

CHAPTER 18

'Your brother has been trying to reach you,' Paula said. 'I didn't even know you had a brother.'

'You don't know everything,' Grant countered into the receiver.

'Sad, but apparently true,' Paula said.

Grant could hear the guffaws come across the radio in answer to their conversation. He replaced the receiver and let his fleeting smile go. What did Evan want? His brother hadn't called him once since his injury. He was too helpless, or thought he was. Whenever Evan wanted to abuse Grant, he had his mother call.

So why the sudden initiative?

Dreading what he might have to say, Grant considered letting it go until after the case was wrapped up. He hadn't said it was urgent.

Grant pulled into the parking lot of the elementary school and finally let his curiosity get the better of him. He dialed his parents' number.

Evan answered. 'Nice of you to get back to me.'

'Well, some of us work.'

'Some of us are paralyzed.'

'You could still work. Who ever said a lawyer needed legs?'

'I thought you said it was a heart we could do without,' Evan reminded him.

'I think lawyers could do without both.'

'Well, I'm glad we've had this pep talk. Almost makes me not want to help you.'

'Help me?'

'Yeah,' Evan said. 'What a switch, huh? Slap yourself a couple of times and let me know when you've revived.'

'What is it, Evan?'

'I kind of like you asking me something,' Evan stalled. 'I might drag this out some more. But I won't.'

'Good.'

'Listen, I've been following your investigation – can barely keep up with the body count – '

'Evan, get to the point.' Grant interrupted tersely.

'Anyway, you know I did a lot of defense work for people connected to politics? So, I see this Carl Lawrence – the stepdad of your victim – and I remember some rumor I heard a while ago. And I make some calls . . .'

'What rumor?'

'Patience, dear brother,' Evan answered. 'My sources tell me that the rumor about Lawrence when he got married to Risa's mother is true. Nobody could ever prove it, though.'

'The rumor?' Grant asked, though he thought he knew.

'That Carl and Sophia Lawrence fabricated the tale about her old billionaire husband beating up on her. Carl had decided to run for office and needed both an issue to emotionally charge his campaign and a telegenic wife on his arm. Sophia caught his eye and fit the bill. The only problem was, she was married. So they, or some brilliant advisor, comes up with the idea of making her husband look bad, so she had to get away, and Carl comes conveniently to her rescue. So, they had to create a couple dozen bruises, a couple black eyes. *Voila!* Media-sanctioned freedom for Sophia and a domestic violence issue for Carl. What do you think?'

'I think I don't want to believe it but I do,' Grant admitted. 'I don't know what it has to do with my case, if anything, but it's enlightening.'

'Just thought you ought to know, for whatever it's worth.'

'Yeah,' Grant said. 'I appreciate it.'

As he hung up he marveled over the fact that thanking his brother felt both unfamiliar and right. Not just because Evan might have helped him but because Evan might have helped himself as well. Grant tried not to hope for more. He didn't want to be disappointed.

He also tried not to dwell too much on the information Evan had given him. It tended to confirm some of his suspicions. Like the expensive Scotch in Skin's motel room. Skin looked as if he was on more of a beer budget. Of course, what people spent their money on was not completely predictable. He'd worked on a case where an oil company heir had bought only generic brands at the grocery store and another where a mother of five worked two jobs just to be able to pay for her habit of French wine every evening.

Just the possibility that all this somehow revolved around Carl Lawrence made Grant nervous. He was powerful. He was connected. He could screw up Grant's career worse than he'd done all by himself. But that wouldn't stop him. The fact that Britt was home with only one volunteer police guard did.

He dialed Jewel's number. Britt answered.

'How is everything?'

'The same as when you left ten minutes ago.'

'You're sulking.'

'How did you guess?'

Grant blew out a breath of impatience. He was trying to keep her safe and he got nothing but grief. Of course, if she'd been compliant he have been suspicious, so he ought to be thankful. Her intractability was reassuring in a perverse way.

'Don't let anybody in the house except Dean. Got it?'

'What, do you think I'm stupid?'

'No, I think you're fearless, and that's what scares me.'

Grant hung up before she could answer. He'd revealed too much of his feelings merely by calling then to say something sentimental like that. What was he thinking? He hoped Britt was too grouchy to notice.

He had called ahead to the school district police and while he'd talked to Britt a patrol car had pulled into the lot and the officer had unlocked the door. Grant got out of his car and waved off the officer's offer of help.

Inside the building the hall resonated with silence. Grant found himself walking more carefully and tried to shake off the sensation of visiting a ghost. He hadn't liked officious Joe McGown, but he realized now it had been more because of his obvious interest in Britt than because of what kind of person he was.

As he approached Britt's classroom he tried to imagine how Joe had walked into the room to find Skin rifling through the children's environment. Had Skin continued searching after whacking Joe on the head? No, he'd said he'd been interrupted. Skin had probably thought he'd knocked him out and ran before he could regain consciousness. The envelope might still be there.

But where? Grant opened the door and tried to ignore the stench of death that clung to the room, despite the overwhelming odor of disinfectant. He stared at the long shelf of books. 'Under the fishy', Lucy had said. He didn't see a fish bowl. But of course, how could a fish survive alone all summer? Britt had forgotten to tell him someone must have taken it home for the vacation. He walked up to the shelf and scanned it for evidence of a fish.

The namecard with 'Goldy' written in careful block letters was the giveaway. Grant crouched down. Which of the dozens of books under it would it be? Surely Risa would have chosen a book that she would remember later? He tried to think of what he'd learned of Risa in the past few days.

Suddenly the image of the babies crawling across the wrapping paper on her locker and the words of her best friend rose in his mind: 'Risa loved babies.'

Hadn't he picked a book about babies up off the floor when he'd helped Britt clean up earlier?

What was the title?

His eyes landed on it. *Baby Love*.

Heart beating in his throat, he reached for the book's spine. Wouldn't he have seen an envelope sticking out of the book? Was it gone? Or was his guess wrong, and it was another book entirely?

He pulled the book off the shelf and opened the cover. Nothing – although it was large, about thirteen inches by nine inches, and would completely conceal an envelope if one was hidden in the pages.

Stemming his urge to shake the book violently, hoping something would fall out, he systematically turned page by page. At page twenty-three he found it. A plain white envelope, with nothing written on the outside. It was sealed. He sliced it open with his pocketknife and peeked inside to see negatives. He resisted the urge to hold them up to the light and slipped the envelope into his blazer's interior pocket. Replacing the book, he stood up to go. Then a thought caught him. What if Risa had chosen that particular page for a reason? He ought to check just in case.

He returned to page twenty-three. It was a picture of a baby and a man. The man had his arms crossed across his chest and was frowning, as if reprimanding the baby. The baby sat on the floor, tearing up a piece of paper and smiling up at the man as if she didn't care what the man thought of her. Grant eyes dropped to the text which said: 'Daddy is mad at Baby. He thinks Baby did a bad thing. Baby Louisa doesn't understand.'

This was the second reference to Daddy. The CD in the player set on pause at the song about 'Big Daddy' and now the envelope in the book. Grant wasn't sure Risa had consciously left these clues, but he sure as hell didn't believe in coincidences either. He had planned to go see Britt after he'd dropped the negatives off to be developed. Now he knew he'd better go see Neil Reeve first.

Britt felt like a caged tiger. Full of predatory energy and nowhere to go. Pacing only intensified her restlessness. She thought of a thousand things at once but nothing made sense. Her fractured consciousness sensed some important connection begging to be made, but she couldn't seem to settle down enough to make it.

Grams watched her surreptitiously over the top of her glasses, which were aimed at the magazine she'd held on the same page for a half-hour. Tori had gone to bed at nine o'clock, both excited and nervous about her first work in three months. She had to be at the shoot on the Riverwalk at five o'clock the following morning.

'He should have taken me with him,' Britt mumbled.

'You're going to wear your legs down to stumps if you don't sit down and rest them. They're short enough already,' Grams added to soften her warning.

'I think I need to go running,' Britt announced.

'That's just what you need,' Grams grumbled sarcastically.

'I haven't had a good run in a week and you know I can't think straight when I haven't cleared my head with some exercise.'

'You don't need to think straight; the police need to think straight,' Grams cautioned with a frown. 'Every time you start thinking, period, you run off and get into trouble.'

'Well, I'm going anyway.'

'You can forget that, girlie. Dean Rogers is reading *War and Peace* out front and, since that dreadful tome has to be the most boring in history, he's bound to notice if you go bouncing by. That is if he isn't asleep.'

Britt let her eyebrows fly up. Grams shook her head in answer. She stuck her tongue out at her grandmother, who burst into laughter.

'Go to bed, Britt. No matter what, our bodies still need sleep – and you can let your brain tackle all that rattling around in your head. It will all make sense in the morning.'

'All right, Grams, but first I just need some air. I'll sit out on the back porch for a few minutes.'

Jewel gave her a measuring look, then nodded. 'You never could lie, and your eyes say you're not going to give us the slip. So, go get your air. Quickly, though. I'll check to be sure you're inside before I turn in.' She stood and kissed Britt's cheek before she walked down the hall.

Britt stepped outside. The backyard was small, maybe thirty feet by sixty feet, and enclosed by a high brick wall covered in English ivy. She walked around the perimeter of the wooden deck, peeking at the full moon sky through the thin canopy of her grandmother's favorite mesquite tree. She listened as her footsteps resonated through the panels of wood; she felt a need to walk more heavily than usual, as if she could make her steps company.

Britt had never been bothered by having to be alone. Before Risa was born she had often been alone with her books, while her mother took Tori everywhere and her father worked. Tonight, however, she felt a keen loneliness she'd never felt before. A need. It wasn't the loss of Risa; it was more urgent. With sudden startling certainty, Britt realized that whom she was missing was Grant. It frightened and frustrated her. How could she possibly have gotten so close to him in so short a time? And what would she do when she didn't have an excuse to be around him any more?

The camera shop on Broadway which the Terrell Hills Police Department usually used to develop its film was long closed, but Grant called and woke up the manager, and he agreed to meet Grant at the shop at dawn the next morning. As Grant headed the two miles to Neil's address in Olmos Park, his beeper went off. It was his parents' number again. Evan probably.

Grant considered calling him but just then he pulled up in front of Neil's townhouse. He looked up and saw a light on in the second-story window. Grant didn't want to give Neil a chance to see him sitting out front. He wanted the element of surprise.

Evan could wait.

Walking to the other end of the deck, Britt stomped her feet angrily, feeling the echo in the wood. A prickly sense of another presence made her slow. Before she could turn around the wood echoed with a step that wasn't her own.

'I'm glad to find you still awake.'

Britt spun to face the vaguely familiar voice. 'Mr Lawrence.'

'That's rather formal for your stepdaddy, isn't it, Brittany?' He took a step closer.

'Not for one I've never met,' Britt retorted softly. She still hadn't recovered from finding him there. In the spilt second between the fall of his step and the sound of his voice Britt had allowed herself to hope it was Grant returning. Instead, Carl Lawrence stood not ten feet from her, looking as if he'd been invited to a midnight barbecue. Why was her mother's husband in her grandmother's backyard in the middle of the night?

Carl brushed a leaf of English ivy off the leg of his western pants. He grinned the big wide, vote-for-me smile Britt had seen him use for potential constituents.

'I didn't realize how gol'durned late it was when I struck out to talk to you. Then, I didn't want to ring the bell and wake your grandmother. Our seniors need their rest. From the front walk there I heard someone walking out back here and hoped it might be you. Have a seat.' He motioned at the furniture in her corner of the deck.

Easing behind a deckchair, Britt put her hand on its back. She shook her head. 'I don't need to sit.'

'Aw, come on, sugar. I thought we might get to know each other.' Carl stepped closer.

'Now? After midnight?'

'Well, you see, we might be leaving tomorrow, and I hated to come all this way and not get to know all my wife's children,' Carl said. 'Especially considering this terrible tragedy with Risa.'

Was that a gleam in his eye or the fall of moonlight on his face? Britt cocked her head to see better, but he moved into a shadow and what she thought she'd seen was gone.

'This really isn't a good time to "get to know" me. *I* don't even know me right now. So we'll have to postpone the family reunion,' Britt said, not adding the *forever* her mouth threatened to tag on.

'Well, that's too bad, sugar.' Carl closed the distance between them to about six feet. 'But maybe you could fly on back to the ranch with us and stay for a while. The campaign's heating up real good. It won't be boring; I can promise you that.'

'I don't think so,' Britt answered, edging farther behind the chair, closer to the side of the house. She couldn't exactly describe why Carl made her uncomfortable – his words were friendly enough – but something about the way he delivered them told her he wouldn't be taking no for an answer. She glanced at the sliding glass door, hoping that Grams's face would appear. Nothing but drapes.

Carl followed her glance. 'Expecting someone?'

'Grams is still awake. She was going to check on me before she turned her light out.' Britt felt like a little girl reporting to an over-inquisitive uncle. A chill ran down her spine.

'Well, I wouldn't count on it. You know our seniors sometimes just drift off to sleep without warning.'

Drift off to sleep.

Who else had done that?

Britt's eyes cut sharply to Carl's face. 'What are you talking about?'

Carl guffawed as if she'd just told a good dirty joke. 'You sure are jumpy, sugar. I'm just saying your granny might have drifted off before she wanted to. No offense. I've been known to do that myself a time or two.'

Was she getting paranoid? Carl seemed all right, if a little too friendly for her taste. She forced herself to relax.

'Well, I can see you need a little shut-eye yourself, so if I can't talk you into coming back to the ranch with us, I can at least ask for your help.'

Britt narrowed her eyes. 'Help?'

'It's your momma, Britt. She's all broken up over Risa. She feels all sorts of regret over not spending more time with her, not being there for her. What's more, she doesn't have anything personal. Nothing to remember her baby by. She told me she came here earlier to ask you to let her go through Risa's personal effects and find something of comfort, but you turned her away. Of course we probably could go through the courts and get access – she is her mother after all – but we really don't want to have to put you through all that.'

'How considerate of you,' Britt muttered, crossing her arms over her chest.

'We try to be,' Carl concurred, not acknowledging her sarcasm. Now, I know you and your momma have had some problems, but maybe you wouldn't mind – going through Risa's things to find something for Soph. It wouldn't be so personal then. Might not bring back hurtful memories.'

Britt studied Carl for a moment. He seemed entirely sincere. Except that he was trying too hard. Why? Did Sophia have him twisted that hard around her little finger? Or was he after something else entirely, something Risa had that he wanted? But what? And how? As far as Britt knew Risa had never even met Carl. Her mind rewound to one of their conversations about Carl and Sophia. Risa had been so vituperous against him. Why? Was Carl's underlying attitude more than Britt's imagination?

'No,' she blurted out.

'Well, I don't see what it would hurt – '

'Are you looking for anything in particular?' Britt asked, feeling her pulse speed up with an adrenaline boost. She felt the dangerous territory she might be stepping into.

Carl tensed, his friendly face freezing for an instant. He stepped as close as he could to Britt, his legs against the chair between them, trapping her in a corner of the deck. His smile broadened, but didn't look quite as open as it had before. 'What should I be looking for, sugar?'

'I don't know, Mr Lawrence. If you're not particular I could choose something of Risa's for Sophia.'

'Well, that's sure good of you, sugar, but it would take away the sentimental meaning for Soph, now, wouldn't it?'

'I didn't realize she was sentimental.'

'Now, now, sugar, that's the woman I love you're talking about, so watch it. What I meant was, you might choose a high school term paper and she might rather have, say, something that means more to her. I think you know what I mean.'

All Britt's instincts went on high alert, though she tried not to show it. 'That's the best I can do. Goodnight.'

He held up a hand. 'Don't be hasty, now, until you hear me out. I was thinking you might want to be part of the winning team – there's always a place for an educator on my staff. Maybe in public relations? We'd certainly understand if you wanted to keep your home in good ole San Anton, and we probably wouldn't have to call on you all that often. But you'd be on full salary, of course.' Carl's grin was as wide as the Rio Grande.

And Britt felt her nausea would fill the Rio Grande. 'Is that a bribe? I think you ought to leave.'

Carl gasped in shock. 'Certainly not, sugar. Soph and I had been talking about it for a while. You'd be a real asset.'

'An asset in the political arena? What an insult.'

Carl looked taken aback for the first time that evening. His eyes glinted hard. 'Didn't anyone ever teach you any manners? You need to be hauled over someone's knee and walloped good on your backside.'

'Talk to the woman you love about that one, Mr Lawrence. She didn't seem to think it was important to stick around to teach me any. Now, if you'll excuse me, I'm going back inside. If you want a keepsake, I'd be happy to bring it to your hotel.'

'No,' Carl had dropped the pretense of good humor. 'We're checking out before dawn. I'm making a speech just after sun-up. You can bring it there. The San José Mission.

'And it just better be the right little keepsake, or we're going to have to have a more serious conversation, if you understand what I mean, sugar. Think on it. I'd hate for you to regret not giving your momma what she really wants.' Carl backed up enough to allow her to push the chair away from the wall. She gave him a wide berth as she walked to the sliding glass door.

'Now you better go check on your granny. What happened to Risa should've taught you life is a helluva unpredictable thing.'

CHAPTER 19

Britt didn't wait for Carl to leave before she slammed the sliding glass door and latched the lock.

You know our seniors sometimes just drift off to sleep . . .

Her heart pounded as she let the drapes fall back into place. Risa had drifted off to sleep, not ever to awaken again.

What had he done to Grams?

Running down the hall, Britt called her name and got no answer. A crack of light shone under her door. Britt reached for the knob. It was locked. She thought about getting Tori to help, but she'd taken a sleeping pill before bed.

Yelling her grandmother's name, Britt rattled the door back and forth. Then she ran back to the living room, fumbling with the glass door she'd just locked, not caring if she ran straight into Carl Lawrence in her desperation to get to her grandmother.

She barely noticed that the deck was empty as she ran around the right side of the house to her grandmother's window. As she neared, she saw a bit of curtain fluttering in a light summer breeze. The window was open about a foot.

Britt sucked in huge breaths to keep herself from

fainting. She put her hands on the windowsill and called in through the window. Nothing. She jammed the window up and leaped into the room, tangling her legs in the floor-length curtains. From the floor she could see her grandmother lying prone on the bed, a book on her chest. She stood, grabbing Grams's foot, feeling her heart ready to jump out of her chest.

The nightmare of getting to Risa too late threatened to overwhelm her.

Her grandmother's eyelids fluttered and she sat up.

'Pickles and peachfuzz, Britt, are you trying to scare me out of my wits?'

Before she could even feel relief, Britt rushed to embrace Grams in a crushing hug.

'Ease up, girlie, these old bones are brittle.'

'Oh, Grams, I was so worried.'

'Worried about what?' Jewel searched the coverlet for her glasses and put them on. 'What's come over you?'

'Worried about you. Did you leave the window open?'

'Well, yes. You know I can't stand laying down without some fresh air. Living more than half my life without air-conditioning, I suppose.'

'Why did you lock your door?'

'Lock my door? My bedroom door? I don't ever lock my door,' she argued.

Britt sprang up and tried the knob. It didn't turn. Britt turned around. Jewel looked puzzled. 'Now, what the devil . . .?'

'Carl was here,' Britt said simply.

'Carl Lawrence? Where?' Jewel looked around as if he might materialize.

'He appeared while I was outside. He couched it in a lot of good ole boy bull, but he basically wanted to plead Sophia's case about the keepsake . . .'

'But why were you so worried about me?' Jewel asked shrewdly.

Britt didn't want to tell her grandmother everything and have her worry. 'He just said some things about you that played on my already over-active imagination.'

'Well, Britt, your imagination didn't lock my door, so I guess we'd better tell the police about the esteemed Senate candidate's visit.'

'What on earth are you doing here at this time of night, Officer?' Neil pulled his half-glasses off his nose and let them drop to hang from a chain around his neck. He squinted at Grant, then looked briefly beyond him.

'We need to talk, Mr Reeve.'

'I'm sure you've forgotten; it's *Dr* Reeve. And this is certainly a strange hour for a "talk", as you phrase it,' Neil pointed out.

'Murder investigations don't keep regular hours.'

'No, I don't suppose they do.' Neil stepped back to allow Grant to enter the foyer. He had on what looked like a smoking jacket, or at least what Grant imagined a smoking jacket might look like, as he'd never seen one before. A pipe and brandy next to a fire would have completed the picture but, as it was June, the fire was unlikely, and when Neil led him to his study a highball glass of amber liquid sat next to his recliner.

Scotch?

Neil followed his gaze. 'Can I get you a drink, Officer?'

Opening his mouth to refuse, Grant paused. It might be the best way to find out exactly what Neil did drink. 'I'll take whatever you're having.'

Neil raised his eyebrows. 'I wasn't aware that police drank on the job.'

'Then why did you offer it to me?'

'Decorum, I suppose. It's as hard to break a good habit as it is to reform a bad one.' He sighed with cultured distress.

'I've never had much use for decorum without a purpose, so either give me the drink or don't, but we have to get on with this.'

Slightly flustered, Neil strode to the bar in the corner. Grant pretended to be looking at a photograph of a teenage Tori on the mantel as he watched Neil extract a bottle of bourbon from the shelf. He poured two fingers worth into a glass and handed it to Grant.

Grant told himself that the bourbon didn't disqualify Neil. He kept his defenses high.

'She was beautiful, wasn't she?' Neil observed.

Shooting him a sharp look, Grant kept his voice neutral. 'She still is.'

'No. Not like she was. Liquor, drugs, age creeping up. It's all adding up for her. She's going to have to transition into acting quickly or there'll be nothing left for her except working behind a perfume counter at some second-rate department store. Or marrying well, I suppose.'

He spoke about his daughter so dispassionately Grant felt a wave of revulsion. Tori could have been no more than an abstract image, and maybe that was exactly what she was to him.

'Are you still Tori's business manager?'

'Yes, though it's not worth the trouble. She hasn't had any real modeling jobs in over a year. Her career is over.'

'And Risa had dismissed you as her business manager and had begun proceedings to get Britt named her legal guardian. I bet that was distressing.' Grant forced neutrality into his voice. He didn't like Neil but that didn't make him a killer.

'To say the least.'

'Had you planned to fight Risa on what she wanted?'

'Of course. She didn't know what was good for her. She was only sixteen – '

'But old enough to take off half her clothes for the world and make a million dollars a year that you'd gladly spend?'

'Now just a minute, Officer.' Neil put his glass down on the table with an angry click. He radiated academic irritation, which masked an inner fury. 'If you're trying to pin her murder on me, you are highly misguided. You think I had motives – anger over her mutiny, avarice over the income she threatened to deny me. But, despite the fact that I would never injure my own child I had much more to lose with her unable to work than I would if she were still alive. I guarantee you, Officer, she was on track to take the crown as the queen of supermodels. No one had any doubts about that.'

'Don't forget I heard you planning to turn Risa into a legend.'

'Yes, I did say that, but I wasn't thinking clearly – obviously my shock and grief interfering with my thought processes.'

Grant raised his eyebrows but held his tongue.

'You see, the world has embraced Risa's fate as the romantic tragedy of the moment. She'll be everywhere for a while. But our society in particular has adopted such a throw-away lifestyle that that philosophy has permeated everything. Legends are no longer made. An actor gets more airtime than all of Congress one year and moves into oblivion the next. Even our presidents – when was the last time we had a real legend? JFK, almost forty years ago. It's not that there haven't been good ones in between – our society has just become unable to create a legend.'

Grant paced the room. Neil's mini-lecture was the first thing he'd said that Grant couldn't argue against. But he wasn't here for a sociology lesson.

'Mr Reeve, what do you intend to do with Risa's money?'

'Keep it, of course. Perhaps take some to form a marketing scholarship at Trinity.'

'Not share it with your daughters?'

'No, they are adults. We all make our own way in the world. Parents can provide moral support but I think it's a mistake to subsidize our children in any way once they hit adulthood. It undermines their character.'

'One could say that Risa – in death – is subsidizing you.'

'No, that's not accurate. Her money is just a return on my investment in her as a child. Sometimes it pays off and sometimes it doesn't.'

After Grant had made a thorough check of Risa's old bedroom, he couldn't get out of Neil's house fast enough. Neil's attitude chilled him even more than it would have if the man had baldly admitted to killing Risa. He hadn't killed her physically, but he sure had done his best to kill her spiritually. Grant marveled at the strength of Britt's spirit that she had withstood such emotional desertion. Ironically, Neil's urging of independence from birth had been the one thing that had saved her. Britt had learned at an early age to depend only on herself. Risa had been luckier, having Britt to provide the unconditional love that had made her bloom, by all accounts, into a giving, happy girl who probably had been too trusting.

Not the first time that night – now early morning – Grant wished Britt were sitting next to him in the car. It was probably a good thing she wasn't, though, he reflected, because if she had been, he would have told her how much he respected her, how much he desired her, how much he loved her.

Not that it mattered in the long run.

His only priority was to get this mess of a case wrapped up.

But for the first time Grant realized he was going to do it for her more than for himself.

Dean Rogers, the volunteer patrolman, sat in Jewel's kitchen, sipping the cappuccino she'd whipped up as Britt had come to rouse him off the front porch. Britt was back to pacing, mostly because of her fear that if she stopped moving she would fall asleep. The exhaustion that had followed the adrenaline rush of her encounter with Carl and the scare with Grams had nearly claimed her. But she wasn't giving up yet.

'I really think I ought to be paging one of the detectives or at least the Chief now,' Rogers said, looking down into his cup. He was extremely embarrassed that he'd slept through Carl's visit.

'Let's wait a little bit longer for Detective Collins. I'd hate to interrupt any of them for just this,' Britt said casually, though she was crossing her fingers behind her back. She didn't want to call Ortega or Rangel; Grant's job was in enough jeopardy because of her as it was.

Just then the scratching of metal in the kitchen door lock called their attention. They stared at the door as Grant let himself in with the key Jewel had given him. Britt resisted the sudden urge to fall into his arms. Her eyes searched his face, haggard with exhaustion and his half-grown beard. His gray eyes glanced off hers before piercing Dean. 'I thought I told you to wait out front.'

'Well – '

'We asked him to come inside,' Jewel interrupted.

'Oh? Take off, then. I'll call if I need you again,' Grant dismissed him. Dean went quickly, with a grateful glance at Jewel.

Grant's eyes returned to Britt and she felt warmth spreading in the wake of his gaze. His eyes warmed a degree or two and the lines in his face relaxed. Britt felt a change she couldn't define in the way he looked at her – more tender, caressing. She wondered if her eyes were giving away her quickening heartbeat, the sudden sensitivity of her skin at his presence. She looked quickly away.

But not quickly enough. Jewel caught on, as usual. 'Now, Grant, we had a visitor.' She held up her hand as she stood to halt the question about to come out of his open mouth. 'I'll let Britt tell you about it. And I expect you to stay and guard us since you dismissed that nice young man. Now, I'm sure you'll find a place to sleep. I'll be up precisely at six a.m., for your information.'

With a hug for Britt she was gone. Grant's eyes twinkled in his otherwise expressionless chiseled face. 'I could swear she was trying to tell us something.'

Britt couldn't keep the smile off her own face. Shaking her head, she glanced down the hall. 'She sure is a smartypants.'

'That she is,' Grant answered seriously, the twinkle becoming a warm glow as his eyes traveled down the column of her throat to where her skin disappeared beneath the cotton of her scoop-necked T-shirt, then to her fingers holding her coffee mug.

'Do you want a cup of Grams's cappuccino?' Britt asked.

'That's not what I want, but I guess it will have to do,' Grant answered.

'Would you rather have coffee, tea?'

Grant arched his eyebrows. 'Aren't you going to finish that famous line? You haven't gotten to what I want yet.'

Britt couldn't stop the blush that flamed across her cheeks. She turned to the cappuccino-maker, not trusting herself to meet his eyes and keep her pride.

'But first – ' Grant's voice remained casual ' – I want to hear about your visitor.'

'It was Carl,' Britt answered, grateful for the opportunity to throw static into the sexual electricity flowing between them.

Britt felt his tension before his tight voice asked, 'Carl tried to talk to you?'

'He did talk to me.' Britt kept her back to him.

'That Dean – I told him – '

'No, I was outside, in the back. Dean never saw him.'

Grant's hand grabbed her arm. 'What do you mean, you were outside? Are you begging to be the next victim?'

Yanking her arm out of his too tight grasp, Britt faced him. 'I am not. But you go traipsing off to find evidence. To *do*. And you leave me to *sit*. If you'd taken me with you – '

'Don't give me that,' Grant snapped. 'I shouldn't have taken you on half of what I have.'

Suddenly contrite, Britt looked up at him with her golden eyes shimmering. 'I know. I'm sorry.'

Grant's jaw flexed. 'Don't be. We're all responsible for our own actions.'

'If that's the case, then I'm responsible for what happened when I went outside. And if I'd ended up on a slab at the morgue, then – '

Grant's hands clamped down on her shoulders. He shoved his face in hers. 'Don't say that. You hear me? Don't ever say that again. That's the reason I can't let you be responsible for your own actions, because you don't value your life as much as I do.'

His words hung heavy in the silence in the kitchen, seeming to grow and fill the air. Their eyes locked. Britt finally spoke in a voice soft as a whisper but strong as a yell. 'If you value my life then you have to trust me.'

'I do trust you.'

'Then trust my judgment too.'

'That's much more difficult,' Grant said with a straight face, but his tone broke the tension.

'Thanks.'

'All right, pour me some of that junk and tell me about Carl.'

'First tell me if you found the envelope.'

Grant sighed and rubbed his hand along his jaw. 'I found it in a book about babies. It was negatives. I'm taking them to be developed first thing in the morning. Now your turn.'

Britt recounted her conversation with Carl as she made him a sandwich. It felt good to keep busy – she didn't want to think about what Grant had meant about valuing her life – was that at all like love? – and it kept her from watching his face grow progressively more thunderous.

Several minutes ticked by in silence. Britt wandered over to the kitchen window and looked out at the shadows in the moonlit garden. She sensed Grant's eyes on her but didn't turn to meet them. She reveled in the feel of his gaze and tried to set it to memory so she could call it up again when she was lonely and he was out of her life forever.

'Why did it take you so long to get back to me?' Evan complained. 'I waited up half the night.'

Running his hand across his eyes, Grant prayed for patience. 'It's a long story. I got stuck in an interview.'

A ribald laugh shook across the phone line. 'Interview. I bet you were interviewing that spitfire you brought by here – a horizontal interview. Hoo-ee. She sure wasn't your usual Barbie-doll type. No, she had character with a capital C, and she practically oozes sensuality. Got to hand it to you. She's wrapped around your finger . . . or is it other body parts she's wrapping herself around?'

'Can it, Evan. I think your fantasies are overtaking your judgment,' he said mildly as he watched Britt come from the bathroom, towelling her hair dry. It hung in black ringlets around her face, still flushed pink from their shower. She gave him a look that was half-courtesan and half-ingenue. How could she send his blood boiling with a mere glance?

'I think you're living your fantasies, and I'm jealous as hell.'

'I think you're digressing, or is this the reason for your call last night?' Grant craned his neck to watch her pull on a pair of sensible cotton panties. How did she make them look like the sexiest French lingerie?

'Hell, no, I didn't call to razz you about your love life. I remembered something about the Lawrence dude that might come in handy. One of my old clients says it's an inside joke in political circles.'

'What is?' Grant asked distractedly, eyes on Britt as she pulled up a pair of faded blue jeans.

'Oh, Sophia calls Carl "Big Daddy".'

Britt and Grant tiptoed down the hall at 5:58. They'd only had about three hours' sleep, if that considering they'd done more than sleep once they got to bed. But, strangely, Britt felt energized. She looked at Grant, who'd been brooding ever since his short conversation with his brother. He'd said his brother was just passing on a piece of gossip. About whom or what he wouldn't say.

She fought the urge to push. They'd been more intimate than ever before that morning, sharing more than their bodies, baring their souls. She prayed he wouldn't shut her out now that they'd woken up to the case. Britt knew she should appreciate the mixed blessing.

The case was what kept them together, but it was also keeping them apart.

Grant refused to speculate on what the negatives would reveal. She thought he was trying to figure out a way to keep her out of the culmination of the case. But she also realized – now – why he was doing it. Because he was concerned for her safety. Not because of the case but because he cared about her. But, even knowing that, Britt knew she still wouldn't let him box her out. She couldn't compromise herself. Even for Grant. And if he asked her to, he didn't really love her.

At precisely one minute after six, Jewel emerged from her bedroom. She peeked into Tori's room on her way down the hall.

'Well, your sister's gone,' she called. 'Maybe she's actually back on track. Now if we can just direct her to some worthwhile work, there's hope for that girl yet.'

'You've got to let her make her own decisions, Grams, that's part of boosting her self-esteem. We'll support with our mouths shut.'

Grant made as if he was choking on his waffle. Britt glared and Jewel winked at him. 'My words coming back to haunt me. Well, girlie, if you can do it I certainly can.'

Picking up the breakfast plates, Grant thanked Jewel. 'I appreciate the lodging, Mrs Reeve.'

'You're welcome, young man. Don't think it's a regular thing, though. This was a unique circumstance.' She drew her brows together but couldn't hide the smile that teased the corners of her mouth.

'Yes, ma'am, I agree. Unique.'

'Where are you two off to now?'

'We're going to pick up the developed photos from Risa's envelope, then I'll bring Britt back here.'

Jewel's eyebrows rose skeptically. Britt narrowed her

eyes at Grant but didn't speak. She slipped her feet in to some running shoes and went to the kitchen door. 'Let's go.'

Grant looked at Jewel as they left. 'Don't open the door for anyone, and call the station if anyone tries to get in.'

The manager must have been watching for them, because once they'd pulled up to the photo shop he walked out to meet them, holding an envelope.

Grant thanked him and handed the envelope to Britt as they pulled out of the parking lot and drove around the corner to a residential street.

Unable to wait, Britt opened the envelope and pulled out the eight-by ten glossies. She held her breath as she looked at the first one. A panoramic photo of a large mansion surrounded by lush grounds then desert. The next photo showed a picture shot through a window; a woman sat at a mirror, a man stood over her. Britt peered closer.

She gasped. Grant pulled to the curb and put the car in 'park'.

'Who is it?' he asked, without the urgency Britt had expected.

'Carl and Sophia. But you knew that, didn't you?'

'I suspected,' he answered as he picked up the photos as Britt discarded them.

It was four rolls taken in succession. All displayed an electronic date. They had been taken on two separate occasions over a two-week period of time.

'This was before Carl and Sophia got married,' Britt said suddenly. 'This was while she was still married to her second husband.'

'Well, it's been proved infidelity for politicians isn't enough to lose an election over; there must be more to it.'

The photos began to reveal Carl making Sophia look bruised and battered. Most of it was done with make-up. But at one point he even cut her scalp with a knife. He lashed her with a horse whip. On both occasions Sophia emerged from the house looking like a battered woman. Here was the proof that either Carl was an abuser or he had helped pin false abuse on another man – or maybe some of both. Here was enough to make Carl lose not only this election bid but any in the future.

Here was the motive. But did they have enough evidence to arrest Carl?

'Look at this,' Britt said, handing him the last picture. It was a photo of a contract. 'It's Risa's handwriting.'

> *I, Risa Reeve, hire D'Wayne Flanders, also known as Skin, to find and take photos of my mother, whom I haven't seen since I was six months old. I am doing this to satisfy my curiosity. I am agreeing to pose (fully clothed) for three rolls of pictures for Skin in exchange for this service.*
> *Signed, Risa Reeve.*

'But how did Carl know about the negatives? Do you think Skin tried to shake him down and told him Risa had the negatives?'

'It's likely. Skin probably didn't even realize who Carl was, that this was explosive information. All the media coverage at the time was very localized to Texas. He probably didn't realize Carl was blackmail bait until he came here.'

'Then how did Carl know Risa had the pictures?'

'Maybe she told him? They were in Dallas at the same time. Maybe Risa tried to blackmail him as well.'

'But why after all this time?'

Grant shrugged.

'And, Sophia, I knew she was cold, but how could she do this to her own child?'

'Maybe she didn't know anything about it.'

Britt thought back to Sophia's visit. 'Yes, she did. It was probably her idea.'

Britt and Grant looked at each other. His hand covered hers. 'Are you all right?'

'I'm fine,' Britt said, clear-eyed. 'I want to know when we can go get them.'

'We aren't – '

'Grant,' Britt cut in, 'you know we probably don't have enough to arrest them now. This shows motive but there's no concrete evidence either of them was involved. The most we can hope for right now is to go public with the photos and ruin his campaign, but that leak of evidence would ruin your career. However, if I took just the photos to Carl, told him I understood what he was getting at and found these, maybe he would relax and slip up.'

'Yeah, relax enough to kill you,' Grant said with a decisive headshake. 'Forget it, Britt. I'll go bring Carl and Sophia in for formal questioning, but no wild scheme. It's too dangerous.'

'You know they'll get off. They'll get some high-powered lawyer in there and plead the fifth. You think he was stupid enough to leave prints anywhere? And we know now that even DNA won't sell a jury.'

'Enough.' Grant lifted his hand from hers. 'I don't care if Lawrence walks off scot-free, I won't put your life in danger.'

'But don't you see? My guilt won't let me *have* a life until I do whatever I can to make Carl pay. I have to let go to go on.'

CHAPTER 20

Sophia sat in the limousine as it moved through the bricked streets of downtown San Antonio trying not to think. It was easy as they moved through the nearly three-hundred-year-old city that had integrated the modern so well. But as they traveled into the residential area just south of downtown Sophia could no longer look out the window. She did not want to see those not as comfortable as she was. 'Underprivileged' was a concept she could talk about but not see. Seeing it made it too real.

So she was forced to think about The Problem. She and Carl had to get those explosive negatives before they left or all her hard work shedding her husband, snaring Carl and building him up in the public eye would go to waste. Sophia hated wasted effort.

She also despised people with no foresight – people who could not see a way to any means to reach the desired end. And through a cruel twist of fate she had given birth to two such children. Couldn't everyone see she and Carl were meant to go all the way to the White House? Some silly negatives that didn't hurt anything but a rich old man's reputation couldn't mean more than that.

Carl hung up the telephone, slid the screen between the passenger compartment and the chauffeur and then looked at his wife. 'Well, Soph, any ideas on what we do if she doesn't produce what we're hoping?'

'I have some ideas, but few seem to work with just the two of us and a press conference. Why don't you want to get a couple of your security staff to help?'

'We've talked about this before, Soph,' Carl explained with exaggerated patience. 'If we involve anyone else we add to the potential for leaks and exposés. Not just for now, forever. It's bad enough having involved that nurse to get the drug. Even though we have something on her, you never know when it can blow up in your face. No, whatever we do, we have to do it alone.'

Sophia nodded once. She saw the sense in what he was saying, she just didn't like it. It made her life difficult. She could deal with difficulty – one didn't allow oneself to be carved with a knife without being able to withstand difficulty. She just didn't like it.

'Do you have the codeine?' she asked.

'Yep. And I got the syringe. I hate to use it, but your eldest is a smart one and a fighter. I got to admire that. Wish she'd taken me up on my offer. She'd kick butt and take names for our camp if we ever converted her. Maybe I should try again?'

'Don't waste your time. We just show her the fatal alternative if she doesn't give us the negatives. It's that simple.'

Grant decided that taking Britt with him would be the only way to keep her out of trouble. No one else had succeeded in containing her. He planned only to go into the San José Mission and ask Carl and Sophia to come with him to the station for some questions. That way he'd have an eye on both the suspects and their next intended victim.

Even then he realized the plan seemed too easy. But he couldn't call Chile or Rangel would get involved, and he might yank the case out of his hands completely. Grant realized he'd lost his perspective, but he had to get rid of any threat to Britt before he turned it over.

The weathered, carved limestone bell tower and domed ceiling of the two-century-old mission church came into sight amid the fast food stores, gas stations and pawn shops, like a reminder of history that time had forgotten to claim.

But once they turned into the side street that led to the mission grounds they too stepped back in time. The trees surrounding the walled compound effectively hid the rest of the modern world and Grant could almost imagine the ghosts of Native Americans housed in its walls from centuries before.

'It's eerie, isn't it?' Britt said, her eyes roaming the limestone wall that rose twenty feet into the air.

Grant slipped the envelope with the negatives under his seat. The photographs were on the seat next to Britt. He turned them face down, then got out of the car, going into the trunk for his tape recorder.

Two television news vans drove off past them, but Grant relaxed as soon as he saw the white limo parked along the sidewalk. They hadn't missed Carl.

Britt got out of the car, her untucked T-shirt billowing in the slight early-morning breeze. Grant did a double-take. He could've sworn it had been tucked in when they'd started out, but he was running on sleep-deprivation so he didn't trust his memory of an inconsequential detail like that.

Silently they walked together to the front gate of the mission grounds. Their hands brushed. Grant resisted the urge to take her whole hand in his. He put the feeling of fullness her mere presence gave him out of his mind. He had to focus. Get the job done and get out of there.

Once inside the heavy wooden gate, he looked across the eight-acre compound for a gathering indicating the Senate candidate's presence.

'There they are.' Britt pointed to the group outside the church. The church's side faced them, giving them a clear view of Carl and a small media following in the rear courtyard, with its layers of Roman and Franciscan arches above and a maze of walkways, shrubs and potted flowers below.

As they watched, Carl gave a big wave and Sophia blew a kiss and the reporters dispersed. Grant had to call on his memory of high school history to remember that the limestone wall that ran around the entire mission was echoed by a second wall, ten feet inside of the first, enclosed on top with wood branch ceilings. This had once provided living space for the mission inhabitants – the Spanish soldiers, Coahuiltan Indians and priests – and parts were now open for park visitors. So, when the reporters turned in their direction, Grant grabbed Britt's arm and they ducked into an open door on the right wall. Inside, they retreated to a corner of the stuccoed interior, through a doorway and to a circular room with a wooden shelf made of branches at head level. Four lookout holes the size of Britt's hand were spaced below the shelf; six holes smaller than a fist were spaced along the wall on top of the shelf.

Grant moved Britt against the wall, away from sight should someone look through the holes. She leaned against the roughened walls, cool despite the sweltering humidity of the summer morning. Grant's hand caressed her delicate face, and he dipped his head for a sweet kiss, breathing in her nutmeg scent.

As he pressed his body to hers Britt pulled away abruptly and moved to the opposite wall. Grant watched her in confusion, but didn't have a chance to ask why she'd rebuffed him because the sound of voices approaching called his attention.

Britt's eyes met his across the space, and they both held motionless.

'It's a nice touch, them wanting to go into the church alone to pray for Risa,' piped a soprano.

'You're too sentimental,' a male voice scoffed. 'It's an expert touch. You are sure to mention it in your voice-over and they win points from all the mush-hearted guillibles like you. Plus, it's a diplomatic way to end the interview and get rid of us. Who could argue against praying over the dead kid?'

A muttering of other voices wasn't quite distinguishable as they moved out of earshot. Grant watched as they came round the outside of the wall and loaded their equipment into their vehicles. A couple of the print reporters looked twice at his car, but so few covered any news of import in Terrell Hills they couldn't be sure they recognized it.

Grant waited until they'd driven out of the parking lot before he nodded to Britt. He wanted to ask about her strange behavior but reserved it for later. Hand on the small of her back, he guided her back out to the walkway.

Carl and Sophia were gone. Britt took off down the path. Grant could hardly keep up with Britt's quick strides. He put one arm on hers to slow her down. Britt slowed just slightly. As he opened his mouth to ask why she'd pulled away from him, Britt nodded at one of the four-foot-high structures that looked like rock igloos scattered through the grounds. 'Wonder what that is?'

'It's a *horno* – a Spanish oven,' Grant said, adding, 'History minor in college.'

Britt regarded him with interest. 'What was your major?'

'Political science.'

She grimaced. 'And I thought I liked you.'

Grant put his hand on her arm. 'Just liked?' His tone was casual but the thread of seriousness too obvious.

Britt slipped him a sidelong glance and a quick, sly smile, but for once he couldn't read her emotions on her face.

Just the time for her to master the art of obscurity.

They walked along the wall of the church, past the steps leading to the bell tower then around to the front doors. Britt's eyes strayed to the two crosses marking graves in front of the church. Seeing her gaze, Grant called her attention back to him. 'Why don't you stay at the back while I talk to them?'

Britt nodded. Grant realized – after it was too late – that she had agreed much too easily.

They opened the doors and looked into the white-stuccoed interior of the church, beautiful in its simplicity. The arches of the cathedral ceiling were painted in stripes of blue and burgundy, small pieces of framed metalwork were hung on the walls in lieu of stained glass windows and a plain but dramatic three-tiered black metal chandelier hung from the ceiling. The altar was tall, with rough-hewn wooden backing that ran halfway up the wall. After this quick appraisal of their surroundings, Grant looked past the twelve rows of wooden pews to where a man and woman sat.

Wordlessly, Grant pointed to a place against the right wall, next to the sacristy. Britt moved there, her eyes locked on the man and woman. Just as she saw Grant reach the pair, a hand snaked out of the sacristy, clamped on her arm and pulled her in.

Grant stopped just behind the pew and cleared his throat. Sophia turned around and her mouth dropped open with surprise. Her companion turned his head.

It wasn't Carl.

Grant kicked himself for not noticing that. While the man was the same height and weight as Carl, he was dressed in a modest plaid shirt and he was older than Carl, with a lot more gray in his thick hair.

'Mrs Lawrence, where is your husband?'

'Sir, these people have asked reporters to let them alone while they pray.'

'It's all right, Father,' Sophia said, observing Grant coldly. 'This is a policeman.'

Father? Grant had thought priests wore black, or at least a collar. This guy looked just back from fishing . . .

'Is there some problem, Officer?' he asked.

Grant opened his mouth to answer, but glanced back at Britt first.

She was gone.

Carl dragged Britt through he sacristy and out into the rear courtyard of the church. He kept a hand on her arm, though he loosened it as they stopped.

'I hope you've brought something to please Soph,' Carl said genially, though the hard light in his eyes defied his tone.

'I brought some pictures taken of you and Sophia scheming – '

'We call it strategizing, and where are the pictures?' His eyes flicked from hand to hand.

Britt reached up under her shirt, but he stayed her hand. 'No, sugar. I'll get them.'

Shrinking from his touch, Britt held herself still against the limestone arch. His fingers played too long on the bare flesh of her abdomen before landing on the photos tucked into the waistband of her jeans and extracting them.

'Too bad,' Carl murmured as his hand drew away from her midriff.

'Too bad what?' Britt asked.

'Too bad I'm going to have to kill you.'

Britt gasped but tried to hold tight to her cool and not give in to the threatening faint. The sunlight shining through the varied arches in the courtyard wavered and grew dim for a moment before she steeled herself against it.

'Why would you want to do that?' She jutted her chin up to look defiant, even though her stomach clutched painfully and she prayed Grant had missed her by now.

'Because I don't see any negatives here, and that makes me angry. It makes me think you're trying to double-cross me, sugar. I'm too wily an old coyote to fall for that.'

'But I know where they are. If you're wily you'll know it's foolhardy to kill me without knowing where they are.' While he considered that, Britt watched his face. Had he seen Grant? Did he know she wasn't there alone?

'Aw, there's always your sister and your granny. Tori's weak; we could buy her – or buy enough stuff for her to put up her nose to keep her quiet. And your granny; you know how vulnerable she is, don't you, sugar?'

Britt felt her fury building to blot out her fear. Carl saw it too, and before she could scream his hand produced a piece of wide tape from his pocket and he clamped it on her mouth.

'Britt – Britt?' Britt heard Grant's voice through the

thick limestone walls of the church. His voice was faint but she could feel his desperation.

Carl's eyes narrowed at her. 'Brought help, did you, sugar? Well, sorry to say it won't help you now.'

Britt kicked out with her leg and just barely missed connecting with his groin. Carl feinted and chuckled. 'I was right. You are a fighter. This might be fun if we weren't being chased. Risa – she gave in to her fate with no fight at all, and that greasy photographer was too stupid to know he was killing himself. This might be sporting, a little like hunting a sassy doe. I know I'm gonna get her, but I like her to give me some fun first.'

Narrowing her eyes, Britt would've let her fury over being compared to a doomed deer overtake her fear and caution had her mouth been free. Her facial muscles pulled and pushed behind the tape, her words becoming a strangled moan in her throat. Carl produced the roll of tape from his western jacket and tried to wrest her hands behind her back. Britt twisted and writhed until Carl, face glistening with sweat, gave up and wrenched her hands to the front and taped them together before flinging the roll of tape into a bush. Not being able to separate her hands threw her balance off, so when she tried to kick again she landed in a heap on the ground instead. Carl chuckled again and lifted her up, dragging her through the corridor of arches, the shadows and light crossing over his face in an eerie, surreal effect – the shadows highlighted the menacing glow in his eyes; the sunlight emphasized his amicable, creased cheeks and smiling mouth.

Carl dragged her up the handful of steps leading to an iron gate. Opening it, he pushed her through and pulled her along to a series of limestone outbuildings at the back of the church. A short bridge led across a dry ditch and Britt pounded her feet on the wood slats. It didn't make enough noise to be noticed. Britt felt her stomach heave with frustration at her helplessness. But she felt an instant of control when she noticed Carl's sudden distress. He grabbed her around the waist.

'Shut up. I could end your fight right now.'

At the first outbuilding on the back side of the church, which announced itself as the oldest mill in Texas, Carl dragged her down the flagstone stairs that led into the building. As he was stepping down Britt leaned on the wood railing and kicked out at him, connecting with his hip. The impact threw him over the opposite railing and into a seven-foot-deep, rock-lined pit. Without looking back, she ran, following the path, down the stairs that led under the mill. She realized too late it was a dead end.

Britt held her breath and heard Carl swearing as he hauled himself out of the pit. Now Britt's breath sounded as if it was roaring out of her nose. Surely he would hear and find her. She had to get the tape off her mouth. She looked at the rough rock wall and bit down on the inside of her mouth as she scraped the side of her face against it and peeled the tape away. She felt the agonizing tearing of skin, smelled the metallic scent and tasted the sickly sweet taste of her own blood. Breathing shallow, silent breaths through her now free mouth, she settled back against the rock wall, listening to his footsteps above. Suddenly she felt a presence to her left.

Swinging around, she faced it – a huge wheel with large, tilted wooden slats hung parallel to the ground, affixed to a large wooden rod that led to the mill building above. It must have been the flour sifter, long ago. A loose rock clicked down the chute from above, hitting Britt on her raw cheek and reminding her she was trapped and bound to be discovered. Soon.

Desperately, she began sawing at the tape on her hands

with the rough side of the metal. She heard Carl's steps above her head, headed for the mill doorway. Realizing she was running out of time, Britt stopped the sawing with only one hank of tape free; her hands were still together, but she had more leverage now. She stepped up on the flat of the wheel; one of the slats gave. Leaning back into the rock wall, she yanked and pulled it loose. It was six inches thick and four feet long. Britt held it, ready, as she heard him walking down the rock steps. Her arms ached from their awkward angle. Her muscles began to tremble and twitch with the weight of the wood. Carl's face appeared around the corner, leering. He pulled a syringe from his pocket and he advanced, slowly descending.

'I'm too old to be chasing you around,' he said in a smooth, self-effacing way. Britt had the sense he was trying to 'sell' her. Sell her into accepting her own death willingly? Had he done this to Risa? Sweet, compliant Risa? Britt felt her rage returning, pumping energy into her flagging muscles as Carl continued, 'Though this will be a memory I will keep for quite a while. That could comfort you a bit as you go to sleep. Gone, but not forgotten.'

'That's what we'll say about you,' Britt countered.

Carl guffawed. 'Still a fighter. I wish my Senate opponent was as worthy a competitor. You know, when Risa came to Dallas to meet with me and Soph she was so righteous. Said we should quit the campaign because we weren't moral people. As if that makes a difference. If we went back to a private life she would destroy the negatives, she so naively promised. As if we could let her continue on as usual, knowing what she did. What a fool.'

Britt felt a surge of pride, knowing Risa had died trying to make a difference. Trying to do something both brave and good.

Carl jerked forward suddenly with the syringe extended. Britt wielded the wooden slat with all the strength she had and any other God could spare. 'You're the fool,' she screamed as she brought the slat down on his head.

The syringe grazed her arm, ripping her T-shirt. As Carl slumped against the wall of the mill's open basement she ran, up the stairs, around the enclosing railing and toward the church. Gulping for air, Britt pulled open the doors to the church and looked in. It was empty. She was about to call Grant's name when she heard hers yelled from behind her. She spun, but saw no one. The sound ricocheted off the walls of the compound. She realized with despair he could be anywhere.

She thought she saw a shadow fall beyond the rear courtyard of the church and ran toward it, but it was Carl, staggering, holding his head. She changed direction, but too late. He caught her arm and flung her across one of the *hornos*. He fumbled in his jacket as his body kept her pinned to the domed rock.

Then Britt heard Grant's voice, louder and clearer and closer.

Carl swore and yanked her back, shoving her inside the door of the *horno*, kicking her out of sight with his feet. 'You stay in there. If you try to come out, I'll jam this needle in. The codeine won't take two hours to kill, like it did when your sister drank it. It will put you to sleep right away. If I don't have a chance, you don't either.'

Britt hit her head on the rock as he shoved her in. Her face scraped against the rough rock and her feet felt numb. She heard voices approaching. She could hear Sophia's high shrill one and Grant's slow rumble, as well as a soft-spoken tenor she assumed was the man who'd been sitting with Sophia in the church.

'Lawrence,' she heard Grant say, 'You tell me where Britt is or I'll kill you.'

'You mean Brittany?' Carl asked smoothly. 'Is she here with you? I haven't see her.'

Grant studied Carl closely. His jacket was streaked with white lime dust and dirt. The side of his forehead was red and swollen. His slicked-down hair was mussed.

Grant knew Carl was lying. He just had to keep control over his emotions enough to think clearly. He didn't care now if Carl walked off to win the Senate campaign. He'd do anything to get Britt back. Alive.

'Mr Lawrence,' the Father put in, 'can you help us?'

'I'm afraid I can't. I was exploring some of the outbuildings – that fascinating mill. The remnants of the drainage ditch . . .'

'What happened to your head?' Grant asked.

'Oh, this.' Carl touched his forehead. 'What a fool I am. I was looking so hard at the historical marker I fell into one of the pits outside the mill.'

Grant looked in the direction of the mill, but the church obscured his view.

'Carl! We need to get you some first aid,' Sophia exclaimed, her hand flying to her own throat as if she were the injured one.

'I'm fine, Soph. Just embarrassed that I let it get the better of me.'

'Grant was tempted to drag the Lawrences back to the station right then, but if Britt was lying dying somewhere he still had a chance to save her. He couldn't leave. Not yet.

'Oh,' Sophia shrieked. They all looked at her. She pointed back toward the church. 'I heard something over there. Do you think it's Brittany?'

Grant measured her with a glance. It was hard to say whether or not she was telling the truth. He couldn't take the chance. The priest grabbed Sophia's arm, and they were heading through the courtyard toward the sacristy door. Grant swept his arm toward the church for Carl to precede him. A reluctant look crossed Carl's face before he broke into a smile. 'I'd be happy to do whatever I can to help you, Detective.'

They walked to the church in silence, Grant trying to shrug off the feeling he was being called by a silent voice. Was it Britt, crossing over into another world? Frustration and despair clouded his brain. He shook them off. He had to think clearly. Even if it was too late.

Britt wriggled and squirmed and inched feet-first along the packed dirt, out of the tiny door of the *horno*. She was free of Carl, but now he was with Grant, his syringe a deadly secret weapon. What was more, she was beginning to feel woozy – different from her fainting spells; this was a numbness, a friendly floating. Her hand went to the dried blood on her upper arm. She was beginning to think Carl had got some of his drug into her. She hoped it wasn't enough to make her lose consciousness before she warned Grant.

She walked slowly and deliberately to the wall of the church. She pressed her hand on the cool limestone for balance. She shouldn't barge into the church. Carl might stick Grant with the needle before he could draw his gun. A diversionary tactic. That was what she needed.

Supporting herself on the wall, she walked to the door of the bell tower. Slowly she climbed the tight spiral staircase, encased with stucco walls. Her thighs burned when she reached the top. Shaking her head, she tried to clear her mind. A high-ceilinged room was before her, with a door to the right leading to the choir loft and a thin staircase on the left continuing up to the belfry. The staircase didn't look strong enough to support the weight of a small cat, much less a person. How did they ring the bell, then? Then she noticed the rope hanging from the ceiling just a foot from her head. The bell rope?

Without thinking, Britt pulled over and over and the bells chimed, resounding through the limestone walls. She heard shouts from inside the church below.

Britt smiled with relief. Now that she had the diversionary tactic, she could show Grant where she was. She opened the door to the choir loft and looked down from its balcony into the church.

There was no way out. Once again she was trapped.

When the bells began to sound, Grant looked over at the priest. His surprise was all he had to see. He knew it was Britt.

'Where?' he shouted at the Father.

The older man pointed to the choir loft. Grant looked up and saw Britt come through the door. The relief he felt was palpable. A warmth spread through him, swelling his heart. But an instant later he saw she was not all right. She staggered slightly and grabbed at the railing for support with her bound hands. He saw her ripped shirt and the blood. She turned her head and he saw the raw, bleeding scrape on the right side of her face.

'Grant,' she called, with a weary smile that became a grimace as her muscles moved under the injured facial tissue.

'Are you hurt?' he called back.

She shook her head. 'Not really, but – '

'Just wait there. Sit on the floor. I'll be right there.'

'The stairway on the left wall outside the church,' the priest called.

Grant started for the front door, but the sight of Carl, appearing at the railing above, stopped him.

'Stay right there, sugar,' Carl called. Sophia gasped and grabbed the priest's arm.

'Go to hell,' Britt called, her elfin face pinched in an attempt to focus her eyes. She shook her head.

'My child,' the Father warned.

'Hold on, Britt. I'm coming,' Grant yelled up as he raced out the door.

'Not fast enough, my boy,' he could hear Carl call down as he raced out and around the building. He had to hunch over and climb the torturous spiral stairway. He rigidly controlled his breathing so Carl wouldn't hear his approach. He looked through the door to the choir loft. Carl wielded a syringe and crept toward Britt, who stood at the end of the railing.

Pulling his gun out of its shoulder holster, Grant wanted to yell at her to huddle down near the floor, to climb back behind the choir's folding chairs. But it wasn't her style. She was going to fight. He felt an unexpected rush of pride. He prayed it wouldn't be pride for a dead woman.

Carl called to her in a hushed, controlled voice as his last step took him within reaching distance. 'Because I'm a gentleman, I'm going to give you another chance to produce those negatives. Or tell me where they are. You and your boyfriend, here, could make a deal.'

'Maybe we could,' Grant offered from the doorway.

Carl craned his neck to look back at Grant while trying to keep an eye on Britt. Grant realized he could use their opposing positions to distract him, if only Britt could be quick enough to get away.

'No, we aren't making any deals. I'm going to see you pay for what you did to Risa.'

'Even if you have to pay too?' Carl asked, grinning cruelly as he held the syringe up high.

Britt's eyes met Grant's, and he could see what her answer was going to be. Could he change her mind? Probably, he admitted, but he wanted to know she'd changed the answer in her heart as well.

After a few seconds of silent communication, he read his own hope in her eyes as they went from bleak to warm. She didn't want to pay with her life, after all.

I love you, Grant mouthed, keeping his gun trained on Carl.

I know, she mouthed back.

Grant fought a smile at Britt's totally characteristic reaction. Always had to have the last word – even in a life-threatening situation.

'No secret signals,' Carl warned, nervous with the exchange. 'Or it's over. Now.'

'It was over a long time ago for you, Carl,' Grant responded,

Enraged, Carl held the syringe out in front of him, pointed it at Britt and addressed Grant. 'It's never over until the person who has the power says it's over. You've got the gun, but the bullet could go right through your girlfriend, here. I, on the other hand, have the ultimate deadly weapon. And the beauty is I probably already got her with a fatal dose. But you don't know if she's a goner or not. One jab and I could make sure. So guess who has the power right now?'

Britt caught Grant in a look that said '*Do it*'. Right as Carl grabbed for her she dove for the floor. Grant pushed away the images of Evan's bloodied body, his ruined life, and squeezed the trigger. Carl fell across the choir's folding chairs with an anguished moan, landing right on top of his own syringe.

Grant heard the sirens first and wondered who'd called the cops. The priest stood in the church aisle, with Sophia gripping his arm. Britt stumbled over a fallen folding metal chair to reach Grant's arms. Keeping one eye on the prone Carl, Grant reveled in the feel of her vibrant body, knowing they had each conquered their own personal demons while conquering a demon in the flesh.

After dark, Ortega peeked in Britt's hospital room. Though she was still groggy, she recognized him and waved him in. Grant, whose back had been to the door, swiveled around. His face tensed when he saw his friend and colleague.

'Well?' he asked.

'So like a *gringo* – ' Chile winked at Britt – 'especially Tom Collins, here, who is the ultra-*gringo*. You guys always have to go straight to business. But we Mexicans want to know about your family, your health, your peace of mind. You think having this brush with disaster it would change you, but, no.'

'Who says my "well?" wasn't an inquiry into your health?' Grant countered with a hint of a smile.

Chile's eyebrows rose dramatically as he shot Britt a conspiratorial look. 'A joke? Maybe he has changed, no?'

'So – you didn't answer the question,' Britt added, weakly but gamely.

'Ah, *si*, I feel fine – except for the *menudo* I had at lunch is causing me a little heartburn . . .' Chile rubbed his stomach. 'And you?'

'They administered the anti-toxin, though they say they don't think she got enough to do any permanent damage. The doctors said she has to be kept awake for most of the next twenty-four hours.'

'That shouldn't be hard for you two. It seems you don't do much sleeping when you're together anyway,' Chile chided.

Britt blushed. Grant drew his black brows together for a reproving look. 'It's serious, Chile. They think she got enough codeine to down at three-hundred-pound football player, but she didn't lose consciousness. Too stubborn, I guess,' he said, with admiration glowing in his eyes.

'Now correct me if I'm wrong, *amigo*, but wasn't this the trait you were complaining about just a few days ago?'

'You complained about me?' Britt asked, aghast. 'I don't believe it.'

Grant fought the grin that was now more seriously threatening at the corners of his mouth. 'I guess some of your less attractive traits might come in handy every now and then.'

'Like my tenacity?' she offered.

'I could think of a few things I'd want you to be tenacious about,' Grant agreed.

'Or – as you so often put it – my big mouth?'

Chile waved his hands in the air. '*Esperas*. It's getting too hot in here for me. Let me tell my tale and I'm gone. *Adios*.'

Grant kept his eyes on Britt, but spoke to Chile. 'Don't rush off on our account.'

'Right, *amigo*. I'll be *rapido*. First, no luck finding the negatives. They weren't on Lawrence. The only thing we can guess is Sophia got them when she threw herself on him before he got in the ambulance – though she denies it and a search of her purse, hotel room, limo turned up zero. My guess? They're history.'

'I'm sorry,' Britt whispered to Grant.

'It's okay, I hid them in my car, and anyway I made a deal with God. You making it was the only thing I asked for.'

'*Dios* got a little too generous,' Chile joked. 'Because Lawrence is going to make it, too. Your bullet collapsed his lung, and he shot enough codeine into himself to be fatal, but unfortunately the paramedics got him in here fast enough to both repair the lung and deliver the antitoxin in time.'

'On the road to recovery, so he can be on the road to the Senate again,' Britt murmured with distaste.

'I don't think so,' Chile said with a wicked grin.

'Why not?' Britt asked.

'Because the whole thing – with him kidnapping you, threatening you with the syringe – the whole episode is on film.'

'What?' Grant and Britt asked in unison.

'A photographer freelancing for one of those tabloid magazines hid out in the church to get pictures of Carl and Sophia praying. When he saw you being snatched up, he followed and got the whole thing from start to finish.'

'He watched it all and never came to help?' Britt sat up in bed, indignant. Grant pushed her gently back down. 'What if Carl had killed me?'

Chile shrugged. 'No telling. But for once the greed of a tabloid *puta* works to our favor. The cops confiscated his film and it's got Lawrence holding the hot tamale. He's not going anywhere but the county jail when he gets out of the hospital.

'Sophia, though, is looking like she's taking a walk. All the photog got was her looking stunned, gripping the arm of that poor Padre.'

'She's probably already filed the divorce papers and is trolling for husband number four,' Britt commented, closing her eyes.

'It's likely,' Grant agreed. 'But she'll end up with someone she deserves. Give us men some credit; we good guys usually end up with pretty good girls.'

'Speak for yourself,' Chile interjected.

'You have Genie.'

'Nah, she kicked me out.'

'Again?' Grant asked, then waved off Chile's coming explanation. 'If you tell that story you'll surely put Britt to sleep.'

'Okay, later, then,' Chile agreed. 'Now on to your job.'

Grant's jaw clenched. Opening her eyes, Britt reached for his hand. At first he almost pulled it away, but then he relaxed – a little – and left his hand in hers.

'You're still Detective Lieutenant – in fact if Rangel could promote you without leaving himself out of a job, he would. The city council has declared you some kind of hero and is going to do a whole ceremony for you next meeting.'

Grant groaned. The city council which probably would have happily lynched him a couple of days ago was now singing his praises. 'Ah, politics in the town of four thousand.'

Britt caught his eye and grinned, dimple and all. He knew it had to hurt, but this was all he'd ever hoped for – to see her smile again. To earn back the respect he'd lost was an added bonus, but he didn't want to do it at the expense of his loyal partner. Grant looked at Chile. 'That's not fair to you. You ought to move back to the number one guy.'

'Are you kidding, *amigo*? You think the extra two chillidogs a month you earn is worth the extra hassle for me? No way. There's a reason I didn't pass the probationary period in the lieutenant's job before you came. I couldn't quit, so I had to slouch it to stay in the sergeant position. What a pain in the . . .' Chile paused in deference to Britt '. . . you-know-what.'

'You know, you have to watch out for those pains in the you-know what,' Grant remarked with a fond glance at Britt. 'Sometimes, if you stick it out, you find out they're worth it – and more.'

EPILOGUE

Britt sat on the bench, watching idly as the little girl dipped her feet in the water of the lily pond. The early summer sun filtered through the trees in the grounds of the McNay Art Museum. She threw her head back into one sunbeam, letting it bathe her face with warm light. She breathed in the scent of rosemary from a nearby bush and, as they often did, her memories linked to the aroma and she recalled the first day she met Grant.

A bittersweet day – much more sweet than bitter now, with the passage of time.

Another natural fragrance began to overpower the rosemary: a familiar, sharp cedar scent.

Britt's eyes opened slowly. He stood before her, bending over to brush his lips against hers. Britt longed to reach up and pull his face deeper to hers. *Later*, she promised herself. His lips lingered a second longer, sending a teasing tongue down the crease, before he pulled away and sat down next to her.

'Do you remember when we first sat on this bench?' Britt asked.

'Is this one of those questions like, do you remember the name of the song that played the first time we held hands on a night of a full moon?'

Britt jolted his leg with her knee. 'Seriously.'

'Seriously, yes, I do.' Grant looked into her eyes. 'Your leg touched mine and I thought the instant bolt of sexual lightning must have been visible. I got as far away as I could for fear it would drag me back to you.'

'I thought you were treating me like a leper.'

'I was, I was scared of you. And scared of myself when I was around you. I thought you were bad for me.'

'And now?'

'Well . . .' Grant teased.

Britt crossed her arms over her chest and pretended to frown. 'You'd better say hi to your daughter before you have two women mad at you.'

'Sonrisa,' Grant called. The little girl with his probing gray eyes and her mother's wild mahogany curls waved and came up to plant a kiss smack on his lips. Her godfather, Chile, had named her the Spanish word for 'smile' – for giving one to her parents when she was born. That her name was also an indirect legacy of Risa was no mistake.

As he straightened, Grant used his forearm to shield his eyes from the setting sun. 'I really need a pair of sunglasses.'

'No!' Britt and Sonrisa shouted in unison.

As a baby, Sonrisa had plucked Grant's sunglasses off his face then stamped them to fragments with her little feet, saying they made it too hard to 'see Daddy's feelings'. They'd never let him get another pair since.

Sonrisa laughed, dimples dancing, and skipped back to the water.

'Do you miss Risa more when you come to places like this, where you have such strong memories?'

'I used to, but I'm beginning to understand something I didn't realize before.'

'What?'

'That part of her is always with me – one way or . . .' Britt looked to the water, where Sonrisa was teasing the turtles with her toes . . . 'another.'

The little girl let out a yelp when a turtle nipped her toe, and this time Britt smiled and didn't say a word.

THE EXCITING NEW NAME IN WOMEN'S FICTION!

PLEASE HELP ME TO HELP YOU!

Dear *Scarlet* Reader,

Good news – thanks to your excellent response we are able to hold another super Prize Draw, which means that **you could win 6 months' worth of free *Scarlets*!** Just return your completed questionnaire to us **before 31 January 1998** and you will automatically be entered in the draw that takes place on that day. If you are lucky enough to be one of the first two names out of the hat we will send you four new *Scarlet* romances, every month for six months.

So don't delay – return your form straight away!*

Looking forward to hearing from you,

Sally Cooper

Editor-in-Chief, *Scarlet*

*Prize draw offer available only in the UK, USA or Canada. Draw is not open to employees of Robinson Publishing, or of their agents, families or households. Winners will be informed by post, and details of winners can be obtained after 31 January 1998, by sending a stamped addressed envelope to address given at end of questionnaire.

Note: further offers which might be of interest may be sent to you by other, carefully selected, companies. If you do not want to receive them, please write to Robinson Publishing Ltd, 7 Kensington Church Court, London W8 4SP, UK.

QUESTIONNAIRE

Please tick the appropriate boxes to indicate your answers

1 Where did you get this Scarlet title?
   Bought in supermarket ☐
   Bought at my local bookstore ☐   Bought at chain bookstore ☐
   Bought at book exchange or used bookstore ☐
   Borrowed from a friend ☐
   Other (please indicate) _____

2 Did you enjoy reading it?
   A lot ☐   A little ☐   Not at all ☐

3 What did you particularly like about this book?
   Believable characters ☐   Easy to read ☐
   Good value for money ☐   Enjoyable locations ☐
   Interesting story ☐   Modern setting ☐
   Other _____

4 What did you particularly dislike about this book?
   _____

5 Would you buy another Scarlet book?
   Yes ☐   No ☐

6 What other kinds of book do you enjoy reading?
   Horror ☐   Puzzle books ☐   Historical fiction ☐
   General fiction ☐   Crime/Detective ☐   Cookery ☐
   Other (please indicate) _____

7 Which magazines do you enjoy reading?
   1. _____
   2. _____
   3. _____

And now a little about you –
8 How old are you?
   Under 25 ☐   25–34 ☐   35–44 ☐
   45–54 ☐   55–64 ☐   over 65 ☐

cont.

9 What is your marital status?
   Single ☐   Married/living with partner ☐
   Widowed ☐   Separated/divorced ☐

10 What is your current occupation?
   Employed full-time ☐   Employed part-time ☐
   Student ☐   Housewife full-time ☐
   Unemployed ☐   Retired ☐

11 Do you have children? If so, how many and how old are they?
   _____
   _____

12 What is your annual household income?
   under $15,000 ☐ or £10,000   ☐
   $15–25,000   ☐ or £10–20,000   ☐
   $25–35,000   ☐ or £20–30,000   ☐
   $35–50,000   ☐ or £30–40,000   ☐
   over $50,000   ☐ or £40,000   ☐

Miss/Mrs/Ms _____
Address _____
_____
_____

Thank you for completing this questionnaire. Now tear it out – put it in an envelope and send it, before 31 January 1998, to:

Sally Cooper, Editor-in-Chief

USA/Can. address	*UK address/No stamp required*
SCARLET c/o London Bridge	SCARLET
85 River Rock Drive	FREEPOST LON 3335
Suite 202	LONDON W8 4BR
Buffalo	*Please use block capitals for*
NY 14207	*address*
USA	

DEALL/9/97

Scarlet titles coming next month:

KEEPSAKES Jan McDaniel
They're enemies – but can they ever be *loving* enemies? Simon Blye and Yardley Kittridge are business rivals. But more than that, Yardley is certain Simon has stolen something precious from her. So how *can* she want a man she should detest?

IN SEARCH OF A HUSBAND Tegan James
Rue Trevallyn appears to have it all, but her life is thrown into confusion when her fiancé disappears just two days before their wedding. Going in search of John, Rue has no choice but to accept help from the mysterious Marcus Graham, who tells her: 'I want you . . . in bed and out of it!'

SHADOWED PROMISES Vickie Moore
Psychic Lark Delavan is trying to solve a crime that took place a hundred years ago, when she suddenly finds herself accused of murder – in the present day! Will attractive lawyer Thomas Blackwell be able to save her?

DEAR ENEMY Maxine Barry
Keira Westcombe knew gossip would be rife when she married a man old enough to be her father. But she doesn't care! She certainly has no intention of explaining herself to Fane Harwood, her stepson. Let him think what he likes!

Did You Know?

There are over 120 *NEW* romance novels published each month in the US & Canada?

♥ **Romantic Times Magazine** is **THE ONLY SOURCE** that tells you what they are and where to find them—even if you live abroad!

♥ **Each issue** reviews **ALL** 120 titles, saving you time and money at the bookstores!

♥ **Lists mail-order** book stores who service international customers!

ROMANTIC TIMES MAGAZINE
~ *Established 1981* ~

Order a <u>SAMPLE COPY</u> Now!

FOR UNITED STATES & CANADA ORDERS:
$2.00 United States & Canada (U.S FUNDS ONLY)
CALL 1-800-989-8816*

* 800 NUMBER FOR US CREDIT CARD ORDERS ONLY

♥ **BY MAIL:** Send <u>US funds Only</u>. Make check payable to:
Romantic Times Magazine, 55 Bergen Street, Brooklyn, NY 11201 USA
♥ **TEL.:** 718-237-1097   ♥ **FAX:** 718-624-4231

VISA • M/C • AMEX • DISCOVER ACCEPTED FOR US, CANADA & UK ORDERS!

FOR UNITED KINGDOM ORDERS: (Credit Card Orders Accepted!)
£2.00 Sterling—Check made payable to Robinson Publishing Ltd.
♥ **BY MAIL:** Check to above **DRAWN ON A UK BANK** to: Robinson Publishing Ltd., 7 Kensington Church Court, London W8 4SP England

♥ **E-MAIL CREDIT CARD ORDERS:** RTmag1@aol.com
♥ **VISIT OUR WEB SITE:** http://www.rt-online.com